J. M. Benj

The Robbery Report
By Glorious

*To my Homegirl Kara
From Glorious...*

A NEW QUALITY PUBLISHING
Published by A New Quality Publishing L.L.C
A New Quality Publishing
P. O. Box 589
Plainfield, New Jersey 07061
anewqualitypublishing.com
anewqualitypublishing@yahoo.com

Copyright © 2011 by A New Quality Publishing
All Rights Reserved

Trade paperback printing 2011

ISBN-13: 978-0-9817756-1-6
10 9 8 7 6 5 4 3 2

First Paperback Edition
Printed in United States

Cover designed by Raheem Hardy
Edited by Kiesha Smoot
Interior design by Pisces

PUBLISHER'S NOTE

This is a work of fiction. Names, characters, places, and incidents either are the product of the author's imagination or are used fictitiously. Any resemblance to actual events or locales or persons, living or dead, is entirely coincidental.

Without limiting the rights under copyright reserved above, no part of this publication may be reproduced, stored in or introduced into retrieval system, or transmitted, in any form or by any means (electronic, mechanical, photocopying, recoding, or otherwise), without the prior written permission of both the copyright owner and the above publisher of this book.

The scanning, uploading, and distribution of this book via the Internet or via any other means without the permission of the publisher is illegal and punishable by law. Please purchase only authorized electronic editions and do not participate in or encourage electronic piracy of copyrighted materials. Your support of the author's rights is appreciated.

Acknowledgements

I would like to thank God for giving me the gift to write. J.M. Benjamin for giving me the opportunity to be heard. I promise I won't make you regret it. My moms Sylvia Davis for always standing by me no matter how much hell I put her thru. My daughters Shakiea and Nakira, my son lil' Glorious. My grandbaby's Amaya and Brianna. My brother's Raheem, Rameek, Faruq and Salidin. My grandmother Ophilia, Aunt Audra and uncle James, Uncle Sean and his wife Kimla. My family in Raleigh N.C. it's too many of ya'll to name, but I love ya'll!!! My family in Philly Joyce, Becky, Trish, Andra, Billy, Queen, C.T. and if I missed you don't be mad, love is love. Intell and Phillis keep ya'll flame burning. My aunt Tracy and cousin Zaheer in Brooklyn also the Rocks stay up. To all my home boys M*Easy, Jahleer, Bang Boy, HK, BV, Young Hunter we in the building, L.B. on top. Peace to the Gods Lord True, Power. My cousins Wild Style and Dan in Richmond V.A.. My sister Tony, holla at ya boy. R.I.P. to my father Les, Skip, My grandpops Stormin' Normin, grandma Telly and Money makin' A.D. MBP we doin' it for you baby!!! Tiaa Griffin ya support is very much appreciated. Emond and April what-up. My strong people Cheri and everybody in dat wild as house. To all the people who read my book in the box and gave me the encouragement I needed to keep it movin'. Kool, Spit, Hood Nicka, Sincere, Zero, Big Nicka bust at me. Magic...Major Papers, Gator I see you fools .Lil' Ronnie hold ya head. Freedom Born, F.J, Casse, Born Unique, I.B., K.C., Miseka we doin' it baby. Big ups to my A New Quality Publishing family. To everybody in the building hold ya head up high, you bigga then that .To all my haters I need you, I need you to hate so I can use it for my energy. Picture me Rollin'...

Glorious

Dedication

I dedicate this book to the people who mean the most to me; my mother, children and grandchildren.

I love you all

Kevin "Glorious" Gause

Prologue

Fall 2004...

G Millions stood posted up in the recreation yard of the East Jersey State Prison in Rahway New Jersey the way he was use to back in his hometown of New Brunswick on the block. You couldn't tell him he wasn't on the streets at that moment. He was in a zone. From where he stood, he had a clear view of nearly everybody and everything in the yard, minus a few blind spot the guards that watched from the towers neglected.

To all of the new and other inmates who didn't know any better, it would have seemed as though G Millions was about to put in some work for whatever reason. It was surprising that the guards positioned in the towers did not say anything to him the way his tan colored, jailhouse fitted cap was over his brow. Normally they had a problem with inmates wearing their hats in this manner but they said nothing. The cold glare he bore in his eyes was concealed by the way he sported the fitted. The pulled down cap also altered his identity from security cameras.

On any other day causing havoc for G Millions may have very well been the case, but not on this particular Sunday. He had just come from the visiting hall after his ride or die chick had delivered what he had been waiting for all week. Now, he was about to put in work but the work he had in mind to put in had nothing to do with violence. He was on a mission to get money.

Famous knew exactly where his partner in crime could be located. They had discussed everything on more than one occasion. As soon as the officers cleared him to enter the big yard, he immediately shot across the occupied basketball court and through the workout area until he was next to G Millions. At first glance, the two could easily be mistaken for brothers. They were both 5'10" and stocky only Famous weighed in at two hundred and ten pounds while G Millions was ten pounds lighter. They both had smooth coffee brown skin, but the distinction of the two was their eyes. G Millions eyes were freakishly light brown and looked odd on a person of his complexion, where as Famous' eyes were black and lifeless. They both sported their hair in waves although most of the time they kept them hidden under skullies, do rags, fitted's, or some type of headgear.

"What's really gangsta my gee?" Famous asked, giving him a pound.

"More or less, out here about to make it happen, you know how we do," G Millions responded.

No sooner than they begin to diddy bop around the yard, a couple of prisoners approached them.

"Ya'll straight?" The inmate fiend with no front teeth in his mouth asked.

"What you need fam?" Famous replied. But before the inmate fiend could place an order, G Millions interjected.

"Nah B, keep it movin'," G Millions snapped. "Ya'll paper ain't even proper enough to see me or my dude. When our lil' manz and 'em come out here, holla at them," he ended.

Although they followed G Millions's last instructions, one of them was mumbling something under his breath. Instantly G Millions addressed the situation.

"Keep running your mouth and It's gonna win your ass a helicopter trip straight to the Trauma Center," G Millions warned. His words and demeanor caused the dope fiend to quickly make his getaway.

"Ha ha, G. you's a slick talking muthafucka. You need to be performing in front of millions," Famous laughed causing his partner to join him. "Seriously though, Lady Pink was looking gorgeous out there on the dance floor with her mean ass," Famous changed the subject. "Not only is that broad fatal, but she don't fucks wit' nobody but you. But shit the way you was bustin' her ass, I see why."

Had it been anyone else G Millions would have taken offense to what was said but he knew what his friend had said was meant as a compliment. All he could do was shake his head and laugh.

"Yo B, you's a silly ass joker. But what I'm trying to figure out, is how you know what I was doing when you was busy diggin' Candy Girl's back out?" he countered humorously.

"Right, right, true, true," Famous retorted.

"Dig, as for me and Lady Pink tho, it's more to it than that. I never really told you the full story," G Millions began. "I nourished shorty's mental back to health, that's why shit is deep with us. Not to mention the way I bagged her. It's only right for her to be loyal, you smell me?" He paused to make sure he had his partner's undivided attention before taking a trip down memory lane of how he and Lady Pink met.

"One day I was breezin' through in that red 325i I used to have, remember them shits had just come out back in the 80's. I was killin' 'em with that joint. My shit was only a year old," G Millions bragged. "It was nice as hell out so you know I had the top dropped that day, with "Who Shot You" pumpin'. Man, that day that piff had me stuck, so I'm zoning to the beats when out of nowhere Lady Pink jumps in front of my ride. Luckily, I snapped out of my zone just in time to swerve around her. She was in the middle of the street distraught and doped up; trying to get away from some young boys, she'd just robbed for a bundle. The broad blew my high! Now you know I was pissed. So I hopped out my G Ride to see what was really good. I remember barkin' on her on some other shit. More or less, she might as well have said fuck what I was hollering 'cause when she seen them little fools whose shit she took coming for that ass, she jumped right behind me. One of the youngin's started spazzin', callin' her all types of dope fiend bitches and talkin' about how he was gonna kill her. I felt sorry for her ass so I said ya'll ain't got nothing better to do but beat up fiends? And a broad at that! And that's when one of the lil' dudes told me she had a bundle of dope in her hand and she ain't pay 'em for the shit. Youngin' was heated, but I couldn't help but laugh. But he wasn't feelin' that. He asked me what the fuck was so funny? So now I'm in the middle 'cause he try'nna talk slick to me. You already know I wasn't smellin' that. I had to let his ass know ASAP what it was. I gee checked the lil' joker on some real shit and told him don't let his mouth write a check his ass ain't prepared to cash." G Millions chuckled as he revisited the story.

"Instead of the lil' nigga fallin' back he pops more shit like fuck what you talkin' bout ole' head I want my shit!"

"Say word," Famous laughed.

"Word to my mutha."

"Lil' nigga called you 'ole head? I know you dumbed out." Famous couldn't stop laughing knowing how much being called old bothered G Millions.

"You already, that's when I snapped and pulled out my Ruger and before the young boy could react, I smacked him upside the head with it. But when I smacked him, I squeezed the trigger by a mistake. A round let off in the air and 'ole boy fell, so his homeboys thought he got shot. They straight dipped and left their own people for dead."

By now, Famous was bellied over in laughter.

"That shit was funny as hell. The lil' dude got up shook as hell with his hands raised in the air. Then to top it off the joker pissed himself. I kept my gun trained on him, but I looked at Lady Pink and snapped. I asked her what she take from these fools. She had the nerve to say she ain't take nothing but a bundle. Now I got the dummy look 'cause this chick really did take the shit, and I pistol-whipped dude and everything over some bullshit, so I felt a little fucked up. I pulled out my bank, peeled off five big faces, hit dude off, gave him my number, and told him to hit me when he was ready to re- up. It was the least I could do. He looked at me like I was crazy, but he took the doe and spun off. Really though, I was mad at myself for even getting caught up in that bull shit, but at that point fuck it. I turned to Lady Pink, told her to get in the fuckin' G ride, and made the mistake of calling her a bitch. That's when she wigged the fuck out."

"Who you calling a bitch?" G Millions tried to mock her tone.

"She tried to give me attitude but I shut that shit down and told her to get her young ass in the car. Real talk, even on that shit she was a bad young piece. I remember me tellin' her that."

"All that paper and pussy you was getting and all the pussy you could've got and you was lustin' over some young fiend," Famous joked.

"Shut the fuck up you silly ass nigga," G Millions retorted irritated by his friend's humor at his expense.

Seeing that he had gone too far Famous, apologized. "My bad my dude, you know I'm bullshittin' go head."

"Like I was sayin' tho, so I'm try'nna figure out why she fuckin' with this shit and she starts talking that I'm grown shit, and I do what the fuck I want, with her hands on her hips and shit. I was feelin' her cocky attitude but I checked her with all that other shit. I pointed out to her how had it not been for me, doing what she wanted, would've got her ass kicked. Even she had to laugh with me on that one. Once I told her who I was she went crazy, saying how I was this legend and asked me why'd I waste my time getting' involved in her shit? I told her I got involved because I know what it's like to be fucked up and need help. That's when she told me how I had a loyal bitch for life. The rest as they say is history," G Millions ended

"Yo it's hard to believe that ole' girl was ever fucked up in the game like dat, now she damn near flawless like DeBeers ice, wit' her Lisa Ray lookin' ass," Famous said in admiration.

"Yeah, I told shorty if she stay loyal and wanna ride wit' me, she had to get her shit together and clean up. She agreed, so I took her to ma dukes house. You know how my mom's gets down, tender loving care, nursed her right back to health. She got that monkey off her back." G Millions looked up over at the watchtower as if in deep thought before continuing. "Once she kicked that shit, I came through, scooped her and we spent the day rippin' thru the mall. It was on from there."

"I see ya work playboy." Famous praised his comrade for how he managed to get Lady Pink right. "She makes sure we eatin' betta in here then a lot of jokers is on the streets."

"Yeah, she definitely plays her position to the fullest," G Millions, stated modestly.

"Man B, I do my numbers, but I gotta give you your props. You the best that ever did it. You got her and wifey holdin' it the fuck down!"

"Yeah Fame, when it comes to love I don't lie and they respect me for it. Both of them know where they stand and they comfortable wit' it. It's all good though, there's enough of me to go around."

G Millions last statement caused them both to double over in laughter.

"G, you a wild boy. Most people would take you as being cocky, but I know you just confident bro."

"Man, you know I don't give afuck about what people think. They don't feed us. I work hard for the shit I got. More-less, you already saw me and YoYo's house. She got her own career and don't have to spend a dime 'cause I take care of all the bills. Then on top of all that, I put in my quality time. So when I'm doin' what I do, she give me my space, feel me?"

Famous nodded his head, absorbed in his own thoughts before speaking. "Damn G, Lady Pink's picture could be in Webster under gangsta bitch. I'm surprised she don't be wildin'."

"Yo B, is you stupid or is you retarded. You act like you ain't heard a word I said!" G Millions snapped, throwing his hands up in defeat, feeling as if his partner in crime hadn't paid attention to a word he'd just said.

"You ain't scared to talk to me like dat!" Famous shot back wittedly, giving them a good laugh.

"Let me explain this shit to you some more. Lady Pink is laid up wit' all of the same luxuries that me and YoYo got in our house. Plus you already know how she does hers. When I'm out there she has me during business hours, and her evil ass is good with a once a month gangsta fuck. She not into all the romance shit. From where I snatched her, to where she at now, she gotta love it, feel me."

"Yeah, and if you was anybody else, I'd call you a trick ass nigga. But I have to admit, ya shit tight. You the first one called out every visit, that's gangsta. Both of your shorty's love they self some G Millions, I bear witness to the greatest."

Famous playfully ruffed up his partner, while they enjoyed a good laugh.

"Hey you two, knock it off before I write your asses up for horse playing!" The prison guard warned from the watchtower.

G Millions and Famous waved there hands in the air apologetic as they continued to walk their laps around the yard.

"You know you need to knock it the fuck off B," G Millions said, while still chuckling. "You act like Candy Girl don't be kicking in the door, waving the four-four." He went on to point out quoting a Biggie Smalls line.

G Millions knew from experience that when dealing with other bosses you had to stroke their egos at times to avoid jealousy coming into play. Even though he knew his boy was not your average joe, he still felt his comment was in order.

"Yeah G, my baby does her thing. I told her to double up next week when it's my turn to bust a move, 'cause we got work to do."

"You already know, as long as they hold us, we gonna make 'em pay!"

"No doubt! We not only have to seize this opportunity, but every suitable circumstance we come across. Individually we hold it up. Together we can't be stopped, ya dig. I promise you we gonna shock da world!" An excited G Millions exclaimed.

"Why the fuck wouldn't we?" Famous agreed. "Wit' you holdin' the title for the smack king and me bein' the cocaine cowboy, we gonna take our game to a whole nother level. I'mma be haulin' in so much of that pure raw, they gonna call me the abominably snow man!" Famous boasted, giving them yet another good laugh.

When Hamma, who was the enforcer of the team, caught up to them, they were on their fourth lap. A hammer is what the old school gangsters called their guns and being as though Hamma kept plenty of them and didn't have a problem using them, the name fit him perfectly. Thus, he wore it with pride.

"My niggaz!" Hamma said as he approached his comrades and gave them hood love. "What you two fool's up to?"

"Man, you know Fame think he the late great Richard Pryor. Son got mad jokes," G Millions informed him.

"Seriously though B," Famous addressed Hamma, his mood swinging from playful to serious. "I told you to make sure that clowns money touched, not butcher 'em up. You make my job harder 'cause now I gotta double up next week just so we can reach our quota and get our money back in order."

"I know what you said Fame, but da nigga got loose so I had to tighten his ass up," Hamma justified.

"Tightening his ass up is one thing, but you murderized the muthafucka! Now don't get me wrong, I don't give a fuck about the nigga. But a dead man can't pay his debt."

"Take it out my pay," Hamma shrugged his shoulders.

"That ain't the point; we don't need that type of heat."

"You already know that, that's what I do. Murder is my pleasure, not money. So the next time, if you don't want a muthafucka dead, send Gangsta, he got more patients than me."

The words that just came out of Hamma's mouth amused G Millions so much that he just had to interrupt this one.

"Who the fuck you think you foolin'? Both ya'll niggaz psychotic!" G Millions snide remark eased the tension and replaced it with laughter.

They were still enjoying their laugh when Hamma's little brother Gangsta walked up. Gangsta loved to be the center of attention, although most of it was negative. He savored the feeling of importance, especially when dealing with family. So when him and the rest of the homies walked up on the trio having their moment, there was no way that he would miss the opportunity to take center stage. He wasted no time.

"What the fuck is this, an OG party?" he questioned playfully and continued his performance.

"Ya'll fools always plottin', plannin' and muthafuckin' strategizing'! Hamma I know that code that went off was your work. That's what the fuck I'm talkin' bout!" he commended his brother for his recent slaying in the jail. "And I'm glad you didn't caught for that shit," he added, giving his brother a handshake and hug.

Some prisoners stole glances, secretly wondering if he was crazy as he went on his tirade. The other prisoners that knew him kept it movin'.

"G Millions you's a pretty muthafucka, give me a kiss." He puckered up and made kissing noises.

"Fuck you punk! Stop playin' so much, we got work to do," G Millions said while handing Gangsta a skullcap containing numerous bundles of heroin.

After taking a peep inside the hat, Gangsta distributed the drugs to the rest of the crew. Then everybody gave each other hood love, which consist of a sideways hand slap, followed by a hug, after which Gangsta and the rest of the convoy of hustlers strolled off.

"Famous you's a sweet muthafucka too," Gangsta shouted over his shoulder, not willing to let Famous escape the wrath of his sense of humor.

"You betta get ya punk ass outta here lil' nigga. I don't give a fuck how many bodies you got. You ain't too good to die." Famous's response gave everybody a good laugh.

As soon as their crew blended in with the crowded yard, G Millions, Famous and Hamma began discussing their plans upon their release. There was no doubt in either man's mind that once the doors opened and they were able to walk up out of them, the streets of New Jersey would have hell on their hands...

Chapter 1

Summer 2002…

"The Making of The Team"

Usually it is considered a blessing to get rain during an armed robbery. In fact, any form of bad weather could naturally provide the perfect camouflage for the criminal element. However, the heavy downpour proved to be a hindrance for Hamma and Gangsta in their quest to rid themselves of their relentless pursuers.

Although in the past, Hamma's superior driving skills had made it almost impossible for any law enforcement agency to catch him. However, now the way the rain came down like cats and dogs, accompanied by the high rate of speed he was traveling Hamma's vision was almost completely impaired, making it difficult for him to dig into his bag of tricks. Not even the rapid motion of the windshield wipers could provide him with any relief. In fact, he might as well not even have had them on.

What started as a one agency pursuit quickly turned into three agencies on there heel's. The robbery took place in Asbury Park but as they made their getaway, Neptune and Ocean Township joined in on the chase.

"Stop playin' with these muthafucka's before the helicopters come!" An agitated Gangsta shouted.

"I got this," Hamma smiled, and remained calm.

"Normally you'd been shitted on these fools!" Gangsta ranted. "You playin' games like we ain't just body a bitch or got this hostage."

"Well get rid of the hostage! That'll give you one less reason to aggravate me!" Hamma paused and looked over at his brother.

Gangsta was really pissed off and the poor hostage was the one to bore the brunt of his anger. First, he blew out the back window with his shotgun, then hoisted the hostage up and tossed her out of the window, sending her tumbling and sliding on the asphalt. His actions caused the police cruisers to swerve and crash into one another. This gave Hamma the opening he needed.

He broke down a block before Asbury Circle, hopped on the wrong side of the street, hooked a quick left on All Burn Street and then vanished.

"That's my big bro!" Gangsta shouted.

"You already know I got the illest wheel work in the nation," Hamma bragged and they laughed.

Happy to have pulled off another successful robbery, Gangsta began to count the take as the two brothers replayed the events that led up to the chase and ultimately their getaway.

They had known that this particular Burger King closed at 11:30 pm, so the two brothers eased up in the establishment around 11:20 pm, being the dynamic duo that they were, both men already knew their respective positions. As always, Gangsta would hold down the front, while Hamma hopped over the counter and headed toward the manager's office.

"All you muthafucka's on the floor!" Gangsta ordered.

Simultaneously, Hamma entered the manager's office and put the ratchet to her head.

"Alright bitch, you know what it is. Be nice and live, don't make it a homicide!"

After seeing the Grim Reaper sitting on the barrel of Hamma's .357, the manager literally loss control of her grippers and shitted on herself as she struggled to open the safe.

"Please don't kill me?" She pleaded.

"I ain't gonna tell your ass no more, open the muthafucka' before I put your brains on this fuckin' wall an open it myself!" He ordered with finality.

The manager got so frightened that she went into shock. Hamma took it as her being rebellious and pulled the trigger. The blow from the .357 slug nearly decapitated her, leaving a mass of blood, bone and brains scattered about the office.

Hamma having clinched his thirst for murder filled up his duffle bag and headed for the front door. That abundance of police cars entering the parking lot did not falter the two brother's determination to avoid capture and make it out with the loot and their lives.

Gangsta thought fast and snatched up one of the employees as they headed for the door. Hamma was the first to exit with his ratchets singing as if they were trying to win American Idol. He backed the police down long enough for Gangsta to reach the car with the hostage. He pushed the hostage into the backseat of the stolen Acura Legend. Once the hostage was in the car Gangsta let his guns go off long enough to make sure Hamma was able to make it behind the wheel and show why he was an All-American.

"Forty-seven hundred punk ass dollars! I'm tired of this shit B!" Gangsta shouted. "We been getting' it in for thirty straight days and nights and we ain't even come up on thirty gees. All we got is a slew of bodies to show for our work."

"You're right little bro, but you know I like murder more than money. However, this shit do got us on fire." Hamma looked to the sky as if in deep thought.

"You know, all you been doin' is poppin' muthafucka's," Gangsta said glancing over at his brother with a smile on his face.

"We might as well just turn these shits into robbery homicides. Fuck it! When we run up on these pussies ain't no need in lettin' 'em live after we go up in their pockets, safe, ass or wherever else they got our paper. Besides, your body count higher than mine," Gangsta clowned as the two shared a laugh.

"That's bullshit nigga."

"Shit if it is. Count how many robbery reports been made on the strength of us, without somebody getting popped and then count how many you laid down," Gangsta challenged.

"Fuck it!" Hamma shouted, before raising his hands in defeat.

"You ain't never lie. Hopefully this bitch ass nigga Money Mike got more in his safe than we've seen all month so you can shut the fuck up. If you keep crying what are the babies, gonna do? Oh yeah and just for the record, if that fool act loose, I'mma tighten his ass up!"

The two brothers were still laughing when they pulled up to another Acura Legend that they had stashed so that they could switch up and continue their robbing spree. They thoroughly wiped down the car they abandoned. Then headed for the room they had rented at the Travel Lodge in order to change their gear and prepare for the next episode.

"We've been putting in work forever lil' bro," Hamma stated, while sitting on the bed and adjusting his bulletproof vest.

"Yeah, it's nothin' though, just another day on the job," Gangsta agreed.

"I been thinkin' 'bout the shit you been rappin' bout and you right, it is about time for a promotion."

"Hell yeah big bro, we came a long way." Gangsta smiled. "And I still remember our first taste of blood."

After his last statement, Gangsta proceeded to take a trip down memory lane. "You know that nigga Stocks was feeling some type of way because we ain't respect him as bein' the man of the house. How could we tho? All that time we held the crib down, and he came out of nowhere on some takeover shit. Then on top of that, he goes and steals mommy's love. That fool had to get it. Too bad we didn't know mommy was pregnant with lil' bro at the time, we might have given him a pass."

"Shiit that fool was outta here regardless!" Hamma interrupted and they both laughed.

"You probably right, 'cause mommy wasn't tryin' to hear shit we was tryin' to say so we had to take matters into our own hands," Gangsta agreed and then he continued.

"That shit was too easy. We already knew he'd be at the Sportsmen remember, that was that nigga favorite spot."

"Yeah," agreed Hamma. "All we had to do was squat and wait for him to come out."

"It was cold as hell that night," Gangsta remembered.

"Yeah and your anemic ass wanted to leave."

"But I didn't," Gangsta bragged. "I'll never forget the look on them niggaz faces when they realized they got caught slippin'," Gangsta added, and then stared off in a distance as if he were traveling back in time.

Stocks exited the bar with his partner Ness. Hamma and Gangsta could hear that the two men were engrossed in a conversation that apparently had started in the bar and spilled out into the streets. They hadn't planned on Ness being there, but Hamma caught Gangsta's nod signaling for him to get at Ness. As Stocks and Ness walked in their direction, Hamma and Gangsta stepped out from behind Stocks customized van. Stocks and Ness were instantly startled until they saw who it was. They made the fatal mistake of letting their guard down.

"What the fuck you two lil' niggaz doin' out here, ain't it pass your bed time?" Stocks asked as Ness chuckled in the background. The smell of strong liquor was confirmation for Hamma and Gangsta that the men were drunk or close to it.

By the time the men saw the twin 380's pointing at them, it was too late. They never knew what hit them. Hamma and Gangsta didn't bother to respond to Stocks humorous comment, not verbally anyway. Wasting no time, they took the two mens' lives like thieves in the night without giving it a second thought. They ran through Stocks and Ness pockets faster then Maurice Green in the one hundred meter dash, taking anything of value and then walked off as if nothing had ever happened.

"I guess we was built for this shit little bro," Hamma replied bringing them back to the present.

"Yeah, 'cause after our first hit shit came as natural as learning to walk," Gangsta agreed.

After strapping their vests up tight, the two brothers checked their ratchets then snatched up the duffle bag and duct tape. Once they were satisfied everything was in order, it was time for some action.

"Let's go get our paper from this clown," Hamma said, breaking the silence.

"Yeah, that lame ass nigga been holdin' on to our bread long enough," Gangsta concurred.

When they got back to the G ride, the first thing they did was hit the CD player.

"Keep your eyes wide open/ you're surrounded by crooks/ shit is real around here niggaz looking for a jux!" G- Unit's "Beg For Mercy" roared through the speakers. This was one of their favorite songs to listen to on the way to a job. They kept the track on repeat all the way to Money Mike's house.

Gangsta turned down the music when they got to his block. The first thing the two brothers noticed was that their marks Cadillac Escalade wasn't in the driveway.

"Just like I thought, that fool still at the club," Hamma says, talking to himself.

"Let's get this money baby," Gangsta reply excitedly, nearly exiting the vehicle before it came to a full stop.

By the time the G Ride came to a complete stop, Gangsta already had on his ski mask and the passenger door open. Within seconds, he was in the yard headed for the back. When Hamma caught up to him behind the house, they both entered through the basement window, which they deemed their best route in to the house.

"Unh...unhhh...shit yeah." The sounds of a female's moans could be heard through-out the house causing both Hamma and Gangsta to stop in their tracks.

"You hear that," Hamma whispered.

"Yeah, it sounds like it's coming from the bedroom," Gangsta replied in the same low tone, wasting no time heading in the direction of the moans with Hamma dead on his heels.

When they peaked in the room sure enough, Money Mike's girl was on the bed butt naked, watching porn, with a dildo and a pocket rocket on her clit. The site of the beauty lying before his eyes caused a bulge in Gangsta's pants immediately. Noticing the lustful look peering through his brother's mask, Hamma whispered, "We ain't here for that B."

"Man, that bitch got my joint harder than US steel. Shiit, that nigga must not be handling his business. Fuck that shit, we got to wait anyway," Gangsta rationalized while heading towards the bedroom.

Gangsta stood at 6 foot 1 ½ inches, with skin dark as night, weighing in at 195 pounds, deep beehive style waves with a dangerous swagger. Therefore, he had no problems when it came to bagging females. Although Hamma's physical features resembled that of Gangsta's, he rocked a baldhead instead of waves and a long scar on his face in which he obtained during a childhood game on a broken fence.

Hamma's disposition was deadly and the opposite sex could somehow sense it. This made him not as lucky with the females as his brother. So, he couldn't understand why Gangsta had to mix business with his own perverted pleasure. He shook his head then went on about his task of searching the house to see what he could find.

Money Mike's lady was so engrossed in pleasuring herself, that when she finally looked up and discovered Gangsta standing over her with his dick out and his gun at her head she was startled, embarrassed and of course scared.

"Shhh, don't even think about screaming!" Gangsta warned.

"Please don't hurt me?" Evette pleaded.

"I don't wanna hurt you," Gangsta calmly stated. "I just wanna make you feel better then Money Mike and those toys." Gangsta assured her with a lustful grin on his face.

Evette cringed at his words and her heart dropped in her stomach from the look in his eyes.

"Just relax ma and do as I say and you'll be good," he stated.

Gangsta pulled out the duct tape and instructed her to turn over onto her stomach. Against her better judgment, she complied with tear-filled eyes. Gangsta taped her hands to the headboard and placed a pillow under her stomach so that her ass sat up perfectly. Even though Hamma didn't approve of his actions, Gangsta couldn't resist the opportunity of bedding the beautiful high yellow amazon who was stacked in all of the right places. *Hamma gonna have to get over this one* he told himself.

After taking a few seconds to admire his handiwork and her beauty, he stood there stroking his erection, unable to believe how Money Mike could leave something this flawless unattended.

"Please don't do this," Evette pleaded, but her cries went unanswered. Deciding not to waste another minute, Gangsta kneeled down, spread Evette's ass cheeks apart, and dove in headfirst. To his surprise, Evette responded by pushing her ass up towards his face to make sure, he got it all.

"Umm, damn," she moaned from the tongue-lashing Gangsta was displaying. I don't know who you are, but that shit feels good as hell," she managed to inform Gangsta.

"I'm here to jux ya dude, but you fine as a muthafucka , so I just had to have some of this here," Gangsta lifted his head long enough to say how he felt.

"A'ight then, shut up and handle your business nigga," Evette panted. Gangsta had no way of knowing she was a stone cold freak and that Money Mike wasn't handling his business in the bedroom. Just as Evette could not have known how much her aggressiveness turned Gangsta on. Gangsta ended his oral assault on Evette and without notice or warning plowed his manhood into the tightness of her waiting ass hole as he filled her womb with the dildo she was playin' with when he first entered the room.

It took all of two minutes for Evette's contracting anal muscles to suck Gangsta's cream straight to the top.

"Ohhh Shit! Unnn uhhh bitch!" Gangsta screamed as he pulled out and sprayed his juices all over her ass and back.

"Damn nigga, that's all you got?" Evette exclaimed. "The next time you wanna take some ass, at least make it last!" She clowned him.

"Fuck you bitch!" Gangsta shouted trying to mask his embarrassment.

"That's what I thought you were supposed to do. All you did was play with a bitch emotions, shit I could have got my own self off!"

Hamma stood in the doorway in laughter.

"A'ight, now back to business. The bar is about to close, so that fool will be here in a minute!" Hamma announced while still snickering.

Gangsta was now seething. He retrieved his hawk, cut Evette loose from the headboard, and took her downstairs to the living room where he tied her to the chair that Hamma had already set up. Meanwhile, Hamma unscrewed the light bulb to give them an advantage on their unsuspecting mark.

"Do you really think I wanna fuckin' sit here and rap, when there's cars to be copped, chicks to be slapped, guns to be cocked, clicks to be clapped," Cam'ron's; Green Lantern freestyle mix CD blurred thru Money Mikes high tech sound system, which announced his arrival to the awaiting home invaders.

Two minutes later, Money Mike placed his key into the keyhole, and entered his home.

"Damn, it's dark in this muthafucka," he mumbled to himself. "Where's this silly ass bitch?"

After seeing, that the light didn't come on when he hit the switch his instincts caused him to draw his weapon. He gripped it tightly and proceeded to walk thru his living room. However, he did not get far before Gangsta ambushed him, perfecting a move so often seen in the many karate movies he'd watched throughout the years. He swept Mike off his feet in one swift motion, causing him to accidently squeeze the trigger on his .9mm Glock.

Not knowing whether anyone had been shot, Hamma quickly screwed the light bulb back in, which temporarily shocked everyone's eyes. As soon as Gangsta adjusted his eyes to the light, he quickly snatched the gun out of Money Mike's hand before he got any bright ideas. But after seeing a hole in the middle of Evettes' head, busting a move was the first thing from the hustlers mind.

"You made me kill my bitch!"

"Fool, you better anti-up before ya'll be twins," Gangsta warned.

"Fuck ya'll!" Money Mike rebelled.

"That's the best news I've heard all day," Hamma smiled.

"Bwow!" The slug tore right thru the middle of Money Mike's face.

"You's about a simple muthafucka!" Gangsta yelled. "Now how we gonna find the safe."

"Shut the fuck up with your freak ass," Hamma shot back. "While you had your face all up in that bitch's ass I found everything we need. It would have been a lot easier for that nigga if he had opened it. But now we just have to carry it and open it up our muthafuckin' selves!"

"Could we have just one smooth jux?" Gangsta joked.

"You got some nerve, you perverted ass nigga. Besides where would the fun be without drama?" Hamma joked, giving them a good laugh.

After they went to stake their claim of the safe that Money Mike once owned they proceeded to make their getaway.

It took the remainder of the night to pry open the safe. But there hard work and persistence finally paid off in the wee hours of the morning when they gained access to what they committed murder for.

"Pay dirt!" Gangsta shouted, as he pulled out bundles of money and nearly a half of a kilo of cocaine from out of the safe.

It took the brothers about 45 minutes to come up with a total of $33,500.

"That's the shit we been looking for. Now let's go see my nigga Fame and get right!" Hamma exclaimed.

"Yeah, now we can split what we came up on during our little spree and give them $30,000 of what we just hit that fool Money Mike for and the yayo. He told us to come see him when our paper got right. This should be a hell of a start."

"Sounds like a plan to me little bro. Now he will see that we can be team players."

"Hahaha, yo big bro, I was just thinking about the day he made us that proposition," Gangsta said as he revisited the day he and Hamma met up with Famous and G Millions.

Spring 2001...

G Millions and some of the hustlers from the area were shooting cee-lo.

"I got $3200 in the bank." G Millions scanned the feet of the other hustlers, mentally counting the money in front of them and making sure that the $3200 was covered. "Chicks pay just to see me walk!" He slyly remarked, as he shook the dice and shot them across the concrete.

"Trips," He bellowed seeing he'd rolled an unbeatable point as the three dice all landed on the number four.

As soon as he bent down to collect his winnings, Hamma stepped in the middle of the circle brandishing his sawed off shotgun, while Gangsta threw a duffel bag on the ground.

"Fill that shit up!" He ordered. "Ya'll know what it is."

The hustlers quickly complied, knowing the money and jewelry were replaceable. After the duffel bag was full, Hamma and Gangsta began to exit the way they had arrived. They were so focused on what they had just robbed the flashy hustlers for that they had overlooked the number one rule of fast money by neglecting to check for weapons.

G Millions and the other hustlers patiently waited until the thieves got out of range for the sawed off shotgun to be effective. Then all hell broke loose. Furious about just being robbed, they all pulled out their guns and opened fire on the thieves. Hamma let loose with his sawed off, but just as predicted, he was too far for it to be effective. The thieves could actually hear the bullets whizzing by there heads and bouncing off the walls and gates, as G Millions relentlessly pursued them thru the complex.

Hamma and Gangsta was confident that they had put enough distance between themselves and their pursuers until they took the wrong turn and a fence stood between them and a successful escape. Left with no choice they scaled the fence with the zeal of a Marine. By the time, Gangsta threw his weapon over and followed suit, he was struck in the back by slugs from G Millions 9mm. With lady luck smiling down on them, he landed on the same side of the fence as his brother. However, he was wheezing and struggling to catch his breath.

"You a'ight big bro?" Hamma yelled.

"Fuck no, I'm hit," Gangsta responded calmly.

As soon as Famous came around the corner to see the source of all the commotion, G Millions hopped over the fence with murder in his eyes. Seeing that Hamma was wheezing and was no longer a threat, he put his ratchet to Gangsta's head with the intentions of getting back at Hamma next. Just as he was about to pull the trigger, Famous pushed his arm away, sending the round into the air instead of Gangstas' skull where he felt it belonged.

"Easy cowboy, I fucks wit' these fools," Famous informed.

"I can't tell," G Millions barked. "They in ya hood takin' money like they invisible or bulletproof.

"Oh, don't sweat dat shit my nigga. They ain't gettin' off that easy," Famous explained. "We gonna see where they really at wit' they shit."

On the strength of his partner's word, G Millions reluctantly took the ratchet out of Gangsta's face and they all tended to Hamma.

"You lucky you listened to me and wore that vest," Gangsta told his brother.

"I don't wanna here dat shit right now," Hamma responded. "It feels like my back broke. I'm just glad dat pretty muthafucka can't shoot straight."

"Keep poppin' shit and my man ain't gonna be able to save you or ya brotha!" G Millions hissed thru clinched teeth.

"You ain't gangsta enough to make a bitch out of me fag!" Gangsta retorted.

"Come on now fellas," Famous stepped in and took control of the situation. "I grew up wit' all of ya'll. Me and G Millions eat together. You two muthafucka's runnin' round here doin' petty robberies." Famous pointed a knowing finger at the brothers.

"Don't think that I didn't know that ya'll been robbin' our people. But we past that now. What I'm gonna do is put ya'll onto a little spot, it's in Asbury Park, where you're not really known and them fools are gettin' plenty of money. Ya'll go out there and get ya'll money right, then we'll show ya'll what it's really about, ya dig!"

G Millions felt it in his gut that he should have pushed them. But Famous made the call and he rolled with his partner's decision. Hamma and Gangsta were glad he had.

"Yeah, I guess they made us an offer we couldn't refuse." The brothers laughed returning to the present. Hamma hopped on route 18 headed back to Exit 9...

Chapter 2

End of School 2003...

"A Change of Scenery"

YoYo was thankful that her final exams were over with and the school year was coming too an end. So today, she decided to walk home instead of taking the school bus. She wanted to clear her mind after a long day of testing and enjoy the nice weather. However, the wonderful thoughts of her promising future and the good weather that she relished was quickly replaced by doom and despair no sooner then her Nike Air Max's touched the top of the hill which lead to her project building. She wanted so badly for her and her family to move out. There was not a day that went by that some type of drama didn'tt unfold down there. But, for some strange reason she felt that today would be different, as if it would hit closer to home.

Although 176 Memorial Pkwy consisted of a mere four buildings and was the only high-rise housing project complex in the town that the streets had dubbed New Gunswick, just like any other project in America, a feeling of hopelessness and depression festered deep within the guts of its residents. Which is why, YoYo enjoyed school and any other activity that helped her to escape the environment, even if only temporary. Unfortunately, there was never a shortage of events to remind her of her present plight.

After standing at the elevator for five minutes, YoYo realized that it wouldn't be there to pick her up today because as usual it was out of service. Her stomach flipped and bile threatened to escape from her mouth at the very thought of having to take the staircase. At least on the elevator one may only have to bare the odor of urine and vomit because it was used regularly when working, but the staircases were an entirely different world within itself. One never knew what they might encounter traveling thru that world.

Hoping not to encounter sex, violence, feces, cat sized rats eating the garbage discarded by the tenants, needles, crack stems and everything else imaginable and unimaginable. YoYo inhaled deeply, *here goes nothing* she thought as she tightly clutched her book bag and made a mad dash for the stairs cursing the very conditions that she was forced to endure.

Just as YoYo was about to thank God for blessing her with a clear path to the three-bedroom apartment on the sixth floor that she shared with her mother, two older brothers and little sister, she turned the corner to her hallway, and ran across the same dope fiend that she encountered daily. However, today, instead of him begging for money to cop his next bag, he was sitting on the floor in an upright position with his back against the wall and his head cocked to the side with a syringe still hanging out of his neck. YoYo decided to disregard him and simply retreat to the safety of her home.

Once inside she poured herself a jar of a mixture of tropical punch and lemon kool aid, pressed the television remote, grabbed the phone, and sat Indian style on the couch. She then dialed her girlfriend Shakira's number.

"Hello," Shakira answered after the customary two rings.

"Hello, may I speak to Shakira please?"

"Girl, don't you know my voice by now? And stop trying to sound all proper whore." Shakira's voice boomed cheerfully through the phone giving YoYo a well-needed laugh.

"Girl you just don't know how good it is to hear your voice. I called myself taking a therapeutic walk home from school and I wound up having one of Pee-Wee's greatest adventures."

"I'm not sure I want to hear this one, but tell me anyway," Shakira joked.

"Haha, girl you's a fool. You gotta hear this shit though," YoYo assured her girlfriend and started revealing her adventure.

"I decided to Nike Air it home being as though it was nice outside. Don't ask me why I took my dumb ass down Remsen Avenue, instead of just staying on Livingston. Sure enough, those fools were up there shooting as if they were trying to show each other how the West was won. Despite the bullet that chipped off a piece of the wall right next to my head, I took that in stride and kept it moving. Then when I got to the top of the hill Ms. Betty's snotty, nose badass kids tried to snatch my coach bag. All it took me was a few hooks off the jab to make it thru that one.

"Haha, no you didn't put it on them kids like that," Shakira interrupted.

"Shit, I don't know why not. The fools know better. Humph, if they can act grown, they can take a grown ass whuppin'," YoYo told her, giving them a good laugh.

"Wait, wait, let me finish girl, so when I finally get to the building, Science and that fool Me-Me from Jersey City got like nine niggaz lined up, ass naked in the breezeway robbing them. Needless to say I saw a lot of big guns."

"Ha, ha, ha, girl you stupid," Shakira cut YoYo off again as they both cracked up with laughter.

"Hold up, hold up, wait a minute girl. I'm almost finished," YoYo said as she composed herself.

"Now me bein' the rider I am, I made it thru all of that. But just when I think it's all good, I turn the corner on my floor and dope fiend ass Paul sittin' there with the spike still hanging from his neck."

"Was he dead?" Shakira asked.

"Don't know, don't give a fuck!"

"You ain't call 5-0 or nothin'?"

"Hell to the no! I ain't no fuckin' witness, I mind my fuckin' business!" YoYo stated matter of factly.

"Damn, you a cold bitch YoYo."

"Shiit, the world is cold. If you're soft, you're lost and losin' ain't in this bitch's plans. I done see and heard it all, so don't much phases me anymore."

"Anyway, enough of that shit. You tryin' to depress a bitch," Shakira said, changing the subject. "I had mad fun at Sal's skip party, that shit was fire wasn't it!"

"You know I don't usually skip school, but it was kinda fun until that crazy ass pitbull got loose. I bust my damn nose tryin' to get away from that fuckin' dog." YoYo twisted up her nose as if Shakira could see her.

"It's all good though, 'cause when it was all said and done, you got a chance to slide off wit' G Millions the boss," Shakira giggled.

"You ain't neva' lie, G Millions that nigga. Let me tell you how he put his thing down!" YoYo shifted on the coach excited, as a surge of energy shot down to her toes and she began to tell her girlfriend about her episode with the love of her life.

"Somebody must have told him what happened to me because one minute he was in the other room with his homies. The next minute he had a towel on my bloody nose ushering me out of the door and into his G Ride. By the time, we got to his house the bleeding had stopped. So as soon as we got inside, he took me to his room, went, and got me some ice to stop the swelling. The pain had me cryin' like a baby, so he cuddled me up and whispered some sweet shit in my ear to comfort me. Then he licked away my tears. Girl, I'm telling you the boy nice wit his!" YoYo paused to emphasize her point.

"Come on YoYo stop playin' and finish." Shakira found herself playing in her coochie, thinking about G Millions doing the same nasty things to her that he did to her friend made her wet.

"A'ight girl, listen, to this. He took me into his arms and started kissin', lickin' and suckin' me from my ears, to my neck and titties. Then he moved my thongs to the side and started finger poppin' my coochie while he was still suckin' on my titties. I'm tellin' you, my pussy was saturated!"

"Would you just tell the damn story!" Shakira hoped her friend didn't hear her heavy breathing.

"Check this shit out. My baby took his time and licked, kissed and sucked his way down to my toes. Then he worked his way back up to my kitty cat. He went back and forth from my coochie to my ass until I just couldn't take it anymore. I had to have that dick. So I pulled him up, put my tongue in his ear and told that nigga I am ready. After teasing me for a minute by rubbing it around the opening and on my clit, he slid it in nice and slow, just the way I like it. Girl, I thought I was in heaven when he started slowly building up the momentum. Once we got our momentum going, he started fucking the shit out of me. I must have cum like three or four times before, we came together. Girl that shit made me forget all about my nose."

"I know that's right," Shakira said after she had brought herself to an orgasm.

"My coochie is throbbing right now."

"That nigga a freak huh," Shakira rhetoricaly said a little envious of her friend. "Girl you're lucky as hell, I wish Famous showed me that type of attention, he's selfish as hell. G Millions need to talk to that fool before he loses a good thing."

"Girl please, you know Famous is too busy flossin' to show anybody else some love. Plus G Millions told me that you are too clean for him. Famous likes grimy bitches 'cause that way he already knows what to expect. With them he doesn't have to worry about getting his little feelings hurt."

"When is G Millions getting you out of there?" Shakira asked, not wanting to discuss Famous any longer.

"My mom said I gotta wait until I graduate. That shit ain't comin' fast enough either. I got a partial scholarship to U Mass and G Millions is gonna pay the rest. I'm going for Computer Science you know I fucks wit' them computers heavy."

"What you worried about school for, all of that money you got around you?" Ya brothers got the projects under siege and ya man and his homies got Uptown, The Ville and from what I hear, they're even fuckin' around down I-95."

"Shakira believe me when I tell you G Millions bring more to the table then a hard dick. Just look around you, most of our peers are either dead, locked up or strung out on drugs. One way or the other their lives are over with before they even graduate high school. Ain't nothin' promised to us girl. My baby gives me the hope I need to make it out of here. I hate to even think about it, but he in the game heavy. So he's headed for either prison or the grave. He even told me himself to pursue my own career just in case something happens to him, that way I will be able to make it on my own." YoYo expressed, with tears beginning to well up in her eyes.

"Damn, that nigga really love you huh?" Shakira said attempting to comfort her friend, and feeling a ping of guilt about being envious of her girlfriend.

Before YoYo got a chance to respond, the thunder of machine guns and semi-automatic weapons interrupted their conversation. Although gunfire was a regular occurrence in the projects, her woman intuition kicked in and told her something was not right.

She moved as if she was no longer in control of her own body, the phone slipped from her grasp and hit the couch before breaking into pieces on the living room floor. TuPac's song, "Death Around The Corner", seemed to be magnified in her ears as she bolted towards the window. No sooner then she looked out of the window she saw what appeared to be her two brothers sprawled out on the blacktop in pools of blood and the hoodied assailants sprinting towards the highway.

YoYo, her mother, and sister damned near knocked each other over trying to get through the door at the same time, each hoping that their vision was deceiving them from such a high point of observation. Not even bothering to check the elevator, the trio of women ascended the stairs with the grace of a gazel. When they finally made it, down the flights of stairs and to the crime scene, their vision was confirmed when they stared at their worse nightmare. Two more family members lost to the game.

After she snapped out of her temporary paralysis of disbelief, YoYo noticed that her mother and sister were just standing there frozen as if in complete shock. At that moment, a light bulb went off in her head telling her she had to be the one to take charge because neither her mother nor her sister would be of any help. Although she didn't want to disrespect her brother's corps, she knew the police and the media would disrespect their memory with talks of drug deals going bad and all the other malarkey that they could come up with when somebody was murdered in the hood. The very thought of that happening was the encouragement she needed for her to take action.

One by one, she relieved them of their money and weapons. Then she fled into the building to stash everything then to call G Millions.

When G Millions received the phone call, he was uptown on Remsen Avenue in front of S & B's ready to bite into his fish sandwich. He knew who the caller was due to the particular ring tone belonging to YoYo. He immediately placed his sandwich in its styrofoam tray.

"Hey pretty mama. What's really?" He asked cheerfully.

"My two brothers just got gunned down in front of my building!" A hysterical YoYo cried.

"What! I'll be right there!" G Millions yelled and ran to the driver side of his BMW.

Before he pulled off, G Millions removed his Nextel from his waist and chirped Famous.

"Bleep…bleep…bleep…What's good?" Famous voice came over the radio.

"Yo Fame, YoYo's brothers just got pushed, meet me down bottom!"

"Say no more!"

G Millions gave the coroner, police, and every nosy neighbor in the projects time to clear out before stepping on the scene.

"I'm tired of this bull shit, my baby is pregnant, and I'm getting her the fuck out of here. I don't give a fats rat's ass what her mother talking about! G Millions informed his homies who were waiting for him when he pulled up.

"More or less you already know I'm with you home boy," Hamma assured him.

"I've been looking for a reason to pop off my new tech!" Gangsta added, with a devious look on his face, rubbing on his tech.

"That's why ya'll my fam, but breathe easy cowboys. I just wanted ya'll to meet me because I didn't know what to expect. Just be ready to make them fools have to fill out them robbery reports on Mother's Day. In the meantime hold me up while I go check on my shorty."

With that being said, Famous and Hamma posted up, while G Millions and Gangsta ascended the stairs to YoYo's apartment. When they came out of the stairwell and turned the corner, YoYo was already waiting for them in her doorway. Upon seeing her baby, she ran into G Millions arms.

"You could take me now. My mother said I don't have to wait until I graduate. She couldn't stand to lose me right now, she'd never be able to forgive herself," YoYo informed him while breaking their tight embrace and looking him in the eyes.

"That's what it is then baby. Pack your shit and let's get the fuck up out of here."

"Everything I really care about is already at your house. The few things that I have here won't take me long."

G Millions and Gangsta followed YoYo into the apartment and waited in the living room for her to return with whatever belongings that she would be taking with her.

"Where is her fine ass sister?" Gangsta asked with a smile.

"Why nigga? What you gonna do, kill da bitch?" G Millions chuckled. "'Cause you don't want no ass."

Before Gangsta got the chance to come back at him on some slick shit, YoYo walked back into the room holding a suitcase and a gym bag.

"I'm ready daddy," YoYo informed, as Gangsta ceased the opportunity to be a gentleman by relieving YoYo of her bags.

Once they got downstairs to the G Rides, Famous and Hamma were there waiting, ready to fulfill whatever action the situation demanded.

"You a'ight lil' sis'? I'm sorry for your loss," Famous offered while giving her a comforting hug.

"Yeah, thank ya'll for being here for me," The teary-eyed YoYo replied.

"It's nothin' lil' sis', you family," Hamma added, giving her a hug also.

"A'ight, ya'll fools can stop hugging all up on my baby now," G Millions giving everybody an uneasy laugh. "Seriously, though, I'm takin' my baby somewhere to try to ease her mind a little bit. I'll get up with you fools later."

With nothing else needing to be said, they gave each other love, hopped in their vehicles and went their separate ways.

As G Millions powered his drop top 325i through the streets of New Brunswick, he and YoYo were deep in their own thoughts. No longer able to sit idly and watch his baby drown in her own misery, he placed his hand on her leg and gave her a comforting rub.

"Why is this world so fucked up G?" YoYo asked through hollow eyes searching for answers, knowing that G Millions always said the right things at the right moments.

"The world ain't fucked up; it's the people in it. In this day and time, everybody is for self and muthafucka's is grimy," G Millions explained. That's why when you meet somebody that's genuine you have to ride with them until the wheels fall off, you feel me. They don't make them like us anymore sweetheart, we the last dinosaurs, that's why we're so good together, and that's why we gotta make it last forever."

"Daddy, you always know exactly what to say. You make me feel special even in tragedy," YoYo thanked him, before kissing her lover on the cheek.

"It's nothing baby girl, the truth is easy to speak. Plus you already know I'm feeling your pain as far as your brothers," G Millions sympathized, and rubbed his free hand thru her hair.

"I know daddy, just promise me that you'll be careful. I couldn't bear to lose you right now. I'll fly straight over the cuckoo's nest."

After they shared a well-needed laugh, G Millions addressed his baby again. "I ain't going no where. Besides that, if I die, how the hood gone stay fly? Everybody in it is eating off me and Fame one way or another." He assured her. "So trust me when I tell you, niggas wanna keep me around."

"Daddy, I wish my brothers would have been as sharp as you. They were getting all that paper and didn't want to leave the projects. My mother and sister act like they don't want to leave the buildings either. I just can't understand," YoYo's pleading eyes searched for answers.

"Baby girl, some people are just content playing the hand that life dealt them, instead of adding wild cards to increase their chances of winning, feel me!?"

As soon as the last words escaped his lips, G Millions pulled up to their favorite hotel.

Once inside, he led YoYo straight thru the lobby and up to the bar, instead of the front desk. After him and YoYo were seated comfortably, he motioned to the bartender to come and take his order.

"I'm ready to get right my dude," he informed the bartender, who now stood directly in front of him.

"What about the young lady?" The bartender asked.

"We've been coming here long enough for you to know that she don't drink in public."

The bartender remembered that what G Millions spoke was the gospel so he hurried up and spent on his heels to make sure that he satisfied one of his best tipping customers.

G Millions shook his head in amusement as he pulled his jack off his hip and pressed the speed dial button for it to connect him to the front desk.

"Hello, may I help you?" The clerk answered after the fourth ring.

"Yeah this is G Millions; I need you to hook up my favorite suite."

"Okay, it will be ready in ten minutes sir."

"Thank you!"

When he looked up the bartender was taking a double shot of gin, a double shot of Hennessy, a bottle of Remy Martin and a cup of Ruby Red grapefruit juice off the tray and placed it in front of them.

"That's why yo ass so crazy now," YoYo said, frowning up her face. "But I'll be glad when we go upstairs so that I can get right too. After the day I had, I need it," YoYo sighed.

"Excuse me sir, your room is ready," The bartender informed granting YoYo her wishes.

They decided not to waste any more time getting to the confines of their room, so G Millions grabbed his concoction off the bar, and replaced it with a hefty tip. Then he took his girl by the hand and led her to their suite.

"Open the door girl."

Without saying a word, she swiped the room key card and pushed the door open. The site before her eyes sent a serge of mixed emotions thru her body. She wanted and so desperately needed to enjoy this moment to allow her man to help her escape reality, even if only temporarily. However, she couldn't help but feel guilty for enjoying herself after her brothers were gunned down just hours ago, not to mention that her mother and sisters were left in the apartment to grieve on their own.

Tears begin to well up in her eyes as she looked at the multicolored roses at her feet and the candles lined up along the bed. She walked down the path of roses that led to the cart that was set up for a candle-lit dinner for two. G Millions politely slid one of the chairs out for her and assisted her into it before he sat across the table from her.

From where she sat, she could clearly see the separate paths of rose petals leading to the Jacuzzi, then from the Jacuzzi to the bed, and they were scattered about the bed as well.

"You are so good to me daddy," YoYo sniffled, wiped her eyes and then continued. "I don't mean to keep talking like this, but I've been through so much. Everything that I love I lose. Having you seems too good to be true."

G Millions got down on his knees between her legs, placed his hand under her chin, and raised her head so that he could look into her light-brown eyes before speaking. "Look baby girl, I'm good and oh yes I'm true, but ain't nothing too good for you pretty mama, you hear me?"

Tears began to resurface in her eyes as she shook her head indicating that she understood.

"Now close your eyes, I got somethin' for you." G Millions walked over to the closet and retrieved a black polo bag before returning to his position between her legs. "Don't open your eyes yet. I need you to take off all of your clothes."

"Boy you nasty. What are you about to do to me?" YoYo asked suspiciously.

"Girl just do it."

Although the suspense was killing her, she complied with his request and stripped down to her maroon laced thong revealing the body of a goddess. G Millions stood up in front of her and placed his 24 inch platinum chain weighed down by an ice infested Lot Boy medallion. He bent down and placed a diamond ankle bracelet set in platinum around her ankle and stayed on one knee. When he grabbed her hand but didn't move nor utter a word, curiosity got the best of her causing her to open her eyes.

"Aghhh," she screamed then jumped up and down, "Yes, yes, I will... I will..."

"Hold up girl, calm down. You didn't even give me a chance to do my thing," G Millions teased smiling up at her.

"Ohhh, okay, okay but that has to be house money and that right there!" YoYo squealed with excitement, pointing at the 5 karat Princess cut engagement ring that G Millions possessed. YoYo was so excited that she started to walk in place fanning her-self unable to stand still.

"Baby girl, until you came into my life, I never imagined that I could love someone as much as I love you. Now that you've come into my life, you've changed me forever. I want you to be my wife?" G Millions proposed.

"Yes...yes...yes!" YoYo screamed, cried, and dove down on him, knocking him to the floor.

The young couple rolled around in the rose petals, kissing one another playfully until they worked up an appetite and decided not to let their food go to waste. Looking across the table at his soon to be life long partner, G Millions couldn't help but feel as if he were the luckiest man in the world. Standing at 5'7", weighing 135lbs., with flawless honey brown, almond shaped eyes, that were a shade darker then hazel. Her hair stopped somewhere in the middle of her back, immaculate hygene, accented with brains and a genuine personality. YoYo was truly a black rose growing from the concrete.

"Why you looking at me like that?"

"You belong in Hollywood."

"I know you're not trying to get rid of me already?" YoYo teased. "The only way I'm going there is if we're together."

"Yeah, Hollywood would meet a real live dude like me, accompanied by his first lady." G Millions flashed his million-dollar smile.

The young couple enjoyed their meal and played affectionately until their plates were empty.

"Daddy you always taking care of me, making sure I'm always good, so tonight I wanna do something special for you," she chimed like a school girl. "I wanna be your freak. Where the weed at, I know you got some, you know that shit gets me horny as hell?" She stated.

"That's what the fuck I'm talkin' about, here light that shit up gangsta?" G Millions said excitedly getting turned on from YoYo's words as he passed her a blunt he already had rolled.

"Let's go get a bottle of Rose, smoke a blunt together, and get right so I can show you how much I appreciate having a good man in my life."

"That's what it is." He smiled, and then walked around grabbed YoYo by the hand then they followed the path of rose petals to the Jacuzzi.

Once in the bathroom YoYo helped G Millions out of his clothes, stepped out of her thong and together they eased down into the hot lathery bubbles. Before getting comfortable YoYo stood back up, grabbed a fluffy white towel and then hit the button to the radio. The sultry sounds of Soul To Soul's "Let Me Love You Down" gently exited through the speakers. She then placed a fluffy towel at the edge of the Jacuzzi and patted it.

"Sit up here daddy," she whispered while gyrating her hips to the rhythm of the music.

She bent down and collected some bubbles, then slowly and sensually lathered herself up, while grabbing her firm breast and caressing her nipples to an erection, all the while swaying her way back to an upright position. YoYo took her time, spent around, and teased G Millions with her pleasantly plump derrière. What seemed to be the perfect amount of bubbles slid off her glistening skin. The platinum and ice sparkled like a beautiful rainbow after a mid-summer rain shower.

She turned back around to face him, and then ever so slowly took his protruding manhood into her mouth. She gently caressed his balls, placed each one of them into her mouth, and then slowly made love to his shaft with her tongue. Knowing her man, she felt him tense up with pleasure. Needing to have him inside of her, she eased her mouth off him, straddled his erection reverse cowgirl style, and rode him as if she were on a bucking bronco.

Just seconds away from a sexual explosion the door burst open and her son little G Millions entered the bedroom and dove onto the bed. His actions startled YoYo and woke her from her dream. The same re-occurring dream that she'd been having ever since G Millions incarceration in "04".

Little G was still jumping up and down on the bed, while his mother sat up trying to collect her thoughts.

"Come here baby," she said to her son while grabbing him up into her palms, kissing and squeezing him tightly.

"I love you too mommy!" He responded, while he wiped away his mother's wet kisses.

Although Little G Millions seemed to be naïve to what was going on in the adult world what they didn't know was that he was soaking everything up like a sponge.

"Ms. Pink is here mommy."

No sooner than he got the words out of his mouth, Lady Pink entered the room.

"That little boy is something else. He looks and acts just like his daddy," Lady Pink stated then she set on the foot of the bed.

"I know that's right. If I didn't know I had carried him for nine months myself, I would have sworn his daddy gave birth to him. It looks like they left me out of that event," YoYo agreed and they shared a good laugh. "So did you cop the S600 or the Quatruporte?"

"I had to cop that Quatruporte. That shit so mean and vicious. I got so much shit in it that our baby is definitely going to be the only king to wear that crown." Lady Pink paused before continuing. "I'm telling you girl that shit is pearl white sitting on sprees, with wood grain smelling like fresh trees, fully loaded with screens and DVDs," Lady Pink boasted.

"Ha ha, girl you are too much. You been around G Millions way too long. I bet you don't even realize that you're starting to talk slick just like him," YoYo remarked.

"That fool gets his swag from me," Lady Pink smiled.

"Whatever bitch," YoYo teased and they laughed again.

"You think he gonna like his welcome home gift we get him?" Lady Pink asked.

"Girl, are you kidding me? That fool's been hollering about that car since it came out. If it had a place for him to stick his dick then he might dump both of our asses. Please tell me that you didn't have a pussy put in their too!" YoYo had them cracking up.

After sharing a sisterly hug, YoYo got out of the bed to take a shower and get dressed. She was happy that one of her re-occuring dreams was finally about to become a reality again...

Chapter 3

Nightfall was approaching as G Millions and Famous took in the polluted air of the summer breeze. Tonight was late night recreation for the facility and G Millions and Famous took advantage of the extra time to discuss plans and often reminisce about life outside the prison walls.

"Yo G, remember when we were growing up and shit used to be fun when we first got in the game?" Famous asked G Millions as the two of them strolled the yard.

"Yeah, we were some wild dudes," agreed G Millions letting out a slight chuckle.

"Oh shit," Famous yelled out. "Speakin' of being wild dudes, how about that time when we were at your crib and that shit popped off with Ms. Dee Dee?"

"Now that was some ill shit," G Millions laughed as the two of them travled back into their childhood...

"Thursday nights at Willies and Pearls"

Winter 1982...

Every Thursday night, Willie and Pearls house transformed into a gambling spot afterhours. It transformed into a place where the grown and sexy crowd of the area could come in and unwind without having to worry about being shot, stabbed or thrown out of a cab.

Being as though most of the people who frequented the house practically knew one another, something as small as a scuffle was a rarity.

Willie and Pearl also provided plenty of good food, music and an upbeat atmosphere, which made the perfect retreat from a hectic workweek, as well as the everyday struggles in which life had to offer. For the most part the crowd that they catered to worked at decent jobs and or had side hustles.

The boosters came through, as well as people buying small quantities of powder cocaine from Willie or one of the other smalltime hustlers. There was never a dull moment and the fun usually lasted until Sunday, Monday or when everybody was broke.

G Millions and Famous were very observant. They paid close attention to everything that went on around them and soaked it up like Brawny. While the grown-ups thought they were too young to understand what was taking place, the youngsters clung to every word that they heard spoken, and stored it and everything that they witnessed into the memory bank.

They took a piece of all of the best game that came thru which they thought would be of some use in the future. In fact, it was starting to pay off for them already.

"Willie, you need to stop letting that boy sit on your lap while you're gamblin' and packaging up that shit!" Pearl fussed. "The little fucker already thinks he grown!"

Willie took a long, slow, drag from his Kool cigarette and blew a stream of smoke upward, which mingled in with the rest of the smoke that lingered in the air amongst the lights before calmly responding. "Listen baby, I understand where your coming from. But dig this here; I ain't tryin' to shelter my little man. He's a third generation hustla. His grandfather was a hustla, his father was a hustla, I'm a hustla, hell you are too." Willie took another drag of his Kool, this time almost burning his fingers, before he continued. "Hustlers aren't made they are born, it's in the bloodline. You heard what grandma Telly said, the little muthafucka sold some old shoes to the woman in the store for some candy. I'm gonna school him right; he's gonna be a millionaire in his lifetime!" Willie was now worked up and full of animation, causing everyone at the table to laugh.

Willie wasn't G Millions biological father, however, he loved him like he was and treated him like it too. He provided him with all of the latest gear and games. Of course G Millions loved to stay fresh but he'd much rather do what he was now rather than playing his video games.

"By the time that little nigga got finished runnin' around for me last week. My wallet was short eighty-five dollars. Shiit, I thought it was a part of ya'll's hustle. But it's clear that the boy is absorbing all of our shit and using it against us," Joe spoke up supporting Willies theory.

"Yeah and that little fuck of yours ain't far behind," Pearl cut in, not willing to let Famous ease out of this one looking like a saint.

"You won't get an argument out of me. Shiit, the other day I caught him and about eleven older kids behind our building shootin' dice and he was leadin' the bets. If I wasn't so proud of him, I would have put my foot in his ass." Everybody in the room burst out laughing except for Rose who didn't find any humor in Joe's last statement.

"Ya'll laughin'. That shit ain't funny!" Rose's sudden seriousness was to no avail because everyone was well aware of her mood swings when she exceeded her drinking limit.

"I told them about hangin' out with the older kids. They are going get their little asses in trouble." Pearl tried to support her friend, but the men were not having it.

"Hell, they can't play with kids in their own age rang, they're moving twice the speed. They even run circles around the older boys in the neighborhood. Face it ladies, they are ahead of their time." Willey smiled.

"They learned from the best," Joe bragged, creating more laughter.

"I hope both of you prepared for the monsters you're creating," Rose refused to lose the debate.

"Shut your drunken ass up woman! I had just about enough of that Mother Theresa shit you talkin'. You get high, gamble, suck dick and everything else around them. Now all of a sudden we're creating monsters. Bitch please!" Joe snapped.

"I bet I won't be sucking your dick no time soon sucka!" Rose retaliated.

"Stop fronting woman, you know you can't keep your mouth off this one eyed spittin' cobra," Joe teased, instantly defusing the situation.

There was never a shortage of wars of words at Willies and Pearls. Things just wouldn't be right without some riffraff about one thing or another. The best part about it was that although someone might get a little overly excited. It wasn't common for anyone to really catch feelings. Tired of having their parents talk about them as if they were not sitting there; G Millions and Famous gave each other the eye. That was their signal to slide off of their fathers laps and head for the sanctuary of the basement.

As they passed by G Millions' room, in route to their destination, they were stopped short by what sounded like bed springs squeaking. Deciding to investigate their suspicions, they saw G Millions' uncle Head giving it to some lady from behind. Her face was buried in the pillow while his uncle sexed her doggie style.

Famous peeped the look in his partner's eyes and already knew what it was, so he whispered. "Let's keep it movin.'"

"Hells no, follow me partner," G Millions said mischievously, as he burst into the room with Famous right on his heels.

Startled by the unexpected youth Head spun around and aimed his .38 special in their direction, not knowing who it was or what they were up to. When he saw who it was, he waved them off. "Get ya'll little bad asses out of here before I shoot both of you mutherfuckas!" Head was growing very agitated because not only did they blow up his spot, but also they interrupted his groove as well.

"Uncle Head, you nasty," teased G Millions.

"Can I get some?" Famous chimed in excitedly.

"You can't handle this grown woman pussy!" Head shot back. "Now get the fuck out of here!"

While Head exchanged words with the youth, his companion tried to hide her face with a pillow. But it was too late because they could spot Ms. Patrice's ass from anywhere. She stayed prancing around in some daisy dukes with her butt cheeks hanging out on a regular basis for them not to notice. The sexy Ms. Patrice was fair skinned with bright eyes, long pretty hair, full breasts, full buttocks, hips and lips. Clothes seemed to be against her religion because her assets stayed on display. She had been the fantasy of G Millions and Famous masturbation sessions on numerous occasions.

"This is my room uncle Head," G Millions reminded his uncle.

"How much you want little punk?" Head saw right through his scheme.

"Me and Famous need some new kicks."

"Well take two hundreds off my stack and get the hell out!"

"Good lookin' out Unc!" G Millions smiled.

"Don't Unc me, you little bastards," Head yelled at them and smiled to himself. "Ya'll getting too big for your britches."

"Let me just see her titties!" Famous blurted and he and G Millions laughed their way out of the room closing the door behind them.

When they finally made it to the basement, G Millions lit up a blunt filled with skunk and hash.

"Let's count our loot and product," he said in between pulls.

"That shit stink yo," Famous complained followed by a futile attempt to fan the smoke out of his face before continuing. "Put in a tape G, I'm tired of that shit they listening to upstairs." Famous screwed up his face showing his displeasure.

G Millions ignored his partner's attitude and popped in their Kurtis Blow cassette, while pulling out a half of a pint of Hennessey. Famous retrieved the digital scale and some cuts for the cocaine and heroin that they had just smuggled from upstairs. At the tender ages of twelve, they already knew how to cut coke, dope, play poker, shoot dice, sex girls, and a lot more boys their age should not know.

You rarely saw one without the other. Everyone thought they were first cousins. Not to mention the fact that their birthdays were only eleven days apart and their parents grew up together the same way they had. Joe and Rose were actually Famous's real parents and had been together since high school, which was a rarity in the hood.

G Millions and Famous had all of the little girls turned out off their swagger and most of the boys despised them. Willie made an accurate assessment when he stated that they ran circles around cats as old as eighteen years old and had some even older getting money with them.

"Yo B, we gonna be millionaires!" exclaimed an excited G Millions, while preparing the drugs for packaging.

"And hood famous!" Famous matched his partner's excitement.

"Let's hurry up and get this done so we can bag it up.

"This some good shit," G Million said, wiping the mixture of cocaine and heroin off of his nose.

"You sniffin' that shit? Fool you crazy," Famous warned.

"Fuck that, this shit got me feelin' real mellow, like I ain't got a worry in the world." G Millions paused, glared at his partner through glossy eyes and continued. "Now when you get tired of doin' Willie and Pearls job, let's get this done. I'mma needs you to help me trick Ms. Dee Dee down here so I can hit her with this dope dick!" G Millions' southern drawl and cool demeanor caused both of them to laugh.

"Yeah, she'll let us both hit it for a speedball and a couple of dollars," Famous added between chuckles.

An hour later, their task was complete.

"We got twenty-five bundles of dope, eighty twenties of coke and $680 cash, not bad for a couple of 12-year-olds," G Millions informed, while splitting the take.

"And that ain't including our weed flow and the doe we're already stackin'," Famous agreed.

After the two young ambitious hustlers gave each other a front hand slap followed by a high five, they took their time cleaning up and stashing their material.

***

Meanwhile upstairs everybody was enjoying themselves. The card game was slowly turning into a party.

"Oowww, this is my jam, where's my baby at?" Pearl inquired loudly while snapping her fingers to the rhythm of the music.

"Right here!" Willie answered.

"I ain't talkin' about you fool, I'm talking about my baby boy."

"I wish you would make up your mind woman! When he here, you don't want him around. Now that he found something to do, you want him around."

"You know she can't live without that little boy," Rose cut in.

"He probably downstairs with Famous adding up all that money and product they don't think we know they got us for," added Joe.

"So that's how my kid keeps my hair and nails done every week?" Pearl rubbed her chin as if in deep thought. "I knew that little nigga was pulling a fast one on me when he told me he kisses the girls."

"You are so naïve when it comes to that boy. He can do no wrong in your eyes." Willie brought her out of her brief stupor.

"You damn right. Ya'll got some nerve though. You had the little fucker in silk boxers before he even got off the potty. Not to mention the ice you put in his ear after I told you not to get it pierced, talking about some he a hustler's poster child," Pearl argued playfully musing Willie in the forehead.

"Them little niggas got it made," Joe said.

"That's what it's all about. We came up, so ain't no use in them struggling. Lord knows we did enough of that for three generations," added Rose.

"I know that's right, that's why I got my baby out of Brooklyn when he was four," Pearl stated matter of factly.

"Yeah, his little ass would be wildin' on the island right now if you would have stayed in New York!" Willie joked.

"There go my baby!" Pearl yelled excitedly when G Millions and Famous emerged from the basement.

"Ya'll smell like a pound of reefer!" Rose twisted her face up in displeasure. "You two been smoking that stuff again?"

"It was good too!" laughed G Millions. "Where ya'll get it from?"

I'll always love my mama, 'cause she's my favorite girl…" blared through the speakers saving G Millions from a pop in the mouth for his last remark.

Pearl and Rose started singing along and snapping their fingers.

"Ahhh, come on baby let's dance?" Pearl grabbed G Millions by his hand.

"Yeah, everybody knows you're a momma's boy!" Famous teased, right before his mother had grabbed him by the arm and dragged him to the middle of the dance floor.

G Millions doubled over in laughter at the site of that.

"I should kill you, you cheating muthafucka!" Flirt shouted, prompting everybody to stop doing what they were doing and investigate the ruckus that was taking place at the poker table.

"You're too sweet to cheat!" Vick retorted.

His comment sent Flirt over the edge. Before anybody could react, Flirt reached across the table and slashed Vick across the face.

"What the fuck is wrong with you fool?" Willie yelled. "You gonna cut a nigga in my house with my family right here!"

Flirt quickly began to explain his actions after remembering what happened to the last fool that was crazy enough to act up in Willie and Pearls house.

"Come on now Willie, we been doing this a long time. You and I both know I ain't mean to disrespect your house. But I caught that cheating muthafucka with an extra card in the game," Flirt paused to see if his words were having an effect on his friend. "Shit, I noticed every time he played his game he won. I knew I was gonna catch him cheating and put blood on my knife!" Flirt justified.

"Yeah, well clean that shit up and both of you get the fuck out of here. Ya'll can kill each other on the streets if you want, but not in here," Willie informed.

"Flirt you 6'5" 320lbs and you're always cutting a muthafucka!" Joe yelled. "Shit nigga, your mitts are the size of bear claws. Why didn't you just smack earth, wind, and fire out of that muthafucka?"

"Shit, I let his bitch ass off easy by cutting him. If I hit 'em, I really would have opened his ass up or broke something!"

"That fool lyin'. He know he's too lazy to fight," Willie joked.

"Hell, I'm too old!" Flirt shot back, relieved that the heat was off him.

Pearl called Vick a cab to take him to Robert Wood Johnson hospital. Although it's real name was Robert Woods, everyone called it Robert Hood because everybody that worked there was from the ghetto, including a hand full of doctors.

While all of the commotion was going on, G Millions and Famous took the opportunity to convince Ms. Dee Dee to meet them in the basement.

"What ya'll lil' fuckers want wit' me?" Dee Dee faked an attitude, already knowing the answer to her question.

"We want some grown woman pussy," Famous informed her with a shit-eating grin on his face.

"You bad little fuckers are always up to something."

"Yeah, we are some bad fuckers and we want to fuck you bad." G Millions flashed his million-dollar smile.

"Show us those juicy titties?" Famous added, grabbing a hand full of both.

"How much ya'll got anyway?" She asked, deciding not to waste anymore time.

"We got coke and dope," G Millions answered wit' the quickness.

"Ya'll learn how to eat pussy yet? 'Cause when I do my speedballs I like to have my pussy licked.

What Ms. Dee Dee was about to do was considered child molestation in a court of law, but the game had no age where she was from. Seven to seventy, you were subjected to whatever the game had to offer, especially if you chose to play it. G Millions and Famous already understood that and had no qualms about it.

"You fine as hell Ms. Dee Dee, but I don't know who been up in that pussy," Famous protested.

"Shit, ya'll don't know who them pissy tail little girls been kissing either, but ya'll keep ya tongues down their throats," Ms. Dee Dee faked as if she was offended before continuing to lay her thing down. "Now let me give ya'll lessons on how to eat some coochie so ya'll can have them young whores chasin' behind ya'll for something other than lunch money. And I'mma give 'em to ya'll for cheap," she said as if she was doing them a favor. "Give me a one on one," she said referring to a bag of dope and a $20 piece of coke. "Plus I'm going to give ya'll a session that will have you ahead of the game."

Without hesitation, Famous went into his bag and handed her a one on one. G Millions followed suit by peeling $40 off his knot and handing it to her. Once that was settled, Famous popped in a Keith Sweat tape to prepare for her strip show while she mixed both products together into a speedball. After she got right, she gave them a strip show that was out of this world, for them anyway.

"That's right ma, get busy," Famous encouraged while licking his lips. Ms. Dee Dee ass cheeks clapped with each move she made as her titties bounced up in down. She ended her performance with a full split and began rubbing her clit then licking her fingers.

When her show was complete, she lay on her back, cocked her legs open and gave them an on the job pussy eating training. She took her time and pointed out all of the areas that turned women on.

As soon as their session was over, she got onto her hands and knees and allowed G Millions to penetrate her, while she gave Famous head. They fully enjoyed the action that she was giving them. They took turns bouncing and flipping her every which way possible. The high from the speedball was in full affect causing Ms. Dee Dee to attack their youthful organs like a prisoner on death row and they were her last supper. Her drug-induced thoughts took her into a world of her own. She was so caught up in the moment that she did not know she had been caught in the act until she heard the familiar voices.

Words could not describe the reaction of Pearl when she walked in on what was taking place. The Heineken bottle that she held up to her lips dropped to the floor as her motherly instincts kicked in.

"Unh uhh bitch!" Pearl screamed trying to get over the shock.

"What the fuck you doin' to my babies?"

While Pearl was talking, Rose was stalking. Ms. Dee Dee's high was blown as she looked up at the two women in horror. There was no way for her to justify having a mouthful of Famous cum and an asshole full of G Millions.

Rose made it over to the bed in two quick strides, snatched Ms. Dee Dee by her hair, and hooked her in the face repeatedly. By that time, Pearls initial shock wore off. She joined in on the party after picking up the discarded Heineken bottle. She smashed Ms. Dee Dee's upside the head with it.

By the time Willie and Joe ran into the room, ass and titties were everywhere and so was Ms. Dee Dee's blood. Her face was badly bruised from the ass whupping the women had put on her.

"Hold up, hold up, ya'll gonna kill her!" Willie yelled while trying to break up the fight.

"That's exactly what we're trying to do." Pearl struggled to break free of his grip so that she could finish Ms. Dee Dee off.

"What's this shit all about anyway?" Joe questioned.

"This whore was trying to pass her diseases off to our kids, with her trifling' ass!" Rose shouted, still raining blows down on Ms. Dee Dee.

Willie knew that he had to think fast, so he tossed Pearl aside, snatched Ms. Dee Dee up, and ushered her through the basement door.

"I should call the police on her ass!" Pearl screamed.

"Ain't no police comin' to this house!" Joe interjected. "Shit, the way ya'll kicked her ass, ya'll might be the ones to end up in jail!"

Both Pearl and Rose saw the logic in Joe's statement and began to calm down.

"Where them little fuckers go that fast anyway?" Rose stood with her hands on her hips, looking around the room.

G Millions and Famous shared a good laugh as the present came back into their view. The prison yard was getting ready to close as their mother's voices echoed inside their heads.

"It's almost over Fame," G Millions said giving Famous a hug.

"No doubt baby," were Famous' parting words.

"Next day."

"You already know.

Chapter 4

Summer 2003...

"The Out of Town Caper"

Candy Girl was as fine as they came and didn't need anyone to tell her. She stood at the petite height of 5'4", 36-24-36, with the complexion of banana Now and Later and felt she tasted every bit as good too. Her green eyes and red hair made her exotic enough to have all of the men chasing, eight to eighty, blind, cripple and crazy. They all wanted to taste the candy. Even the women both gay and straight had tried to take a taste.

Candy's parents were wealthy and loved to spoil their only daughter. Credit cards from Visa to Master Cards were always made available to her for whenever she wanted. So when you spoke about Gucci, Prada, D & G, and any other designer label she had a taste for you were speaking her language.

She had been out of school for a whole year now and her parents had decided that it was time for her to do something with her life, get a job, attend school, or do something. This revelation would come to surface tonight. Candy Girl was relaxing in her room listening to her Usher CD, when her mother entered and sat on the bed. Candy Girl became agitated by her mother's sudden intrusion.

"Hey baby-," her mother said affectionately rubbing her hair.

"Me and your father need you to come downstairs so that we can all talk."

"Okay mom, I'm right behind you," she answered before hitting the stop button on her CD player.

She followed her mother downstairs where her father was waiting for them in his Al Bundy chair, with hand in his pants and all.

"Hello ladies, it always fills my heart with so much joy to see my two favorite girls together," her father said to them with a smile.

"Your father thinks he has game," her mother joked.

After sharing a family hug, Candy Girl's father turned serious as he spoke with a somber expression on his face.

"Listen baby, you are the best part of the love that your mother and I share, which is one of the reasons we always made sure you never had to struggle the way we did coming up. We've kept you around for a year after you graduated for our own selfish reasons."

"We didn't want to let you go," her mother cut in.

"But we've come to the painful conclusion that we have to let you experience the world for yourself." Tears began to build up in her father's eyes as he spoke.

"We will miss you baby, but we're not going to be around forever." Her mother stepped in, seeing things were getting very touchy. "So you have the choice to either go to school or get a job."

"What? Ya'll kickin' me out?" Candy Girl joked, which lightened up the mood a little before she continued. "Seriously though, I know it seems as though I was just being content with ya'll taking care of me, but I just needed a break from school, now I'm ready to return. I was looking at Clark University in Atlanta Georgia."

Her parents looked at each other and smiled. "Okay then it's settled, I'll make the arrangements," her father assured, relieved that they were all on the same page.

***

Within a month's time, Candy Girl's father had made true on his word. He moved her into her own apartment in Atlanta Georgia and enrolled her into Clark. Candy Girl was excited to be in a big city. Florida was nice, but Atlanta was a completely different crowd of people. Everywhere she looked, she saw black people living how the white people lived in Florida.

The first day after her parents went back home, she was so enthusiastic about going to school in Atlanta, that she woke up early just to make sure that her hair and makeup was perfect. When she finally arrived on the campus, she was like an excited tourist. The first thing that she had to do was go to the guidance counselor's office in order to get her schedule. While standing in line Candy Girl noticed a girl eyeing her.

"Hey girl, that Christian Dior is fire," the girl named Angie complimented, pausing to see if Candy Girl was sociable. After reading her receptive body language, she continued. "What's your name and where are you from?"

"Thank you," Candy Girl responded, hoping to be meeting a new friend. "My name is Candy Girl and I'm from Florida."

For some reason she knew at that moment she could fuck with Angie.

"My name is Angie; I'm from right here in the "A", a hood called the bluff," Angie informed, with her hand extended.

With the preliminaries out of the way, the two girls agreed to meet after class.

As soon as class let out, Angie ran up on Candy Girl right outside of the lecture hall.

"Hey girl, do you want to go to lunch?"

"If you are treatin', I'm eatin'!" Candy Girl joked.

"This is my town. Why wouldn't I welcome my new road dog?" Angie grabbed Candy Girl by the arm and led her to the student parking lot. "Let's go!"

"This how you doin' yours?" Candy Girl asked, inspecting Angie's dolphin green Yukon Denali sitting on 22's.

"The "A" is good to me." Angie smiled and hit the remote on her key chain.

By the time the girls reached Benihana, one of the Atlanta's popular restaurants, they had covered a lot of ground. After discussing, each other's life styles and what they liked to do. They discovered that although they had different backgrounds they had everything in common. The main thing was that they both loved digging in ballers pockets.

"Damn Angie, you sure we don't know each other from another life? It seems like you slid out of my mother's ass!" Candy Girl joked and they laughed.

"Girl you're cool as a fan." Angie playfully tapped her new friend on the shoulder. "Some friends of mine are throwing a party at 112, you wanna come?"

"Why wouldn't I?"

On their way back to school, they exchanged numbers. Candy Girl was feeling herself because she was already seeing so much of the "A" and Angie was just what she needed to help her put her hands on what was really good in the city. She was smart enough to know that it wasn't going to be dudes riding by honking their horns at her as she walked by that supplied her demands. She didn't care if they were in a Benz or a Bentley, she needed to be in the game and Angie was her way in.

The first impression was the best impression. So Candy Girl knew that she had to be tight tonight. She started making preparations as soon as she got home. The first thing that she did was called Angie to find out where she could go shopping.

"Hello," Angie's groggy voice came thru the receiver.

"What's really good?"

"My pussy," Angie joked.

"That's a little more info than I need. But anywayz," she disregarded Angie's statement.

"I need to know where I can get a fresh outfit that will have dudes down here droolin'."

"Talk slick girl!" Angie smiled.

"The best local spot is the Lenox Square mall, you can't go wrong there. I would come with you but I got a few errands to run."

Candy Girl took the directions down, hopped in her G Ride and shot to the mall. She wasn't in the mall for no longer then a half an hour before she spent a stack of her emergency money on a Gucci purse with some matching sandals. She didn't have an ounce of remorse either because she knew that it was an investment. One of these fools would pay it back and then some she reasoned.

Angie came thru to pick her up at the witch's hour. But unlike Cinderella who had to be home at 12 a.m. or she would turn into a mere maiden, Candy Girl's glamour would just begin to unravel for all of what seem to be 200 club goers' to witness.

"It's kinda early for 112, the ballas don't usually start fallin' up in there until around 1:30 or 2 o'clock," Angie informed

"It's whatever wit' me Ang., I'm riding shotgun."

"A'ight, we gonna parking lot pimp until that time."

When the two girls pulled into the club parking lot, Candy Girls eyes lit up as if she'd seen a pot of gold. All different makes and model SUVs', cars and bikes reminded her of a Funk Master Flex car show. You name it and it was parked there. Young men and women alike were putting their thing down early.

However, it would be them, who would prove to be the showstoppers. All eyes were on them when they jumped out of Angie's big truck. Angie was freshly clad in Lou V and Candy Girl could have put a Gucci model to shame.

The Hotlanta air was refreshing and the young hustler's and hood models alike took the gorgeous evening as an opportunity to show their peers how good life had been to them. When the girls finally made it thru the parking lot and up to the line, some dudes Angie knew from the west side of the city called them up to the front.

"What's good besides your beauty Ang?" Crazy D flirted.

"Ain't nothin', me and my girl come out to do our thing," Angie responded, popping her legs back, knowing how crazy it made men and women.

"Well you already know your money aint no good to me and my homeboys," Crazy D said while scanning her entire body

"I know crazy; ya'll always hook a sista up."

With that said, the guy's paid their way in 112. It was packed. This is gonna be a good night Candy Girl thought to herself. As they were walking to the V.I.P, one of the guy's spoke to Candy Girl as he guided them to the roped off table with his name on it.

"What's yo' name shorty?" Los asked in his L.A. accent.

"Candy Girl," she responded looking him up and down.

"Yeah, well I can see why," Los flirted. "Are you as sweet as you look?"

This lame ass nigga couldn't come up with nothing better than that she, that's what they all say, Candy Girl thought to herself.

"That's what they tell me," was her response.

"Well maybe I'll get to find out," Los pressed.

"Be easy big time, we just got here. I came to mingle," Candy Girl smiled flirtatiously before asking. "What ya'll do anyway?"

"We own a car wash on the west side among other things," Los grinned slyly.

After the waitress came through with a couple of gold bottles, the guy's left the V.I.P to get their mack on, while the ladies continued to dance by themselves and enjoy the champagne.

Security was escorting a group of hustlers to a bigger V.I.P section than the one they were in now. As they floated, pass one of the hustler's grabbed Candy Girls hand.

"Come on ma," Richie Rich proposed full of confidence.

When Angie saw her friend hesitate, she whispered in her ear. "Girl, you know who that it is? That's Richie Rich; his face is plastered on billboards all over the city."

"You ain't gotta tell me twice," Candy Girl whispered back while taking the hustler's out stretched hand.

For the rest of the night Candy Girl partied as if it were her last night on earth. When the club was about to let out, she sought after Angie in order to let her know what was good.

"Girl, I'm about to see what that nigga Richie Rich is working with," she announced.

"Go ahead and do ya thing girl, I'm straight."

Minutes later, she was riding shotgun in Richie Rich's Phantom. Thirty minutes thereafter, she was arriving at a five star hotel. Everything else was a blur.

It was three in the afternoon, the next day when Candy Girl woke up. She was a little disappointed with her-self for missing school, but the envelope left on her pillow along with a letter from Richie Rich helped her to get over it.

"Take these two gees, you earned it. I have this room until next week, so whenever you leave just tell the housekeeper to clean up the room.

You the Best Ma (Smile), $ Richie Rich $."

She had doubled her pocketbook investment she thought to herself but it bothered her that she had no recollection as to what she had actually done to earn it. She massaged her temples to try to ease the pain from her splitting headache. She realized she must have had way too much to drink not to remember her rendezvous last night with Richie Rich. It had been a long time since she had been that tore up.

Candy Girl finally surrendered to the fact that she wasn't going to be able to remember. So she called the front desk and had them fetch a cab.

It was about 5:30 p.m. when she left the Swiss hotel. The first thing she did when she got in the house was check her answer machine. There were thirteen messages, ten from her parents and three from Angie. First, she called her parents who were easy to convince that she had a long day at school and was asleep. Then she called Angie who picked her cell phone up on the first ring.

"Girl, where you been?" Angie yelled through the phone. "I was worried to death when I didn't see you at school!" She scolded, without giving her friend a chance to answer. "If you're going to run with me, you have to be more responsible. I party, but I remember what I'm here for and if we're going to be road dogs, you've gotta do the same. Can I get that?" Angie's voice was full of concern.

"You got that," Candy Girl answered, knowing that her friend was right.

"Did you get paid last night?" Angie asked cheerfully, easing the tension that was previously lingering in the air.

"You know I did!" Candy Girl squealed excitedly. "Good looks for everything girl!"

"That's what's I'm talking about."

Angie was happy for her friend and she hoped that she was sincere about keeping her focused because she didn't want her getting sucked in by the Bermuda triangle like effect that the "A" had on some people.

"Girl, I gotta tear the mall up today and wash my Benz, you ridin'?" Candy Girl invited, thinking about the DKNY sundress she saw the day before.

"Yeah, come and scoop me. I have to take care of some business there myself."

"Got you."

Twenty minutes later...

Candy Girl scooped Angie up in her fully loaded candy apple red CLK, with red interior and 20" chrome verticals on all four corners and they were off to the mall. After they purchased a few items, Angie took her friend to the same car wash on the Westside that she took her truck too. She knew Candy Girl would be fully satisfied with their services because every time she left there it looked as if her truck had been detailed and ready for the showroom. The best thing about it was that it was free.

While they were waiting for the Benz to finish being washed and cleaned, Carlos from the club walked up.

"Hey ladies. What's goody wit' ya'll?"

"Hey," they sang in unison.

"Angie you didn't tell me you were coming to my carwash."

"You didn't ask," she answered playfully.

Throughout the entire exchange, Los couldn't keep his eyes off Candy Girl. She was looking right, sporting some form fitting Baby Phat jeans, a red silk blouse knotted up in order to expose her flat mid and cute belly button. She rocked her favorite red Coach bag, Vera Wang shades, with a pair of red open toed sandals to show off her perfectly pedicure toes bringing her ensemble together perfectly. She was most definitely easy on the eyes and had Los mouth watering.

"I told you your money no good where ever I'm at, so the car wash is on me. And I wanna see you tonight," Los pushed up after snapping out of the trance Candy Girl had him in.

"A'ight, you seem to know how to treat a lady of my caliber, so I'm game." Candy Girl accepted while eyeing him up and down knowing that she had him.

"Take this stack and go get your hair and nails done. I want you at your best tonight."

"Thanks. She will," Angie said, snatching the money out of his hand after noticing Candy Girl's hesitation.

"It's nothin' boo, I'll see you at eight," Los assured Candy Girl before retreating to his office.

A couple of minutes later the Benz was ready and just as Angie predicted Candy Girl was thoroughly satisfied with the job.

"Damn Ang, I'm souped and impressed," Candy Girl exclaimed. "I came to Atlanta not knowing what to expect and I've already met my long lost sister and two of the richest niggas in the city."

"Don't be surprised, this is the land of opportunity for our people. Brothers can come down here broke one day and be a hundred thousand strong the next. And the good part about it is that they don't mind sharing it with sisters like us. Especially when they see us trying do something with ourselves by going to school, starting a career or business or something."

"I hear that girl," Candy Girl said, giving Angie a high five.

"Listen, Monday night me and one of my girls is going to a female review at the strip club, you in?"

"I feel kind of funny about going to watch a bunch of women shake their ass. But hey, I gotta admit, I come up fuckin' with you Ang, so count me in."

"Right answer, 'cause the ballas will be in the buildin' girl!"

The two women squealed with excitement and gave each other a high five to solidify their date.

***

Monday night rolled around swiftly and both Angie and her home girl Lady Pink were good and pissed off by the time Candy Girl arrived to pick them up. But Candy Girl who was perky and cheerful couldn't understand why the girls were so upset with her for being a little late. Her self-centeredness caused her to over-look the fact that she had plenty of time to prepare, thus there was no reason for her tardiness. Angie quickly got over it though. However, Lady Pink half spoke to her the entire night.

Lady Pink had a completely different agenda and she wasn't going to allow Candy Girl or nobody else to fuck that up for her. Her boo G Millions had put her up on how deep that spot be with balling cats dropping stacks as if it was nothing. So what she was preying on would be there. With her beauty and style, one would never expect her to be a predator. But they were dead wrong.

While Angie and Candy Girl did their one-two, playing for what she considered pennies Lady Pink decided to put her plan in motion for the big bucks. While wiggling her way to the bar, she thought about how she did what she did for pleasure. Lady Pink enjoyed holding her lover down and couldn't wait to catch a dog chasing her tail or his dick, depending on how you want to look at it.

When she reached the bar, she pulled out a big face hundred and asked for a double shot of Grey Goose with pineapple juice. Her ears, neck and both wrists were on freeze, so she caught the attention she was looking for. Her predator instincts let her know that her trap was set. Keeping her game face on, she got up and left a Jackson tip for the bartender, and made her way back to the table where Angie was sitting there talking to some average dude with paper confirming her earlier thoughts.

Lady Pink was chilling sipping a drink, feeling it when the DJ put on "Shake That Ass Girl" by 50 Cent, which instantly got the club jumping. A stacked deep chocolate dancer by the name of Juicy came over to their table looking every bit of her name.

"Ya'll want a lap dance?" Juicy asked seductively.

"Play ya position ma!" Lady Pink accepted in a sexy tone.

She knew she wasn't gay so she had no problem supporting a sister's hustle. Plus, she had to admit the chocolate sister was gorgeous and if she did swing that way, Juicy would be hers. But being as though she didn't her and Angie just rewarded Juicy for the ass poppin' show that she put on by throwing her ones. All eyes were on them as the crowd of dudes surrounded the table and joined in throwing cash at Juicy while poppin' bottles of champagne. Candy Girl was on the other side of the club doing her one two until she met Famous. Although Angie told her that Lady Pink was from Jersey, she would've have never thought he and Lady Pink knew each other.

Major Papers, who was in the cut witnessing the whole scene, was amazed at how live the beautiful women were. Bottles were being sent to their table all night and they emptied them out as if they were Kool-aid. Usually Major Papers would have been over there to stake his claim but for some reason the apple that had his eye, had him slightly intimidated.

After guzzling down the last of his yellow bottle, Major Papers finally worked up enough courage to make his move. He was surprised at how receptive Lady Pink was to his advances, although he shouldn't have been because he usually got his girl. Lady Pink played her position well and by the end of the night, she had him wrapped around her finger. He even went so far as to put his platinum chain with an iced out medallion that read Major Papers around her neck. *Got 'em,* she thought to herself.

Angie had been in the "A" forever, but she'd never seen this dude, which was probably because he was from New Orleans, and claimed that he was just visiting like Lady Pink. However, the way everyone was catering to him, the girls knew better. They didn't doubt that he was from "N.O.", but he had to be heavy in the "A" to receive the type of treatment he was.

As the night drew near an end, the girls were too intoxicated to drive, so they allowed Major Papers and his boys to talk them into going to breakfast. The agreement was for them to have breakfast together and by then the girls would be sober enough to drive themselves home. Of course, that never happened. They ended up in the mansion Major Paper's had rented for the week while he and his people were in town. After pairing up, they continued to pop bottles until 7 a.m. The evening didn't end for them until after the maid cooked them breakfast and they feed their intoxicated systems.

Lady Pink woke up around twelve-noon and went into the bathroom to call G Millions.

"Bleep…Bleep… What's really Gangsta ma?"

"Bleep…You know how I do; I found what I came for."

"Bleep…Say no more."

Lady Pink ended the call and returned to the room. She was relieved to see Major Papers was still fast asleep.

"Hey baby, I have to go, I have a lot to do before I go back to Jersey," Lady Pink woke him up.

"When am I going to see you again beautiful?" Major Papers asked, still groggy from his champagne induced sleep.

"Whenever you send for me," Lady Pink responded innocently, before kissing him on the cheek.

"Here, take this," he handed her a stack of bills consisting of twenty-five hundred dollars. "That should be enough to get you to New Orleans." He put his hand under her chin and looked her in the eyes before continuing. "Whenever you're ready, need anything or just want to talk, don't hesitate to hit me up."

"Aw, aren't you sweet," Lady Pink said, allowing a tear to escape from her eyes.

"I will." She gave him a hug and then went to go find her friends. She woke them up and

Major Papers got one of his dudes to drive them to their car. No sooner than Candy Girl put the key in the ignition, they start their girl talk.

"Did ya'll get some booty last night?" Angie asked with a lustful smile.

"Hell to the naw, that nigga was too busy worshipping me to try. Not that he would have gotten any anyway." Lady Pink turned around in the passenger seat and gave her girl a high five.

"Not only did I get some, but I ran that niggas pockets too," Candy Girl bragged. "Shit, that nigga was so drunk, he didn't even notice."

"My dude must have had a little dick, he didn't even try to touch me," Angie said feeling cheated.

She would much rather believe that a man is either gay or have a small dick, if he didn't try to make a move on her. To her it was inconceivable that he just may not have been interested.

"I slept like a baby. I laid my head on ole boy's big ass stomach and was out in everything but my shoes. I'm going to visit him next week. He gave me paper for the flight and everything," Lady Pink said in a tone that told both girls that they needed to take notes.

"You make me sick; you always get the good ones," Angie whined.

"That ain't no coincidence Ang. I'm a predator, my instincts never fail me," Lady Pink smiled mischievously.

"Bleep...Bleep..." The alert sounded on Lady Pink's Nextel before Angie got a chance to respond.

"Bleep...Hey daddy!" She perked up.

"Bleep...Hey baby. Bleep... Listen, shit up here on fire, so I'm on the red eye tonight."

"Bleep... Okay, chirp me with your time of arrival before you leave Jersey."

"Bleep...No doubt."

Lady Pink was happier than a kid in an arcade with a pocket full of quarters when she got off her phone. She loved G Millions and couldn't wait to see him. He took her off the streets and upgraded her to the baddest chick in the game and he had been her best friend ever since.

***

Later that night, G Millions flight arrived. When he arrived at 10:50 p.m., Lady Pink was right there waiting for him. When he descended from the ramp, she ran into his arms and showered him with hugs and kisses as if she hadn't seen him in years.

"Hey daddy, did you enjoy your flight?" She asked cheerfully.

"Yeah ma, it was all good. I had my concoction and watched the DVD we made with Chinchilla Black to promote Pay Dirt," G Millions answered, as they made their way thru the crowded airport with their arms intertwined oblivious to both their admirers and their haters.

"I'm glad you came daddy," Lady Pink said, pecking him on the cheek. "I hope you're hungry too, because I'm taking you to the hottest seafood spot in the "A", and then we're off to the Embassy Suites."

"You sure know how to spoil a nigga," G Millions smiled. "I get two seafood platters tonight huh?"

"Fuck you nigga, wit' ya nasty ass," Lady Pink responded, smacking him playfully up side of his head.

"That's what I want you to do," G Millions said thru lust-filled eyes. "You lookin' good as hell and for some reason I've been horny as a muthafucka for you."

"You know I live for you boy. Let's go eat, because you got my coochie wet as hell right now," she replied in a sexy voice while rubbing the bulge in his pants.

The Mickey and Mallery type couple jumped into Angie's Denali and headed for Spondibita. G Millions filled his gangstress in on what was going on back in Jersey, while Lady Pink filled him in on all her marks. By the time they devoured their delicious meal, the couple couldn't wait to get to the Embassy Suites to devour each other.

Their passion for each other had built to an all time high by the time they entered the suite. But they were still patient enough to get comfortable before they did their thing, knowing it would be more enjoyable that way. Lady Pink bought an already rolled blunt along with G Millions notorious concoction and sat next to him on the couch. The Carl Thomas CD and dim lights put the icing on the cake, making the mood perfect.

"Damn, baby, I was already buzzing off of them Long Island iced teas now I'm really feelin' it fuckin' wit' you," Lady Pink said seductively.

The effects of alcohol and piff had her feeling extra frisky, making G Millions the beneficiary of an erotic striptease. Satisfied that she had her lover hypnotized, she brought her show to an abrupt halt and dashed for the shower. No sooner then she turned the water on; she felt a hard slap on her ass. The sting from the slap turned her on immensely and the jiggle from her healthy ghetto booty made his already hard penis feel as if it was going to burst.

When they stepped into the hot steamy shower, they wrestled playfully, kissed passionately, and felt each other up. After washing each other slowly and deliberately, thoroughly enjoying each other's bodies, they were ready to take their foreplay to the next level. Lady Pink dropped to her knees and started handling G Millions sex mic like a professional porn star. The hot water, steam, and euphoric feeling from the piff and alcohol made them feel as if their bodies were one. She licked, sucked, and jerked him off intensely until he blasted off into her mouth. Not missing a beat, she continued her rhythm until he was ready again.

Lady Pink led G Millions out of the shower by his erect member to the suite's huge bed and pushed him onto his back. As she made her move to straddle him, he motioned for her to sit on his face. Grabbing her by her fleshy butt cheeks, he guided her motions as she gyrated her hips and rubbed her moist opening on his mouth, while he licked, sucked and tongue sexed her to a body quivering orgasm. Not giving her a chance to recover, he made love to her in every position known and unknown to man until they were both drained of their juices. While she lay in G Millions arms, fully satisfied, Major Papers became the topic of their pillow talk.

"What's really gangsta wit' ole' boy you been hollerin' at?"

"I don't know exactly what dude holdin', but from the way they treat him here, he heavy. More-less you already know I know how to pick 'em daddy. I learned from the best." She smiled up at him and gave him a peck. "That fool not only gave me $2500 to come see him, but he let me hold on to that flooded platinum chain over there on the dresser not knowing if he'd ever see me again."

"It's amazin' how gullible these trick as niggas is," G Millions said with a disgusted look on his face. "And to think it be them dear mama ass niggas getting' all that scrilla."

"Most of them cats be some ole' lucky niggas who just happened to run into a good connect. Then they hire a bunch of cock ridin' ass niggas who be ready to bust their guns for 'em and everything. They don't ever think that it would be a bad bitch like me that would come along and end their career."

"I heard that hot shit, that's why I fucks wit' you." G Millions smiled. "You came a long way ma, go ahead and do what you do so I can come down and get my scrilla ole' boy holdin' for me."

"You know I got you daddy," Lady Pink assured him.

"No question, you always hit a three pointer and the clutch like Robert Horry to win the game for me," G Millions complimented her, letting her know that he was confident in her abilities.

"I'm gonna find you a connect too daddy."

"Yeah, that's all we need. Johnny is good people, but he can't give us the numbers I'm looking for. Shit, we serve him cocaine after our juxes." G Millions paused in deep thought. "Then we can take our foot out of the mediocre hustler's ass. Not that I don't enjoy it, but I like the luxury of knowing where my next meal is coming from, ya dig!"

"I heard!" Lady Pink jumped into his arms and they playfully rolled around on the bed.

The next day she called Major Papers in order to set up the trip and he was happy to hear from her.

"Get on the red eye right now!" He exclaimed happily through the phone.

"I can't right now, but book me the first flight out in the a.m."

"No problem, I'll call you back later with that information."

"A'ight sweetheart I'm looking forward to seeing you."

"You ain't the only one."

"Fo' sure!"

The next day…

Throughout the whole ride to the airport, something weighed heavily on Angie's mind. It wasn't until they got to the flight area that she decided to speak up.

"What type of freak shit ya'll into?" The bewildered Angie frowned up her face. "He knows you're going to New Orleans to see another nigga and he's cool with that?"

"I'll explain it to you later." Lady Pink smiled, and looked at her pink diamond infested Rolex watch for women. "Get G a rental and make sure he enjoys himself."

"You know I take care of my peeps," Angie assured.

Angie watched as her friend disappeared up the ramp. Then she headed back towards her truck determined to get Lady Pink to teach her how to step her game up.

Lady Pink's flight arrived in New Orleans at 11:37 a.m. The airport was too crowded and all she brought with her was a pink and white Louis Vuitton carry on. So she headed straight towards the exit. Just before she made it to the glass door, her Nextel chirped.

"Bleep…Bleep… What's good gorgeous?"

"Bleep… Walking through the airport"

"Bleep… It's good to see you had a safe flight," G Millions said upon hearing his gangstress voice.

"Yeah daddy, I'm safe. I am headed for the exit now."

Upon seeing what was waiting for her, she stopped dead in her tracks.

"Daddy you wouldn't believe this shit. This lame ass nigga got this fool in front of a Maybach holding up a sign with my name on it. Let me go," she took her finger off the chirp button just as she reached the Maybach.

After informing the driver of her identity, she asked, "Where is Major?"

"He had to take care of some business," the driver answered politely in a foreign accent. His flawless charcoal black skin gave her a hint that he was from somewhere in Africa. But after further inspection, the tribal marks that appeared to be burned into his face confirmed her observation. After taking a few seconds to weigh her options, she twisted up her face, pouted her lips and decided to call him.

"Hello."

"What's up with this shit?" Her Jersey accent and street attitude kicked in as she let him know that she wasn't feeling him not showing up personally. "You got me all the way down here and you can't even be here to greet me?"

"Be easy baby girl, I want to give you all of my attention, so I'm getting some last-minute business out of the way," he reassured her, thinking that her little tantrum was cute. "My driver will take you to get something exclusive to wear. We have a big night ahead of us."

Although the all-day shopping spree eased her attitude towards Major Papers and she was a little tired by the time she made it to his mansion, she immediately perked up at the sight of it. Why'd this fool bring a chick, he don't even know, to a place like this, she thought to herself.

Unable to contain her excitement, Lady Pink chirped G Millions to share their good fortune as soon as the driver was out of earshot.

"Bleep...Bleep...Daddy."

"Bleep...Yeah?"

"Bleep...Daddy this fool is loaded," she informed him bubbling with excitement. "His mansion looks like Tony Montana's shit, you hear me."

"Bleep...I heard that gangsta shit," he nonchalantly informed her. "I'm on the next thing smoking in the morning to make sure everything goes smooth."

"Bleep...Angie taken care of you daddy?"

"Bleep...Yeah, Angie good people, she taken me clubbing tonight."

"Bleep...I heard, go enjoy yourself, I'll holla tomorrow."

"Bleep...You already know."

G Millions wasted no time making flight arrangements to New Orleans. Only then would he be able to enjoy his night out on the town.

By the time Major Papers finally came home, they only had an hour to get ready and make it to their engagement on time. Lady Pink showered and got ready in the master bedroom, while Major Papers did the same on the other side of his mansion.

Major Papers was immaculately dressed in a wine colored tailor-made Roberto Cavalli silk suit with a matching tie, triple Italy knots, a burgundy silk shirt, a hanky, and some chunk gators. His one pinky ring glistened rays like the sun thru a magnifying glass. His Glashutte original watch screamed taste, while his platinum and diamond bracelet confirmed the fact that he had major paper.

He knew there wouldn't be another man at the reception that could stand next to him, so he was ready to make his grand entrance. Lady Pink had to make sure everything was in place causing her to take a couple of extra minutes in order to get ready. Major Papers was beginning to get a little impatient while waiting to see if the goddess that he had chose would live up to the esteem in which he held her in. After all, he did meet her in a club, a strip club at that. The luxurious foyer of his estate was very comfortable. The water fountain was strategically placed in the middle of the floor in order to provide a sense of peace and tranquility to the callers whom usually awaited him, but now he sat as if he were a guest.

When Lady Pink appeared, she quickly erased all doubt that he may have had. She stepped out on his balcony looking absolutely breath taking. It was at that moment that he made up his mind to do everything possible to make her a permanent resident of his estate. Her beige colored chiffon silk Christian Dior evening gown fit her perfectly, revealing all of her curves and just enough cleavage. The pink and white diamonds that shimmered around her neck, wrist, and ankle amplified her smooth light complexion, making her look like the goddess of the sun. Her stiletto heeled wrap around Jimmy Choo's made her calf muscles and fleshy buttocks flex and protrude to sexiness. Her walk down the half-moon curved stair well was graceful and confident, which turned Major Papers on. He was excited to the point where he found himself rubbing his crotch and literally drooling at the mouth by the time she drew near him.

"Damn baby, you're going to be the hottest chick at the reception," he complimented.

"Thank you, you know I have to represent you to the fullest," Lady Pink said innocently before placing a sensual kiss on his lips, savoring her taste Major Papers took her hand and led her out of the door.

When they arrived at the reception hall, the traditional red, black, green, and yellow African colors captivated Lady Pink. Never before had she witnessed such natural beauty. The majestic deep chocolate women had radiant skin and long, silky, healthy black hair. The men were beautiful as well, with the same tribal marks as the chauffeur.

As they mingled through the crowd, Major Papers introduced Lady Pink to everybody who was somebody. She learned throughout her travels that she was attending a celebration of the son of Major Papers African connection Lummumba.

The moment Major Papers introduced Lady Pink to Lummumba; he instantly took a fatherly liking to her. So finessing the number to his brother Hotep in Brooklyn wasn't a hard task. The atmosphere was so jubilant that Lady Pink almost wished she was there for pleasure and when it came to an end, she wished it could continue. This would definitely be a night to remember and if she had it any other way, it would have been spent with G Millions under different circumstances.

***

Three days had passed since the reception and Major Papers still hadn't made a move on her. *This nigga got the full court press on, but he's just like the rest. As soon as he does what he wants, he will change up. The only one I can count on not to do that is my baby G Millions*, Lady Pink reasoned with herself

The loneliness she felt from being in the huge mansion compelled her to call G Millions.

"Bleep...Bleep...Daddy."

"Bleep...What's good ma?" He spoke cheerfully through the phone.

"Bleep...You baby," she asnwsered, smiling as if he could see thru the phone.

"Bleep...How's things coming a long?"

"Bleep...This dude think he got him a keeper. He been wining and dining me for the last three days. He even trusts me enough to leave me here by myself. So when he's gone or asleep, I cut off his security system and handle my business. He even went so far as to send his whole staff home on the strength of me. A proposal gonna be next, so I'm ready to put an end to this thing," she said. "Come on through I'm ready to be out."

"Say no more."

With that said, G Millions snatched up the keys to his Cadillac Escalade rental, thankful for modern technology in the form of the navigation system, which made it easy for him to learn the route to and from Major Papers' mansion.

Major Papers came home earlier than Lady Pink had expected. She hoped that G Millions reached the mansion first so they could just take what they came for and be out. In their line of work, she was used to nothing ever really going as planned. Which is why she had mastered the art of improvising and that's exactly what she did.

In a matter of minutes, she had Major Papers laid back on his Shaq sized waterbed pouring his heart out to her.

"Baby girl, you are an amazing woman. I can truthfully say that I've never encountered a woman quite as diverse as you," he complimented her. "When I first laid eyes on you at that strip club, you were the life of the party amongst the ballas. Then tonight you awed some very influential people. Thus the qualities that you possess are rare in this day and time."

"Maj, I just be myself," she said candidly. "One of the biggest problems of society today is that everybody wanna be everything and everyone but themselves."

"I couldn't have said it better myself, which is why I need you by my side." He paused to check for a facial expression before continuing. "Lummumba told me he gave you the number to his brother in Brooklyn. For him to do that, he must've been feelin' you, because that just doesn't happen." He smiled. "I can see that you are a woman who values her freedom. But baby there's no need for you to have that number. You're welcome to stay here with me, I'm willing to share all of this with you. He made a sweeping motion with his arms. "I know we don't know each other well enough to be in love, but I can see you love this lifestyle and when you get to know me, you will love me too. Stay here with me and you will be set for life," Major Papers assured her while retrieving a black velvet box, from which he produced a five-karat pink diamond engagement ring set in Platinum.

Lady Pink should have won a lead role in Hollywood how excited she acted. Once she calmed, she fell into his arms and gave him a passionate kiss. She put her hand down his silk polo boxers and stroked his member rocking him up instantly. She felt G Millions presence just as Major Papers started gyrating his hips to the rhythm of her hand.

"Hold on baby, I want to do this right," she whispered in his ear as she ran her hands up his chest to his shoulders. "Sit up and let me give you a massage."

"Damn baby, you should have done that first," Major Papers said, a little frustrated with the sudden halt in action.

But he was close as ever to her forbidden fruit, so he just went with the flow.

"Relax baby I got you."

Once she saw that she had him open, she reached under the pillow. With one swift motion, she put one hand on his forehead and pushed the ice pick thru the back of his head.

"Hocus...Pocus...Muthafucka!" She yelled, her face contorted as an orgasm gushed into her panties.

Although Major Papers wanted to bring her to an orgasm, he would have never thought it would be at the expense of his own life. He laid there wide eye as the Grim Reaper came for him.

"Damn baby, that was intense," G Millions stated, while walking in to the room holding the bulge in his sweatpants and flashing his million-dollar smile.

"The only thing better is you daddy." A wicked twinkle danced through her eyes before getting back to business. "Now let's get what we came for and be out."

G Millions was proud of his baby. He couldn't help but smile to himself as she led them to the game room which was located in Major Papers lavishly furnished basement. The game room looked more like a club complete with a huge bar containing every kind of alcohol imaginable.

Lady Pink already knew the layout so she walked straight to the Ms. Pac-Man opened it up and pulled out around a million in jewels.

"Diamonds are a girl's best friend," she joked while moving on to the Space Invader machine.

After repeating this process to several other video games, they ended up with 80 bricks in total. Then they went to the Donkey Kong and Donkey Kong Junior machines and pulled out countless of eggs of dope. G Millions lit up with excitement. There were over one thousand eggs staring him in the face.

"Ain't this some shit daddy? This dude got the ice with the female games, the coke with space games for the up high and the dope with the gorilla machines 'cause that's damn sure what your going to have fuckin' wit' dat shit," she said imitating a gorilla, giving them a good laugh while she popped open the pinball machine bringing them $350,000 in cash.

Lady Pink was able to successfully use Major Paper's security system to her advantage using it to track his movements when he was home and doubling back when he was abroad.

"Dats what the fuck I'm talkin' bout."

"That was that fat muthafukas petty stash," Lady Pink informed. "We would have come off better kidnapping him."

"Nah baby, we ain't have time for all of that. We're already out of our element as it is. You sleep walked him perfectly. If we can't get right off of this, then we never gonna get right. Now let's claim our treasure and ride." G Millions kissed her.

Lady Pink smiled. The couple loaded up the Louie luggage; Major Papers had brought for Lady Pink, with money and product and then headed for the Escalade. G Millions, who always thought ahead, had already arranged to get their score on the first thing smoking back to New Jersey...

Chapter 5

When G Millions and Lady Pink stepped into their meeting spot back in New Jersey, Famous was sitting in a lounge chair with Candy Girl on his lap.

"What the fuck is this?" Lady Pink screamed, flipping on them while pointing at Candy Girl."

"She's reppin' me now," Famous calmly informed her while sporting a smile that he knew would aggravate Lady Pink even more.

"How do you know she don't get down like me?" Lady Pink continued her line of questioning but with a little more resolve.

"I had your girl Angie punch her thru the computer for me." Famous grinned from ear to ear. "Her days of dippin' in trick ass niggas pockets are officially over."

"Wasn't you supposed to be in school?" She now directed her questions at Candy Girl seeing that she wasn't going to get anywhere with Famous.

"Yeah but I'm going to transfer to Rutgers so that I can be with Famous," Candy Girl answered proudly.

"Ya'll muthafuka's is crazy," Lady Pink stated, throwing up her hands in utter disbelief and defeat.

"Fuck ya'll writin' a book or somethin'!?" G Millions snapped. "We're supposed to be celebrating our latest come up and ya'll up in here wit' dat bullshit," he chimed, bringing the minor disagreement to a halt. "Ya'll need to tighten' up."

After everything settled down in the room, G Millions and Lady Pink both filled Famous in on the score while G Millions concoction flowed freely thru their cipher, skipping Famous of course.

"Damn homey, we holdin' like dat?" Famous asked excitedly.

"Yeah B, now we don't have to sell them other niggas weight and take it back no-more," answered G Millions.

"Yeah, and you betta not o.d. on all that smack," Famous teased.

"Fuck you fool, I can afford to sniff the whole Peru if I wanted to, I gets it in," G Millions smiled with a quill to his nose as he spoke.

"No doubt home boy, you and that evil ass bitch of yours scored big for the home team on this one," Famous concede.

"I got bigga balls then you fool!" Lady Pink cut in.

"Whatever, just don't stick me wit' dat ice pick," Famous joked and they all laughed.

Five days later:

The eagle had finally landed. G Millions, Famous, Lady Pink along with Candy Girl assembled in Lady Pink's condo in order to ration out the loot. G Millions hit Famous off with the 80 bricks of coke, 50 thousand cash and the jewels of his choice. He also instructed him to make sure Johnny ate because he always came thru for them. Lady Pink received 50 thousand, the jewels of her choice and he would later purchase her the Porsche Cayenne SUV that she'd had her eyes on ever since she became his rider.

Candy Girl was blessed with ten stacks and the jewels of her choice welcoming her to the family. G Millions took the same split that he gave Famous and Lady Pink. His main concern was that the whole family ate. As long as they were happy, he was happy.

It was up to him to make sure that they had financial security and longevity in the game. He was the thinker. That's what made him the leader and everybody knew it without it having ever been said.

When Lady Pink spoke to Hotep, he informed her that one of his brother's stores was closed due to the sudden death of it's manager. He also let it be known that it would be painful for his brother to believe that she had something to do with it. However, he would agree to a meeting.

G Millions was now faced with a dilemma. He knew he'd be taking a grave risk putting his and Lady Pink's life in jeopardy by agreeing to meet up with Hotep. He knew he had to be all the way on point after making his decision and that's exactly what he intended to be...

Chapter 6

Early 2004...

"New Brunswick's Finest"

Sgt. Shyster paced the floor of the narcotics division of the New Brunswick police headquarters accompanied by detectives Doloch, Gruff, and several other narcotic officers who were assembled together for a special meeting regarding G Millions, Famous and company. The two-some had been a thorn in the N.B.P.'s side ever since they where juveniles and although they were one of the most elusive and profitable tandems in his thirty year experience, Shyster planned on bringing their run to an abrupt end at all costs.

"I'm really getting tired of these G Millions & Famous characters! These two assholes are running circles around all of us and my boss got his foot square up my ass!" Shyster pointed to himself before continuing his tirade. "Produce is his favorite fucking word and if I don't we're all gonna be shoveling shit for a living!"

Shyster was now beet red with sweat running down his forehead.

"Sgt., it's amazing how these assholes got everyone in the city and who knows where else on their payroll or purchasing their narcotics from them," Doloch added kissing Shyster's ass as always. "What's even more amazing is that out of all the people that we've arrested none of them are willing to talk. We can't get anyone to role over on these pricks."

"Yeah, them people get selective amnesia," Shyster joked. "But if you give them some fried chicken and watermelon, I bet they'll remember."

"What the fuck was that supposed to mean?" Doloch snapped. "I don't find shit funny," the black narcotics detective chimed.

"I'm not talking about you, you're different," Shyster said trying to ease the sudden tension that he'd caused.

"That's exactly what I'm talking about. You're always coming sideways out of your face with some bullshit!" Doloch pointed an accusing finger in the face of his superior.

"I'm just calling it the way I see it," Shyster shot back smugly. "These nig-, I mean petty thugs are sticking together."

That was the last straw. Doloch lunged over the table, grabbed Shyster by the throat, picked him up off the ground and shook him like a rag doll. The other narcotics officer's saw that things had gotten why out of hand, so they ran over and broke up the quarrel. Luckily, for Shyster they were there because had they not been, he would have undoubtedly been choked to death in a few more seconds.

"Come on fellas the bad guy's are out there," Gentry said attempting to calm his fellow officer's down.

"Fuck that, I'm tired of this shit!" Doloch yelled. "I'm always the first one out of the car during street raids conducting illegal searches, lying on the bible and a whole bunch of other immoral and wrong shit for the right reasons." He was so angry that he was foaming at the mouth, his breathing was heavy, and his nose was flaring. "I don't have to put up with this shit!"

"Okay, you've made your point," Shyster conceded, finally realizing that he had went too far.

Once the situation was defused, Sgt. Shyster officially got the meeting underway. "With what intellect we gathered thru our informants, these guy's don't make street sales and are selective, with who they do business with." Shyster paused and scanned the room making sure that he had everyone's undivided attention. "They have been a pain in my ass since they were kids!" Shyster furiously pounded the desk in front of him.

After giving his team his spiel, Shyster concluded the meeting. It filled him with immense pleasure to know that he had all of his men on the same page. This was exactly what he needed to make his plan a success. *Yeah, it's only a matter of time now*, he thought to himself. Leaning back in his swivel chair, rubbing his potbelly allowing his mind to drift back to 1988, which was the first of many run-ins he'd have with the New Brunswick hoodlums.

It was still very misty outside after a couple of hours of rain. All of the throw back narcoses including his self-led by Lt. Klazza had set up a perimeter around the 176 projects.

One of James Mack's stoole pigeons had informed him that the Macy's Blvd. Posse' from uptown had assembled in Feasters Park known as Infer-Red Park. He also told them that they had a small arsenal, walkie-talkies, police scanners and bulletproof vests, plotting revenge for one of their slain homeboy's "Chicago". Word of the incident had traveled thru the underground like wild fire. The murder of Chicago was the cause of an ongoing war between two sections of the small city.

At the time Shyster was a young up and coming detective hoping that he could somehow change the world. So hearing his colleagues out-look on the young kid who was gunned down just hours ago disturbed him greatly.

"Every time these niggers decide that they want to kill each other, my boss comes down on my ass to produce," Rock Face complained.

"Yeah, then once we do produce, the prosecutor makes deals with these scum bags and then their right back out on the streets giving us ulcers," Banski added.

"It doesn't help us none that most of these pricks are juvies and they know that they don't have to serve any serious time if any at all," Det. Jones agreed.

"Yeah, and we even have to watch what kind of ass whipping we put on them," Rock Face joked and they laughed. "Seriously though, it's getting increasingly dangerous out here. You patrol thru uptown and everybody is wearing army fatigues, ski masks, and black timberland boots. Hell, the monkeys already look alike, now you really can't tell them apart, and on top of all that they have the nerve to be taking pot shots at us." Banski paused to light a cigarette. He inhaled deeply and blew out three smoke rings before continuing. "Then when we go down to the projects, not only do we get fired on, but they throw shit out of the windows and off of the roofs. How, the hell, are we supposed to protect and serve? Shit we're the ones who need protection!" Banski chuckled nervously.

"Yeah, we don't get paid enough for this shit," Det. Jones agreed.

"You can bet your sweet ass that when we move on them there's going to be problems," Rock Face warned his troops.

"Let's move on them now!" An eager Shyster shouted.

"Easy cowboy, were not going anywhere off of the word of a snitch. If his information turns out to be legit, then we'll go in and make our arrests after the cock suckers run out of bullets," Rock Face explained.

"Meanwhile let innocent people get killed?" Shyster questioned with discussed.

"What the fuck are you on some type of we are the world crusade?" Banski's statement reeked of sarcasm, causing everyone except Shyster who failed to find any humor in his statement to laugh.

"Son, it's against them, we have to save our asses. The sooner you learn that the longer you'll survive," Rock Face advised.

Before Shyster could muster up a response, Lt. Klazza pulled up next to them with the frequency to switch their radios on and then he pulled off. The taillights on the Lt's cruiser hadn't even disappeared yet when a small army wearing ski masks and camouflage emerged out of nowhere. They were well organized and had all angles covered. The officers never had a chance to react before all hell broke loose. Gauges started pumping, and ratchets started singing as a fierce gun battled erupted.

Just as planned, the team of Dt's didn't make any attempts to move in on the youth until the gunshots subsided. When they moved in, the project youth that were still able to, made their escape by using the many options that their buildings had to offer to assure them a swift and easy get away.

The uptown youth used the blanket of darkness in order to make their escape. They also had the luxury of the busy highway and some were even brave enough to use the buildings also. Having left bodies sprawled out to be hauled off to the hospital and morgue was enough motivation for them to make their getaways to success.

However, some weren't as lucky as the others were. Several chases had ensued by way of both foot and automobile. It would be Shyster, Rock Face, Jones, and Banski who more than earned their pay on that night. They were the ones who stumbled upon G Millions and Famous in the middle of their scramble for their freedom.

It was by sheer coincidence that the four Dt's happened to be cruising up Commercial Ave looking for shooters when G Millions made a right turn in front of their unmarked car. The youth were headed back uptown when the Dt's hit their lights and sirens in a futile attempt to get the fleeing Honda Accord to pull over without incident.

"They're not stopping!" Shyster said with a surprised look on his face.

"You can bet your sweet ass they're not stopping!" Rock Face shot back, feeling the need to confirm his earlier statement.

***

Meanwhile in the fleeing stolen Honda Accord, Famous reloaded the weapons with the speed and precision of a seasoned vet. "Don't stop my nigga," he stated calmly.

"You thought I was?" G Millions shot his partner a glance as he'd just said the dumbest shit in the world. "Yo, help me put some distance between us, so we can bail in the park!"

"Say no more!" Famous position himself out of the window so that he could get a clear shot at the pursuing vehicle.

Although they had to swerve to avoid the fury that jumped out of Famous's pump action shotgun, the authorities refused to be denied.

"I can't believe these little bastards are trying to kill us!" Banski shouted.

"You better believe it," Rock Face hollered while they exchanged shots on the way up Commercial Ave.

G Millions was determined to ditch his pursuers, so he hit his brakes, hooked a right onto Comstock and another quick right into the parking lot of Infer-Red Park. Then he pulled up in front of the basketball court where he and Famous bailed out and made a dash for it. But the detectives had already predicted that move and were on their asses. The police cruiser hadn't even come to a complete stop when they bailed damn near the same time as the youth.

Famous ran with the determination of an Olympic track star in quest of a gold medal. He dashed thru the park, across Handy St., thru the graveyard, hit Seamen St., and disappeared into a brown colored house. This was one of many at their disposal just for situations like this.

G Millions wasn't so fortunate. The 5-0 decided to make him the object of their pursuit. G Millions led them on a foot chase thru the park where they threw shots at each other. He crossed Macy's Blvd and hit all of the backyards that would lead him to his destination.

The backyards were so dark that you could barely see your hand in front of your face and Shyster wasn't as familiar with the area like the youth he was chasing. So, he proceeded with caution. G Millions emerged from the backyard laughing to himself at the rookie cop that he'd left in his dust. He was so caught up in gloating to himself that he literally ran into a police car as he attempted to cross Remsen Avenue. By that time, police were everywhere. They even seemed to be emerging from the ground.

When they exited their vehicles, they had their guns drawn and when they converged on him they forcefully cuffed his hands behind his back. The entire ruckus drew a huge crowd begging to get unruly. To avoid a major confrontation with the angry Black & Latino crowd, he reminded the officers that their prisoner was a juvenile and ordered them to take him to the station house without any further brutality. In his heart of hearts, he felt that anybody who had the audacity to fire on his officer's, deserved a good ass whipping. But his experience and common sense told him that this was not the time or the place for it.

Famous called everybody and their mothers from the confines of their safe house so that they could go down to the precinct to raise hell so that they wouldn't be able to do what they wanted to do.

Willie and Pearl were the first ones to reach the station house demanding to see their baby. The shift commander having already threatened the jobs of every officer on duty was now sweating bullets because there was no way that he could allow them to see their boy now even if he wanted to. But he was somehow able to keep his wrinkled up face emotionless, however his long nose that was now beet red gave away the fact that he was covering something up. Neither parent brought the story that he was trying to sell of their son already having been sent to the youth house with a court date for the next day.

After another hour of hell raising, Willie threatened to have the whole police forces jobs and assured the shift commander that he would be in court the next day, with lawyers present. Then he and his wife reluctantly left the station house.

The interrogations that were being held in the rear of the police station were hopelessly at a stalemate, leaving the arresting officers to ponder their next course of action. G Millions and the other youth that were captured in the melee were all tight-lipped making it almost impossible for the officers to determine who actually possessed the chrome .357 and the double-barreled sawed off shotgun that they recovered from the scene after the gun battle. Although the officers knew the weapons they recovered were only a fraction of the weapons fired, they still needed answers and they where determined to get them. They were so determined in fact that Lt. Kannon decided to interrogate G Millions personally. It infuriated the Lt. to know that this little two-bit thug had the balls to fire on his officers, killing one, but to have total disregard for the law would not be tolerated.

"Who the fuck do you think you are shooting at my officer's!" Lt. Kannon screamed, not really expecting a logical answer.

"Fuck you and your officers. I ain't shoot at nobody!" G Millions yelled back in defense.

Lt. Kannon's hand was on fire after he smacked the youth so hard; he sent both G Millions and the chair he was cuffed to tumbling to the floor. The Lt. picked him up and leaned in so close to his face, that the aroma of his hot stinking breath assaulted the youth's nasal passage.

"Now you listen here you little fucking monkey, I've had enough run-ins with you already to know that you ain't gonna talk. That's why there are no tape recorders, lawyers or anyone else to witness this conversation." He paused to look into G Millions eyes. "You see, I don't give a fats rat's ass if you little niggers want to kill each other. But all of this open season on my officers is gonna stop," Kannon snarled, now foaming at the mouth.

"You ain't smart enough to catch me, you stale donut eatin' cock–suckin' muthafucka. You ain't got no gun with my prints on it. If it wasn't for your bitch ass snitches, all of you muthafuka would be runnin' around with your thumbs up ya asses." G Millions decided to push'em to the limit. "But guess what? I don't give two fats rat's asses about you, your officers or your snitches. You got a job to do and I got a job to do. Only time will tell who's gonna do the better job," G Millions calm sarcasm was enough to not only make the Lt.'s color return to his face, but he was now beet red.

"You little fucking punk!" He screamed at the top of his lungs.

"I'll kill you myself if I have to! You think you're smart, I'll show your smart!" He threatened before storming out of the room, leaving G Millions.

Detectives Shyster, Rockface, Banski and a few other detectives stood there with shocked expressions on their faces as the LT. stormed by them mumbling all types if obscenities to himself. His spark plug figure reminded them of Barnie Ruble and it took all the restraint that they had not to laugh. The youth that had managed to strike a cord in the LT. like no other just sat there flashing his million-dollar smile, refusing to allow all of the beating he took to defeat him. It was at that moment Shyster had to almost admire the young thug. He had more balls then a pinball machine and he knew that he was gonna be a major problem in the future.

Yep, they don't make them like they use to, criminal or detectives. He's truly one of the last dinosaurs. Too bad I'mma have to take him down. A wicked grin spread across Shyster's face at the thought, while he picked up the phone & placed calls to both the D.A. and the judge.

Although the Macy's Blvd. days were long gone, the elements still existed thanks to G Millions and Famous. Even though he couldn't prove it, Shyster knew that they were the moving force behind the robbery reports as well as most of the other illegal activity that plagued his city. *This city isn't big enough for the three of us* Shyster thought to himself as he began to put his plan in motion...

Chapter 7

Summer 2004...

"All in a day's work"

G Millions and Famous had picked an ideal place for their latest venture, a recording studio. The spot located on Jersey Ave in New Brunswick, provided easy access to all the wanna bee artists no matter where they were in the city. Famous who was always looking for a way to get his name in lights, jumped on the opportunity to buy the fully equipped studio for a mere fifteen stacks and a lease pick up. Although the equipment was not state of the art, it was of good quality and would sustain until they truly got serious about getting an artist signed. This was exactly what Famous planned to do as soon as his street dreams became a reality. He knew of several artists who were more then capable of getting his feet in the door. It was only a matter of meeting the right people and making the right moves to get their demo some airplay on the top radio stations.

It only took G Millions and Famous a minute to see that the third floor unit that they shared with a bail bonding company was an atmosphere that they could get used to. But to make it more pleasing to them they piped out the offices and lounge area with thick wall-to-wall carpet, plasma TV's, wall decorations, big plants and anything else that they felt would give it a more comfortable and professional feel. A temporary employment agency occupied the second floor along with a warehouse.

This was a perfect set up for G Millions and his crew. With all of the other activity going on around them, it made their traffic seem normal. Not to mention the fact that for an additional thousand dollars got them a duplicate key to every door in the building and the code to the alarm system as well. Although as small as these things may seem, they were very conducive to their business.

Today was one of the many days that Famous had gotten the chance to enjoy having added Pay Dirt Entertainment to his portfolio. As always, the lounge area was packed with scantly clad hood models and young gangstas as well. The aroma of every brand of exotic bud on the market filled the air as if it were cigarette smoke. Hennessey, Remy Martin, Patron, and Champagne flowed like water. The hypnotic soul grabbing street bangers from the label's headliners Chinchilla Black and Throw Back blurred through the speakers. They could not get enough of "Gangsta Degree" which was destined to become a street anthem and hood classic. Everybody in the studio was high except Famous who only got high off knowing he was the 'cause of the police filling out their Robbery Report and of course, the fast money and chicks that came with it. He also loved to gamble and stay fresh to death.

On this occasion, Famous sported a cross-colored red Polo button up on top a crisp white tee and Evisu jeans that he had just popped the tags off an hour ago. The Japanese designed jeans hung perfectly over his Prada shoes. His platinum chain hung just the right length in order to show off his iced out Pay Dirt medallion which rested right above his belly button. The way his Glashutte original hung perfectly from his wrist, one could have gotten the impression that it was going to slide off, however that was just another one of his eye-catching illusions.

Famous was definitely true to his name and he loved every minute of it. So why would today be any different? He and G Millions was blowing up rapidly. On top of that, he was flanked by his two top guns Hamma and Gangsta.

The family's personal barber Sincere was giving him his weekly razor sharp haircut, preparing him for his trip to Atlantic City, while they all sat around and traded war stories.

"Damn pretty boy, you goin' outta town again, while we in the hood gettin' ugly?" Gangsta teased.

"Shut the fuck up. You in the hood gettin' ugly 'cause that's what you like to do," Famous retorted as Sincere straightened his head trying to get the perfect angle for the third time since there exchange. "You always tryin' to put shit in the game, " Famous continued once Sincere released his head. "You got bread and shit sweet for you right now. You doing just what you niggaz love to do. Oh, and don't think you slid that pretty boy shit by me either chump."

"You ain't never lie. I live for this shit. When we go to Cancun, All Star weekend, Freak-Nik, Mardi Gras and all of the other main events, I get home sick like a muthafucka. You is a sweet nigga though Fame," Gangsta smiled and everybody in the room burst out laughing.

"Fuck you lil' nigga!" Famous shot back, enjoying the laugh just as much as everyone else did in the room.

"What time we out Fame?" Hamma asked once everybody settled down.

"Soon as we ease up outta here, we gone. I'mma go throw on the fresh linen, silk, and reptiles. Then we're on the parkway my gee," Famous informed.

"Shit sun, you could have called me to Sin City to cut ya hair," Sincere cut in.

"Nigga I know you don't sit down and pee," Famous shot back. "Ain't nothin' up in here but gangstas and closed mouths don't get fed."

"Plus that P.Y.T you got at home ain't havin' it," Hamma exposed, referring to Sincere's pretty young girlfriend, putting Sincere in the position to either have to go with them or look soft in front of the fellas.

"Man I'm the king of my castle my dude," Sincere attempted to defend himself.

"Get yo ass in the car then fool and stop being sensitive," Famous added. "You part of the fam, you dear mama ass nigga!"

"Word sun, if your baby mama let you out of the house, you betta ride and see how the real playa's play," Hamma filled him in. "Fame hit them spots so much he got a credit line, free limos, and the whole nine. Shit, I wouldn't be surprised if we fly in the private jet to Las Vegas."

"Where we ballin' at?" Sincere asked, relieved that the convo was shifting away from him.

"I fucks wit' the Wild Wild West heavy in A.C. 'cause I'm a cowboy and the Palace in Vegas 'cause I'm a King," Famous bragged.

"Fool, you ain't shit." Gangsta couldn't resist the opportunity to aggravate Famous. "Anyway, give us a robbery report on all that action from the prior day."

"You ain't gonna be satisfied until I make you Famous sun!" Famous snapped.

"You fools might as well be married!" Hamma intervened. "Just give us the robbery report B."

Famous shrugged off Gangstas antics and was now in his glory. He loved to take center stage and relive the events of the past.

"Dig this; you know it was my turn to make that trip up top," he began. "So I fucked around and took my new addition to the family, Al Capone. You already know he tried to live up to his name fo' real. I don't know what I was thinkin' about, takin' that lil' young nigga with me anywhere. It's like he's a drama magnet."

"Nigga you know why, you needed him to hold ya shit," Gangsta interrupted and everybody including Famous broke out into laughter.

"Yo, you gonna let me give the report or what?" Famous asked in between chuckles.

"Do what you do B." Hamma was anxious to hear how it went down.

"A'ight, as I was sayin'. I go scoop the lil' nigga, more-less I was strapped to death wit' my vest and two ratchets. He knew how we get down, so he G'd up from the feet up, flashin' his tech. I see he ready to flex. Bein' as though I ain't too keen on drivin' in New York, I park my Lex in a garage down town, and we hop on the train headed to the BX. Once the train stopped on 42nd St., some Dominican cats hopped on the train wit' duffle bags. Check how this lil' nigga starts right in," Famous spit shaking his head as he reflects back on the scene on the train.

"He leans over to me and whispers yo B, I think them niggaz holdin'. I remind the nigga we ain't come for dat and try to tell this lil' nigga to let dat that shit go but, this muthafucka gonna say I needs dat for somethin' on some 'ole persistent shit. So, I told this nigga again B to dead dat shit thinkin' dat would be the end of it." Famous's tone changes as he shakes his head with a grin plastered across his face. "Shiit, I might as well had of told him to go ahead and pop off, 'cause before I got a chance to stop the nigga he was backin' them cats down. I gotta admit the lil' nigga is smooth, 'cause from the outside lookin' in, you would have thought they were having a conversation and them Dominican's was just giving this nigga a gift or something. But I knew what it was, so I had to hold the lil' nigga down until the next stop. We didn't even check to see what he got 'em for. So, now we gotta get off the train and catch a cab to the BX. Then we get to the spot and the order ain't ready as always. So we go up in our regular restaurant to get something to eat and kill some time. While we up in there, this badass shorty struts up in there looking better then somethin' just comin' off a Paris runway. That's my word B, that bitch belongs on the big screen. Shorty was wearin' that shit too! Some brown capris', showing off her curvy ass hips, thick thighs, and shit. She had on this halter top that was so tight I thought them titties was gonna pop out at any moment B and this bitch had jet black hair that stopped just above her perfect apple ass. Her home girls was the truth too she had butter pecan skin and it was flawless, and you know I love a chick with pretty skin," Famous licked his lips before continuing. "So this wild cowboy ass nigga tryin' to holla at shorty, but he ain't got common sense enough to figure out that she don't understand English. So he takes it as a dis, grab shorty's ass and put his tongue in her ear. Then when shorty smacks sparks out of his ass, he got the nerve to get mad and whipped the tech out," Famous laughs as he plays the tape back for his team.

"Get the hell outta here," G Millions joined him in laughter.

"I'm dead ass. Dude puts the tech to her neck and cuss her out in Spanish. I didn't even know the nigga knew that shit." Famous had to pause until the laughter subsided in the room.

"Now I gotta be on some we are the world peace maker shit and make him chill. Shorty stepped off and came back like fifty deep. I'm thinkin' we bout to have a shoot-out like the wild wild fuckin' west when my man Poncho popped up and squashed the whole little drama and shit. Baby girl was on fire tho'. She really wanted them papi's to do us. So now, we back in the buildin' handling business. We get the pack and jump in my man Eric's Lincoln Town car. That's the luxury service dude I told ya'll I be fuckin' wit' when I busts my sessions. So, now we in the backseat of the car and we finally get a chance to see what's in the bags from the subway. As soon as Al Capone opened up the first bag, I knew it was Pay Dirt by the way his eyes lit up. These fools got three bricks of yayo in one bag and thirty three thousand cash and four Glock 27's in the other. I can't figure out for the life of me why niggaz put ratchets in a duffle bag! Anyway, that got my spidey senses tingling. Now the little nigga got me off my Gunswick bullshit. So I tell Eric to take the scenic route. By the time we get to the Westside highway, I'mma little aggravated and frustrated because we ain't run across nothin' worthwhile. I steal a glance at Al Capone and he sittin' there lookin' like he has a secret that nobody else know about but him. Now I'm pissed 'cause he done got me started and now it look like ain't nothin' poppin'. But just when I get ready to say fuck it, I peep something. Once Pone's peeps it too, it was on."

"Shine that's mine," the lil' nigga said with slobber running down his mouth."

"I told Eric to pull over. Eric tried to reason with us talkin' all dat scary shit, talkin' bout what's wrong wit' ya'll this ain't the time or place. I had to calm the nigga and let him know we had him and to fall back. I know he didn't want to, but he pulled up next to the GS, me and Pone had spotted. As soon as the car stopped, we hopped out and stalked our pray, no words needed. Pone pinned down shorty and I step to dude. Once we re-up on him, I realized he was Muslim. He said some Muslim shit saying how happy he was to be getting' some help. He ain't think he was getting the type of help we came with tho. Me bein' the pro I am, I whip out and pin him down. When dude see the ratchet, he like, "Brotha-," Holdin' his hands up wit' a funny ass look on his face. The way he said it was comical as hell B. It took all that I had not to laugh in his face. So, check we strip ole' boy and his shorty for their jewels, my man had fifty-three hundred in his fuckin' pocket and a hundred grams of raw heroin in a brown bag we took everything. Yo, I'm a predator and a hustla," Famous boasts.

"We know all that, just finish the story nigga," Gangsta cut in, interrupting Famous's animated account of his robbery report.

Famous just ignored him and returned to the stage.

"Whatever nigga, but check, so we hop back in the Lincoln, Eric takes us to my Lex and we hit him wit' a stack for his troubles. After we put everything in the stash box, we jump on the road headed back home. Now, the whole ride back home, this lil' nigga keep aggravatin' the shit outta me talkin' about he hungry and shit. By the time we get to Rahway, I'm tired of hearing his shit. So I stop at the White Castle. While we up in there, drama the last thing on my mind. Shit, I'm thinkin' about them double cheeseburgers and onion rings. Why these bitch ass niggaz gonna come up in there on some brolic shit, tryin' to stunt for their hood rats? These clowns had the nerve to step to Pone and me on some gorilla shit like, look at these bitch ass niggaz. I should smack the shit outta you niggaz and make ya'll come up off of that shit."

"Me and Al Capone looked at each other like this fool can't be serious. These silly ass niggaz standin' in a pit of gators and don't even know it. Their broads found all that sucka shit hilarious. I'm hot as hell and I can see Pone is too, but we keep our cool. Seein' that we wasn't feedin' they bounced, or so we thought. We should have known better though. They never even ordered anything. So we grab our grub and step outside, these fools leanin' on my joint playin' us all the way out. Man, we look at each other, drop our bags, and whip out our hammers. The dudes scatter and leave the broads standin' there lookin' stupid. You already know we had to teach them a lesson. We ran up on the broads and pistol-whipped 'em like they was dudes. The whole while we puttin' it on their ass we're schoolin' them about runnin' wit' lames. We like, bitch, ya'll thought that shit was funny huh? You thought them lames was hard huh? I can't tell, they left ya'll for dead. We left them silly ass bitch's lookin' like the female versions of that Martin episode after Larry Hit Man Herns got at him." Famous's humorous punch line caused the whole room to erupt in laughter.

"Damn, I missed that shit," Gangsta said, still a little hype from Famous' war story.

"Fame you a lucky nigga," Hamma added.

"Fool, I ain't lucky," Famous bragged. "I'm good."

"Fuck them lame ass niggaz," Gangsta said still wishing he had been there.

"Yo B, it seems like every mark you hit be holdin'," Hamma spoke still insinuating that Famous was lucky.

"Hey man, what can I say, I know how to pick 'em. Just like an eagle can spot a mouse from 100 miles in the air, I can see straight thru a niggaz pockets," Famous exaggerated in order to get his point across. "But yo, on some real live shit, the boy Al Capone gonna put mad food on the table when he settle down. The boy a natural."

"Shit, you ain't gotta spend ya money in Vegas. You gonna be spending them other fools money," said Sincere.

"Man, that shit ain't 'bout nothin'. Let me take you to school real quick. As long as I keep that Pyrex leanin', and bring that work back proper," Famous paused. "And as long as them lames out there holdin' my paper waitin' for me to come get it, I can travel around the world wit' my mind at ease. On top of all dat, I be so relaxed and confident I win more then I lose. That's why the casino owners be pacifying me. They be chasin', but you know Wild E Coyote never caught the Road Runner and the Road Runner ain't got shit on me!" Famous concluded and they laughed, appreciating the life Famous brought to a simple haircut.

Twenty minutes later Famous, Hamma, and Sincere were all climbing into their awaiting Benz limo. The limo emerged on the New Jersey State Parkway and headed for exit 38. As soon as they arrived, Sincere got to see first hand what Hamma told him in the studio was not only the truth, but it may have been an under statement. The red carpet treatment was in full effect from the time the limo driver opened the door to let them out. Hamma was already used to the treatment, so he acted as if he was running for mayor. The fact that he was being cordial to every one that they walked by on their way to the suite was kind of funny. Sincere on the other hand was amazed by the vastness of the casino, as well as the large assortment of slot machines, roulette tables, crap tables etc. He was also taken aback by the lively atmosphere. For some reason he was expecting it to be more laid back. Famous was on his cell phone trying to appear important as if he was some type of hot shot business man. Although he was discussing business, there was a little bit of pleasure involved also. He was letting his A. C. shorty Hassanna know he was in town.

"Hey boo!" Hassanna greeted him, enthused to hear his voice.

She knew her lover by his Usher ringtone.

"What's really, pretty chocolate?"

"You, sometimes me," she slyly remarked.

"I'm out your way, you comin' thru so I can make you Famous or what?"

"Why wouldn't I?" Hassanna said. "Plus you know I got them contacts on track for you."

"Well what da hell you still on my jack for? Get your black sexy ass over here." They both laughed and disconnected the call.

The lavish suite they blessed Famous with every time he graced Atlantic City with his presence was more evidence of the royal treatment he received at the Wild West.

"Damn, you the man homey!" Sincere said excitedly as they entered the suite.

"I thought you knew," Hamma replied.

"Ya'll fools must drop a lot of cash here?" Sincere questioned still a little overwhelmed by the vastness of the suite.

"It ain't that, we just consistent. Plus not only have me and G Millions been comin' here for years. But my pops used to run thru here when it was just the Caesars. Gambling is in my blood B. Sure we drop our share, but when you go hard like me you can't lose. I'm a made nigga, I keeps them pots leanin' and infer reds beemin', ya dig! They can't stop what's hot!" The chirping of Famous's Nextel interrupted what would have been another performance.

"What's really?" Famous answered.

"I'm downstairs," Hassanna's informing voice came thru the phone,

"Who you wit'?"

"My peoples."

"A'ight."

Hamma and Sincere was mixing Remy Red and Absolute, puffin' a blunt of haze when Hassanna walked into the suite followed by four hood model chicks. They were all fresh to death with the latest designer labels and their maintenance was to the ceiling.

The women were no strangers to made men, which made it easy for them to get comfortable and play their positions. A constant flow of champagne, piff and Grey Goose had the girls gettin' loose. Hamma was used to this action, but Sincere was in heaven as the girls each took turns licking and sucking each other and them too.

Famous and Hassanna was off in their own world handling their business. The two met four years ago on the board walk and they'd been mixing business with pleasure ever since. Up until the day that he met Hassanna, Famous was under the impression that A. C. was just boardwalks and casinos. However, a quick tour of the city showed other wise. Hassanna wasn't a stunning beauty, but she was the blackest, sexiest hood model he'd ever laid eyes on. Standing at 5'7" she was the answer to his Serena Williams' fantasy. He also liked the fact that her maintenance was immaculate. She also, was about her money and like him; she didn't drink or do drugs.

When the couple entered the room, they took care off business first because that always made the pleasure more enjoyable. Hassanna placed forty grand large on the dresser, which she gave him every week for the two kilos of coke that he fronted her. In return, he would re her up with two more.

Damn I'm good, that's two for one all day he thought to himself while she freed his manhood from his linen pants and placed it into her mouth.

After showing how much they missed one another, they hit up the casino so that Famous could do what he did best which was play poker. There was no doubt in his mind that he was gonna come up.

Famous followed the country singer Kenny Rogers' song. He learned fast early that as long as you know when to hold 'em, fold 'em and walk away, you'll never have to run.

Famous would jerk off some chips every now and then, but not tonight. He was focused. He had his poker face on. Tonight he planned to show his team how he earned the love and his royal treatment from the Harrah's establishment and any other gambling joint that he graced with his presence.

Most of Famous' trips to Atlantic City were productive and this one wasn't any different. Being as though Hamma was always straight, Famous put five stacks in Sincere's pocket. He'd come to A. C. with twenty thousand dollars in spending money and two bricks for Hassanna. After hitting the poker table for thirty thousand along with the 40 thousand from the last two bricks that he'd left for her, he had no choice but to be satisfied with the days work.

Hassanna didn't have to twist his arm to get another round out of him. However, there wouldn't be any cuddling or pillow talk. After there sex session ended, so did his time in the city. Famous had already booked three round trip tickets for him and his two comrades. Hamma, Sincere and himself hopped on the first red eye available slated for Vegas.

"See what ridin' wit live niggaz like us gets you," Famous bragged as they boarded the flight.

"Hell yeah, I never had this much fun in my life," Sincere admitted.

"The fun has just begun B," Hamma informed. "Wait till we touch ground in Vegas."

"Just stick around B, I'mma make you Famous," Famous spat his trademark response as they laughed...

Chapter 8

Summer 2004...

"San Juan"

G Millions swaggered up into Infer-Red Park still trying to process the disturbing information that he'd been receiving all day long. If you were to judge him by his demeanor, you would never be able to tell that he'd reached his boiling point. He'd long ago peeped that the ones who make it in this game never seems too fazed. Whenever a situation arose, he handled it as if it were nothing.

Jessie was his head whom he had been feeding, clothing and putting healthy portions of food on his table. Although none of the above was about nothing to him because he did, what he did out of pure love. Which made it much more disturbing to him that the same guy that he'd been showing so much love to, had his knife in his back twisting it, hard.

How you gonna cut ya dick off like that? Don't this fool know the streets talk like Kelly and Regis. So either he a dumb ass muthafucka or he just don't give a fuck. Either way, I got somethin' for his tough ass-, G Millions thought to himself.

No sooner than he reached the middle of the park, all different colored dots illuminated his body, resembling a rainbow in the dark. He smiled to himself with pride thinking about this thing that he'd put together. I'm a bad muthafucka he smiled inwardly.

"You fools betta act like ya'll know who in da building'," G Millions announced.

"You betta act like you know we don't mind killin'," the young gifted and pitch black Saint I's joked.

"Watch ya mouth lil' nigga." Normally he would have said something slick back but today G Millions was not in the mood. "Ya'll fools ain't got nothin' betta to do then play wit' dem dots," G Millions shot back, more of a statement then a question.

"That's what you pay us for Big Homey."

"What's really wit' da flow out here?"

"Steady."

"I heard," G Millions answered before switching his attention to one of his up and coming stars. "Jux I need you to take a ride wit' me."

Jux was tall and lean; he was also the owner of the green dot. The over sized white tee in which he sported couldn't mask his chiseled upper frame as he hopped out of the tree and strolled over to his big homey.

"You fools be easy!" G Millions yelled as he and Jux turned to walk away.

"You already know we gonna hold it up, we learned from the best," Saint I's answered.

Saint I's last statement caused G Millions to smile. While the gangstas had mad love for their big homey and would pop their things for him in a heartbeat, they were all play fiends and there was no doubt in his mind that them multi-colored dots where escorting them out of the park.

As soon as they got into G Millions rented Expedition, Jux found Styles P's Gangster And A Gentleman CD and they cruised the hood. Each of them was caught up in their own thoughts while track 7 oozed thru the Expo's factory made sound system.

"Are you ready to get some real paper lil' homey?" G Millions broke the silence.

"Why wouldn't I be?" Jux answered as calmly as possible trying to conceal his excitement.

He knew that whatever it was that G Millions came and got him for, if he handled it successfully, he'd be in the big leagues thereafter.

"You know that ole' head Jessie?"

"Yeah, I know that cat."

"Hocus Pocus," G Millions retorted using the familiar code his team knew meant murder.

"Say no more."

Jux had no problem with putting in work for nothing. But for G Millions to come and scoop him personally, that had career advancement written all over it.

The next day:

G Millions sat in the parking lot of an auto body shop located on route 27 on the Franklin Township side of the small highway. He chose to sit in that particular spot so that he could get a clear view of Jux in action. Jux was unaware of the fact that he was being watched as he posted up in between the low housing income three-story housing projects on the New Brunswick side of the highway.

Henry St. was a walking zombie zone for those who were spaced out on dip, crack, smack or one of the many other mind altering drugs that was readily available in the housing projects. The individuals' who weren't spaced out on drugs, were too busy hustling, gambling and talking shit to even notice the youth posted up in between the buildings plotting. Nobody in particular had their fangs sank into Henry St., it was a free for all. Hustlers came from all over the city in order to get their grind on. So nothing seemed to be out of the ordinary. Jux was just another youth on the set to get a small piece of the pie.

At exactly 4:30 pm, Jessie came thru just like clock work on his Honda CBR 600 which was one of the many perks that he'd acquired while fucking with G Millions. Jux spotted him as soon as he turned onto Henry St. He slowly and methodically eased from in-between the buildings. When Jessie got close enough for him to get an accurate shot, fire leaped from the barrel of his. 9mm as he squeezed the trigger with purpose, two bullets ricocheted off Jessie's helmet and bike, while others found themselves a home in his flesh. The impact from the high capacity slugs sent him tumbling and sliding on the burning hot asphalt. His bike seemed to have forgotten that someone had been on it as it continued to roll until it hit a parked car. The zombies snapped out of their daze and the hustlers disregarded their Remy Martin bottles and their blunts as the sudden eruption of gunfire and the thunderous sound of crunching metal interrupted every ones comfort sending them running and ducking for cover. Jux was satisfied with his handiwork, so he calmly strolled over to the stolen Honda Accord, he had strategically tucked away on a back block for his smooth getaway.

When Jux heard the echo of the approaching sirens, he jumped into the car and turned on his police scanner to listen.

"Cccrrr…we've just received a call reporting shots fired on Henry St. caller states that a Black male with a bullet wound to the neck and several to the upper torso area, " The voice of the dispatch instantly got Jux's blood pressure boiling.

The information he had just heard filled him with so much anger and frustration that he damned near put his fist through the dash-board. Not to be denied, he immediately made up his mind to finish the job. He started up the stolen Honda, pulled up by building 912 and waited for the ambulance to pass by.

G Millions was puzzled about his little homey's behavior so he pulled into the parking lot of the Chinese restaurant across the street. His question was quickly answered when the ambulance sped by and Jux jumped behind it completely disregarding the police cruiser that escorted it.

Jux was determined to finish his mission. He caught up to the ambulance, stuck his arm out of the window and started dumping on it while trying to run it off the road. The blur from the police sirens along with the flashing red lights quickly snapped him back to his senses.

My wheelwork will get me out of this situation just like any other one, Jux thought to him self. He banged a hard right on French St. barely missing an elderly couple who was taking their daily stroll. After hopping back off the curb, Jux banged another hard right on Joyce Kilmer Ave. and the chase was over with as quickly as it began.

I know how to pick 'em, G Millions thought to him-self while listening to the events unfolding over his scanner.

***

An hour later Jux sat up in Pay Dirt Studios waiting for his mentor. He paid no attention to the up and coming gangsters or the hood models that were having their customary session. When G Millions entered the building, everyone tightened up not wanting him to catch them out of order. He caught Jux eye, which gave his young gunner a signal to follow him into the office.

When they reached the office, G Millions peeped the unsettled look on Jux's face. Young Jux had the look of a prize fighting pit-bull that had let his master down and expected to be starved, or even worse, one between the eyes, just as he'd seen so many others.

"Yo B, I don't know what that wild cowboy shit was that you pulled out there, but I ain't mad at ya." G Millions assured his new young protégé', while flashing his million-dollar smile.

"I feel like I let you down big homey," Jux expressed with sincerity. "I should have finished him."

"Listen B, you did the damn thing. Your relentlessness got our point across. So when that fool get out of the hospital and heal up, you gonna bang his ass again." G Millions felt his blood pressure building up all over again just thinking about the shit that Jessie tried to pull. "Every time he heal up, you gone bang 'em until he stop breathin', ya dig?"

"Now that's gangsta!" Jux replied relieved at the way things were working out.

"I hope you don't have any plans," G Millions said while studying Jux facial expression. "We gonna hit P.R. so I can show you what real millionaire status consists of and at the same time give the streets a chance to settle down."

"Are you kiddin' me?" A smile graced Jux face, revealing the excitement he felt about riding with his big homey. "If I did have somethin' to do, that shit would be on da burner so that I could ride wit' you. I heard you are the real, for real. But ain't nothin' like baring witness to it, ya dig!"

The two conversed a little more while passing G Millions concoction back and forth before exiting the office to have a little fun with the rest of the home boys and hood models

***

The next day at 1:10 pm, they hopped on a flight headed for San Juan. Upon their arrival, they rented a room to hold them over until the condo that G Millions had booked was available. They hadn't even gotten the chance to put their bags down before Jux was setting fire to a blunt of haze, hooking up the play station and popping a yellow bottle for a toast to San Juan.

After they got right, they clowned around a little bit before taking a shower to get ready to see what San Juan had to offer. When the men stepped out of the hotel, they were shining as always. Looking for something to get into, they hit the strip so they could do a little bar hopping. But it didn't take too long for the jet lag from the flight to set in. They decided tomorrow was always another day and went back to the hotel for some z's.

The next morning the San Juan sun bogarted its way through the glass sliding doors, setting the stage for an early rise. Eager to get the day started G Millions and his new young gunner gathered up their belongings and went to seal the deal on the condo. The sweet elderly woman who dealt they dealt with made the process easy, thus the paper work and the money exchange was complete in no time.

Jux was just going thru the motions. He wasn't able to fully enjoy himself until he smoked his first blunt. Unlike the hotel room, the condo gave them a feeling of a home away from home. The condominium itself was very spacious and exquisite in its own right. But what made it so captivating to Jux was that it sat on the 19th floor, and from the balcony, you could see the whole island.

By the time they finished unpacking, the hunger pains had started to set in. G Millions couldn't even pronounce the name of the restaurant across the street from the high rise, but its' food spoke for itself. From where they sat, they found entertainment in the people of all colors, shapes and sizes who sauntered in and out of the E.J.J. hotel that they could find humor in. The gorgeous women of San Juan must have been getting their beauty rest.

As soon as they finished eating, they went shopping to fill up their fridge in the condominium. After they went shopping, they threw on some shorts and hit the same beach that they'd been watching from the balcony.

G Millions enjoyed being able to show Jux that there was more to life then the streets of New Gunswick while at the same time taking full advantage of what San Juan had to offer. The two of them soaked up the sun, sipped on casaba melon juice, jet skied, and para-sailed over the beach. Their day ended on the balcony of the condo, inhaling the fresh San Juan air and some good haze, while looking over the island plottin' their adventures for the night.

By the time night fall had replaced the day time, G Millions transformed and looked spiffy in his silk linen, closed toe gator skin sandals, with both his ears and neck on freeze, topped off with Cartier frames and Cartier watch to complete his assemble. Jux chose to go the sporty route with his Kenny Anderson New Jersey Nets throwback, Iceberg shorts, white New Balance known as New Brunswicks in his hood, a red doo rag beneath a Nets fitted cap and his Pay Dirt chain swingin' from his neck.

Strip bars and nightclubs lined the streets in San Juan, all the way down to Rio Pedro. Jux was in awe seeing there were clubs everywhere.

"Damn B, the strip clubs pop all night!" Jux exclaimed excitedly.

"I thought New York was the city that never sleeps. Shit, this the one!" G Millions was just as excited. They did their one-two, mingling a little, but for the most part, they were just feeling there way along the strip. After watching a few miamian's shake their asses and having their full share of Puerto Rican Rum, they went back to the room, watched a little B.E.T. and took it down.

The next day they enjoyed being able to lie back in their lawn chairs, partake, in their daily ritual of casaba melon and haze. Watching the gorgeous women of San Juan act a fool on their jet ski's, gave the two of them a great feeling of rejuvenation. Today would be the day that they found some action. However, as it turned out the action found them. On their way back to the condominium, they were stopped by the security guard.

"Where yuh from New Yawk ?" He questioned with a slight Spanish accent.

"Nah, Jerze," Jux answered.

"O jah, mi from Camden," he announced in his West Indian accent. "Mi been on dis island for a minute now. Come tru di next day 'bout eight, mi give jou island tour," the security guard offered.

After they lined up the tour with the security guard, they went back up stairs to plan their night on the island. While sitting on the balcony they could see police boats racing up and down the water chasing suspected traffickers.

"Damn, in our hood it's cars, here it's boats," Jux expressed, learning another thing about San Juan.

"Yeah B, shit goes down all over the globe," G Millions response was accompanied by a feeling of frustration and hopelessness.

"Fuck that shit man," Jux said feeling G Millions vibe. "Dude at the LQ said the strip clubs is what's really gangsta. Lets' get jig and see what it's hittin' for."

"I'm wit that."

Lucky 7 was the first spot they hit. The cover charge was only five dollars and came with a ticket for a free drink. The scenery was reminiscent of a salon in an old cowboy movie only bigger. Two minutes into their bottle of Moet and three shots of Henny they had ordered to get started, two cuties from Honduras pushed up on them for some action. The language barrier saved them a whole bunch of unnecessary rap, so they were able to shoot straight upstairs and get it in.

The next two shorties were even finer than the first. They had not even gotten a chance to sit down and get comfortable in their booths before the girls pushed up. Not wanting to disappoint the ladies, they took them upstairs and gave them a shot at the title. After about an hour of bumpin' and grindin', they went back downstairs, had another shot before heading next door to the Hawaiian hut.

"Damn my nigga, if we would have come here first, there would have been no Lucky 7," G Millions stated lustfully.

"This is the candy shop fo'real!" Jux said, unable to decide which flavor he wanted. "Chicks backed up in this muthafucka and they drop dead gorgeous!"

"From now on, we gotta choose our hoes wisely, 'cause every time we go upstairs and come back down, some badder pieces push up," G Millions informed.

"The way we shinin' and the way they pushin', they must think we superstars," Jux smiled.

"Not only are we superstars, we millionaires, so get use to it lil' homey," G Millions corrected and encouraged.

After a few drinks and some careful observation, they took two more trips upstairs and they were done. Deciding to call it a night, they headed back to their condo, hit the shower and clasped into a coma.

***

The security guy resembled Daddy Yankee and turned out to be cool as hell. Jux was low on smoke, so the security dude went to the projects and copped them some. While he was gone, G Millions and Jux went to the beach where they met a shorty from Amboy who didn't speak a lick of English. However, she did lead them to a bathing suit contest where the security dude caught up to them an hour later.

"Mi see jou enjoyin' San Juan." He smiled knowingly.

"Fo sure!" G Millions agreed with his eyes still glued to the beautiful honeys strutting their stuff in skimpy bathing suites.

"Yo, take us to the mall so we can get fresh," Jux cut in, changing the subject.

On their way back to the condo, they decided to hop on a trolley to peek at San Juan. As the trolley approached the same projects, that the security guy copped the haze from, all hell broke loose. The sound of shotguns and automatic weapons erupted, drowning out the hustle and bustle of the daytime activity and the click clacking of the trolley car. Both women and children alike ran for cover, spilling out of the buildings in droves, trying to seek refuge from the murder and mayhem. Bullets and shotgun pellets lodged in cars, shattered windows and found homes in innocent bystanders.

G Millions, Jux, the security guy and the rest of the trolley passengers all looked on as the scene unfolded like something straight out of a western movie. The trolley screeched to a halt as a huge Puerto Rican man standing every bit of 6'4" 270lbs, toting two .50 cal desert eagles was thrown to the ground by slugs to his legs, ass, and back. Determined to go out in a blaze, the giant popped the clips out and reached for back up. But his pursuers were upon him before he got a chance to make his move. Seeing that there was no way out, he sucked in a chest full of air and rolled over to face his pursuers. Two of the men brandished Nine's while the other gripped a shinny chrome pump action shotgun. The giant looked at his .50s' and saw that the slides were back and his clips were all the way on empty. In one last attempt out of desperation, he slid his hand to the small of his back for his back up, but the trio was on him. The guy with the shotgun must have been the leader because he stood in the middle of the other two and took control of the situation by putting the pump in the giants' mouth as he started screaming something in Spanish. What he said was foreign to G Millions and Jux do to the language barrier, but judging from the spittle flying from his mouth, not to mention his facial expressions, it was obvious that he was pissed. In hood terms, G Millions translation was, "Nigga you know you done fucked up." After getting whatever burden he carried off his chest, he squeezed the trigger on his pump and grinned wickedly while he watched the giants head explode like a time bomb and splattered like a melon with an M-80 inside of it. Without hesitation, they witnessed as his cronies stood over the giant and dumped the slugs from their .9mm's into his already lifeless body.

The area fell silent, as gun smoke and the stench of gunpowder lingered in the air. In no time, the assailants quickly disappeared back into the shelter of the buildings.

"I thought we were supposed to be getting away from this type of shit," Jux laughed breaking the silence.

"Shit, at least this is one time there's drama and our team ain't involved," G Millions spoke aloud, but to know one in particular.

"Now jou see why me didn't bring ja'll down here wit' me to score dat haze. Des is every day ting," The security dude added, letting it be known that San Juan ain't all fresh water and warm weather.

"Man, we ain't no stranger to danger," Jux offered.

G Millions just grinned. He was thinking the same thing.

At the same time, the security dude was completing his sentence, some old dude was dragging the corps out of the street, and the driving was cranking the trolley back up.

No sooner then they got off the trolley in front of the pool hall right down the street from the condo, the security guy's friend Felix walked up on them. After going through the formalities, they all went and had a few drinks at the bar. Felix, who could easily play Tony Montana's son in a Scar Face sequel, made his living spitting Reggae Tone, and the way G Millions and Jux had it on; you could not tell him that they weren't producers.

After a couple of games of pool and some small talk, they all went back to the condo. Felix had eighty bags of San Juan's finest smoke and could flow, so he fit right in. They sat in the room until about 3:30 a.m. high and horny. Felix suggested they hit the strip to scoop some young and tender hookers and that's exactly what they did.

At about 11:30 a.m. the next day, or the same day, G Millions walked over all of the naked bodies that where sprawled about the house attempting to get to the kitchen. His intent was to eat one bowl of the Fruity Pebbles just to put something in his stomach, but they were so good, he ended up eating the whole box. This same ritual got him thumped upside the head when he was a kid by Pearl on so many occasions he remembered.

"You're not the only one in this house, you greedy fuck!" The verbal abuse she would spit ran concurrent with the thump.

G Millions had to let out a slight chuckle just thinking about his mother while milk dribbled down the corner of his mouth.

We can eat as much as we want to now mother, ya boy done came up, he thought to himself while placing the bowl into the dishwasher.

After smoking a blunt on the balcony, G Millions took a nice hot shower. When he stepped out of the shower, he was feeling refined and restored so he decided to get dressed and head to the beach. The casaba melon, which was always the first thing he got when his feet touched the sand, was a welcoming refreshment to his taste buds. The sun had already reached its peak and it had to be the hottest day of the year, wanting to do something different G Millions decided on going scuba diving.

While on the boat, he met a couple of other people who turned out to be cool as hell. The exotic fish that swam freely had the group captivated. The stiff ass instructor tried his best to put a damper on their fun, but he and the others weren't having it. They started a little game, which was to see how many stingrays they could hit by swimming to the bottom of the ocean to find a bolder, swim back up, and drop it. G Millions lost, only hitting three out of ten. However, for the first time in his life, he actually enjoyed losing.

After scuba diving, he jumped on the eighty-cent ferry in route to see the beautiful Bahamas. Just like San Juan, the Bahamas was gorgeous as were the women. However, he didn't come for that, so he simply admired them from afar. Before he knew it, a couple of hours had passed so he decided to head back to San Juan. He greatly appreciated being able to find sometime to be alone with his thoughts, away from the constant drama that surrounded him and his life.

When G Millions reached the sidewalk outside the condominium, he heard the same whistle that he had been hearing since he got to San Juan and as before, he ignored it and headed to his room. The security dude was gone by the time he stepped into his temporary place of dwelling. However, Jux, Felix, and the girls were fresh and ready for the day's adventure.

"I went down and rented the skies home boy," Jux informed.

"That's what it is." G Millions looked to the ceiling as if to gather his thoughts. "But dig this B, I think I got a fan club smellin' my gangsta."

"Why you say dat?"

"Cause every time I come thru, they be whistlin' at da kid," G Millions smiled causing everybody to burst out laughing.

"What da fuck is so funny?"

G Millions failed to find the humor in the situation.

"That's the San Juan Mascot. It's called the Coque, they whistle instead of rivette," Felix explained, and they all laughed.

After the little tummy tickler, they all filed out of the room in order to hit the jet skies. Once on them, they raced up and down the shores, riding waves the size of buildings. G Millions and Jux wound up venturing out a little further then they should have, idled their jet ski's and then set fire to some piff.

"Yo B, I know I'm not buggin'," Jux squinted his eyes as if trying to be sure him self. "You see dat?"

"Dats, dat piff B. But you ain't buggin'."

"Sharks!" They both yelled and hauled ass back to shore.

G Millions and Jux enjoyed their vacation, but like all good things, it too had to come to an end. On their way out, they saw security dude and thanked him for the tour. They also told him to keep his job and assured him that they would holla back. Felix had been aggravating G Millions ever since they'd met but he had also grown both he and Jux. G Millions told him to pack a light bag and when they left the island so did Felix…

Chapter 9

"They Cheating"

G Millions' and Famous' flight were scheduled to arrive at the Newark International Airport within hours of one another. Famous's flight was the first to arrive, so he decided to wait for his partner instead of meeting him in the hood. They had just recently ended a telephone conversation which he wasn't to comfortable with. He and G Millions had grown up together and he knew him better then he knew himself, so it wasn't hard at all to figure out that something was wrong.

Famous also knew that this wouldn't be a good time for Sincere to be around, so he sent him straight home. Meanwhile all him and Hamma could do was wait inside off to the right of the bar for their comrade. The Virgin Pina Coladas and some slick talk made the forty-five minutes they'd been talking feel like only five. Then, they got up and strolled over to the flight area where they were greeted by Lady Pink.

"What's goody wit'cha' sis'?" Famous asked while they exchanged a hug and kiss on each other's cheek.

"You know me, I'm doin' what I do," she responded while they broke their embrace.

"What's dat? Staying fine as a muthafucka," Hamma joked.

"Fool you betta watch ya mouth, my ice pick made it thru." Lady Pink rolled her eyes and neck, giving them a good laugh.

A couple of minute's later G Millions' flight was gliding down the runway. When he appeared from out of the tunnel, Lady Pink disregarded the rest of the passengers. She ran into her lover's arms and gave him a full and passionate kiss on his lips.

"What's really gangsta pretty mama?" G Millions searched his rider's eyes for answers.

"I gotta holla at you daddy."

"A'ight, give Jux your Porsche keys," he told her. Lady Pink handed Jux her keys without question.

"Jux, you, and Felix cop a suite at the Hyatt," he instructed. "We'll get at ya'll later."

When Felix saw that the Cayenne truck was pink, he didn't give it a second thought. His only thought was how fly the Porsche truck was. He was feeling New Jersey already, thus he was ready, willing and able to play his position.

On the limo ride to New York, Lady Pink brought G Millions, Hamma, and Famous up to speed on what took place during their absence.

"That sucka ass nigga Shyster put together some bogus ass indictments against ya'll. Him and the narcos raided a couple of spots, but they didn't get anything but a few burners that a couple of lil' homeys had on them. Plus they pinched Gangsta wit' a tech and got warrants for ya'll." She pointed at them.

"So more-less they ain't got shit," G Millions stated nonchalantly.

"More-less, Gangsta said that all of ya'll got distribution charges, but we all know that, that's bullshit 'cause don't nobody in this car go hand to hand on no local shit. And Hamma is just Hamma," Lady Pink said and everybody laughed.

"Girl, you wild as hell." G Millions managed in between snickers. "You find a way to make everybody laugh even when ain't shit funny."

"They can't be serious," Famous added.

"I keep tellin' you to let me eat that nigga," Hamma shouted.

"I dig where you're coming from, but we ain't gonna do them table scrap getting' fools no favors. He's too dumb to put together a good case on us. Our lawyers will tear their ass up." G Millions scratched his chin in deep thought. "Plus if we get at this cat, the big boys gonna step in. Shit, I'd rather deal with Shyster. We'll get around him like we been doin'. So we gonna make bail and it's gone be business as usual. Oh yeah, speaking of bails, did you pull Gangsta yet?"

"You already know I'm about my business daddy."

"Fo' sure, but you know I got class so I gotta ask." G Millions rubbed Lady Pinks shoulder. "Famous I need you to get all of your paper work together and rent out the block so that the peasants can eat. We're going to turn ourselves in, make bail then fuck the game up. Hamma, I need you to chirp Gangsta and tell him to shoot down V.A. and stay wit' my sister until we bail out," G Millions instructed. "I'll see ya'll at the spot."

Everybody met up on 39th St between 5th and 6th Ave in lower Manhattan to support Pay Dirt. Chinchilla Black and Throwback were on the venue to open up for Beanie Segal at club Speed. This was a good look for the family. If they did their thing, that would put G Millions one-step closer to being a legit millionaire.

After Pay Dirt performed, they made their way over to where G Millions, Famous, Lady Pink, and Hamma were. On their heels was Gangtsa followed by at least thirty BG's sporting either Pay Dirt or Exit 9 tee's representing the hood. The family showed each other love and popped a few bottles before Lady Pink and G Millions bounced back to Jersey. Famous and Hamma stayed with Pay Dirt.

***

When G Millions and Lady Pink reached the comfort of her condo, he gave her a monthly sex session before taking it down for the evening.

G Millions got up bright and early the next morning and made his way home to put in some quality time with YoYo, Lil' G Millions and his well-mannered championship breed Presh Caurio dogs Sable and Lynx. The Presh Cario was a mixture of Great Dane, Bull Mastiff, Rottweiler, and Pit Bull. They actually looked like big versions of pit bulls and were used in England to guard the Kings castle. So what better way to keep his castle along with his Queen and Prince secure was G Millions logic.

It always brought him a great deal of pleasure to walk into his extravagantly furnished room and see his wife and son sleeping peacefully on his oversized bed. It was at that moment that he decided to consider making his money work for him legally. All of his hustling, robberies and body count had afforded him the good life thus far. However, the recent turn of events made him realize that the fast money would someday slow up. Even with his last heist, everything was lovely, but now a nice chunk of his cash would have to go on bails lawyers etc. That accompanied with their everyday living expenses threatened to put a dent in his balance sheet. So he would definitely have to intensify his gangster and expedite his business ventures as well.

G Millions decided that he wanted to surprise wifey and his little man. He went down stairs and cooked them breakfast consisting of pancakes, turkey bacon, scrambled eggs with cheese, freshly sliced cantaloupe and orange juice. He then placed the breakfast on a tray along with a long stemmed white rose, took it up stairs to the bedroom and woke his family up to breakfast in bed. He gave YoYo a kiss and his son a hug. Judging by their facial expressions it was plain to see they were both surprised and happy to see him.

"When ya'll get finished eating get dressed, we goin' to Great A," he announced and left the room before anyone had a chance to answer.

Satisfied that he had just made his family's morning, G Millions set out for the kennel to do the same thing for Sable and Lynx. The huge dogs went bananas as soon as they saw their master. No sooner then he opened their cage they were all over him. After confirming that their master loved them, they wolfed down their food and took off around the yard as if it were their first time out in years. G Millions got a kick out of watching his pony sized dogs, dash around the yard, as if they were still puppies. It felt great to be able to enjoy one of the rare moments that he got to spend at home, savor the small things in life and most important spend time with his family.

An hour had passed since he had come outside with Sable and Lynx, which was plenty of time for them to get their exercise. Once he put them back in their kennel, he chirped Famous and headed for the house.

"Bleep...bleep...bleep...Famous!"

"Bleep...What's really gangsta B."

"Bleep...7A."

"Bleep...I heard, I'll be right thru."

"Bleep...Bring Candy Girl, it's a family affair."

"Bleep...A'ight."

By the time G Millions showered up, thoroughly groomed, and got fresh, Famous and Candy Girl were sitting in the living room being entertained by little G Millions and enjoying every minute of it. YoYo discovered his dancing skills from just the two of them sitting and watching music videos. Her baby would imitate the dancers. She loved to see him do the Harlem shake the most.

Forty-five minutes later, they were walking around Great Adventure. Little G Millions wanted to take a ride thru the safari, but this was one of his few requests that he was denied, out of fear of the animals scratching up the G Ride. So instead they made it up to him by hitting all of the major rides such as King Da Kah, Batman, Rolling Thunder, Lightening Loops, the water rides etc. After, they took time out to enjoy the live entertainment. The adults had fun as if they were kids again. And little G Millions simply had fun. A little exhausted and famished from all of the walking and waiting on the long lines, they stopped at an outside dining area in order to rest their feet and get a bite to eat.

It was like déjà vu for G Millions to be sitting in this particular dining area, the same one they used to sit at in their high school days when Franklin High School would take them on their field trips.

"Yo B, you remember 1984 our sophomore year when the school brought us here?" asked G Millions.

"Yeah, we were some wild ass young boys." Famous smiled.

"Shiit, we even got the celebrity treatment back then. Our whole team was G'd up in Polo, Bally's, British Walkers, shell toed Adidas, Pumas, Le Tigre, Kangols etc." G Millions smiled at the memories. "The world wasn't ready for us yet. Everywhere we went shorties wanted to take flicks with us."

"We ended up havin' to get up out of here too, fuckin' wit' lil' Tommy's silly ass." Famous laughed as they began to take a stroll down memory lane with G Millions leading the way.

"Word, we was mobbin' thru the park like thirty deep wit' our mini Louisville Slugger baseball bats, when we walked up on that giant ass white dude slappin' his wife around. Lil' Tommy was like hey...hey...what are you doin' over there? In that stupid ass deep voice he be makin'," G Millions recalled.

"Yeah, he was a funny ass joker," Famous took over. "And dude was like mind your fuckin' business, you fuckin' nigger. Now why he go and say some shit like that for is still an unsolved mystery," Famous laughed.

"We was on him like piranhas," G Millions joined back in.

"Then one of them good white Samaritans must've called the park rangers on us. They gonna ask us did we have anything to do wit' what happened on the other side of the park and asked us to leave. Like we were gonna say yessir boss we's did it." Everybody started cracking up laughing at G Millions account of the events.

Famous picked up where he left off.

"Yeah, we had to take our party to the bus after that. We even ended up turning the bus driver out with our skunkweed and mix tapes. We had all that hot shit back then, Big Daddy Kane, PE, G-Rap, Slick and Doug E. Fresh. We had the bus fogged and rocking." They all shared another laugh.

At the end of the day, everyone had thoroughly enjoyed themselves. The mood was still up beat even after G Millions and Famous prepared their families for the war that they had coming with the law, as well as their future. It was probably the plans that they had for the future that kept everybody optimistic. That kept everyone sane. After putting the final touch on their plan, Famous and Candy Girl returned to their big beautiful home to try to make little G Millions a running buddy.

"You and mommy are my role model," Lil G Millions announced proudly. "Ya'll are the coolest parents in the world and so are Famous and Candy Girl too." he stretched his little arms in order to emphasize his point, while his father tucked him in.

"Listen here little fellow. It's alright to have role models, but you have to be yourself at all times. If you have people you look up to, instead of immolating them, you take their strengths and add them on to yours to make you a stronger person." G Millions searched his son's eyes until he was satisfied he understood him before continuing. "You also have to keep doing well in school. Don't ever let anyone tell you that it's cool to be dumb because it's not. It's the smart person that makes it in this world. You understand?"

"Yes daddy." Little G nodded his head.

"Good, now show me what you got," G Millions said and they did their secret handshake.

"I love you son."

"I love you to daddy."

G Millions gave his little man a kiss then went into his bedroom to be with his wifey.

When he entered the room, YoYo had Mary J. on for the mood, while she was in the bathroom putting together a nice milk bath for her and her G Millions. He was exhausted from the festivities of the day, so he lay across the bed attempting to relax.

YoYo sensed that her man had something on his mind, so she walked sexily over to him and whispered in his ear.

"What's wrong daddy?" She rubbed his back and shoulders purposefully trying to rid his muscles of tension.

Without saying a word, he rolled over and grabbed her by the back of her head and kissed her as if it would be their last. After seeing stars like she always did whenever they kissed, they went to the bathroom to relax in the hot milk bath Yo Yo had prepared for them.

Determined to make him forget about his worries, YoYo bathed her man as if he was a baby while they continued their foreplay. The couple's passion and lust lead them back to the bed where YoYo took total control. She pushed him on his back, climbed on top of him, and started licking and sucking on his neck, then she worked her way down his chest and then his balls.

"Ahhh shit girl!" He murmured as she sucked his sack while stroking on his now erect dick.

After thoroughly licking and sucking his balls, she placed his giant sized sex into her mouth. He closed his eyes and played in her hair trying his best not to cum too fast.

"Um-uh nigga, open up your eyes and look at me," she ordered and then went up and down on him, while rubbing his pre-cum all over her face." Cum daddy," YoYo purred while lustfully looking him in the eyes.

"Oouaah shit girl, I'm cumin'!" G Millions yelled as he exploded in her mouth.

She caught and swallowed every drop of her man juices. YoYo wasn't at all surprised that he was still standing at attention because he never let her down. Refusing not to let him down either, she climbed on top of him and slid him inside her wetness.

"Damn baby, you gotta have the best pussy on the planet," G Millions whispered while grabbing her by her perfectly round butt cheeks and followed her rhythm. This time they reached their climax simultaneously. Yells and moans echoed through-out the house. Having satisfied the yearning for each other that had been mounting up ever since the breakfast in bed, YoYo nestled in his arms and the two lovers engaged in pillow talk until the wee hours on the morning.

***

The next day G Millions, Famous and Hamma met with their attorney's at the bail-bondsman's office, which was located in the same building as their studio. The purpose of the meeting was to make preparations to turn themselves in. After a brief discussion with their lawyers and the bail-bondsman, they were able to determine the best way to post bail without having to worry about the feds getting involved.

Once they made it down to the police precinct and thru the booking process and questioning, Shyster set a ransom bail as always and as expected. The lawyers were pissed, not only about how crooked the New Brunswick P.D. were, but also the whole Middlesex County court system.

The system gave Shyster, who was only a lieutenant for the narcotics division of the police force the power to set bails. He also encouraged his detectives on his task force to conduct illegal strip searches, lie under oath and to top all that off, any plea bargain that was negotiated as a result of an arrest by him or anyone on his task force, had to be approved by him.

The whole system from the municipal court judge to the superior court judge and the prosecutors all worked together. In the town, the quality of lawyers didn't even matter. You could have the late great Johnny Cochran and the entire dream team and wouldn't get a motion granted, a reasonable bail or a fair trial thought G Millions and Famous. Their motto was, "Take it up with the Appellate Division."

G Millions bail was set at a half of a million, Famous was a quarter million, and Hamma's was a buck fifty. The lawyers advised them not to post their bails at the station house, but wait until they were lowered by the bail unit and make bail from the county jail.

They ended up sitting in the county for three days. When it was all said and done, G Millions bail was reduced to a quarter of a million, Famous a hundred thousand, and Hamma's was seventy five thousand. No sooner then they received their bail slips; they were on the phone with their lawyers, who gave the okay to the bail-bondsman to post bond immediately.

When they stepped out of the county jail, they were embraced by the humidity of the early summer evening air. G Millions was tearing open the plastic bag which held his belongings so that he could raise hell on his jack about nobody being their to pick him up, when a beautiful white Mercedes stretch pulled up. Not knowing who was in it nor possessing their ratchets all three of them thought about retreating into the building. However, Lady Pink and Gangsta quickly erased their thoughts when they hopped out.

Once they pulled off G Millions instructed Lady Pink to get Jux on the jack and have him round up Butta, Al-Capone and Grass and have them at the studio.

Upon their arrival, the atmosphere was in full throttle as always. After everyone had poured their choice of drink, rolled their preferred smoke and settled in, the meeting was called to order.

"More-less, ya'll already know the sucka shit Shyster tryin' to pull. Wit' his last stunt he showed us that he will stop at nothin' to bring us down. Even if it means cheatin', he figures that if he kills the head the body will fall. But what he fails to realize is that our structure is organized so that there's always somebody to step up. Everybody in this room has been there and done that. So all we have to do is continue to play our positions flawlessly and him and his sucka ass squad will continue to grasp at straws." Pausing to take a swig of his concoction, a few long drags off piff and a quick glance into the attentive eyes around the room, he continued his commentary. "The narc's got a job to do and so do we. We just have to do ours better. We are a family gathered around money, if we can't gather around money, then what we stand for ain't about nothin'." Once again he paused, took a few swigs, a few puffs and continued. "More-less, I already know I don't have to ask nobody to leave this office if they're not ready to put this thing down. There's no big I's and little U's in this team. Everybody has to play his or her position and we all eat lovely. Jux, get two good men and put one in charge of smack and the other in charge of the yayo uptown. You give them the work, collect the bread and see Lady Pink. Butta, you got the projects. Al Capone you got the Ville, Class Pl and Henry St. Grass, you got Parkside and the South Grove. The gloves is off, ya'll tell all them fools out there to break bread or fake dead, you hear me? Let's go out there and get those millions," G Millions said, which concluded his halftime at the super bowl speech.

The young gangsters filed out of the room buzzing with excitement about their future. Before they cut into G Millions and Famous, they were mere small-time street hustlers, robbers and shooters at best. Now that their big homies saw their potential and helped bring the best out of them, their every intention was to make them proud. However, this moment called for a celebration with all of the hood-models, good piff, and champagne and gangster music. This would be a celebration to remember.

While the YG's went on to celebrate, it was strictly business for G Millions and Lady Pink. There was a lot to do in such a little time and the clock was ticking…

Chapter 10

End of 2004...

"On the come back"

G Millions had just breathed a breath of life in his team sending them to enjoy the celebration in high spirits. Now it was time for him to do him. G Millions swept everything off of his desk causing Lady Pink to freeze with a puzzled expression on her face. As far as she was concerned, the meeting was a success so his look threw her.

The open hand from G Millions caught her completely by surprise.

He pushed her onto the desk, spun her around, pulled her capris down to her ankles and buried his tongue in her ass. As bad as she wanted to protest, she just couldn't, it felt too good to her.

"Aghhh shit nigga, you on that freak shit tonight," she screamed and let out a sigh of joy while she continued gyrating her hips.

She reached back and spread her ass cheeks apart so that G Millions could get to it thoroughly. Now that his hands were free, he used one to show her some attention by rubbing her clit and sliding his fingers in and out of her goodness, while using the other to show attention to her body, by caressing and needling it like a sensual massage.

"You like dat?"

"Ooooh shit yeah daddy, that feels sooo good," she panted.

G Millions was turned on even more by her pants and moans, which caused him to intensify his love making to her butt-hole, giving her a feeling so amazing that she thought that she would pass out. Satisfied with how he got her sex cat gushing its' hot wet juices, he switched the attention of his fingers to her ass. When Lady Pink was turned on, her womanhood got, so wet and her juices flow so freely that it looked as if she were urinating. In fact, the first time that it happened that's what he thought she was doing and flipped. Now ever since that day he discovered she was a squinter, it had been his mission to see her waterfall.

Once he quenched his thirst, he made his way back to her butt-hole, to the cheeks and slowly worked his way up her back and ears.

"You love this shit don't you girl," he whispered in her ear.

At this point, it wouldn't have been surprising if her cries of pleasure were loud enough for the youth on the other side of the door to hear.

G Millions took advantage of Lady Pink's unbelievable wetness by using it's juices to lubricate her butt-hole.

"Yes, that's right daddy, put it in my ass," she cooed, while pushing her ass into him.

G Millions not wanting to deny her any pleasure fulfilled her wishes by easing it in slowly as she wound her hips like a Jamaican girl dancing to a classical dance hall tune. After getting, it all the way in, he picked up the pace until they were humping like jackrabbits.
"This dick good ain't it."
"Yes, that's it daddy, right there, give it to me just like that," she panted in her best freakish tone. "Ahhh yeah daddy, I wanna taste your-."
The combination of her dirty talk and her anal muscles gripping his dick was too much for him to bare.
"Oh fuck I'm cummin'!"
Upon hearing her daddy's cries, Lady Pink's butt made a suction noise when she came off his length. She quickly turned around and put it in her mouth. His length almost gagged her as she tried to shove it down her throat. Luckily she was used to it, thus was able to recover just in time to receive his massive amount of fluids. Her own juices flowed like the Nile River as she made every ounce that pumped out of him disappears. After taking a moment to savor the flavor, Lady Pink was the first to speak.
"Damn nigga, I like aggressive, but you ain't have to smack the shit out of me like that."
"I know ma, but I was watching this crazy ass triple x movie earlier and saw how much Lexi loved that shit, so I had to catch it, ya dig?" G Millions flashed a wicked grin.
"Fool this ain't back in the day when you watch those Bruce Lee movies and come outside all amped up, kickin' niggaz heads off!" Lady Pink said, rolling her eyes and snapping her neck.
"Stop stuntin', you know you smellin' my gangsta."
"Fo sure, I came as soon as you smacked me," she said and they laughed.
After the couple straightened out the office, they went out and enjoyed the celebration with the rest of the family. It made the young gangsters feel good to know there big brother and sister didn't think that they were too big to be amongst them. They also owed them something that couldn't be repaid with nothing but loyalty.
With the family going hard in the streets, the next eighteen months flew by. They also promoted shows, sponsored cruises, bus trips, and vacations. You name it they had their hands in it, anything to stack a dollar. Surprisingly, besides a few robberies there wasn't any blood shed. But like in all walks of life, they knew nothing good last forever. Their balance sheet was looking proper when the bottom fell out of this one. Both G Millions and famous along with Hamma and Gangsta blew trial and now they were about to pay the price for telling Middlesex County to pick their best twelve.
Everybody including the judge, prosecutor, and even the courtroom sheriffs was

surprised by the verdict. Their lawyers were outraged and their families devastated. No one could understand what could have possibly been on the jurors minds. It seemed as if they had their minds made up that the defendants were guilty and nothing, including the facts were going to change that.

Their trial was a prime example of a glitch in the Middlesex County judicial system. Instead of having jurors composed of their peers, there was eight middle aged to elderly white people and four Clarence Thomas type Negroes who couldn't possibly understand what went on in the hood, or could conceived the thought that an officer of the law could lie under oath or do anything underhanded just to secure a conviction. As a result, they assisted Shyster in his modern day kidnapping.

After being convicted of a fabricated observation sale, with no pictures, video tapes or even phone taps, just the word of an un-produced snitch. This made both G Millions and Famous realize that they could no longer take anything for granted. This also made them determined to turn the set back into an opportunity. Shyster and his lackeys would surely pay for their act of treachery. The near future would reveal that boxing them up was the worst thing they could have done.

No sooner then they hit the building, G Millions bumped heads with his long lost peoples EQ. EQ was also from Exit .9, New Brunswick. He was at the end of his 15 with a 7 1/2 year stint for armed robbery. After being the subject of several robbery reports, EQ was finally cornered off while coming down the stairs of a drug spot whose door he had just kicked in, in broad daylight. Realizing that he was trapped, his plans was to go out in a blaze of glory but the robbery squad got the drop on him struggling to carry the safe with both hands.

Now five years and three months later here he stood, face to face with his old Pop Warner tailback. Although the two of them hadn't seen each other since then, they became close again in no time behind the walls of the Rahway State Prison. Back in the days as a New Brunswick Raider fullback, EQ would open up gaping wholes for G Millions to run thru. Now that they were in the box, EQ would do whatever needed to be done in order for G Millions to be able to run his smack down thru the building with virtually no interruptions. His loyalty was fierce and so was his murder game, which was why G Millions dubbed him Lucca Brassie. Lucca wasn't an offensive tackle huge; however, he was a presence and a monster. So he ended up being the perfect compliment to Hamma and Gangsta.

***

It took fifteen months for G Millions, Famous, Hamma, and Gangsta's appeal to be granted. All four of them had managed to throw their time back and would be touching the streets within days of one another. Today would be G Millions day, so the family all met up in the mess hall for breakfast to show their love.

"What's really gangsta wit' cha fool?" Famous exclaimed, giving G Millions a brotherly hug.

"It's over B!" G Millions answered excitedly.

"Don't get out there and get on no gay shit chump," Gangsta teased.

"Fuck you, you young punk," G Millions shot back causing everyone to laugh.

"Seriously though, hold it down out there B!" Hamma stated.

"You got both of my bad ass sistas mobbin' thru to scoop you huh?" asked Famous.

"Why wouldn't I?" G Millions flashed his million-dollar smile. "More-less you already know its millionaire status all day homeboy. But it don't stop wit' me, the whole family gonna touch in style. Then once we all out there we gonna have a home coming extravaganza bigger then Howard Home Coming, ya dig!"

G Millions made his way to four upper level on the fifth tier back to his cell where he spent his unwanted vacation. He reflected back on how he used his time behind the wall to get his mind right and focused his energy on his legal businesses so that when he was ready to retire from the game he'd see enough profits to legally support his lifestyle. As soon as he bent the corner to his tier, there stood Lucca Brassie leaning on the bars in front of his cell. His enforcer smiled uneasily as he approached.

"Lucca Brassie, what it do?" G Millions asked while trying to read his eyes.

"You already know what it is homeboy. All you gotta do is give me some rachets, a vest and cut my check and I'll murder the Pope for you B!" Lucca informed with a serious smile.

"Breath easy homey, I already told you, you're a made man now," G Millions assured and patted him on the shoulders. "The family will be here to pick you up and make sure you have everything you need. So put ya feet up 'cause shit about to get sweeter, ya heard."

G Millions being the natural born leader that he was knew that his job sometimes entailed him being a gangster-oligist in other words a gangster psychologist, so it was easy for him to detect Lucca's apprehension due to all of the broken promises that was made by the many others who came and went in the past. But Lucca would soon bare witness to the greatest. He would see to that personally.

"Damn B, ain't nobody ever show me this type of love. I'm going to shadow you like the secret service do the President," Lucca said in a sincere tone.

"It's nothin' B, that's what I do, I'mma team playa. I'd rather my whole team drive Benzes together, then me pushing a Rolls Royce or a Bentley by myself, ya dig," G Millions explained.

Lucca got a little sentimental as they gave each other hood love before leaving the tier. G Millions walked into his cell to make sure he had everything together.

***

Three hours later, G Millions' door to his cell shook. He knew that was his signal that meant it was time to go. He grabbed his fish net laundry bag, which possessed his legal work, mail and pictures and made his exit. As he made his way through the tier's corridor, he received big love from dudes who had great respect for him from all parts of the tri-state area.

The hate from the correction officers lingered heavy in the air as he strolled through. He could actually feel their eyes burning a whole in his back all the way, up until he reached the middle door. The reception there was much warmer because one of his peoples, Tasha, was working looking gorgeous as ever. Tasha was one of the cool C.O. chick's that didn't take any shit, especially from other officers. She felt G Millions swagger from day one, so she fucked with him heavy hence the reason for all the hate from the other officers. She was a contributor to why G Millions lived so well during his bid.

"Hey G!" Tasha smiled at him when he stepped thru the inner steel door.

"Hey Tash," G Millions smiled back. "What's really gangsta wit' ya fine ass!?"

"Boy you crazy, make sure you stay your behind out there," she advised.

"That's the plan ma," he retorted smoothly. "This little punk ass fifteen months taught me something," he assured her.

G Millions sensed it in Tasha's body language that she wanted to give him a hug good bye and he felt the same way. Tasha made his time in the box a lot easier. They had talked about everything from relationships to politics whenever the opportunity presented itself. She really became a good friend and in another day and time, in another world she would have been his. He let her know how much he appreciated her friendship during his bid and if she ever needed him, he was there. After a minute of awkward silence, she bust through the outer door and waved at G Millions.

***

Little G Millions was the first one he spotted when he walked down the stairs and into the hallway of the front house. He stood in between the two glass doors as if he owned the joint. The front house was packed with cats from the camps, halfway houses that had come in for various appointments, and front house workers along with officers.

G Millions sat down on one of the wooden benches and patiently waited for his check and for the lieutenant to sign him out. A few cats he knew struck up conversation with him and the others added their two cents. G Millions hated that shit and normally would have addressed it, but he wasn't about to allow anyone or anything for that matter to spoil his day. He was all too glad when the Lt. came followed by the little Indian girl with his check.

Right after he finished with them, he headed for the front door accompanied by wishes of good luck from the inmates who would have given anything to be in his shoes at that moment. When he swung the door open little G Millions ran and jumped into his arms.

"We gone have to find another way to greet each other boy, you getting to heavy," G Millions smiled at his son. This had been the longest time he spent away from him since he was born.

"I know, I've been eating all of my vegetables," informed little G Millions, while making a muscle to emphasize his point.

"Yeah I see," G Millions said feeling his sons muscle on the way out of the door. "Where's mommy?"

No sooner then the words fell off his lips, a snow white 2004 Maserati Quatroporte pulled up. Damn, that shit official! He thought to himself. YoYo and Lady Pink hopped out looking like two movie starlets. His women were hotter then the sun that was blazing on that day of July 18, 2005. All eyes were on them as he swaggered towards the two loves of his life.

When he reached them, they both took turns giving him hugs and kisses, which was a little more attention then little G Millions cared for as his father still held him and his bag in his arms.

Once they were all settled in the G Ride, G Millions took a quick inspection of the upholstery and accessories. He was very proud of how well his women paid attention to him. *They did the damn thing* he thought to himself. YoYo hit the remote to the sound system. The base line dropped and the sound of Jay Z's voice boomed thru the Quatroporte's quality sound system. "Catch up niggas... Damn you fadin' 'em Hov/ how you gave 'em that/ the Audemars Piguet wit' the alligator straps-," All though the song was a little out dated it fit the mood perfectly as if it just dropped yesterday. Yoyo pulled off showing the on lookers how to do it, leaving them gaping and gazing. While inside of the G Ride Lady Pink was wrapping an Audemars Piguet watch around his wrist and kissing him on the cheek.

"Welcome home daddy," she stated warmly.

Just then, her jack started to vibrate on her hip. Seeing that it was the call that she'd been waiting for, she motioned for G Millions to turn down the music, flipped her jack, and took the call.

"What's really gangsta?"

"Them foreigners still in our hood without a green card," Grass stated calmly back thru the phone.

"Go to the studio," Lady Pink instructed. She disconnected the call and replaced the jack back in its holster. "That was Grass on the jack tellin' me that we still got that issue we discussed when you was boxed up."

"You got a pint out on them cats?"

"You already know I'm 'bout my business," Lady Pink said, giving him the people's eyebrow.

"You want me to be done wit' the issue?"

"Nah, I want ya'll to drop me off at the studio and prepare my home comin'," G Millions instructed ignoring Lady Pink's facial expression.

"You ain't coming with us daddy?" Little G Millions asked.

"I gotta go to work son, but I promise I'll see you tonight."

"You're going to work already?" Little G Millions twisted up his face and folded his arms. "You never have time for fun."

"If you got time, you don't have any money. If you got money you don't have any time," G Millions said, patiently schooling his son. "I have to put it in son, so that you, your kids, their kids, don't have to struggle, you understand?"

"Yes daddy."

"That's my little man." He gave his son a high-five as they pulled in front of the studio.

G Millions eased up out of the G Ride and into the building with the grace and power of a panther. Pandemonium broke loose at the sight of his presence. He received mad love as he swaggered thru the lounge area. When he spotted Grass, he pulled him to the side and told him to give his people in the South Grove the night off.

The studio hadn't changed one bit in his absence he thought. The familiar sounds of Chinchilla Black and Throw Back dominated the speakers welcoming him home. *Damn it feels good to be home*, he thought to himself. His Green Team comrades B-Nam, Jahler, Fifteen, and Santino caught his hand signal as he walked by and followed him into his office.

"What's really gangsta wit' you fool?" G Millions asked giving them hood love.

"It's good to have you home B!" Santino was the first to welcome him.

"Yeah, it was a short vacation, that shit wasn't 'bout nothin' B," G Millions responded.

"What's hood for tonight?" B-Nam asked.

"I gotta put in that QT wit' the family tonight. But right now I'm 'bout to show the hood what they been missin', smell me."

"I heard you ain't wasting no time huh?" Fifteen smiled.

"That's why you young fools love me so much."

"More-less, you already be knowin'," Jahler, confirmed his statement.

"What you fools workin' wit'?"

Neither of the youth said a word. They answered his question by lifting up their over sized tee's revealing their .44 desert eagles and slug proof vests.

"That's what the fuck I'm talkin' 'bout. All I need is for ya'll to box them lames in and I got the rest," G Millions paused, searching their eyes for understanding. Once he was satisfied that he had it, he finished. "Pull up the G Ride and I'll be right out."

Now that he was alone in the office, G Millions went behind a framed poster sized picture of him and Famous leaning on the window seal of his Aunt Joyce's house in West Philadelphia and punched in the combination.

He retrieved his twin .45's and his jacks. He closed the safe and went to the closet where he quickly shed his state issued denim dickey suit and replaced it with his vest and army fatigues. He prepared himself for his mission with purpose. The hood was about to find out ASAP, that not only did he have muscle, but he also he was the muscle.

After he strapped up and was on the way out of the door, G Millions hollered at Grass.

"Yo son, what you workin' wit?"

Grass simply responded to the question by handing him the duffle bag at his feet, which contained his tech .9mm. He didn't have a problem giving it to his boss because there was much more where that came from.

On their way to South Grove, G Millions inspected the paperwork and photos that Lady Pink had given him. Once he had completed his review of them, he conducted a thorough inspection of his weapons. They were pulling up on Phillips Rd. just as he completed the inspection.

G Millions instructed the Green Team to post up while he crept thru the parking lot, up thru the wall. In no time, he spotted what he was looking for. With his tech raised, he eased up on his pray with the grace of a ballerina. His foes were so engulfed in their conversation that they got caught sleeping and G Millions was there to make sure that they would never wake up again.

"Blllat. Blllat. Blllat. Blllat-." His tech sung them twenty-four good night notes.

Their so-called leader was lifted up off his feet and came crashing down into the bushes. The rest of them who tried to take flight met their fate by the burning led spat from the desert eagles of the Green Team. G Millions calmly placed his tech in the small of his back, walked over to the bushes, and emptied the clips of his .45's into the already mangled body of the so-called boss. It didn't matter that dude had already went to see who he believed in. G Millions came to show the hood what they had been missing. Mission accomplished a satisfied G Millions thought.

When they pulled back up in front of the studio, YoYo and Little G Millions were already waiting for him. He hopped out of the Green Teams G Ride and into the Maserati with his family, giving them both hugs and kisses. YoYo pulled away from the curb and whisked G Millions away before he changed his mind and headed home.

***

A feeling of rejuvenation swept thru G Millions body upon entering the comfort of his home. He could hardly believe he was there after fifteen whole months. He felt sorry for his comrades who had to do real numbers. Visiting the studio was one thing, but his lavish castle was a whole other ball game. YoYo and Little G Millions started the pampering immediately. They led him to the dining room table and made sure that he was seated comfortably at the head of the table before going to retrieve his meal. He hadn't realized how hungry he was until they started placing dishes in front of him. One whiff of the lamb chops, macaroni and cheese, rice smothered in gravy with finely cut garlic, broccoli and corn bread awakened senses that he'd forgotten existed.

After ripping thru his first meal home as if it was his last super, answering a million and one questions, getting beat half to death by his son in Play Station 2, and tucking him in, he finally got a chance to go to his bedroom and unwind with his baby.

When he stepped thru the door, he was pleased to see that YoYo had the mood set perfectly. Fuck the negligee, pumps, and all of that other glamorous stuff. She had on the sports bra, daisy dukes looking nice and raunchy with the fluffy Majenta slippers. She knew just what her baby wanted, and exactly how to give it to him.

"Differences" by Genuine played in the background enhancing the mood. She walked around the room seductively shaking her nice jingly booty like a hoochie mamma, giving him a little show while she had his feet soaking in a Whirl Pool foot massager. She followed that up with a manicure, pedicure, hot bubble bath and a full body massage. By this time, they were both hot and horny. YoYo took G Millions manhood into her hand, then went down and sucked his balls one at a time while stroking the length of his erection. She slowly worked her way back up to his body, placing passion marks on all of his hot spots before slowly inserting his love muscle into her goodness. After they made love in every position and having multiple orgasms, YoYo lay curled in his arms happy to have her man home. To say he was happy to be home would be an understatement for G Millions...

Chapter 11

Spring 2005…

"The Home Coming"

After Cory, the crack head gained entrance to the check cashing joint Jux put two slugs in his face while Al Capone pumped three in his chest. They no longer had any use for him and they'd be damn if they were going to take a chance on a crack head bringing down the organization. So, they dumped his body into the dumpster behind the building. Cory was a specialist at breaking and entering whom Lady Pink hired to take with them on this particular job. The check-cashing joint that they were robbing was nothing more then a regular building with a few extra reinforcements and alarms designed to keep the average crooks out. However, their hood took pride in being above average. When the Robbery Report came out, the word average wouldn't be anywhere to be seen, not in a good light anyway.

This jux was something that G Millions had plotted, planned, and strategized for Famous, Hamma, Gangsta, and himself. However, a lot has changed since then. There was a lot going on that G Millions had to focus his energy on. He put Lady Pink and two of his young gunners on the job, which would pay out lovely if, executed right.

There was nothing the youth would have rather been doing then what they were doing now, they sat in the check-cashing place waiting for the owner to come and open it up for the first of the month's traffic. They knew kicking it with the homies all night wouldn't rake in the cash they were about to score for the family.

G Millions thought ahead while planning this jux. He didn't want any unnecessary bodies, especially in broad day light. He decided the best route to take would be to have them break in and wait.

Jux and Al Capone were up in the spot smoking piff and sharing a fifth of Hennessey, while Lady Pink sat in a stolen Pontiac GTO listening to her police scanner, while stroking her chopper AK 47 as if it were a cat, ready for whatever.

"Yo B, we 'bout to have a wild ass day my nig," Jux chased his words with a swig of Henny.

"Hell yeah, after we go and get our big homies, it's on and poppin'," Al Capone agreed.

"This that piff right here B." Jux looked at the blunt and shook his head up and down as if agreeing with his own statement. "We 'bout to shock the world!"

***

The night flew by and the owner came in at 6 o'clock sharp, just as planned. When he opened the door and entered his establishment an unfamiliar scent alerted his nostrils, but he brushed it off at first. However, when he walked thru the security doors the smell had gotten stronger. Although business had been running smooth for the elderly Chinese man in the poverty-stricken neighborhood for the past thirteen years without interruption, something didn't sit right with him this day.

***

Jux and Al Capone found the puzzled man humorous. While he stood there scratching his head pondering on his situation. The two crooks watched and laughed to themselves, while playing connect the dots on the Chinese's man body. The owner finally derived a conclusion but by the time he reached for his cell phone and pistol simultaneously, it was too little, too late. The two robbers emerged from their place of hiding.

"The only use you'll have for that jack is to make funeral arrangements," Jux stated frankly.

"Pop the safe young fella!" Al Capone demanded, getting straight to the point.

"Ahhh" The owner who was in his late 60's lost control of his bowels, which made no difference to the cold blooded Al Capone, who still hauled off and smacked him upside of his head with his pistol.

"I told you to pop the muthafuckin' safe not shit ya-self fool!" Al Capone snapped, losing patients.

"Damn, that nigga stink!" Jux added, holding his nose and twisting up his face.

"If you don't hurry up and pop the safe, you gone be stinkin' for real!" Al Capone issued his final warning.

"I think my dude serious young fella," Jux mocked. "If I were you I'd pop that safe."

The owner finally conceded to the warnings of the two robbers and opened up the safe revealing stacks and stacks of cash and several moneybags. Moving swiftly, the two youth filled up their duffle bags with the paper.

"Pop!"

Al Capone put a slug in the old man's face leaving blood, brain and skull fragments all over the walls floor and safe. Then they eased their way out of the back door and made their way to the awaiting GTO.

A broad smile formed across Lady Pinks face as soon as she saw the young gangsters approaching the G Ride with the loot. When they got in and closed the doors, she pulled off smoothly and swiftly, making their getaway from the scene of the crime. Once they switched up G Rides, they went to the Hyatt to get cleaned up.

G Millions, YoYo, and the rest of the family were already getting fresh when they arrived.

Everyone was buzzing with excitement, while they got fresh and prepared to bring Famous, Hamma, Gangsta and Lucca Brassie home in style. YoYo got the keys to the vehicle containing the loot from Lady Pink and made her exit to complete the final stage of the robbery, which was to secure the take and abandon the getaway car.

Candy Girl and her girlfriend from Atlanta were excited and having their own conversation off to the side catching up on what was going on down in the dirty south when G Millions walked up on them.

"What's really gangsta ladies?" He asked with a smile.

"Famous!" Candy Girl answered excited about going to pick up her daddy.

"You already know what's gangsta wit' me," said Angie, "But it's good to see you again though."

"Yeah, you showed me a good time in the "A," now I'mma show you how we get dirty in Jersey, ya dig!" G Millions promised.

"I heard! I'm excited already. I'mma put this good "A" town twat on one of these young gangstas you got runnin' around here," Angie said giving Candy Girl a high five and they giggled like little school-girls.

"Candy, make sure you have everything straight for the show tonight. I got Thomas getting the G Rides in place so we can bounce. Plus he's settin' up the trip for after the show," G Millions reminded Candy Girl before he left her and Angie to resume their conversation.

***

It was a gorgeous day outside when Famous, Hamma, Gangsta, and Lucca Brassie stepped thru the front house doors and into the fresh air and welcoming sun, which was quite the contrast of the gloom and stale dry air that they'd grown accustomed to inhaling.

Although all four men were strong in their spots, they couldn't help but to be overwhelmed by the assortment of luxury vehicles, limos, and SUV's along with the whole family there to greet them and welcome them home.

When they approached their entourage, the first to greet them was the young gangsters whom were in charge of each area of the city, Jux, Al Capone, Butta, and Grass. Next were Chinchilla Black and Throwback followed by the Green Team, Candy Girl, Angie, Lady Pink, and G Millions. When Famous looked over his partner's shoulder, he spotted a familiar face belonging to his half Italian half Greek friend Thomas Goamas leaning on what he would soon receive as a coming home gift. The white 2002 ML60 Mercedes Benz, the fastest SUV in the world was a beauty. It could reach 0 to 60 miles in 4.6

seconds with a super charged V8 5 speed. Famous had been on Thomas since before he went in trying to get the truck from him. So Thomas decided to look him out with it to welcome him home.

Thomas was a 38-year-old entrepreneur that just happened to have the biggest roofing company in New Jersey. If it weren't for his long, straight, jet-black hair in which he mostly wore in a ponytail, he could be mistaken for a light-skinned Black man at first glance. Famous' mind drifted back to 2002 when he was still in his hand-to-hand days they had met on route 27.

Thomas had been parked in his CL55 sitting on 22" Lorenzo's on the prowl for what he liked, that good cocaine. Apparently he couldn't reach his normal connect, so he ended up spending twenty-five hundred with some cats in front of 912, which was directly across the street from where Famous was getting it in at the time. What made them clowns sell a dude like Thomas some bullshit remained a mystery to him. Thomas was far from a sucker the Italian half of him came from his father who was a solidified in the underworld surfaced because to him it wasn't about the money it was about the respect.

It was a good thing for them clowns that they were no where to be found, but as fate would have it he ran into Famous which ended up getting him more then just some good cocaine in the long run. Thomas could tell just by looking at Famous' swagger and looking him in the eyes that he wouldn't get beat again, and if he did it would have been for much more then $2,500.

Famous approached his vehicle openly admiring the rims that the cokehead had on his CL55. He knew from the rip that either he owned a few buildings on the strip, or he wanted to cop a whole bunch of yayo.

"I hope what you got is official, 'cause I ain't into repeating the same mistakes twice, if you know what I mean," Were Thomas's first words to Famous.

"The best way to avoid all that is simple," Famous told him while passing him a $20 half of gram and taking notice to his Italian accent. "Sample this shit here and see for yourself."

Thomas took his time and tested the work. "Yeah this the real deal, but I know you got some raw and uncut."

"Cool, you mind takin' a ride?" Famous asked, sensing Pay Dirt.

"Sure as long as it's worth it," Thomas answered, seeing the dollar signs in Famous's eyes.

Famous took him right around the corner to his spot that he had in the Ville. It was at that moment that the trust factor was added. Thomas also liked the way Famous went out of his way to get him what he needed and he knew that this young fellow knew what it took to get money. So he dropped $5,000 on him like it was nothing and Famous gave it away to him like Crazy Eddie. Although Famous already had customers who dropped more with him, there was something about Thomas and it wouldn't take him long to see that he was absolutely right.

"This ain't shit; I do this at least twice a week," Thomas informed him before continuing. "I don't hustle because I don't have to, but I know the game. Always keep in mind that the heavier you cop, the heavier your stash will be. Meaning keep enough paper for bail and I'm not just talking just no drug bail either. In this life you never know what's going to happen, so you have to keep a good mouth piece on retainer, be able to make a murder bail, and the rest go to poppie."

Although Famous appreciated Thomas's advice, he learned from the best and was already way ahead of his time. In fact, he really didn't have to be on the block. This was just one of his ways to pay homage to the hustle gods who seemed to be smiling down on him since birth.

"Stick wit' me Tom, I'mma make you famous," was all he said.

Before they parted ways, Famous got the description of the clowns that robbed Thomas, they exchanged numbers, and the rest as they say is history.

Thomas had been getting things done for them that would be too difficult for young Black men to have done, ever since that day. Famous would later find out, it was also Thomas, who had booked him and his family the private jet, which would take them to the mansion that they rented for their two weeks vacation in Acapulco. Now he was handing him the keys to a $75,000 truck as if it was nothing. Thomas's willingness to do whatever he could for the hood showed how it paid to be a real nigga. You never knew how and when it might come back to you.

The look on the people from the outside faces showed that their luxurious convoy was shutting it down. G Millions, Lady Pink, Famous, and Lucca led the way in G Million's Mas while Candy Girl, Angie, and Thomas styled in the quarter to eight BMW 745. Hamma and Gangsta pushed the ML60. Jux, Al Capone, Butta and Grass held it down in the brand new triple black Ford Excursion. The label truck was exclusive; it possessed plush leather recliners with white Pay Dirt emblems stitched in the headrests. The extended back was big enough to accommodate eight linemen from a NFL football team. Two 13" colored TV's contained the PS2 hook up with the wireless joysticks, which all of the young gangsters kept one of their own because the gambling got serious. What would start out as $100 friendly bet could quickly escalate to $1000 and better a game. Their most heated games were Roy Jones fight night and NBA Y2K. The Excursion was also equipped with internet access, satellite phones, and stash boxes with heavy metal and ammo. It sat on 29" rims with burnt diamond lug nuts. The sound system consisted of Rockford Fasgata detachable face radio that played CD's, DVD's, I-Pod, Sirius satellite radio etc. And to top all of that off, it had laboratory certified armoring. Although everyone had their own hot wheels, this was G Millions way of showing his appreciation for the hoods undying loyalty. The labels headliners Pay Dirt and the Green Team played clean up in a fully equipped stretch Lincoln Navigator complete with the complementary Moet, but niggaz kept them yellow bottles.

The convoy split up when they reached the highway. The Masareti and ML60 hit Rt. 1 and 9 in order to make a quick stop at Woodbridge Mall so that Famous, Hamma, Gangsta, and Lucca could shed their dickey denims, pop some tags and strap up for their meeting with Hotep. Everyone else hit the Turnpike and headed for their favorite room at the Hyatt in order to prepare for the show that would be popping off later on that night.

After G Millions made sure everybody was straight, he hopped on the turnpike and was Brooklyn bound. It took forty-five minutes to get to Fort Green Park from the mall. Five minutes before they arrived, Lady Pink called Hotep to inform him of their arrival.

Hotep set the meeting up in Fort Green Park so that he could still enjoy his favorite game, Cricket. Cricket is something like the islanders version of baseball, except the ball is much harder, the bat is flat and thick and instead of a catcher, there is a stick set up with a smaller stick balanced on top of it. The object is for the pitcher to try to knock the stick off and the batter to try to prevent that from happening, while everyone else played the field like baseball.

Once they got all of the formalities out of the way, Hotep got the meeting started.

"Pink my brother told me that you were gorgeous, but I had no idea," Hotep complimented. "You young lady, belong in Hollywood."

"So I've been told." Lady Pink flirted.

"Yes, I'm sure you have, now let's get down to business so that I can get back to my game." Hotep cringed as one of the players from the team he was rooting for struck out. "Listen, how do you all say this thing. I'mma keep it gully with you. All of your guns and muscle you brought with you wouldn't have done you any good in my back yard, yours either for that matter. I got enough paper and guns to get at Bush," Hotep stated with an air of arrogance. "My brother was pissed about the shit ya'll pulled in New Orleans. However, he later found out that Major Papers was into another trade from which I'm sure you all benefited from as well. Being as though that wasn't apart of his contract, you guy's saved us the trouble of killing him." Hotep paused searching for some type of reaction, but didn't receive any so he continued his spiel. "Major Papers was a good customer, but he didn't account for a fraction of our income. I'm sure that being as though you felt the need to rob and kill him, you'll be able to at least match his input. Now, I'm not going to tell you how to run your business, that's your business. Lady Pink vouched for G Millions so that's who I'll be dealing with. I don't want to hear about you having any other trades unless they are legal. So stay loyal and we shall enjoy prosperity. I'll contact you in three weeks, have a million waiting for me and we can get started." Hotep smiled for the first time since he laid eyes on Lady Pink.

"No doubt," G Millions agreed.

"G Millions I like your style. You're a man of few words and I can see that you lead by example. Stays focused and always remember; a weak man follows every rule, a strong man interprets the rule and bends it to fit himself. In you I also see strength; other wise my brother or Lady Pink wouldn't have been able to convince me to do business with you," Hotep informed.

"That's what it is," G Millions answered with a nod of his head.

They ended the meeting with a handshake and begun a connection that G Millions hoped would solidify his millionaire status. From that day, forth G Millions had no plans of ever looking back.

The family was in a zone on their way back to New Brunswick. Once again, G Millions and Lady Pink scored big for the home team and for once, they did it without casualties. They made it back to town fast and met up with everyone at the Hyatt. Inside of the suite, the atmosphere was live; everyone acted as if they were sitting on top of the world. After getting right, they got fresh and headed for the show.

***

By the time the convoy pulled up in front of the Franklin Twp. Fire hall, which was located in the middle class section of Somerset N.J., it was packed to capacity. Females you rarely seen came out of hiding, along with every gangster and hustler the hood had to offer. It was a gorgeous night outside, so all of the soldiers sported either their Pay Dirt or Green Team tee's. The family's muscle provided the security and they even gave a few notorious old heads fresh out of the box something to do, so their investment was secure.

The crowd outside went crazy when the hall security announced that the inside was packed so they weren't letting any more people in. However, the black youth settled down, adjusted and started a party of their own outside.

Wizz, Ali Rock, and Nykeem from the South Grove opened up for Pay Dirt and the Green Team who arrived just before they finished. When the convoy pulled up the expression on the peoples faces was as if some a list celebrities were coming thru. All of the soldiers with their tee's on cleared it out for the muscle, followed by G Millions, Famous and the women. Then Pay Dirt and the Green Team hopped out flossing with yellow bottles in hand. The partygoers were shocked, they never thought that it would be done like this locally. So they felt as if they were getting their moneys worth.

The family finally made it inside thru the side entrance and took their time hitting the stage, like stars do. You couldn't tell them that they weren't already signed yet. But they were stars in the hood so it was all good.

The DJ must have spotted them as soon as they hit the V.I.P. area because they could hear him screaming over the mic.

"Are you ready?"

"Pay Dirt! Green Team! Pay Dirt! Green Team!" Was all you could hear the crowd chanting, before going into a frenzy from the anticipation of a hell of a show.

The Green Team hit the stage first and set it off, and then Pay Dirt came on cue for their verses. By the time, they got finished their first song the crowd was out of control! Motherfuckers started brawling so hard that Franklin PD had to come thru. When they hit the lights, the crowd really lost their minds and not even the police was exempt from their wrath. Not wanting to risk arrest, the family got up out of there and headed for the hood. But to everybody's surprise, the hood was on Rt. 27. It was even more crowded up there then it was at the fire hall. Youth was everywhere, foreign cars and hoopties alike were double-parked completely disregarding the fact that Rt.27 was a four-lane highway running in both directions.

On one side of Rt.27 Mr. Lee's parking lot was packed, the hot dog spot next to it was wall to wall with hood-models and gangsters. Across the highway McDonalds and White Castle's, known in the hood as Krenshaw was atrocious! The family couldn't get their big shit parked in anywhere because if they squeezed up in any given spot, they may have had to be the last to leave and they weren't smelling being boxed in. Even in there own back yard, anybody could get it!

Crenshaw was already the spot after the club, parties, or whatever. But this night the family brought the hood out for real. The atmosphere looked like a freak nick. Youth were lined up from Crenshaw to the Ville and Suburban bus station.

Once they finally found a place to line their shit up, they got out and went to receive the love that they deserved for the turn out. Of coarse, their entourage scooped up all of the sexiest hood-model chicks who wanted to ride with the winning team and took them to their suite. The party at the suite might as well been for the guests because the family was too tired and pissed off to enjoy it.

In the midst of the festivities, Famous ordered the family to come together so that G Millions could present them with their well-deserved gifts for holding the family up in the box. He was proud of everybody from Famous to YG's for putting in work, no questions asked. They'd been completely loyal and as a result, everybody's lifestyle had changed tremendously for the better.

Once everybody was in the room G Millions pulled back the blanket revealing some of the jewelry from the New Orleans heist that they did before going into the box and another brief case.

"We ain't gonna make this a long one. As I told ya'll from day, I take care of mine. The first thing I would like to do is officially welcome Lucca Brasssie to the family." The room erupted with loud cheers, whistles, and handclaps showing their love and approval.

After everyone calmed down, G Millions popped open the brief case revealing two nickel plated .38 revolvers, which was Luccas favorite, along with four speed loaders and $25,000 cash.

"This is just a little something to get you started," G Millions said flashing his million-dollar smile.

"I heard you were the black "De Facto" boss of bosses, but seeing is believing!" Lucca thanked G Millions, embracing him tight bare hug and everybody laughed, popped bottles and started lighting up.

Once G Millions caught his breath, he spoke.

"Before ya'll get too bent, remember we got a big trip ahead of us tomorrow. So fuck around and don't be ready if you want to, I'm tellin' you now, the jet ain't waiting on nobody."

With that said, G Millions passed out the jewels and everybody else resumed their activities…

Chapter 12

The next day...

"The Vacation"

The family took G Millions advice and did very little partying and got lots of rest. Many of the young gangsters had never even been out of New Jersey and now they were about to travel to Acapulco New Mexico to have the time of their lives.

G Millions spared no expense and rightfully so, his family went hard in the streets, thus they deserved every bit of the enjoyment that they were about to receive. Being the natural born leader that he was, G Millions recognized this and made it his business to make sure that his team reaped the benefits of their labor. He also knew that a little bit of love went a long, long way. Meaning, they would go even harder for him when it was all said and done.

Some of the more business minded in the family followed his lead and invested in some 24 unit row houses that his man Nasty from Trenton, New Jersey put him up on while they were in the penitentiary. So he and YoYo had been purchasing them ever since he'd been home. He also used the line of work he was in to his advantage. It allowed him to get the units refurbished for little of nothing. Once they were fixed and ready to go, they would contact social services and rent them out to section 8, which was money in the bank, direct deposit from the state every month. The money was so sweet that he didn't even have to hassle with the tenants that paid them their measly $100 out of their pockets. Shit, he figured they needed it more then he did.

No matter what G Millions did, his goals were to make sure Pearl, YoYo, Lady Pink and his little man was secure, a goal in which the property helped him solidify. As for the hood, the smarter ones invested, but the ones living day to day chose not to. Lately G Millions had been working on a plan to take taxes out of everybody's pay like the government. Also to take a percentage of the robberies for bails, lawyers etc. He'd been in the game long enough to know that most of the time you have to think for the people that you choose to surround you. He had it all planned out. When they returned from Acapulco, he'd give everyone raises, that way after taxes they will still be seeing a little more then they already are and as a result, everybody will be happy. But for now, he was prepared to enjoy his vacation just like everybody else.

The atmosphere at the hotel was like that of a high school field trip. All during breakfast and immediately after, both the young gangsters and hood-models were in rare form. No sooner then their toothbrushes were back in the holders, bottles were being popped, and piff was being fired up. Then the arguments start as to who had the biggest or smallest dicks, who's' pussy was the wettest, tightest, sloppiest, driest, tightest, who ate the best pussy, sucked the best dick all this dominated the daily morning topic.

Pay Dirt, Green Team, Felix and a few of the girls provided the live entertainment spitting exclusive free-styles and R&B vocals. After a few hours of fun at the hotel, they jumped into their convoy and arrived at the private airport in Edison N.J. within fifteen minutes. Thoman Coucin, the pimp from Vegas and Shaleek was already waiting for them.

G Millions called Shaleek, Leeka Leek because he loved to smoke water, which was also known as leek. You definitely had to watch him because he would pass you a strawberry Dutch laced with exotic and wet and you'd be drowning in the water world. The brown-skinned 5'11" 260 pound Leeka Leek grew up in the projects in New Brunswick. Seven years ago, he moved to Park Heights in Baltimore where he'd been getting it in heavy. He always made himself available for G Millions when he needed a creeper.

After everyone gave each other the usual ghetto love, they traveled thru the small private airport where the rich whites and snobbish blacks stared in amazement at the young, gifted, and black. They sported the same designer labels as the wealthy, but they put it together in a way only the hood could appreciate. They were truly ghetto fabulous!

The camcorder was being passed around through the family ever since the night before. This trip had the making of a hot video written all over it. With the right editing and music, the footage could go places. They would put it on YouTube first to test the waters. The hood-models were a welcomed distraction to keep the young gangsters busy because too many gangsters in one spot would end up killing one another no matter how cool they were.

By the time, they reached the private jet everyone was more-less calm, consumed by their own thoughts and fantasies. Thomas had hooked the jet deal up with a friend of his who was in charge of getting the New Jersey Nets basketball team to their away games, so their was plenty of room and luxury to accommodate the family. After everybody boarded the jet, they settled down in their plush leather seats and prepared for take off.

Once they were in the air it was on again. The food, drink, and sour diesel were plentiful. Some of the youth watched smack DVD's on the jet's projection screen, while others listened to their I-Pods. Portable CD players boomed while couples became members of the mile high club.

After hours of fun in the air, the jet taxied the runway in Acapulco where a couple of stretch Benz's awaited to drive them to the mansion. The beauty and vastness of the mansion had everyone in awe except for Thomas, who just stood there shaking his head, as the wild youth ran inside in order to further inspect the premises.

"I gotta give it to ya Tommy; you really out did yourself this time!" G Millions excitedly patted Thomas on the back.

"Yeah, you did the damn thing B," Famous added.

"Nothin' but first class for my guy's" Thomas stated modestly. "There are three huge suites in there that's ours. So we better go before them wild ass youngin's' fuck up our sheets," Thomas warned and all three men laughed knowingly.

The three of them took in the scenery of the immaculately manicured lawns, flowers, and giant cactus with appreciation as they made their way into the palace. Once inside, the first thing that G Millions and Famous noticed was the breath taking views and total privacy from every angle. This place was huge, 18,000 sq ft. with 10 other big ass rooms that didn't include the three suites. There was a swimming pool on the roof and another on the ground. Also a steam room, 4 Jacuzzi's, a small gym, 3 wide-screen TV's, multiple bars and private terraces, the place was so big and beautiful that there was not one argument over the rooms. Everyone was so overwhelmed by the space of this spot things just worked themselves out.

There were so many things to do that the family hardly knew where to begin and two weeks wasn't nearly enough time to get it all in. The main thing that caught everyone's eye was the pool on the roof. They never saw anything like it, so that's where the party began.

Lady Pink had already discovered the stereo system with surround sound thru out the mansion, so she took the liberty of loading it up with all of the latest Hip-Hop and R&B.

The party was live and as always, there was never a shortage of food and drink. The bartenders and servers stayed on point with plenty of lobster tails, jumbo shrimp, crab legs, champagne, patron etc. But you know the hood couldn't stay away from the fried chicken, burgers, hotdogs, potato salad, gin, Remy, Heineken etc. For them the party just wasn't right without certain ingredients.

Also from the spot on that roof, they were able to see the beach, spa, boutiques etc. The weather was fantastic and it stayed the same year around. Cousin the pimp and Felix, hit the beach strip and were gone for an hour before returning. They came back sporting sombreros and ponchos with a gang of gorgeous Mexican women to add a little spice to the party.

Money was being bet on every water sport that they could think of. Volley ball, basketball and of course swim races. They even made up a water fight game were there would be teams of two consisting of a male with a female on his shoulder. The object was for the females on the male's shoulders to wrestle each other until one fell into the water. The one still standing was the winner. Once they got bored with the one on one fighting, they had a brawl for it all, with $7500 in the pot, Throw back and one of the Mexican girls won that. So to show his appreciation he rewarded her with a couple of pesos and a promise to let her go down on him. Of course, he told her that in Spanish, the funny thing was that was the only Spanish he knew.

Butta, spotted a golf course, started up an argument about football, and just as planned his prideful comrades fed right into his malarkey. One thing led to another and they all strapped up and went on the green turf of the golf course, where they picked teams. Everybody played except Thomas who took on the task of being a referee. The ante was a thousand dollars a man, which put the pot at sixteen grand. A bunch of young drunk fools playing football was hilarious. The hood-models cheer leaded and everyone assumed that, that's what the Mexican girls were doing also. Only Felix knew for sure.

Cousin the pimp stole the show playing in his green linen pants, eggshell white silk shirt, and cream Mauri's. His theatrics was without parallel. If you could imagine a modern day super fly playing football that was Cousin the pimp. Everything he did had to be pretty and staying clean must have been his motivation as he displayed moves that Reggie Bush would have envied, running touch down after touch down. This was one of those events that you had to see to believe. Americas home video, smack DVD's, gut DVD's etc. best move ever, this footage would truly become a hood classic.

Around midway through the game, gulf course security came and broke up the game. G Millions, Famous, and Felix had to play United Nations to prevent an all out brawl between security and the young gangsters. Under normal circumstances, they would have been the first to set it off, but calmer minds had to prevail on this one. So everybody had to be reminded of what they were there for, plus they were wrong for tearing them people's golf course up anyway. The young gangsters were still a little angry because all they saw was the police fucking up their flow just like they did in the hood. Never the less everybody calmed down and returned to the palace.

The shower situation was funny and it reminded G Millions, Famous, Hamma, Gangsta, and Lucca of the four wing showers on visit day at Rahway State Prison. The only difference was that the four-wing shower's was big and wide open, with ten shower heads for 200 + prisoners. Were as in the palace you had decent size showers three or four at a time. Which wasn't an issue because for the most part with the exception of a few tender dick niggaz handcuffing there hoes, it's been a free for all ever since the night of the show.

Throughout the day and night, the Mexican girls would be broken in as long as they hung around. Plus there would be much more where they came from during the course of the vacation, Cousin the pimp would see to that. As the festivities resumed, the staff earned their pay and was tipped heavy for there troubles. So they didn't mind keeping the food and drink flowing like water and they saw nothing.

Spades, poker, and cee-lo games took place all over the palace. Every square inch of it was being utilized and very much enjoyed. When the nightfall came, it was still beautiful outside and the atmosphere in the palace was like that of a back in the day house party. Everyone felt very free while having the time of there lives.

G Millions caught up to Famous at his favorite spot, the poker table.

"Fame I need you to rally up the troops and meet me at my suite," he requested of him before, easing off to find Lady Pink.

"Where you goin'?" Jux asked, not to happy when Famous got up. "I'm loosing."

"You always gone loose fuckin' wit' me anyway fool." Famous smiled arrogantly. "I'm doin' you a favor by allowing you to keep ya money."

"That's some bullshit B!"

"Listen little nigga, you just heard what the fuck G Millions said. You act like ya'll fools can't play without me." Famous was beginning to loose patients with his little homey.

"Keep fuckin' wit' me and you gonna see what my gun game be like!" Jux persisted.

"Ya last one wasn't impressive." Famous smiled, regaining his composure.

"Fuck you nigga, you know you respect my gangsta!" Jux retorted ending their little verbal sparing match with a smile of his own, while he and Famous exchange playful punches.

After finally getting away from the poker game, Famous caught up to Hamma in front of one of the big screens watching Hard Boiled by John Woo. He wasn't happy at all to have been interrupted from one of his favorite movies of all times.

"Why ya'll always fuckin' wit' me as soon as I get in my zone?" Hamma questioned.

"It must be something important, so put it on pause, and let's ride," Famous said, before heading out of the room.

When the two of them reached the second floor, they found Gangsta in the Jacuzzi flanked by Mexican girls.

"We got a meeting in G Millions suite," Famous informed him, amused by his fake ass Luke impression.

"Ya'll fools sure know how to fuck up a wet dream." Gangsta smiled, looking like the cat that swallowed the canary, just as one of the Mexican girls came up from under the water.

"Damn, lil' bro., what you given out scuba diving lessons?" Hamma joked and they all laughed.

Gangsta exited the Jacuzzi, dried off, thru on his smoking jacket and followed Famous and Hamma to G Millions suite.

***

Meanwhile G Millions found Lady Pink in another Jacuzzi with Candy Girl and Angie. He figured that they must've been plotting on something because they stopped talking as soon as he walked up.

"What you trifflin' ass hoes plottin' on?" He asked knowingly.

"Fuck you, nigga!" Candy Girl sassed.

"Hook a sista up wit' Lucca Brassie?" Angie smiled.

"Hells no!" G Millions shook his head adamantly. "You ain't takin' my nigga to the "A"."

"Who said I'mma take him to the "A"?"

"From what I heard about that cootie cat, he might wanna go." G Millions chuckled.

"Boy you stupid!" Angie squealed and they all burst out in laughter.

"Anywayz, what's really gangsta daddy?" Lady Pink asked, while trying to recover from the laughter.

"I gotta holla at you," G Millions answered, handing her, her robe.

By the time they made it to their suite, every body that G Millions had summoned was waiting for them. Once they were settled down, G Millions ran his story.

"I have a few things on the agenda concerning our hood," he said, looking everyone in their eyes one by one. "The first thing is long term. So this is what it is. I ain't smellin' that shit Hotep was hollerin' 'bout at the meeting." He was now pacing back and forth with beads of sweat beginning to formulate on his forehead, which was an indication of him getting pissed off all over again. "I don't appreciate how he tried to talk down on us like we were some type off common, petty thugs or somethin'. So we gone cop off him for the time being until we can find out everything about him, then we gone bang 'em. He wants' us to bring a mill, to start. Our goal is to get too big for him to serve. So we gotta reach out to everybody we connected with in the box and see what it's hittin' for. We need our product in everybody's hood on the east coast and with the numbers that we're getting our heroin and cocaine for, we can basically give it away like Crazy Eddie as long as them fools spending that paper. Then when the time is right, we gone see who got the biggest muscles, ya dig!" G Millions scanned the room, pleased at the nods of approval he received, he continued. "In between time, I got two banks waiting for us to withdraw our money as soon as we get back. I've been master mindin' this shit like David Grandsaff. My people inside of the N.B. and Franklin PD said that they supposed to be runnin' up in a few of our spots. So we gone rent space for an extra two weeks, that way our people will be safe. Then while they're pulling their fake ass raids, we gone give 'em a real Robbery Report to write, ya dig!"

"Yeah B, but who the fuck is David Grandstaff?" Gangsta asked with a puzzled look on his face causing the room to erupt with laughter.

"David Grandstaff master minded the largest bank robbery in American history. Although he ended up getting pinched, he eventually walked because the alphabet boys put shit in the game and they never recovered the three mill' he came off wit' from the Tuscan National. So even though what I got planned ain't as big, we can make a little bit of our own history. That's the basic's for now, I'll give ya'll the rest of the details when we get back to the town."

"Who the fuck you think you are fool, Simon Bar Sinister, or some muthafuckin' body?" Gangstas outburst gave everybody a good laugh.

"I see you keep a joke, huh." G Millions smiled. "Just for that, all you fool get the fuck out" He held the door open and motioned for everyone to leave."

Everyone was still giggling as they filed out of the room. As dysfunctional as they were, they were still family. Hell, to them they were normal and there was never a dull moment.

Jux, Al Capone, Butta, Grass, and Felix sat in front of one of the big screens engaging in the usual battle of NBA Y2K with yellow bottles in hand and sour diesel smoke in the air. The Mexican girls snuggled up against them unable to get enough of their style. Jux sparked up a conversation about how he had things set up back home uptown while enjoying himself playing the video game.

"Yeah my niggas, after that sucka shit Shyster pulled on our big homey's, I got my people on some gorilla warfare type shit fo'real. My baby gorillas be up in trees camouflaged up, wit' walkie-talkies, police scanners, binoculars and the whole shit, while my pitchers pitchin' out of manholes. I ain't got time to be fuckin' 'round wit them fools. That's why I don't just have anybody on look-out and all the pitchers be wanting is a stem, Suzy Q, some chips and a quarter juice!" He boasts and everybody laughs, while Lebron James glides from the foul line and finishes with a hard dunk shaking the joysticks.

"I feel you my nig., I got the buildings in the projects to protect my squad. So I just keep my perimeter look-outs 24/7, my roof patrol wit' their walkie-talkie head sets and my crossing guards," Butta explained.

"What the fuck you need wit' crossing guards?" Felix asked innocently in his Spanish accent.

"Fool, I just call them crossing guards because they direct traffic," Butta further explained with a smile.

"I got buildins' connected in my spot, so by the time they get past the perimeter and hit any of my pitchin' spots; the work will be in a whole nother buildin'," Al Capone added.

"My shit set up like the old school lower eastside spots, wit' a whole in the concrete wall just big enough for the money to come in and the product to go out," Grass, informed.

The young gangsters continued to exchange slick talk and Mexican girls for the rest of the night.

After a fun filled day of activities, Famous and Candy Girl entered their suite to relax, only to find Lucca Brassie busting Angie's ass.

"Ilk, ya'll nasty!" Candy Girl said while turning her nose up at the pungent aroma of sex that lingered in the air. "Why ya'll ain't doin' that shit in ya'll own room?"

Lucca Brassie turned around and smiled at the couple standing in the doorway.

"Because them wild ass youngin's' makin' porn in ours," Lucca answered, while still stroking Angie doggy style.

"Well ya'll ain't gotta go home, but ya'll gotta get the fuck outta here!" Famous shouted while trying not to laugh.

"Damn, that shit was getting' good," Angie said, smiling.

"Get it good somewhere else. Bye!" Famous shouted back, waving his hand signaling for them to leave.

No sooner then they made it thru the door, Famous and Candy Girl sprayed some Febreeze, changed the sheets, and picked up were their friends left off.

The two weeks of fun in the sun went fast and not a moment was wasted. Within a two week span the family went deep-sea fishing, jet skiing, sight seeing and everything else Acapulco had to offer. They tore up the town and the palace was a constant party. Now it was time to get back to business.

The flight back was a lot calmer then the flight going. Everybody was tired so they relaxed and watched "Heat" on the big screen. Their entrance back in town wasn't nearly as flamboyant as their exit. Although G Millions enjoyed his vacation he was happy to be home so that he could spend some time with his little man and YoYo. Besides one meeting and the robberies that he lined up, the next week belonged to the home front...

Chapter 13

"Two for one"

After the Acapulco trip G Millions stayed in the house for a few days of being tortured by "All My Children", "One Life to Live" and other soap operas by YoYo and "Biker Boys" and "Bike-Fests DVD's by Little G Millions who had a motorcycle fetish. Never the less it always felt good to spend time at home with family. He often asked himself why life had dealt him the hand in which he was now playing and wondered if he could be happy with just being a square. As those very thoughts consumed his mind, a verse by Chinchilla Black boomed thru his high tech surround sound system seeming to answer his question.

"If you see me and I'm drinkin' them drinks and fuckin' them hoes and ridin' them rides, I'm livin' the life! Anything else, I would be livin' a lie-."

His homeboy's lyrics brought a smile to his face as he headed towards the kennel to feed, bathe, and let Sable and Lynx get their exercise. While he took care of his dogs, he plotted, planned, and strategized the details of withdrawing his money from the two banks he'd been scoping out in his head. It sure enough paid to be surrounded by a bunch of loyal young gangsters, because it freed him up to not only put plans like this together, but concentrate on legal endeavors as well.

When Sable and Lynx saw him, they were happy as hell. *They had better be happy as much as I paid for them*, he thought to himself. Famous, Pearl and he were the only ones in the hood with them. In fact, very few people even knew about them. Everyone else had Rotts or Pits.

G Millions also had a thing for gators and not limited to the ones that you wear. Someday soon, he would have a pit full of them. He laughed inwardly as he thought about how many bodies he could throw in it.

While Sable and Lynx frolicked about his vast area of land, he decided to chirp Famous to see what he was up to.

"Bleep...bleep...bleep...Fame!"

"Bleep...What's really wit' ya fool?" His partner's voice came thru the jack.

"Bleep...It's time to do what we do my nig," G Millions informed him. "What you doin' right now?"

"Bleep...Puttin' in the QT wit' wifey. Lucca and Ang. Here to."

"Bleep...Shorty put it on that fool huh!"

"Bleep...Yeah, I think she 'bout to relocate to!" Famous joked and they laughed.

"Bleep...That's what it is, but dig this right here though," G Millions said, getting down to business. "I need you to rally up the boys and meet me at the studio at 1am. Besides our usual suspects, we gone get Lucca and Felix dick wet. It's time to see if they Prime-Time playas for real, you hear me!"

"Bleep...I heard," Famous put his phone in his pocket and his tongue down Candy Girls throat.

By the time G Millions got his in his pocket Lady Pink was chirping him.

"Bleep...Bleep...Bleep...Hey daddy!" Lady Pink's voice came pleasantly thru the jack.

"Bleep...Hey pretty mama! What's really gangsta?"

"Bleep...You already know, you that nigga daddy!" For some reason she was sounding sexy as a muthafucka to him.

"Bleep...What you been doin' these past couple of days?" G Millions asked while trying to force down the bulge that began to protrude thru his Sean John sweats that he lounged in.

"Bleep...Nothin' really, just checkin' on my businesses, relaxin', thinkin' about you, ya know." She paused briefly. "How's YoYo and the little fellow?"

"Bleep...They good, the little fellow ask about you all the time. He loves himself some Ms. Pink. I think he wanna hit that," G Millions joked and they both laughed. "Seriously though, I need you to meet me at the studio at a quarter to one."

"Bleep...A'ight," Lady Pink confirmed before closing her jack and returning to her urban novel.

After getting off the cell phone with Lady Pink, G Millions returned his dogs to their kennel and then he went into his home to prepare for his meeting.

The time for him to go and meet with the family came rapidly. G Millions grabbed his surveillance DVD and wrote YoYo who was at Shakira's house playing spades a short letter just in case she came in while he was out. Satisfied that his home front was covered, he snatched his keys off the mantel and headed for the front door.

***

As always, when G Millions arrived at the studio, he was welcomed with all of the love that he deserved. The atmosphere was ordained with another hit by Pay Dirt on repeat, along with plenty of smoke drink and hood-models. After returning the love, he headed for his office followed by everyone that he summed to brief for the robbery. As everyone got comfortable, G Millions prepared to show the surveillance DVD.

"Fuck we doin', getting' ready for a football game?" Gangsta blurted.

"Shut the fuck up and pay attention lil' nigga!" Famous snapped. "You always got something slick to say out of your mouth."

"Fuck you pretty boy!" Gangsta taunted.

"You couldn't fuck me if I had a pussy, bitch ass nigga!"

"Why don't both of ya'll shut the fuck up!" Hamma screamed. "Ya'll act like ya'll married or something!"

"Come on B, you know a meetin' ain't a meetin' if I don't fuck wit' my homies," Gangsta said with a smirk. "Let's just run up in their though."

"Just sit ya ass down somewhere. You fish tank head muthafucka!" Famous cracked causing everybody to laugh.

Once the laughter subsided and order was restored to the office, G Millions started the DVD. It took a little over an hour to go over every little detail from the entrance, to everyone's positioning, the timing and most important the getaway.

"This shit right here is easy money," G Millions assured them. "Do ya'll think we can put that work in without any bodies?"

"Psss, you can't be serious. Look around you and answer that question for yourself," Lady Pink stated the obvious, while making a sweeping motion with her arms.

Her statement prompted everyone in the room to look around the room at one another. After seeing exactly what Lady Pink was talking about, the room erupted with laughter. The family bonded for a little while longer before everybody went their own separate ways.

***

The next day Famous went to meet with Vinny, his crazy ass biker dude who used to lock down on the same wing with him during his little vacation compliments the state of New Jersey. Vinny could make anything when they were in prison, he supplied Famous and the rest of the homies with Glocks, which is prison term for a fiberglass shanks. These crudely fashioned knives were lightweight, easy to handle and they didn't ring off in the metal detectors.

Now that they were both free, they decided to continue their business relationship, although the stakes were much higher. Last week Famous dropped off everybody's guns in order to be fit for silencers and now it was time to retrieve them.

When he approached Vinny's house, he couldn't understand how someone with paper as long as Vinny's could live so foul. The rest of the neighborhood kept their house well maintained and their lawn, scrubs etc. well manicured. You even had to be careful walking up Vinny's walkway, because it looked as though something may be lying in the shoulder high grass, waiting to jump out and attack you. His neighbors were disgusted, but they knew he'd just done six years for fatally stabbing a friend for not passing a joint back to him fast as he thought he should have. So they were not about to take the chance of pissing him off.

The book bag that Famous carried containing twenty thousand dollars was a mere pittance compared to what Vinny was raking in thru his many trades and Famous knew it, which was another example of why it paid to be good to people. Vinny proved to be a valuable ally.

The front door swung open just as Famous approached and there Vinny stood with his thick beard, mustache, and full head of unkempt hair, looking like a young Grizzly Adams.

"Hey Fabulous, Famous or whatever it is you calling yourself these days," Vinny greeted. "Anyway, it's good to see you."

"My main man Vin the chin. You saying that like you didn't just see me days ago."

"Yeah, yeah, you're right, come on in."

"Why don't you buy yourself another house?" Famous questioned. "Or fix this one up, with all that paper your makin'."

Famous followed Vinny into the house.

"Let's just say, this one has sentimental values, but it serves its purpose just the way it is," Vinny informed with a wicked grin.

Famous is my guy, but if he keep fucking with me about my house. I'm going to fuck him and burry his black ass with the rest of the teenaged runaways I got stashed in one place or the other around this joint, Vinny thought.

"Whatever floats ya yacht Vinny." Famous patronized, snapping him out of his thoughts.

The two men remained silent on their walk down to the basement. When they reached the bottom landing, Famous couldn't believe his eyes, *Pay Dirt.* He thought to himself. Vinny had to have every weapon ever made, from the Billy club, to grenade launchers. Not to mention the garbage bags full of cash and marijuana. He also had a homemade gun range in which he used to test his handy work.

The two stopped at the table where the guns that Famous had given him the money for the silencers sat. After a quick but thorough inspection of his upgraded weapons, he gave Vinny the duffle bag containing twenty stacks.

"Vinny, you do excellent work and your fast." Famous complimented. "We're going to have a beautiful relationship."

"I told you I'm a professional," Vinny bragged. "You wouldn't believe my clientele. The only reason that I do business with you is because you literally saved my ass in prison.

So I know you're a stand up guy. By the way, who the fuck is Vin the chin?" Vinny said and they laughed.

After allowing Famous to finger fuck a few of the other weapons, Vinny was ready to conclude their business.

"Come on Famous lets go test a few of your toys." Vinny suggested, looking at his watch. "I have other business to tend to."

Famous grabbed his .9mm Glock off the table, slung one of his little homey's Mac 10's over his shoulder and followed Vinny to the room that he had sound proofed for his homemade gun range.

"Psss...psss...psss..." As soon as Vinny opened the door and went to enter the room, Famous' .9mm whispered three times, splattering Vinny's blood and brains all over the door.

"Yeah, it works just fine Vinny," he said looking at his .9mm as Vinny's blood and brains slid down the door.

Pleased with his handy work, Famous pulled out his chirp phone and reached out to Hamma.

"Bleep...bleep...bleep...Hamma..."

"Bleep...What's really gangsta my nig," Hamma answered.

"Bleep...Nobody."

"Good, I need you to bring the Suburban to 1179 Hillcrest ASAP," Famous informed him before putting his phone back in his pocket without waiting for a response.

Ten minutes after Famous pulled his ML60 into Vinny's garage, he had it loaded up with the money and the marijuana. Hamma arrived five minutes after that and Famous had him pull his Suburban up into the garage before leading him thru the basement to retrieve the arsenal. The sight of Vinny's dead body slumped over caught Hamma slightly off guard. Although he wasn't a stranger to death, this was the furthest thing from his mind at the time.

" What the fuck happened to him?"

"He wanted me to test out our gangsta machines and I figured we could use all of this shit he had. So I killed two birds wit' one .9mm," Famous joked.

After sharing a good laugh, they both loaded the weapons and ammo into Hamma's truck and headed for their homeboy's house.

***

It took them an half an hour to reach G Millions house. When they arrived, he and his son were playing catch football, while YoYo, Sable and Lynx watched. As soon as Little

G Millions spotted Famous and Hamma exiting their trucks, he ran up to them and gave them both love.

Sable and Lynx wasn't use to people outside of their household, so they got a little restless. Knowing her dogs all too well YoYo quickly exchanged pleasantries with Famous and Hamma before taking the dogs around the back with Little G Millions in tow. Of course, he would have rather stayed and hung out with the big boys. But the thought of an ass whipping from YoYo for being in grown folks business, stifled any would be protests.

When G Millions approached Famous and Hamma he gave them mad love.

"What's really gangsta wit' you fools?" He smiled and embraced them one at a time.

"More-less, you already know, we doin' what we do," Hamma answered while Famous handed him the duffle bag with the twenty stacks, without saying a word.

"What, our gangsta machines wasn't ready or somethin'?" G Millions asked, looking at the duffle bag as if it contained anthrax.

"Yeah, they were ready," Famous, answered. "I got 'em in the truck along with a few other tools of the trade."

G Millions knew his comrade long enough to know that he had a trick up his sleeve. When they reached the ML60 his suspicions was confirmed as soon as Famous opened the doors revealing the garbage bags full of money and weed. A broad smile graced G Millions face as he nodded in approval, after which the trio moved on to Hamma's truck. When Hamma lifted up the back, the cargo area exposed an assortment of weapons; slobber dribbled out of G Millions mouth as he hit the garage door opener and motioned for Famous and Hamma to pull in their trucks.

Once they were finished unloading the SUV's, they kicked their feet up and relaxed in the plush comfort of G Millions basement.

"Ya boy Vin the chin was runnin' his numbers, huh Fame?" G Millions asked, amused by the whole ordeal.

"He was until he fucked up and talked slick to the wrong dude," Famous joked, giving his best impression of a redneck.

The fellas were still laughing when YoYo came down with a tray holding three plates of steak, baked potatoes, and fresh salad and butter biscuits. Then she went and got them a yellow bottle on ice and an ice tea for Famous.

"Damn daddy, what's dat smell?" YoYo asked, frowning up her face.

"That's that exotic ya boy Fame came up on," G Millions answered while grabbing her by the waist and placing a kiss on her soft lips, which was his way of thanking her for the food.

"You want some sis?" Famous offered.

YoYo looked at G Millions for approval at which time he nodded his head in agreement for her to accept his offer. Seeing that it was all good, Famous reached into one of his bags, gave her a generous amount of sour diesel, and at the same time thanked her for the grub. After nodding her head silently thanking him for his generosity, she exited the basement.

Once YoYo was gone, the three men took their time and enjoyed the meal that she'd prepared for them. After, G Millions and Hamma got their smoke on, while Famous began to put the money thru the money machine and took the stage as only he can do.

"Vinny must have been a swami," Famous stated, referring to someone who could predict the future. "That fool damn sure had everything waiting for me. All the bills are separated with no ones and on top of that, I see my homey's love that sour diesel.

A couple of bottles of Crystal, shots of Hennessy and a few backwoods later, they were 180 thousand in cash and 120 pounds of sour diesel richer. The sour diesel was worth $6500 a pound in the streets, so when it was all said and done, Famous came up on damn near a million, even if they let the pounds go for $5,000 and that was including the guns. Plus they were looking forward to the bank robberies that they had scheduled.

The three of them collectively agreed to give each young gangster a $5,000 dollar bonus along with a pound of sour diesel and to put the rest of the product on the streets. Being as though they hadn't planned on the Famous come up, they figured that it wouldn't hurt to show a little bit of love; it goes a long, long way.

Once again, the balance sheet was starting to look good and they had enough guns and ammo to go to war with Al-Qaeda. G Millions took a quick examination of all the newly acquired weapons. He was particularly fond of the big Iraq toys that Famous scored, which consisted of AK-47's, M16's, HK's, MP5's, a grenade launcher, pine-apples and an assortment of big hand guns. *My team gonna be an issue out here in these streets*, G Millions thought to himself as he walked over to Famous and patted him on the back.

"You keep a rabbit in your hat my dude," G Millions smiled.

"It's nothin' B, you know how we do. We been makin' them fill out them robbery reports all our lives and it's only been getting bigger."

"We got the dream team for real, ya heard!" Hamma shouted out of nowhere and they all laughed.

Two days later:

Two teams of four masked gunmen sat on their street bikes in the cabs of two separate Ryder trucks, around the corner from each perspective bank that they were about to withdraw their money from. Everybody had there earpieces in awaiting the signal from Lady Pink who was listening to the police scanner and awaiting a call from her friend in dispatch. The raids on the drug houses were confirmed, and the narcotics officers would be rolling out at any second.

It took ten minutes for Lady Pink to get the call that she was waiting for, after which she immediately relayed the information to both teams. Seconds later, both teams ascended from the Ryder trucks. The timing could not have been more perfect. The way the events unfolded made G Millions look like a genius.

Not only did the teams exit simultaneously, but they arrived and entered the banks at the same time also.

"Psss... psss... psss..." Their weapons whispered to the security guards like clockwork, splattering blood and brains all over the floor and walls of both banks. *So much for a body-less robbery report*, G Millions thought.

"Everybody on the muthafuckin' floor!" Gangsta who was in one bank and Al Capone who was in the other, both barked simultaneously. "You know what it is, don't make it a muthafuckin' homicide.

The thought of what had just happened to the security guards happening to them was enough to make the patrons comply immediately.

G Millions and Famous, who were in the bank with Hamma and Gangsta and Lucca, Felix and Jux who were in the other bank with Al Capone, hopped the counter as Hamma and Jux held down the doors in each of their perspective banks.

"Back the fuck away from the counter and get the fuck on the floor!" G Millions and Lucca barked the same orders, but in different banks

As Famous and Felix hopped over the counter and directed the managers to the vaults in each of the banks. With the tellers secure, G Millions and Lucca swept thru the drive thru windows and emptied the registers of their banks. By the time they were finished, Famous and Felix were coming out of the vaults. Although they all sported leather riding suits and helmets with dark tint, they were careful to retrieve the surveillance videos and then they were out as swiftly and suddenly as they came.

The two teams of four worked efficiently, making the action in the bank go as smoothly as G Millions knew it would. Once the two teams rode their bikes back up into the trucks, they stripped off their riding suites, helmets, disposed of their weapons and exited the truck. Hamma and Jux who were in charge of getting rid of the evidence made their getaway in the two trucks while everyone else escaped in two Dodge Intrepid with the heist paper. When they arrived at the stash house, Lady Pink was already awaiting their arrival. She then took the money to another stash house where it would be secure.

The next day:

G Millions, Famous, and Lady Pink sat in the middle of her living room and counted $750,000 from their last take.

"Now I know how them athletes feel getting all that scrilla for havin' fun!" Lady Pink exclaimed excitedly.

"You ain't never lied," Famous co-signed.

"Between the banks and the lick you hit the other day, our balance sheet lookin' real proper like," G Millions said pointedly. "Fame after you handle your business in A. C. I need you to hop on a red eye to Vegas and clean up whatever money is left so that I can be ready when it's time to holla at Hotep. I'mma hit everybody that put that work in wit' fifty cash and all of our baby gangstas wit' ten cash for doin' what they do in the streets." He paused, looking for his people's approval, before continuing. "I'm also gonna invest some paper in some serious stocks, that's what's poppin' right now. So remember where you heard it first."

"I'm a gambler B and fuckin' wit' you ain't no gamble, it's a sure shot, you already know I'm in," Famous exclaimed.

"And I'll follow ya punk ass to the end of god's green earth, so you know I want in daddy!" Lady Pink added. "Hell, I haven't looked back since you came into my life unless it was to reminisce."

"It's good that ya'll got such strong faith in a nigga," G Millions said. "Ya'll motivate me to be at my best at all times. And for the record, I strongly believe in ya'll," he proclaimed thru the moisture in his eyes.

"A'ight sun, that's enough of that sentimental shit," Famous cracked.

"Let me find out you gettin' soft daddy!" Lady Pink Added.

"Fuck ya'll!" G Millions snapped out of the moment, giving everybody a good laugh.

They all gave each other love after which G Millions and Lady Pink prepared to meet Hotep. Meanwhile Famous placed a call to Cousin the pimp.

"Holla at ya boy!" Cousin' the pimp breathed thru the phone in his best Ron O'Neal impersonation.

"What's really gangsta?" Famous asked.

"My pimpin'!" Cousin answered. "Which one of my Jersey dudes is this, the one that will make you Famous?"

"You already know pimp."

"So to what do I owe the pleasure of you blessin' my jack?"

"I'm comin' ya way on the red eye at 9:45, ya dig."

"I heard pimp, I'll have a couple of thorough breads from out of my stable waitin' for ya. You know it's first class all the way pimp. They'll be in a Carolina blue Rolls Royce," Cousin bragged.

"You big pimpin' for real huh!" Famous said, purposely putting an energizer in Cousin's back to get him started.

"My hoes love me man. Fuck what you heard about how a pimp ain't supposed to stick his dick in his hoes," Cousin the pimp stated, giving Famous a little 101 on the pimp game. "I love my bitch's mane; my hoes got me livin' like a super star mane. I got a fleet of exotic European cars, a mansion, all the platinum and ice a nigga could wear, every flavor and style gator ever made, furs, the list goes on mane. And the best thing about it is that it's all legal dawg. You couldn't pay me to hustle again and I'm too pretty to rob," Cousin the pimp finished with a chuckle.

"A'ight pimp, see you when I get to Vegas," Famous said, with holding a laugh of his own, satisfied with the result of his energizer.

Everybody got a kick out of the way Cousin the pimp talked even though he could be too much at times.

"My bitches will be ready and steady for ya," Cousin the pimp assured before hanging up.

After he got everything straight with Cousin the pimp, Famous went to Atlantic City to go and see Hassanna to take care of their business before going to catch the red eye to Vegas.

As always, G Millions was plottin', plannin' and strategizing' on getting at Hotep. He couldn't shake the thought of how Hotep had tried to play him at their meeting and it was going to cost him in more ways then one. *Fuck what that nigga talkin' 'bout. I'm the real for real!* G Millions thought to himself...

Chapter 14

"Uncooked Beef"

The African drums seemed to beat with the rhythm of G Millions and Lady Pink's heart as the raced thru the jungles trying to elude the pursuit of a bunch of half-naked, black top dark skinned men, whose faces were covered with war paint. They blue darts and hollered a language that neither of them understood, but it didn't take Einstein to figure out that the Africans were pissed. The couple had no idea why though, as far as they were concerned, they were African also. After all, it wasn't there fault that they were kidnapped and brought to America. Hell, they didn't agree with most of the stuff that their country did either, but it was the only home they knew. So they had to get in where they fit in, and instead of dwelling on its flaws, they intended on taking full advantage of its opportunities. The Africans didn't give a fuck about none of that, to them they were just as bad or worse then the oppressor. They should stand up and fight instead of allowing this to happen.

Africans seemed to be coming out of the ground, spears and darts flew by them as they ran for their lives. G Millions tried to shoot back at them, but for some reason his .45 just wouldn't fire. A dart struck him in his buttocks and quickly took effect, causing him to feel paralyzed as he collapsed to the ground. When Lady Pink stopped to help him, she was struck in the buttocks also. Hours later, the couple woke up groggy and strung up over a big, round, black pot like bugs bunny being prepared for rabbit stew.

When Lady Pink pulled the Nissan Maxima rental into the Madison Square Gardens parking garage, she noticed that G Millions was very restless and sweating profusions in his sleep. When she went to wake him up, he reached for his gun, which wasn't in its usual spot on his hip. The only way that Hotep would agree to do the transaction would be if they were unarmed.

"Daddy, what's wrong?" Lady Pink asked. "You're fightin' hard as a mutherfucker in your sleep."

"This bitch ass nigga gotta go!" G Millions yelled, banging his fist violently on the dash. "I can't believe I had a dream about this cock sucka tryin' to get at us! Boof your ice pick ma, we 'bout to get it poppin' in the Garden like Hov at the 2001 summer jam, ya heard!"

"You already know it's whateva wit' me daddy, you know I'mma hold it up. It's all about you nigga!" Lady Pink assured him while thoroughly wrapping her ice pick, before inserting it into her vagina.

They left the rental in the parking space that Hotep had reserved for them and proceeded to the entrance of the stadium where they were checked by a hand held metal detector. Once they made it thru, they headed for the skybox where Hotep was waiting for them. First, they had to make a pit stop so that Lady Pink could retrieve her weapon that she had stashed in her womanly cave.

Once they arrived, they where greeted by Hotep's men who led them to their seats. The view of the Garden floor from the skybox was electrifying, which gave them the full effect of the game. The Knicks's were playing the 76er's and Allen Iverson was unstoppable.

G Millions and Lady Pink had been enjoying lobster tails, a bottle of Cristal and the game, when Hotep sent one of his people to lead them to a small area in the back where they were to finish their business. I'm a fuckin' genius. G Millions thought to himself. He knew that Hotep's arrogance and lack of respect for him would 'cause him to make a costly error. This would be the last time he and Hotep would do business together.

When they reached the back area, Hotep greeted them both with cold indifference, like he was doing them a favor by letting them spend their million dollars with him.

"G Millions, Lady Pink, let's get this show on the road. I have other business to tend to," Hotep said. "Do you have the keys to the Maxima?"

"Fo sure," G Millions answered and handed him the keys.

In return, Hotep handed him another set of keys to another Maxima the same make and model as theirs.

"It's parked on the same level as yours, row 5b. I don't have to count my money do I," Hotep asked sarcastically.

Although G Millions patients had been wearing thin, he kept his composure up until that point.

"I'm a man of my word," G Millions answered calmly.

"Ha...ha... What you got jokes?" Hotep spat with his breath reeking of sarcasm. "You're nothin' but a hoodlum that caught a few breaks."

That was the last straw.

"Hocus pocus!" G Millions exploded as he spit his gem star razor and slit Hotep's throat in one swift motion.

He laughed at the horror in Hotep's eye's as blood gushed from his throat while trying to speak.

Lady Pink followed suit and sprung into action by digging her ice pick handle deep into one of the bodyguards throat.

Everyone in the skybox as well as the rest of the stadium was so engrossed in the game that they had yet to notice that death was among them. The two point guards wearing number 3 were putting on a show of a lifetime exchanging three pointers. The fans were sure enough getting their money's worth. G Millions and Lady Pink were also. By the time the second bodyguard caught his wits and reached for his gun, it was too late. They were on him like piranhas, chopping and poking.

The bodyguard's nerves caused him to squeeze the trigger, shooting himself in the hip. The gunshot snapped everyone out of game mode and it was pandemonium in the skybox. The stampede for the door provided the perfect getaway for the couple.

When they reached the garage, G Millions who was thinking fast enough to take the keys back from the dead Hotep, quickly found the rental with the kilograms of heroin. While Lady Pink hopped into the rental that they came in. The traffic was somewhat slow, but they didn't allow it to threaten their getaway as they maneuvered like that veterans that they were. Once they made it thru the first tollbooth, they began to relax and play a little phone tag on their way down the turnpike back to Exit 9.

"Bleep...bleep...bleep...Did you cum ma?" G Millions teased.

"Bleep...Like I was suckin' on that gangsta dick of yours!" Lady Pink responded in her sexy tone.

"Bleep...Yeah that pussy was sweet." He smiled as if she could see thru the phone.

"Bleep...You know how we do daddy"

The couple went back and forth for the half an hour it took them to get to the ramp on exit 9. Once they cruised thru the easy pass, they headed to Lady Pink's condominium to plot, plan and strategize their next move.

***

Famous was enjoying Vegas already. Cousin the pimp's Rolls Royce was the truth. He had it fully loaded just like the "Pay Dirt" Excursion, except he had a 19" plasma, instead of the two 13" TV's, with the same PS3 hook ups. Everything else was identical from the plush leather recliners, to the internet access, satellite phones etc. Cousin obviously took notes while in Jersey. Cousin the pimp done brought the hood to the lifestyles of the rich and famous. Famous thought to himself as he laughed at his own inside joke.

Before they hit the strip, the girls took Famous to Del Frisco's, one of the many upscale steaks joint that Vegas had to offer. The steaks served at Del Frisco's was so tender that they could be cut with a spoon, which was one of the reasons Famous enjoyed dinning their whenever he was in town. After Famous and the girls enjoyed their meals, they hit the strip and proceeded to clean up the money from the bank robbery. Cousin caught up to Famous right were he knew he'd be.

"Hey dog, what's happenin' wit' ya?"

"Ain't nothin' pimp. I'm just tryin' to get some of this Vegas paper, ya dig."

"Fo' sure dog. But listen here mane, you know I talk too slick for the drug game and I'm too pretty to rob, but I got somethin' for ya sure nuff!" Cousin explained.

"What you takin' so long to tell me for B.?"

"That's what I'm talkin' 'bout right there dawg, that's why I stay fuckin' wit' my Jersey boys. I can count on ya'll to get dirty." Cousin the pimp smiled.

"Stop tryin' to mind fuck me fool and tell me what's really gangsta. I ain't one of ya hoes!" Famous was losing patients.

"You know you gotta work wit' me dawg. My mouth is my money, you see the Paul Wall grill pimp. I got niggaz whips in my mouth," Cousin the pimp said flashing his mouth jewelry. "Anyway, this big money gettin', fake pimp slash king pin cat that I use to send business to, ran off with one of my hoes. But I'm the real deal like Holyfield in his prime, so I knew she'd be back. See you can't fake the pimp game but for so long then you'll be exposed 'cause it ain't in you. This pimpin' thang serious dawg. Pimps are born they ain't made, understand what I'm talkin' 'bout?"

Famous knew that once Cousin the pimp got started it was best to just let him go, so he simply shook his head yes as Cousin continued.

"As you already know, I got a stable full of the baddest bitches in Vegas. So I don't trip about no hoes man. But this nigga broke the platinum rule of pimpin' and he didn't call it in. You already know I love my hoes dawg, that ain't no secret. So I'm callin' the city jail, hospitals, morgue, the birth's mammy and every number I could find trying to locate my hoe and come to find out, this fool harboring' my hoe man. You came right on time dawg; ole boy got the shit right up in his crib. My dude that he cop from, rent girls from me from time to time and he like my style, so he stay close you hear me! Dude just copped 200 of them thangs from my man. You can have that and whatever else you come up on, all I want is my 70 thousand my bitch would have made, plus 30 thousand for distress." Cousin smiled. "I'mma send that same bitch his dick got tender for and she gonna get you in. Ya slammers is still at my crib, so you straight.

"Damn, wherever I go niggaz holdin' my bread for me huh!" Famous wore a look of disbelief on his face. "I got one question for you though pimp. This fool ain't got no protection on all that shit?"

"Dawg, these dudes livin' on this side wit' virtually no interruptions. This a money town and ain't no robbers out here to take it. It's easy enough for me, but it ain't my line of work," Cousin explained convincingly.

Cousin the pimp continued to give Famous the rundown, after which he took them thru the area where the marks mansion was located. *This gone be easy*, Famous thought to himself looking at how the mansion sat out in the middle of nowhere. Plus it had mad woods a football field away, if he ended up having to go that route. As if reading Famous's mind he showed him where the woods came out. That night he fucked as many of Cousin the pimp's hoes as possible.

The next day…

Cousin the pimp's girl Boogie didn't have any problems getting into the mansion. So far, everything was going like clockwork. Boogie waited until everybody was settled in and having fun before she let Famous in. Once on the inside, Famous crept thru the mansion until he found the room that he was looking for. When he rolled up on his mark, dude was sitting up in his Jacuzzi filled with beautiful woman smoking a Cuban cigar, drinking Champaign out of the bottle and one of the woman was feeding him cocaine off of an 8x10 inch mirror, while they watched porn on his 52" plasma screen TV's.

Famous stood in the doorway unnoticed for two minutes amused at how easy these rich dudes gave away their money. The chrome .44 bulldog that sat on the edge of the Jacuzzi didn't go unnoticed by Famous. *This shit about to get fun*, Famous thought to himself. Finally getting bored with the little display going on in front of him, he set it off.

The sight of Famous standing in the doorway with his machine gun in hand caused all hell to break loose.

"Ahhh!" The woman started screaming hysterically.

The mark knocked the cocaine up into the air hoping to distract Famous long enough to have time to reach his .44 bulldog. But little did he know this type of situation wasn't anything that Famous wasn't used to.

"Blllat…" Reacting swiftly, Famous put the laser on the girl next to the marks head and let his machine gun loose.

The blood, skull and brain matter caused the mark to stop cold, knowing that he was next. The women also stopped screaming and looked on in horror and shock, as the events unfolded before them.

"Now shall we try this again?" Famous asked calmly.

It's funny how brains make people think, he thought to himself amused at how quickly everybody was now cooperating by climbing out of the Jacuzzi onto the marble floor.

Famous had Boogie duct tape everybody except the mark whom he had take, him to the stash. The mark led him to a huge walk in closet with mirrors covering the walls, circling the entire closet. Once inside, he hit a switch and a section of the wall popped out and slid to the side revealing a man size safe.

Famous put the beam to the marks head while he turned the dial to open his safe.

"Blllat…" He put one in the back of the marks head as soon as he got the safe open.

He then filled the marks Louis Vuitton luggage with cash, cocaine and jewelry. Once the luggage was all loaded up, he popped open his hawk knife and handed it to Boogie.

"Cut that fools dick off and put it in his mouth," Famous ordered.

Boogie didn't hesitate to do what she was told. Famous put a phone in the marks hand. Although they didn't necessarily agree with Cousin the pimp's line of work, he could always be counted on and he was family. Like Cousin always said, "He didn't put a gun to them bitches head and make them sell pussy." Women always liked to give him their money, and he liked to take it. The message would be loud and clear; you better call in fucking with Cousin' the pimp.

***

Famous and Cousin the pimp had just finished counting the loot when G Millions broke thru his chirp.

"Bleep…bleep…bleep…Fame!"

"Bleep…What's really gangsta wit' you fool?"

"Yo B, I need you to cut your trip short, shit real in the field, ya dig!" Informed G Millions.

"I heard, I'm on the next thing smokin'" Famous assured his partner.

Cousin the pimp had one of his girls book Famous a red eye. Famous gave him a hundred and fifty thousand and some jewelry for his ladies. He would have also given Boogie something for her part that she played so well, but he knew that it would only go to Cousin. So he just gave her an exotic necklace with multicolored diamonds set in platinum. He also had Cousin arrange to get the 170 kilos, and 1.8 million dollars back to New Brunswick. Famous took the money that he came with and was out of there. His only regret was that he didn't get the chance to frequent the places that he liked. It was all good though, he came up as always and there was no doubt in his mind that he would see Vegas again very soon.

When Famous arrived back in Jersey, he was greeted by G Millions and their small but deadly entourage. After showing each other love, they all hopped into the company Excursion and headed for their favorite suite at the Hyatt. On the way down the N.J. Turnpike, G Millions briefed his partner on what took place in the Garden and Famous briefed him on what took place in Vegas. Famous also agreed with the changes that G Millions had in mind. It only took Lady Pink twenty minutes to get from the Newark airport back to town. The young gangsters were mad because they didn't get the chance to finish their game.

All eyes were on them as they strolled thru the hotel lobby. But they weren't strangers to the attention, so they just kept it moving, hopped on the elevator and went to their suite. Once they got inside, they got comfortable and patiently waited to be filled in on what was going on. To unwind, the family ordered room service and laughed at the footage of their vacation and a few of the other main events that they'd attended. After the little entertainment was over with, G Millions started the meeting.

"More-less, ya'll already know we've been scoring big lately, thus our balance sheet is lookin' proper. Everybody in this room is having an all-star season, so more-less you will reap the benefits of your labor. Our family bond is strong and it's about to get stronger. Lady Pink and I just scored big again and Famous hit two licks back to back. The best part of about these scores was that none of them was planned; however, they were well worth it. You can never get enough of that fast money." The suite erupted into a joyful agreement causing G Millions to have to pause until everybody calmed down. "I wouldn't get too excited yet because with prosperity comes consequences in this life of ours." He paused again to examine the expressions on the young gangsters' faces as his last statement-sunk in. to his delight they all had their game faces on, so he continued. "The jux that I and Lady Pink caught was our African connects and although they won't be able to get back, you can best to believe that their people ain't takin' it too good. Therefore, before we allow them to sleep on our porch, we gonna take it to their house. I already got Lord True and Wonderful from Brooklyn on their Deens like the Muslims and we're arranging to get the heavy metal thru the tunnel. In the mean time to be safe, everybody needs to send their family on vacation. Also, there's plenty of more paper out there for us to get, that I've had my eyes on for sometime now. But we'll get back to that later. Right now, I got 30 keys of raw dope, Famous got 170 keys of coke, and that's not including the cash that we divided so that everybody can eat, plus the work that we already got. Everybody in this room will enjoy millionaire status when it's all said and done. Lady Pink, Hamma, Gangsta and Lucca nothin' will change for ya'll except we gone stay closer together, at least until the smoke clears. Jux, Al Capone, Butta, and Grass, I hope ya'll ready for the league, 'cause we pullin' ya'll up. Until we can keep a connect long enough, we gotta do what we do best, make them cock suckers keep fillin' out them robbery reports. So ya'll gone have to pick who's going to replace you, because we about to get into some real live gangsta shit, so make sure whoever you pick is treasure hungry pirates like ya'll and able to get rid of all of this shit we 'bout to dump on them. Make them get blood on their hands like ya'll did. I need ya'll to take care of that ASAP and stay close to us," G Millions finished.

They all agreed and the young gangsters were happy. Not only because they were moving up, but because they also had partners that they grew up with that were just as capable and dangerous as they were, but just didn't catch the same brakes. So they kept them close, so the family wouldn't be missing a beat by putting them in place.

Once the meeting was over, everyone relaxed and did what they do best which was smoke, drink, gamble, listen to music, watch movies, and argue. Famous tricked the young gangsters into playing poker after the cee-lo game wasn't going his way. Then he turned right around and let them trick him into playing play station, knowing that he didn't have any wins.

Hamma and Gangsta argued over who always started the murders when they were on there missions. Lucca was pissy drunk cracking up off the movie Friday After Next. How he could hear with all of the ruckus going on was a mystery.

G Millions and Lady Pink were hugged up, blowing each other shotguns, plotting, planning and strategizing on a new connect and how to keep him alive long enough to get a good run out off him.

The next morning…

Lady Pink and Hamma were on their way to make a run when Lady Pink saw movement out of the corner of her eye. She wasn't sure what it was that she saw but it had ambush written all over it. Without hesitation, she dropped her Mac-11 from her shoulder strap and set it off.

"Blllat…"

"Boom…" Her instincts where correct but that didn't do Hamma any good. A slug from a large caliber weapon knocked him back against a parked car.

Lady Pink grabbed him before he hit the ground and helped him around a car to duck for cover. Once she got Hamma around the car, she continued to go hard.

G Millions got the call from the parking attendant informing him that all hell was breaking loose in the garage and that his people might be involved. Before the attendant got the last words out, G Millions and his troops rallied and headed for the stairs.

Although they were out numbered 20 to 2, Lady Pink and Hamma were holding it down. But Hotep's men were relentless and closing in slowly but surely. Hamma rose and made the fatal mistake of giving up his position in an attempt to get to the Excursion. He knew that once he got them there, they would be safe. But as soon as he made his move, a bullet struck him in the eye blowing the back of his head out as it made its' exit. Although Lady Pink knew that her chances of making it out of this one were slim to none, she didn't panic; she continued to fight for her life.

Luckily, for her the cavalry arrived just as a bullet struck her hand sending her Mac-11 flying across the garage. They came from all angles of the garage and quickly gained control of the shootout. By the time they made it to where Lady Pink was, she was saturated with Hamma's blood as well as her own. Everybody was both furious at the sight of Hamma's out stretched body.

A surge of guilt consumed G Millions, because it was his jux and he knew that he should have made sure that there wasn't any chance at them getting back. However, he was still a thinker and he knew that he had to get his people out of there before the police came and there ended up being more dead bodies. Gangsta stood over his brother's body in disbelief. His brother and mentor were gone.

"We gotta get out of here!" G Millions said urgently.

With that said, everybody scattered to their cars and made a hasty exit. Lucca had to physically snatch Gangsta up and toss him into the truck.

Once the family made it away from the scene, they all met up in their stash house and regrouped. Lady Pink made it out of the gun battle only suffering a small bullet wound to the hand and a graze on her left cheek. G Millions tended to her wounds, while Famous made all of the calls to Brooklyn and Mississippi to put an end to this issue finally.

Gangsta had disappeared and wasn't anywhere to be found. G Millions and Famous shut down the hood for a week, paying their respects to Hamma. Gangsta finally showed back a week later on the day of the funeral acting like a maniac. Watching his brother be lowered into the ground was too much for him. He made his exit before the funeral service was over.

The hood was out in full force so the police didn't dare try to flex. Later on that night, the family threw a party at the Elks on Baldwin St. and gave out 1000 R.I.P. Hamma T-Shirts with his picture on them. Pay Dirt tore it down, Gangsta was still M.I.A. G Millions and Famous both knew that wasn't a good look and hoped the bad feeling that they had wouldn't last. But in their gut, they knew that it was gonna get a lot worse before it got better…

Chapter 15

"Beef cooked well done"

While Hamma's funeral was being held in Jersey, all hell was breaking loose in Brooklyn and New Orleans. There would be no nice funerals in either of the cities, just a picture on boxes, in other words closed caskets. Every club, restaurant, house office etc. that was affiliated with the Africans was blown up and their people slaughtered. *What happened to all of that fools guns and money? He couldn't even get at me, how the fuck was he going to get at Bush? That cock sucka was all rhetoric*, G Millions thought to himself.

They say that you cannot go through life without going through issues and sure enough, Murphy's Law was sure out to get G Millions and his crew. No sooner than one problem disappeared, two more emerged. Gangsta went stark raving mad and because of all of the bodies that had been popping up across the city the big boys, better known as the F.E.D's came to town. Up until this point the family had been making good use of their out of town connects. Now it was time for them to take it to the next level. They had all of the dots, now it was time to connect them. Candy Girl and Angie were down in Atlanta and Famous was chilling at home alone. Being as though them boys were in town, everybody was laying low and being extra careful because ain't nobody know what they were up to and expected to be takin in for questioning any day now.

In the mean time, everyone got new phones and knew not to play themselves or the family on them. They also took precautions on what they talked about and where. The family changed all of the usual hangouts and if you weren't recording, you weren't allowed in the studio. However, even with all of the precautions being taken, it was business as usual. The whole family lived for that fast money and was ready to die for it.

G Millions was greeted at the door by his homeboy Famous with hood love. Once inside of the house, G Millions went straight to Famous's bar, hooked up his concoction, and then lit up a blunt of sour diesel.

"I'm glad that's the only diesel you fuckin' wit now a days," Famous joked.

"Yeah B, even though I stayed fresh and kept my stacks up, that other shit didn't allow me to live up to my fullest potential so I had to shake that gorilla , ya dig!" G Millions smiled.

"It shows to, you a muthafuckin' animal now B. Look at us, we millionaires now and we're on our way to bein' Famous. We came too far to turn back now. So I'll be damn if the F.B.I., D.E.A, A.T.F., C.I.A, or anybody else interrupts us, ya dig!"

"You already know B," G Millions agreed. "I invest my paper 'cause I'm about that paper, but ain't nothin' like that fast money or being the subject of them fools Robbery Reports, plus we been getting it all of our lives."

Famous nodded his head in agreement and then turned the radio up. They sat listening to D.J. Kay Slay drama hour and continued to chop it up, while Dip Set was in the building tearing it down.

"You think our young gangstas gone hold up under the light?" Famous asked.

"Yeah, ain't know doubt we picked winners. Not only that, the way we had them put it in, they gone stand up. Plus they eatin' like a muthafucka and they see how far our hands stretch. We might not be the Mafia or nothin', but we some real niggas and gangstas from everywhere love us. We in the hood for real B, we them niggas that them rappers rap about. So if them fools cross us, where they gonna go? They might as well be dead 'cause they ain't going to be able to enjoy life," G Millions answered.

"You already know I'm wit' you B," Famous assured him. "Just before you came I was thinkin' about how you saved my life when we were kids visiting Andrea and them in West Philly."

"Damn, I almost forgot about that."

"Not me kid. Remember we was playin' chase, jumpin' from roof to roof and I hit a soft spot and almost fell through. While I was hangin', them wild dogs wit' their ribs touchin' and their fangs showing was waitin' on me to drop, when you came back and pulled me up outta there.

"Ever since then I felt safe with my life in your hands 'cause I already know you ain't gonna let me fall B," Famous confessed, getting a little sentimental.

"More-less, you already know I love you like you slid out of Pearl's ass. So my decisions are in both of our best interest, ya dig," G Millions explained. "Just like I get us out of every other situation, I promise you B, I'mma get us out of this one. Either that or we gonna be Famous, CNN specials, Americas Most Wanted, ya dig," he assured his partner and they both laughed.

Once they settled back down, Famous broke the news to his partner that he had been dreading all day.

"Yo B, wit' all the other shit goin' on right now, I didn't want to be the one to tell you Gangsta been runnin' wild like a dog wit' rabbit rabies. He's blamin' us for what happened to Hamma."

"I'm not surprised B, more-less I knew this day would come that day you stopped me from poppin' him." G Millions voice became low, full of both pain and regret. "Hamma turned out to be a team playa, but Gangsta's only loyalty was to that bread. YoYo been got the word that it was him who pushed her brothers, but I had to put business first. No matter what happened I still had a business to run and Gangsta was playing his part." G Millions took a moment to gather his composure. "Fame we put food on a lot of people's tables and we have enough problems outside of the family, so we can't afford to be eatin' up from the inside like cancer. Right now Gangsta is cancer, and he gotta be cut out. So put the word out on the streets it's ten stacks for him dead and twenty-five for him alive. We also don't have anymore use for Shyster's bitch ass, so I'm going to give Leeka Leek a key of that good smack to take care of that issue. We also gotta keep the big boys busy locally, while we take our show on the road.

***

Gangsta was finding out quickly that his strength was diminishing. First, he lost Hamma. Then he crossed the family. Although he still had money, it wouldn't last but for so long with the lifestyle that he'd become accustomed to. Sure, he still had plenty of heart, but that would only take him but so far.

The word spread rapidly thru the ranks and every young cowboy in the hood was out for blood. They already felt disrespected and played out, so they would have pushed him for free. The only reason he had made it this long was because every gangster in the hood was waiting for the order to come down from the top. But now the green light was on him, so not even the two punk ass tech's that he carried would be enough to save him. Gangsta hadn't been in the gutter for a while and he'd been living the life with the bosses, eating shrimp and lobster, popping bottles and hood-models. But the young gangsters were on the rise and he'd find that out very soon.

The youngsters had every intent on cashing in on the bounty on Gangsta's head, not to mention the fact that it would give them the chance to humiliate him for shitting on their hood and bring them closer to Pay Dirt.

***

Leeka Leek had Shyster under surveillance for the past two weeks. The more he stalked him, the more crooked he found him to be. You name it; he had his hands in it. Everything from accepting bribes, to extorting the Mexicans on French Street known as little Mexico. Shyster fed his snitches heroin, had his hands in a few whorehouses and to top it all off, he was having an affair with a Mexican transvestite named Dixie.

Leeka Leek was having so much fun stalking that asshole that he hated to end his surveillance. However, he would have even more fun putting him in retirement. Shyster was one of the main reasons for him moving to Baltimore. Leeka Leek was a stick up kid and Shyster made his job difficult because you never knew what drug spot he would have under surveillance. *Now look who's under surveillance cocksucka*, Leeka Leek thought to himself.

An hour later...

Leeka Leek along with two of his Baltimore bandits sat up in Shysters house with their faces wrapped up like Al-Qaeda rebels. Shyster's wife and daughter were scheduled to arrive home shortly and Leeka Leek and his bandits were eagerly awaiting their arrival. He hoped that the woman of the house would enjoy the little DVD that he'd made for this occasion as much as he and his bandits were going to.

Fifteen minutes had passed before Shyster's wife was turning the key to the front door. When she entered her home, she fainted at the sight of the Al-Qaeda clad bandits sitting in her living room brandishing AK47's. Leeka Leek immediately snatched the daughter up and strapped her with enough C2 to blow up the whole block, while the bandits woke up Mrs. Shyster with a golden shower. When she saw the three big black cocks standing over her, she fainted again.

The bandits got a kick out of her, as they sat her in a chair in front of the TV and sat her daughter right next to her. She finally woke up for the second time to the smell of popcorn. The sight of her daughter strapped with the C2 almost caused her to faint again.

"This is the price you pay for marrying an asshole," Leeka Leek taunted.

"Are you going to kill us?" Mrs. Shyster asked thru tearful eyes.

"You and your daughter will be fine. But I hope you got a big policy on your husband," Leeka Leek answered with an insane chuckle.

"What kind of people are you to terrorize a man and his family for doing his job?" Mrs. Shyster questioned while still sobbing.

"If he was just doing his job, we wouldn't be here. Now, let's see if you still have that attitude after we watch this DVD. Here have some popcorn." Leeka Leek let out a loud roar, causing the rest of the bandits to crack up laughing also as he hit the remote.

The first thing that appeared on the screen was Shyster's shady deals. The bandits just sat, smoked wet and enjoyed the show as Mrs. Shyster found herself eating popcorn, watching in disbelief. As if watching her husband commit all types of atrocities wasn't enough, they popped in a DVD they brought off Dixie for five stacks. By the time that video was over, Mrs. Shyster was on the brink of hysteria, smoking wet with Leeka Leek and the bandits, while drinking Jack Daniels straight from the bottle.

***

When Shyster entered the house three hours later, he was greeted with the butt of an AK47 to the back of his head. He was then awakened two minutes later by a golden shower from his wife.

"What the fuck did you do that for?" Shyster asked, while wiping the urine from his face and spitting it out of his mouth.

"You dirty, low-down, no good, rotten scoundrel! I can't believe I've been so naïve for all of these years," Mrs. Shyster cried.

The menacing laughter from the bandits caused Shyster to see that his ways had caught up to him in the worse way. Not only was his life over with, but he had gotten his family caught up in his shit too. The sight of his only daughter with C2 strapped to her caused a tear to escape from his eyes.

"Awww, that's so touchin'," Leeka Leek commented, sarcastically.

"Listen here champ, I'mma keep it gully wit' cha, it's curtains for you, the jig is up!" Leeka Leek said giving his best Bumpy Johnson imitation. Once he and the bandits were able to stop laughing, he continued. "It's funny how things turn out isn't it champ. Anyway, a mutual friend of ours is a fair man and providing your wife over there doesn't hear the wrong things or names, her and your kid makes it out alive. You also have to anti up all of the information that you have on our friend, or your daughter turns into a suicide bomber in the precinct. She saw the DVD of you taken it in the ass and suckin' the chump off, champ. Never trust a chump. He sold you out for five grand," Leeka Leek informed him and the bandits laughed, while Mrs. Shyster cried some more.

His daughter didn't really know what was going on and Shyster just sat there with a simple look on his face.

The bandits took his daughter outside to the mini-van and waited for the call from Leeka Leek, informing them to either let her go or drive her to the police station. Shyster led Leeka Leek and his wife to his home office and retrieved all of the information that he had on the hood and handed it over to Leeka Leek. Out of no where, his wife aimed his Glock at him and put one in between his eyes. She couldn't believe how he'd stripped her of her womanhood by cheating on her. Not with another woman, but with another man.

She would go with the request of the gunman. The DVD and her silence would assure her and her daughter's freedom. She never thought that she could hate anyone so much, never the less the man she loved, bore a child for and was loyal to since high school.

After handling the situation at the house, Leeka Leek went to the van, unstrapped the girl, and sent her running into the house. He then pulled off slow and easy, thinking to himself how he was about to flood Baltimore with the little pills of heroin. There wouldn't be any weight being sold until he finished that package and got another one. G Millions just made him rich for doing what he always wanted to do anyway.

Leeka Leek rented a Maybach and hit all of the local spots to celebrate his newly acquired fortune. He brought out all of the bars and clubs and showed the Dixie vs. Shyster DVD everywhere he could. After him and his bandits enjoyed a night on the town, they hopped on I-95 and mobbed back to Baltimore.

***

Gangsta had been up for the last three days straight, drinking gin and smoking blunts of wet. Now he was sitting in the cut on Throop Ave. plotting on Infer-Red Park. Shit had been real easy for him lately. *"Why should I run wit' all of them fools when I can just take their money? My big brother is gone, now my only partner's are my techs. These young niggas supposed to be gangstas. I'm the only Gangsta around this muthafucka! These niggas is pussy! I'm tired of these bitch ass niggas usin' my name in vain, they betta read the third commandment,"* Gangsta grumbled to himself.

Gangsta had gotten so caught up in his own bullshit, that he hadn't heard Saint I's little brother Midget creep up on him. Midget couldn't believe that he'd caught the legendary murderer off guard like this. Gangsta was one of the few people that he looked up to besides his brother. He wished he could run with him so that he could learn a few tricks of the trade. But it was too late for all of that now, he'd crossed over and there was no coming back. Now him and Saint I's were about to take Gangsta's name and the twenty five thousand that was on his head. He'd even hold onto the techs for souvenirs.

Midget hit Gangsta in the back of the neck with his taser gun, after deciding that he might as well get it over with.

Midget laughed to himself as Gangsta collapsed to the ground unconscious. Upon seeing this, he called his brother on the walkie-talkie. Minutes later Saint I's and a couple of the baby gangstas came, duct taped him and carried him to the basement of one of their spots.

By the time, Gangsta woke up, not only was he sober as hell, but he was hungry as fuck too. When he was finally able to really focus his eyes, a big ass red nose pit-bull was sitting in the corner looking at him like, I dare you muthafucka, bust a move.

How the fuck did I get myself into this shit and how the fuck I'mma get myself out of it? Gangsta questioned himself. But he decided not to drive himself crazy about it. *Fuck it, I'm a muthafuckin' gangsta, throw the chips up in the air and let them fall were they may,* he thought to himself.

As Gangsta was dosing back off, the gate leading to the basement opened and Midget along with a few of his road dogs came downstairs carrying White Castles, crates, fifths of Hennessey, a big portable boom-box, along with Gangsta's bullet proof vest. Midget fed Gangsta as him and his homeboys listened to a mixed D-Block CD, smoked some sour diesel and passed the Hennessey around the room. Once Gangsta got a little bit of his energy back, thanks to the food and drink, it didn't take him long to get aggravated.

"What the fuck you lil' niggas want wit' me?" He snapped.

"Oh shit, this fool can talk!" Midget teased, causing everybody to laugh except for Gangsta of course.

"Ya'll fools must don't know who ya'll fuckin' wit'," Gangsta snapped again.

"Who dat?" They all asked in unison, laughing in Gangsta's face.

"Oh, ya'll got jokes huh?" Gangsta said in an agitated tone.

"Nah home-boy, we know exactly who you are and you the muthafuckin' joke," Midget growled. "You had it made. Everybody in this basement would have loved to be in your position and your bitch ass couldn't handle the pressure and crossed the street. I can't believe I ever looked up to your bitch ass!" Midget hollered at Gangsta, suddenly getting serious.

"Fuck you, you lil', pretty, chinky eyed punk! You don't know what the fuck you talkin' about," Gangsta screamed at the top of his lungs, while twisting in the chair. "I got more time on the shitter then you got in the game!"

"You know what? Since you are a legend and ya'll say all us lil' niggaz can do is bust our ratchet, I'mma give you a fair one. If you win, I'mma cut you loose, but you banned from the hood. If you lose, I gotta make that phone call I've been putting off," Midget said, unphased by Gangsta's outburst. "Oh yeah, I almost forgot, put this on."

Midget then tossed Gangsta's vest into his lap, as the baby gangsta cut him loose. Gangsta had no idea what he needed with his vest. But what he did know was that he was about to whip Midget's lil' ass.

"Boom!" One of the baby gangstas walked up on him and shot him in the vest as soon as he strapped it on.

The impact of the slug sent him to the damp concrete floor and knocked the wind out of him. It also caused him to throw up all of his White Castle and Hennessey.

"Don't you ever bring ya bitch ass around here wavin' them things at me and my dudes again. You got five minutes to catch your breath and take this ass whuppin'," Midget calmly informed Gangsta, knowing damn well he wasn't gonna make it.

It was at that moment Gangsta knew that it wasn't going to be his day, but he wasn't going out without a fight. He peeled off his vest and sucked it up to the best of his ability. Midget grew up boxing and was currently fighting golden gloves, looking for a shot at the Olympics. So there was no doubt in his mind that he was going to put it on Gangsta, but the shot to the vest was his insurance that he wouldn't have to keep his word and have to let Gangsta go if he did happen to get lucky.

Midget's road dogs cleared out the basement and sparked up another blunt. The pit-bull started to get agitated by the smoke being blown in his face and had to be chained up. Ten minutes later it was on and popping. However, a minute into the fight it was over. The baby gangstas was cracking up because the ass whipping that Midget put on Gangsta wasn't pretty and it was all caught on tape. The fight was actually over with before it was started, but Midget prolonged it a little by playing with his opponent and practicing some of his new shit. It was a shame how Gangsta was going out, but that was the nature of the game. One bad decision or one bad move and your career was over.

They tied Gangsta back up and made the call to Jux. Gangsta was left in the basement for another week until YoYo came back from vacation. It was her idea to leave his punk ass down there until she returned.

***

It was 3:00 a.m. when YoYo was finally ready to take care of her business. After getting back in town earlier that day, she decided not to prolong the inevitable any longer. She put on her black Baby Phat sweat suit, with her black constructs, black Nike gloves, and her Boston Red Sox skully. The cool morning breeze was invigorating to her. When she got into her Lexus, she popped in "Hard Core" by Lil' Kim and lit a blunt of sour diesel to help her zone out to the classic while on her way to meet G Millions and the rest of the family at the safe house.

When she arrived everybody got a kick out of her war wear, but she didn't let them take her out of her zone. *When they see the shit I'm 'bout to put down, I wanna see how funny shit be then*, she thought.

Gangsta put on his poker face when the gate opened and Butta, Grass, Jux, Al Capone; Lucca, Lady Pink, Famous and G Millions came down and formed a circle around him. But once YoYo came in, although he didn't flinch, he knew it was over. She put down the duffle bag and a big ass gas container, Gangsta was hoping like hell that it was water. YoYo didn't waste any time, getting straight to work. Reaching into the duffle bag she pulled out a big ass dog chain, the same kind that held Midget's pit-bull. Then she wrapped it around her hand and punched Gangsta in his face hard, causing him to spit blood and teeth onto the floor.

"Bitch, I should've pushed ya shit back too!" Gangsta screamed, letting his pride and anger get the best of him.

"Oh, you wanna be a tuff nigga huh!" YoYo shouted. "Chain this piece of shit up!"

"Lucca, Al Capone be gentlemen and help the lady out," Famous ordered.

Without hesitation, Lucca lifted him into the air as Al Capone threw the chain over the beam, and then connected it around Gangsta's underarms and around his chest, leaving his feet dangling 6" from the floor.

"Ya'll some bitch ass niggaz!" Gangsta yelled. "Ya'll muthafucka already forgot what I brought to this family!" This was his way of making one last plea for his life.

"Yeah muthafucka, you brought the family a good example of what's going to happen to anybody that crosses us!" YoYo snapped back, before spitting in his face.

Then she suddenly started spazzing out and whipping his ass with the chain that she had in her hand. Everybody just looked on, wishing Gangsta didn't have to go out like that. If he wasn't family, he could have gotten off with one to the head. However, this family was close and it hurt them that this fool would show his ass the way he did. But in the same token, everybody's plate stayed full, so there was no need or excuse for anyone not to stay loyal. Thus, Gangsta was getting what his hands called for and there were no objections.

YoYo was dripping with sweat by the time Gangsta passed out from the pain that she was inflicting. While he helplessly dangled from the chains, she passed out blunts of sour diesel for everyone to smoke while she continued to perform.

"Play the wall!" YoYo ordered once everyone's blunts, were halfway gone.

As soon as everybody was lined up against the wall, she awoke Gangsta by dashing him in the face with the gasoline. Everyone in the room looked in stunned silence as she continued to soak him with the gasoline. Only G Millions and Famous really knew that she had it in her. YoYo walked over to Lady Pink and gave her a high five. Lady Pink passed her the blunt. She took a long pull off it and walked over to Gangsta.

"Hocus Pocus muthafucka!"

She laughed demonically and flicked the blunt on him, stepped back and watched him burn and scream like a bitch.

The sickening stench of gas and flesh caused some of the gangsters to vomit. Everyone except for Lady Pink and YoYo. G Millions weren't the only thing they had in common...

Chapter 16

"Layin' Low Don't Stop the Flow"

With the big boy's still in town, all of the top dogs of the family turned their focus to the legal side of things. While they stayed in the eyesight of the feds the young gangsters were making the moves both in town and out. Without the information from Shyster, whom for his own personal reasons wouldn't have given it up anyway, they underestimated the family and regarded them as just being high strung street thugs.

Although they were provided with as much information as possible by the remaining narcotics officers, they just couldn't see it. But just for them coming to town, they hauled all of the top dogs in for questioning, but of course, they came up empty. Therefore, as far as they were concerned their surveillance had been a waste of time.

Lady Pink, who was already the family's best kept secret, simply put more love into her rim shop. The three units connected to it ran themselves. For the most part, she could be found in the shop. That made her more accessible to the tenants in the rare moments that one of them was in the need for repairs.

She also had a manager in her tattoo shop and massage parlor, who kept her business running smooth. Although they were both childhood friends of hers, she made her rounds to collect her money daily and she went over the books monthly. With the nice piece of change that she was making legally, Lady Pink could have easily walked away from the game and lived middle class comfortable off her businesses alone. That wasn't including her investments with G Millions. But she would be there for her man as long as he needed her, plus she enjoyed putting in work. It was therapeutic for her.

Jux, Al Capone, Butta, and Grass chipped in together and opened up a clothing store. The store consisted of all of the top designer labels, footwear, CD's, DVD's etc... If it was the latest, they had it. When they weren't gambling in the back of the store, or smoking and were taking the business seriously, they shut down the competition like they shut down the drug pipeline going to New York.

Lucca and Felix did most of the footwork for Pay Dirt and the Green Team as far as the promotion, booking shows etc.

G Millions and Famous got more hands on with the crew that they hired to refurbish their 24 unit row houses. They were fully equipped with hard hats, tool belts and the whole nine yards. Of course, they had to bring the hood to the site, with the Akademiks, white tee's and construction Timberlands. They would also go thru the studio a couple of night's out of the week to check on everything.

When he was at the site, G Millions conducted whatever business he could by phone and if his presence were needed elsewhere, Famous would take care of everything on the business end.

After a hard days work G Millions decided to stop by the studio to smoke some sour diesel and sip a few drinks with his artists. Once again, he wasn't disappointed. Throw Back was remixing Jay Z's club classic "Throw ya hands up" off vol.3 for the hood. Chinchilla Black passed him the Dutch Master and a yellow bottle, while Throw Back was spitting his verse, *How the fuck you gone talk about them d's on our heels/ when we just popped them things homey/ them stainless steels/ pockets stay mumpy, plus the ratchet works ill/ any given time the desert eagles in ya grill...* Throw back continued to ride the hot ass beat and commit murder on wax. *These boys are good, the whole world need to hear what they have to say*, G Millions thought to himself. It was at that moment that he made up his mind to focus more of his energy on getting them signed. With all of the other shit going on, he'd been neglecting his responsibility to them. If nothing else he would help, them to start an independent label so that they could be in the position to do their own thing, but of course, he would get a nice return on his investment.

Even though they were under the microscope, the family was able to network and get things done. All of the young gangsters that were in charge of their own areas reported to Saint I's, who reported to Jux, who made sure all of the business was complete. The fresh legs of the family were both business savvy and bloodthirsty. Saint I's little brother Midget, picked his best two little homies uptown and put one in charge of the heroin, and the other in charge of the cocaine. He gave them the work, collected the paper, and reported to Saint I's. One of Butta's little homies Jeffry Dommers did the same down the bottom. Al Capone's little homie, Young Nitty, took charge of the Ville, Class Pl. and Henry St. Grass put his little brother Piff in place in Parkside and the South Groove.

When Saint I's entered the top floor apartment of his rooming house that he had gutted out and turned into a loft, minus the freight elevator, his homey's were there gambling, smoking, drinking and arguing as always.

"Ya favorite DJ aught to be smacked for saying the Ether was better then the Take Over!" Young Nitty hollered.

"D Block niggaz!" Piff spat.

"Word! I fucks with Kiss, Sheek and P," Midget added.

"Yo, the Broad Street bully spit dat heat!" Jeffry Dommers said.

"That nigga Buck serious B.!" Piff shouted.

"Word, I wanna hear him, Young Jeezy and Lil' Wayne put something together," Young Nitty expounded.

"Biggie and Pac fools!" Saint I's cut in.

"Ya old ass would say some shit like dat!" Midget joked, and everybody laughed.

"Fuck you sun, I'm only 19," Saint I's said defensively.

"Anyway, fuck that shit man, those fools got their money. We gotta get our paper right, ya dig. That's why I called this meeting. We got the opportunity to turn something good into something great. Shit is already in place for us, all we gotta do is stay hungry and loyal B. That ain't 'bout nuthin', that's what we do. So let's show these niggaz in the hood how the West was won!" Saint I's rapped, giving his little pep talk, after which they went back to their conversation.

"Yo, when our Pay Dirt and Green Team Niggaz get in place, they gonna be a problem," Young Nitty said pointedly.

"You already be knowin'," Piff agreed. "But the industry act like they don't wanna let no real live Jersey niggaz eat. More-less you already know it ain't the talent. I can count seven rappers in New Gunswick that's better then the top five out right now, smell me!"

"You ain't never lie. Yo, you remember we ran up in that rap niggaz house in Ridgefield and Jeffry Dommers was sportin' ole' boy's chain for like a month straight?" Midget reminisced.

"Yeah, them fools thinkin' shit sweet up in them Jersey suburbs and dudes in their own camp be knowing about that robbery report, and put us right on for a minor cut," Jeffrey Dommers stated.

"It's funny how small the world is, ain't it," Saint I's said and they all laughed.

Later on that day:

Midget and Young Nitty was frequenting Runways, which was the local athletic store set up like Foot Locker and it just happened to be their peoples competition. While flirting with one of the young beautiful Spanish lady's who worked their, Young Nitty peeked the owner carrying the register to the back of the store. Midget was too engrossed in an argument with another store employee about the latest T.O., McNabb saga to even notice what was taking place. Young Nitty finessed his way to the back behind the owner in order to investigate what type of change he was holding back there. Although the store wasn't crowded at the present moment, it was Friday and Young Nitty knew that if the money from the week was in there, it should be a little something for the kitty because Runways short stopped the mall money just like their home boy's store did when people were in a hurry or didn't have a ride.

Just as he'd hoped, the owner had money stacked up on top of the desk about to count it. *Pay Dirt!* He thought to himself, as his eyes made a quick estimate of forty thousand. Pulling out one of his Glock 21's, he eased up on the owner and put it to the back of his head.

"You seen it on the TV, you heard it on the news. You know what it is, be nice and live, and don't make it a homicide!"

A warm stream ran down the owner's leg as he begged for his life.

"Take what you want, please don't kill me?"

"Shut yo bitch ass up! I don't need you to tell me what I can take. Now get on the fuckin' floor!" Young Nitty ordered losing what little patience he had.

As the owner goes to get on the floor, Young Nitty gave him some assistance by putting his foot in the owner's ass. After which he put one foot on the owner's back, flipped open his jack and hit Midget on the hip.

"What's really gangsta my nig., where you slide off to?" Midget's voice came thru the phone.

"Yo B, I need you to knock it off with that Jimmy the Greek shit. I got my foot on the owner's neck," Young Nitty informed.

"I heard," Midget, answered.

Calmly putting his cell phone in his pocket, he pulled out both Glock 21's and pointed them at the employee that he was arguing with. The worker's eyes got as big as silver dollars unable to comprehend what put the youngster in such a foul mood so swiftly.

"Hey dude, I'm sorry you were right, T.O. shouldn't be suspended for telling the truth!" The worker said thinking that, that's what pissed Midget off.

"Shut the fuck up and close this mutherfucker down!" Midget ordered. "Everybody smell the carpet!"

Once the doors were closed, locked and the closed sign was put up, Midget ushered the rest of the employees and the few customers to the back and tied them up. Young Nitty shoveled the cash into one of the store's sports bags, while Midget filled up as many garbage bags possible with every size Mitchell N Ness Jersey both college and pro. He also grabbed; shooting shirts, construction timberlands uptowns, and what ever else he liked. After they loaded up the truck, they went back in to make sure there were no witnesses and retrieved the surveillance DVD.

***

Saint I's, Piff and Jeffry Dommers were coming back from making a porn movie with some girls gone wild for the love of gangsters in Saint I's hooptie. The big white Ford Bronco rode like a tank, but it served its' purpose. Mob Deep's Murder Madness Music was what they chose to vibe to on this occasion.

"Yo B, were you find this old ass Bronco? I feel like O.J. Simpson in this mutherfucker!" Jeffry Dommers joked, causing everybody to be in stitches.

"Fuck you nigga, you act like I don't got them racks on the Range!" Saint I's snapped back, referring to his new hunter green Range Rover sport.

"That ain't got nothin' to do with this big ass tank," Jeffry Dommers continued.

"I'm 'bout to show ya'll why shit like this come in handy," Saint I's retorted calmly as they approached the gun store that he'd been checking out every time that he came from these same young lady's house.

Both Jeffry Dommers and Piff wondered what the fuck he was doing when he steered the truck directly towards the store.

"Yo B, I wish you would drive right, you fuckin' up my high!" Piff screamed over the music.

The truck ran thru the storefront no sooner then Piff got the words out of his mouth, running down the storeowner and his wife.

Everything happened so fast that by the time the shop owner could recover from the shock of the crash and grab his gun, he was taught the latest dance from shots from all three youth's tech .9mm's.

The baby gangsters then quickly jumped out of the truck and spread out thru out the store. They grabbed all of the assault riffles, sub machine guns, handguns and ammo that they could fit into the truck. Jeffry Dommers then found the safe in the storage room in which it took all of them to load it into the truck.

When they were finished loading up the truck, Saint I's pulled it out of the rubble and sat fire to the joint as they made their getaway. They arrived at their little hide away in Franklin shortly after Midget and Young Nitty. Walking into the house was like walking into Foot Locker. Uptowns and construction Timberlands where lined up along the floor, while jersey shooting shirts and other garments occupied just about every other spot in the living room. Midget and Young Nitty were at the kitchen table with bottles of Remy Martin, smoking sour diesel and counting stacks of money.

"What ya'll come up on?" Saint I's asked as his eyes scanned the living room.

"A quick thirty five stacks and that shit on the floor," Midget answered pointing at the gear.

"We caught the runway nigga dozing', so ya'll might as well go shoppin'," Young Nitty added.

"Ya'll fools retarded! What the fuck ya'll take gear for?" Jeffry Dommers questioned.

"Fuck you B!" Young Nitty snapped. "What ya'll worried about how we rob for? Don't nobody say shit when you be scalpin' niggaz! And on top of that, you already know you gonna shop at our store anyway."

"Why the fuck wouldn't I?" Jeffry Dommers said thru a psychotic grin.

"Yo B, we need ya'll to help us unload my truck." Saint I's cut in already headed for the door, with everyone else on his heels.

When they got to the truck the high strung baby gangsters started choosing weapons for themselves.

"Easy cowboys, relax and get this shit in the house, there's plenty of time for that shit," Saint I' assured and they all laughed, knowing that he was right, so they proceeded to unload the truck.

Once they had everything in the house, it took them a couple of hours before they finally got the safe open.

"Next time make sure you make a nigga pop the safe before you push 'em," The exhausted Young Nitty said.

"Fuck you B! What you worrying about how we rob for!" Jeffry Dommers retaliated for Young Nitty's earlier statement, causing everyone to laugh.

After they recuperated from their little tummy tickler, they counted eighty thousand dollars, while plotting, planning and strategizing on how they were going to flex on the supermarket that Piff had his eyes on for some time now.

The next day...

Saint I's, Midget, Jeffry Dommers and Young Nitty sat in a Toyota Camry waiting for Piff's wife Sharrece to call them on the throw away and let them know when to make their move. Sharrece was in the store pretending to be shopping, while weaseling her way to the back of the store. Once there, she would open the back door and let Piff in. When Piff made it into the store, he would open then ease his way into the managers office to the safe undetected.

"Yo B, you know them bitches I left the club with last night?" Midget bragged.

"How can I forget, them bitches looked like something straight out of a Luke video," Young Nitty said, giving him his props.

"You's a greedy nigga sun!" Jeffry Dommers hated.

"Fuck you fool! You got a mouthpiece, plenty of paper, bud, ecstasy pills, and whatever else them smuts like, If you can't get no cunt wit' all that, fool, get some porn and jerk off," Midget teased.

"Yo B, you musta forgot who set off that orgy last night. But that's irrelevant, I wanted some of that exotic cunt you had my nig." Jeffry Dommers smiled.

"Them shorty's was 'bout they business to B. I don't know if it was me, the E, or the butta soft leather in the 745 that got them horny, but dig this here. I'm pushin' it to the limit tryin' to get to the telly and I get kicked in the back of the head. So I'm like what the fuck! I look in the rear view and shorty got home girls leg cocked up suckin' the shit out of her home girl's pussy. So you already know I'm pushing it hard, about to get tickets and the whole shit tryin' to get there, ya dig!" Midget reminisced and everybody laughed and gave each other dap.

"Yo B, what the fuck is wrong wit' you lil' niggaz?" Saint I's snapped. "We about to put it in and ya'll fools hollerin' 'bout some triflin' as whores!"

Midget and Young Nitty looked at each other as if to say, this fool can't be serious! But Jeffry Dommers put it out there.

"Yo B, like what's really gangsta wit' you? You losin' it or something? You got to concentrate now? This is what we do B, it's nothin'! We gonna go in here, get our money and Rosco betta hope they don't get in our way, 'cause if they do, we gone fry them donut eatin' muthafucka wit' these choppers!" Jeffry Dommers stroked his AK47.

Midget and Young Nitty both had smiles on their faces that read Holla at 'em my nigga. Saint I's facial expression had closed casket written all over it, but before he could respond his throw away started humming.

"What's really?" He answered.

"Come get this bread," Sharrece responded.

After hanging up the phone with Sharrece, Saint I's pulled up in front of the store without saying a word. Everyone in the car calmly put on their gas masks, chambered their choppers, and rushed the store.

Sharrece let Piff in thru the back door just as planned, after which she went and sat in the Mitsubishi Eclipse in which Piff had gotten for their getaway.

The young gangsters let off a warning shoot, commanding the whole stores full attention.

"All you cashier muthafucka betta have a plastic bag filled with the money from your register by the time I get there!" Jeffry Dommers ordered. "The rest of you muthafucka nose down-ass up!"

Both employees and shoppers alike were horrified by the gas mask clad gangsters, so there was no hesitation. The mothers did what they had to do in order to protect their children and the cashier complied by loading up the bags.

The manager looked thru the two-way mirror in the state of disbelief. But no sooner then he decided to take action and dial 911, the office door burst open. The manager quickly dropped his jack at the sight of Piff standing in the doorway with a laser from his MP5 pointed directly between his eyes. Piff tossed him a big sports bag, which hit him in his face and dropped to his feet.

"Pop the safe and load up the bag chump!" Piff ordered.

After snapping out of the trance that he was in, the manager did as he was told. Now that the rest of the team's mission was complete, they awaited the signal from Piff. The quick burst from Piff's MP5, along with the police sirens blurring in the distance, let them know, it was time to go. When Piff made his exit, he replaced the contents of the safe, with the blood, brains and bone fragments from the managers' skull and face.

The police were pulling into the store parking lot just as the two cars were making their getaway. The squad cars tried their best to set up a good road block, but never got the chance to because Jeffry Dommers popped out of the sunroof with his AK47, while both Young Nitty and Midget hung out of the windows with theirs.

They all unloaded on the police cruisers simultaneously, sending the officers ducking for cover.

The baby gangster's superior firepower was too much for the first units to arrive on the scene. Most officers where too busy fighting for position behind the engine block of their cars to return fire.

The same held true for the squad cars that had the miss fortune of trying to interrupt Piff's escape route, as bursts of fire erupted from his MP5.

"Ain't no fun when the rabbit got the gun, is it muthafucka's!" Both he and Sharrece laughed hysterically as they left disabled vehicles, along with dead police in their rearview.

The two vehicles full of baby gangsters met at their favorite spot when it was time to get low. Mostly out of state truckers frequented this particular motel and the owner was a friend of Thomas's, making him a friend of the family's.

Once they were settled into the room, everyone gathered around the bed and began counting the money. Young Nitty and Jeffry Dommers were the first to get tired of counting and started to get it in on 06 madden.

"Put my cut on the table," Jeffry Dommers announced, without taking his eyes off of the

TV.

"Yo B, you better pay attention. I don't want no excuses when I put my foot in ya ass," Young Nitty taunted.

"I can't even see on this raggedy ass TV," Jeffry Dommers complained.

"We ain't at the Hyatt fool!" Saint I's came from out of nowhere.

"Damn sure ain't, but we'll be in the buildin' tonight," Piff agreed.

"Piff, who put you on that sweet ass jux?" Midget asked.

"I overheard some white boys in school schemin' on that shit. So I put it under surveillance during my free time," Piff explained. "While you fools was out fuckin' and suckin', I was doin' my homework, ya dig!"

"Aw man, get the fuck outta here nigga, you full of shit! That bullshit ass job ain't take all that, and you was makin' porn videos along with us!" Young Nitty exposed his man, causing everybody to bust out laughing.

The youth continued to have fun passing around blunts and bottles of Moet.

"Yo B, Jux got somethin' O.T. for us to make this ninety thousand look like pocket change. Plus with our scores, we been bringin' a lot to the table, so we holdin' it up ya dig! So lets' get fresh tonight, sip some of that good Champagne and jump it off wit' them hood-models," Saint I's said and once again the room erupt in laughter...

Chapter 17

"If it ain't one thing, it's another"

The family beat the big boys the only way they could, everyone kept their mouth shut. Although that was very rare, these days and normally everybody and their mother usually tried to cut some type of deal in order to cut their time. What they failed to realize was that if they had kept their mouths shut, nine times out of ten, they would not have gotten any time at all. That's what most of the government cases are built on, cooperation. Without that, they would not have anything.

To celebrate being able to spread their wings, G Millions had YoYo book the Pines Minor exclusively for the family. They were also celebrating Pay Dirt's album release Under their independent, label Pay Dirt Ent. The new label was not only a good look for the artist, but it was also a good look for the hood.

While the rest of the family was running around making last minute, preparations for the dinner slash party. Saint I"s, Jeffry Dommers and Piff, who already had their fresh laid out at their suite at the Hyatt, was combing thru every square inch of Mexican Hectors house. Hector was the chief lieutenant of the ruthless local Mexican gang, who up until recently haven't been a problem to the family. Normally they operated from Joyce Kilmer Ave. to Somerset St., with French St. being their main strip, like Remsen Ave. was to uptown.

Jux and Hector had a history together because Hector use to live in his neighborhood on Columbus Pl. Although Hector's family didn't speak much English, they didn't mind Jux coming over to play with Hector and the rest of his brothers and sisters because Jux's family was the only ones to show them love when they moved to the hood. Lately the Mexicans had been slowly but surely inching their way into the family's territory.

Although Jux hadn't really fucked with Hector ever since Columbus Pl., he got at him out of respect and warned him not to venture across Joyce Kilmer. But Hector was high strung and not trying to hear his childhood friend, which led to the baby gangstas sitting on his leopard skin furniture clad in their gas masks, waiting for him to come home.

Midget and Young Nitty were walking thru a mini mall on the outskirts of town, getting their little accessories when they decided to stop in the jewelry store to see if they could find anything to add to their shine for the night. When they arrived at the store, the clerk buzzed them in and they immediately spotted a case of jewelry that they liked. After about fifteen minutes, the store clerk became restless and uneasy, so he walked over to the youngsters and questioned them.

"Are you guy's looking for anything in particular?"

"Not really, but if something catches our eye, we'll holla at you," Young Nitty answered, speaking for both of them.

"What price range are you working with?" The clerk persisted.

Midget and Young Nitty looked at each other as if to say, this clown can't be serious, but they decided to ignore his comment.

"We good."

"Those watches you're looking at start at twenty five thousand," the clerk continued.

"Yo B, didn't my man just tell you that if we needed help we'd holla!" Midget's patients were quickly wearing thin.

"Listen guy's let me be frank with you. This is an expensive store and we have a lot of professional clientele that comes thru that door. I don't have time for you to be in here if you're not going to buy anything," the clerk said, making the fatal mistake of judging a book by its cover.

Without saying a word, Midget reached into the pocket of his butter leather and pulled out knots of money wrapped with rubber bands holding ten thousand each. He then placed them onto the counter, went into the pockets of his Evisu jeans and did the same thing. Young Nitty who already knew what it was hitting for headed for the door. The clerk was too caught up in his ignorance, to even realize that he was in danger. Midget placed the knots back in his pocket while Young Nitty flipped the sign over from open to close. Midget reached into the inside of his leather as if he was going to retrieve more money, but this time he came out with his .45 colt revolver. The clerk damn near fainted at the sight of the grim reaper sitting on the barrel of those big ass cannon with his arms folded.

This can't be happening, this type of stuff only happens in Hollywood, the clerk thought to himself.

"Back yo bitch ass up from that counter!" Midget hissed. "You really need to learn how to treat your customers. All we wanted to do was purchase a nice piece of jewelry, but nah you wanted to be disrespectful. Now where's the safe?"

"It's behind the curtain," the clerk pointed.

Midget hopped over the counter, while Young Nitty was already placing cases of jewelry into shopping bags. The clerk was so shocked, that he could hardly turn the dials on the safe.

"Listen muthafucka, I'm only gonna tell you one time. I ain't got all day, open this muthafuckin' safe right now, or I'll put ya brains on it and open it myself!" Midget said with authority.

That turned out to be all of the encouragement the clerk needed to get it right. After he got it open, he filled the bag up that Midget had thrown in front of him. By the time, the clerk had gotten the bags full; Young Nitty was back with his bags full and the DVD from the surveillance.

"Some people came thru peepin' and shit, but they ain't know nothing. I played it off like I belonged here," Young Nitty whispered to his partner.

"Fuck them. This door got an alarm on it?" Midgets' attention was focused on the clerk.

"Nnnooo," the clerk stuttered.

"If you lyin', you dying," Midget promised.

"No sir, I'm not lyin' swear," the clerk said thru pleading eyes.

"Oh, now you got manners and shit huh! Open the fuckin' door!" Midget demanded.

As soon as the clerk opened the door, Young Nitty put two in his face and they slid out.

***

Piff thoroughly inspected the jewelry that was lying around Hector's house, along with some petty cash and guns, he knew that this was a drop in the bucket compared to what they knew they'd get when Hector came home. Jeffry Dommers was passing time by watching Mexican porn, drinking Corona and Hennessey mixed with Hypnotic, better known in the hood as an Incredible Hulk.

Saint I's got bored just setting around, so he decided to comb thru the house personally, in order to see if the baby gangsters missed anything, when he returned to the living room, they where both smoking a blunt of haze.

"Damn, you fools can't go ten minutes without smokin'!" Saint I's complained.

"They don't call me Piff for nothin'." He smiled.

"You want some?" Jeffry Dommers teased.

"You already know!" Saint I's took the blunt out of his comrades out stretched hand. "Yo B, which one of you silly ass lil' niggaz duct taped the fish?" Saint I's asked in between puffs.

"Fuck you talkin' 'bout homey?" Piff said as he and Jeffry Dommers looked at each other and started cracking up laughing, which let Saint I's know they were co-defendants.

"Ya'll some wild ass lil' niggaz B." Saint I's had to laugh at that one before he was able to continue. "First when I get to the bathroom, I almost bust my ass tripping over the Rottweiler that ya'll had duct taped. I gotta give ya'll your props for that one; ya'll work fast 'cause I never even heard that muthafucka but that was all good 'cause he could've been a threat. Whatever the case may be, I'm walkin' down the hallway, and I see a big ass fish tank on the wall with no fish. So I gotta get a closer look 'cause wit that big pretty ass fish tank, ain't no way Hector wouldn't want to show off some exotic shit in there. So when I go to take a closer look, I see movement at the bottom of the tank. I look closer and see Shark fish, Alligator, and Oscars wrapped wit' duct tape. Yo, some of them muthafucka still alive!" Saint I's reenacted the carnage of Jeffry Dommers and Piff's animal terror's giving the all a good laugh.

A couple of minutes later, the sounds of salsa could be heard booming from Hector's pearl white H2 hummer, with "26" chrome vertical rims.

"Damn B, this nigga livin', we should have been up in here wavin' them things, ya dig!" Jeffry Dommers said, as they watched him pull up.

"Better late then never!" Piff shot back.

When Hector entered his house, he was greeted with the aroma of marijuana, as well as the tech .9mm of Piff. Hector normally walked around like he had big balls, but the sight of the tech-toting, gas mask wearing youth sitting up in his house was not something that he was use to, thus it startled him.

"Get yo rice and bean eatin' ass in here, punta!" Saint I's demanded aggressively.

"What da fuck is dis shit?" Hector spat.

"Oh, you getting' ya cahoona's back huh, let's see how long that's gonna last," Piff mocked, as Saint I's searched him and relieved him of his Glock .9mm and then held it up to his face.

"What you gonna do wit' this muthafucka?" Piff asked, while smacking Hector upside of the head with his own pistol.

"Where the fuck is the safe at, you wet back muthafucka?" Saint I's questioned thru clinched teeth.

"What safe?" Hector answered.

"Wham!" Saint I's hit him so hard with his .9mm that blood and teeth flew across the floor.

Hector living alone in his house limited the advantage that they had on him, so they anticipated a little resistance, but it wouldn't be anything that Jeffry Dommers couldn't handle. So Piff and Saint I's held him while Jeffry Dommers busted up his fingers one at a time.

A half hour went by and they still didn't have the information that they wanted. It was not until Jeffry Dommers busted him in the hip with a hammer found in the toolbox that

Hector finally caved in. After that, not only did he tell them where his safe was, but he also told them everything they needed to know about his boss's where-bouts, where they stashed the mother-load and the whole shit. Jeffry Dommers slit Hectors throat and then the baby gangsters collected the money and more jewels from the safe. Plus some more product from the stash spot, scalped him and they was out.

***

As Young Nitty and Midget made their way thru the alley, they came up on a truck from Best Buy. Thinking that shit was sweet like everyone else, the truck driver was taking a power nap before making his delivery. This made it easy for the youth to ease up on each side of the truck and open the door at the same time.

"Wake up my man," Young Nitty ordered with calm authority, while nudging him in the side with his pistol. "I'm only gonna tell you one time. This truck is too big for me to drive. But if you try some bullshit, I'mma pop ya ass and get job training."

After looking at his two high jackers, the truck driver quickly decided that he wasn't paid enough to play super hero.

"Where to?" He asked, hoping that if he showed that he was co-operating his life would be spared.

Midget directed him to their favorite hotel in the cut. When they finally got a chance to peep out the inside of the trailer, it was filled with all of the latest gadgets, such as XBox 360, lap tops, PSP, all types of video game cartages, cell phones etc. After scanning through their goods, they made the driver unhook the trailer and drive them close to their hideout in Franklin, then torched the truck, and let the driver go but not before taking his ID and two pictures of his kids that he had in his wallet.

It only took them ten minutes to make it thru the woods, to the house and when they went inside it was like deja'vu, Saint I's, Piff and Jeffry Dommers where all in the house counting loot, product and jewelry that they had stung Hector for. As soon as they walked into the room, Piff looked up.

"What ya'll come up on?" Midget asked.

"A little donation from the Mexicans," Piff answered nonchalantly.

"Everyone seems to enjoy donating there shit!" Young Nitty said.

"What's really gangsta wit' that box wit' the ribbon on it?" Midget asked pointing at the box that sat all alone on the coffee table.

"It's a little gift for Jux, check it out." Saint I's tried his best to keep a straight face, while Midget and Young Nitty went to open the box.

When Midget opened up the box, they both looked inside to see Hectors hair and scalp staring them in the face.

"What the fuck!" They both yelled in unison, stepping away from the box.

"Yeah, that fool Jux will get a kick outta that," Midget said gathering his composure and everyone shared a good laugh.

"Ain't nobody do that shit but Jeffry Dommers," Nitty said. " What ya'll fools come up on?"

"A disrespectful jeweler and a sleeping truck driver," Midget answered.

After dumping all of the money and jewels on the table, they lit up some sour diesel, popped some yellow bottles, and talked slick while they tallied up their take. When it was all said and done, Saint I's, Jeffry Dommers and Piff came off with $130,000 cash, 23 kilo's of cocaine, 12 .9mm Glocks which must have been Hectors favorite because those were the only kind of guns he had and plenty of jewelry.

Midget and Young Nitty counted $58,000 cash and an estimated half a million in jewels. That wasn't including the merchandise in the truck. Everyone that was in the house got first dibs on the jewels; their cut off the envelopes for the family and everything else was put up for the kitty.

"I would say we held it up for the family for real," Saint I's exclaimed. "These last couple of days has been lucrative!"

"God bless America!" Young Nitty imitated Don King and everybody laugh.

'Ain't nothin' like makin' them fools fill out them robbery reports," Midget chimed in.

"We gonna shine tonight my nig!" Piff stated excitedly.

"Don't we always!" Jeffry Dommers said with animated sarcasm, giving everybody another good laugh, before they all filed out of the house into the fresh air, on their way to get dressed to impress for the night.

***

Pines Minor had top shelf service, including valet parking. The staff was both amazed and impressed by the style, class and obvious riches of the black youth. Although they knew 9 times out of 10, the youth had gotten their money illegally, there was something to these youth that one had to admire.

Lucca, Alix, and Pay Dirt came thru in the company's Excursion, wearing all different color furs, linen and reptile shoes. Of course Chinchilla Black was flossing a full-length chinchilla coat, with a matching chinchilla fit it hat. The green team pulled up in the ML60 that Famous gave them, rocking money green mink coats with matching silk, lignin and reptile shoes.

Jux, Al Capone, Butta, and Grass were shining in Jux's fully loaded S600 with "22"

chrome gangster shoes. Jux sported a cinnamon fox coat with a matching silk shirt, linen pants, and ostrich shoes. Al Capone had on a gray mink coat with a hood, a matching silk shirt, linen pants, and ostrich shoes. Grass did the black, with a black full-length mink. Butta played the brown, with the tan lining and tan chunk gators.
Saint I's, Midget, Jeffry Dommers, Young Nitty and Piff slid thru in a stretch GS400 Lexus, with full length puffy butter leather snorkels, black silk and linen and black ¾ Mauri gators with a black Boston, Red Sox skull cap pulled low. What they lacked in class, they made up in flash, because their diamonds was glistening from everywhere, including their Paul Wall grills.
G Millions, YoYo and Lady Pink came thru in his Maserati Qattroporte, G Millions donned a burgundy full-length mink, with a matching mink dobs hat, burgundy linen and silk two-piece, with burgundy ¾ ostrich skin shoes. YoYo sported a burgundy Paul Hardy pure luxury part shawl, part mink fur coat, with matching Princes Diana handbag, Chiffons evening gown, open toe ostrich wrap around shoes, and she was dripping with ice.

Famous shut it down when he and Candy Girl came thru in his brand new just seen on that night 2006 Bentley Continental Flying Spur also known as the Flying B. It was all white, fully loaded, with chrome Bentley factory rims. He hopped out in a full-length white mink coat, with a matching mink hat, white silk shirt, and linen pants, running concurrent with white chunk gators and of course, he was iced out. Famous was in all of his, splendor doing what only Famous could do. Candy Girl wore the same Paul Hardy as the other girls, except her collar was red. She also carried a red jet tote to high light her chiffon evening gown by Chanel and red lizard skin shoes. The cameras were flashing like the red carpet at the VMA's. Although everybody shined with platinum and ice, the fresh legs of the family sported the most.
Everybody thoroughly enjoyed the music played by a popular hot 97 DJ, as well as the good food and champagne. The hefty tips made the staff oblivious to the smoke and dice games. Saint I's and the rest of the baby gangsters went around the room passing out gifts and fluffy envelopes of money to the family. Each member paid accordingly. They paid homage to G Millions and Famous with extra fluffy envelopes. The night was winding down when the family gathered around with anticipation to watch Jux open his gift.
The room gasped when Jux pulled out Hector's scalp, and was temporarily frozen with surprise as Jux held it in the air and looked at it curiously.

Then suddenly the room erupted with laughter and toasts. Once the family settled down, G Millions tapped on his champagne bottle with his spoon, satisfied he had everyone's attention he spoke.

"First, and foremost, congratulations to Pay Dirt for your first album."

"Cheers!"

"I would also like to congratulate and welcome our fresh legs, who as you can see from the scalping, are going to be problems!"

"More cheers!" And everyone showed hood love.

After the hugs and daps, the staff was summoned to retrieve their vehicles. By the time everyone headed for the exit, they all were all fully, drunk and excited about their success. Lucca and both groups were the first ones to exit with the rest of the family on their heels.

As soon as Lucca and the two groups walked under the canapé, they were greeted with the Mexicans Uzi as they drove by slowly in their low rider '64 Chevy Impala.

Bullets crashed thru glass, ricochet off metal, and broke chunks of cement walls. Everyone ducked, dodged, and dove for cover. By the time everyone recovered and went to retrieve their guns, the Impala was long gone. When the smoke cleared, Lucca's blood and brains were all over both groups as well as the pavement. Also, a few group members caught flesh wounds, but other than that, everyone else was good.

The bullet proof Excursion pulled up on the scene just in time to minimize the damage that would have otherwise been very extensive because of the ambush.

Not trying to be there for the police or the coroner, Famous left the staff a bonus for damage control and to handle the issue, the family then hopped into their luxury vehicles and headed for the studio…

Chapter 18

"It's on like Donkey Kong"

After regrouping in the studio, G Millions put together a temporary plan to neutralize the Mexicans until he could put together a bigger plan to literally chop Draggo, the boss of the Mexican gangs, head off. Knowing from experience that the Mexicans would be squatting for them to come right back thru, G Millions decided to get all of the families business affairs in order before there would be any retaliation. He appreciated the luxury of having a team of loyal young gangsters. *Fuck what you heard there is honor amongst thieves*, he thought to himself

For the next couple of days, Jux brought in all of the money from the product sales minus the payroll. Saint I's and the baby gangsters took control of the product that needed to be processed, packaged, and distributed.

Just like the young gangsters over them, the baby gangsters never looked at it as if they could have went off on their own and did them because they fully understood the longevity of breaking bread together as a family. Not to mention the fact that everyone ate lovely.

Midget and Young Nitty got the stuff from the truck and gave it out to the family. Initially, they wanted to give it out to the children in the nationhood, but decided that that was not such a good idea. With all of the other bullshit that was going on, all they needed was for the wrong people to hear what they were doing and put two and two together.

***

Lady Pink, YoYo, and Candy Girl decided to do some female boding by doing what women loved to do most, shop. They were strolling thru the Gallery mall in Philadelphia, when they ran into Iwaquim, a dude that grew up on the same floor as YoYo in the projects. Back in the day Waq as they called him, also balled with her brother's on and off the basketball court.

"Waq, is that you?" YoYo asked, and then continued before he got the chance to respond. "I know you wasn't going to walk right by me like we didn't use to ride big wheels and play 1, 2, 3 red-light and shit. You keep acting all fly and shit 'cause you shinin' now, I'mma tell my home girls how good you used to play double-dutch nigga!" YoYo scolded him playfully rolling her eyes and neck.

"Oh shit, what's good ma!" Waq smiled. "I see you ain't doin' to bad yourself," he looked her up and down. "Stop tryin' to play me girl, you know I ain't play no damn double-dutch!" Waq denied, genuinely happy to see his childhood friend.

"I thought that would get ya attention nigga!" YoYo teased, still giggling a little while sharing a friendly hug.

"Yo, stop being rude and introduce me to your home girls," Waq said, looking Candy Girl and Lady Pink up and down lustfully.

"Don't even try it fool! I love you like a brotha, but you a dog and their both married," YoYo informed him.

"I'm appalled!" Waq responded, throwing his hands up in mock surprise, causing them all to enjoy a good laugh.

YoYo introduced Iwaquim to everyone and he joined them shopping, while he and YoYo caught up on who was doing who and what was what.

"So what's been up and how is the family?" YoYo asked.

"Still gettin' that bread and everybody good."

"What you doin' here by yourself?" YoYo continued to probe, knowing that he had to be up to something browsing in Miss Sixty's.

"You know me, ain't nothin' change, that's how I do mine." Waq smiled.

"Un huh, I know ain't nothin' change, that's why I know you still full of shit!" YoYo stated suspiciously. "Now stop playin' and put it out there."

"Why I always gotta be up to something'?" Waq asked defensively.

"Cause that's how you do yours," YoYo said, flipping his words back on him, causing everyone to laugh.

"If I tell you, you must gonna help me," Waq gamed, knowing that if he could get the girls to play, it would make his job a lot easier.

"It depends," YoYo said, folding her arms and rolling her neck.

"More-less, you already know I be the cause of mad robbery reports right!"

"Boy get to the point."

"Damn, you still bossy as hell," Iwaquim said, twisting his face up. "Anyway, since I flat-lined, I've been gettin' it in, in Delaware. My dude plugged me in on this Willie nigga who just had 700,000 E pills shipped to him from Arizona, I need that for somethin'."

"So, what the fuck does that have to do wit' you bein' in Miss Sixty?" YoYo questioned with a puzzled look on her face.

"His bitch got the same taste as ya'll," Waq said, pointing to the shorty that he had been stalking before he bumped into the girls.

"We got you," Lady Pink spoke up for the first time, sensing pay dirt.

"Damn, I didn't know you had a voice," Waq said, directing his attention to Lady Pink. "I thought you were just here to look good."

"Don't let my good looks fool you," Lady Pink shot back, placing her pink Gucci shades on the top of her head. Waq seen the truth in her eyes.

"Do ya'll know what ya'll doin'?" Waq asked, leery of them messing up his score.

"You need help or not?" YoYo asked both her and the girls looking at him as if he was stupid.

"I don't know ya'll, I'm pregnant," Candy Girl came out of left field.

Candy Girl's revelation put a surprised look on YoYo and Lady Pinks face.

"We'll talk later," YoYo said while Lady Pink handed her chirp to Waq.

"Go ahead to your G Ride before she think you're a stalker and call the police. Or if she's like me, bust a cap in your ass," Lady Pink teased and everyone laughed.

Waq did what he needed to do with the chirps and handed Lady Pink back her phone. YoYo still tasted blood from the gangster incident so this little bit of excitement got her pussy wet. Although she wanted for nothing, the chance to show Famous that she could touch something excited Candy Girl also, so it was on and popping.

Iwaquim went and sat in his Cadillac EXT and waited for Lady Pink to chirp him. The girls followed their mark thru all of the malls hot spot, 9 West, Fendi, Gucci, Polo, etc.

"Shiit, this trick bitch know what we like," Candy Girl commented and they all shared a good laugh as the young woman headed towards the counter.

Lady Pink, who was thinking on her toes, hopped in line behind her so that she could eye hustle her name off the credit card. After the cashier swiped the girl's credit card, she got the merchandise and headed for the exit door.

"Ya'll go to the G Ride," Lady Pink instructed.

YoYo and Candy Girl did as they were told, while Lady Pink continued to follow their mark. When she saw the mark was leaving she chirped Iwaquim and told him to get ready. As soon as the young woman made it to her SL600 coupe, Lady Pink sprung into action.

"Cameel, Cameel Saxton, is that you?"

Upon hearing somebody spit her whole name, Cameel let her guard down, but she gave Lady Pink a curious look like she didn't recognize her.

"Excuse me, I don't mean to be rude, but do I know you from somewhere?"

"Excuse me, I don't mean to be rude either but we can do this the easy way or the hard way," Lady Pink mocked, flashing her P89. "Now get your ass in the car."

Not wanting to go out without a fight, Cameel looked around as if she were weighing her options. Seeing that there was no way out, she got in on the passenger side and Lady Pink got in behind her and pushed her behind the wheel.

"Bleep...bleep...bleep..." Lady Pink chirped Iwaquim.
"Bleep...What's really?" Iwaquim asked.
"Bleep...You already know, meet me on market."
"Bleep...I heard."

Iwaquim tossed his cell phone in the passenger seat, excited about his come up. *What a way to reunite wit' an old friend*, he thought to himself. Then he sung the old Peaches and Herb song aloud, "Reunited and it feels so good!" He laughed at his own sick humor.

"Bleep...bleep...bleep...Yo."
"Bleep...Hey girl, is everything going smooth?" YoYo questioned.
"Bleep...Why wouldn't it be? You know how I do," Lady Pink said.
"Anyway, meet me on Market St. I'm in a powder blue SL600 coupe."
"Bleep...Being as though we playin' follow the leader, it's a good thing we didn't come in your pink mobile," YoYo joked and they laughed.

Minutes later, they met up and headed for Dover Delaware.
"Is the address on your card the same address we're going to?" she asked her victim.
"Yes, but listen Miss....I don't know what this is all about, but all I do is work and come home," Cameel tried to reason.
"I guess this is the price you pay for being Willie's wife," Lady Pink responded.
"My husband is a respectful business man," Cameel shot back defiantly.
"You can't be serious. It's unbelievable how naïve you bitches are. I got a bridge for sell," Lady Pink teased and laughed loudly, while retrieving Cameel's credit card.
After their little exchange, Cameel just sat in deep thought with a puzzled look on h face.
"Bleep...bleep...bleep...Yo..."
"Bleep...What's really?"
"Bleep...Yo, you know where 176 Quale Hollow Dr. is?"
"Bleep...Damn, they doin' it like dat?" Iwaquim twisted up his face as if she could see him. "Yeah, I know where it is."
"Bleep...A'ight, take the lead and get us there the quickest route possible."
"Bleep...I heard."
After her and Iwaquim was finished she called YoYo.
"What it is girl?" YoYo's voice came thru.
"What's really gangsta wit' that trick Candy Girl, is she ready to ride or what?"
"Yeah, she souped now."

"That's what it is, all I need her to do is sit in the car and don't touch nothin'," Lady Pink joked and they laughed.

After that, Lady Pink, YoYo and Iwaqium played phone tag the rest of the way to the spot.

***

Felix had been infiltrating little Mexico ever since the incident at Pines Manor. Felix was Puerto Rican but the common language made him acceptable in the Mexican hood, but not in the ranks. He even bagged himself a quiet little Mexican girl and so far, he had been able to identify the money blocks. So whenever he wasn't with his mommie, he was beating the streets for information. Hector had already given up the main information that he needed about the Mexican boss Draggo in which G Millions and Famous were handling that surveillance personally. Felix being in little Mexico was just a clever diversion.

It was a beautiful day outside so Felix decided to go for a walk and pick up a few things. He was walking thru Somerset St. thinking about his days in San Juan when he walked up on a group of young Mexicans posted up in the middle of the block.

"Yo homes. You lost something around here?" One of them asked.

"No my girl lives right around the corner," Felix answered calmly.

"I've seen him around," One of the other Mexicans spoke up, trying to let Felix live.

"Listen bro., I don't want no trouble, I'm just goin' to get some Coronas so I can have a good time with my girl tonight," Felix said.

"Well if you don't want no trouble I suggest you not come back thru here unless you're buying something my man! The first Mexican said aggressively falling right into Felix's trap, taking his passiveness for weakness.

"No problem," Felix said turning as if he was about to walk away. "Rabbit ears muthafuckas!" He spun back around swiftly with his Mac11 in hand catching them totally off guard.

Upon seeing the Mac11 all of the toughness fled from the group of young Mexicans, making Felix's job that much easier.

His Mac11 laid the Mexicans down for good after digging in their pockets.

Felix didn't have to be an expert shooter to find his targets as he stood over them for the kill, so that the message would be clear. Felix laughed to himself as he walked away with some extra pocket change and continued his journey to get some coronas and Dutch Masters so that he could have some fun with his lady just as planned.

***

Felix's gun was still smoking when he returned to his girl's apartment. His mamma seta Rosa was awaiting him looking sexy as hell in her Victoria Secret bra and thong set. She also sported a white Chad Johnson Cincinnati Bengals jersey, which gave her that hood appeal that turned Felix on to the max. Her long, silky, black hair rested in the middle of her apple bottom, and her perfectly pedicure feet blended in with her outfit magnificently. *Damn this bitch does something to me*, Felix thought to himself.

To set the mood, Rosa had the lights dimmed with the scented candles, with Hector Lavor playing mellow in the background. She also had the dinner table set for two, with a tasty meal consisting of fresh lettuce, rice and beans, boneless fried chicken breast and plateaus. She had the sour diesel already rolled up, which allowed them to eat and have a moment of conversation without any interruptions.

Once they were full, drunk and smoked out, the couple found their way to the bathroom for a nice hot bubble bath. After being settled in, in the bathtub, they started their fun off with a tongue-wrestling match, which made Felix rock up and Rosa's nipples swell instantly. Rosa was excited by the effect that she was having on Felix and his dick seemed to be calling her. She heard it talking to her, telling her to come and kiss it because it was feeling neglected. So she gently touched, caressed, and spoke to it in English.

"I'm sorry for neglecting you poppie, it won't happen again," she said in a lustful whisper.

When she looked up into Felix's eyes with her own pretty-light green eyes, she saw that he was feeling good. *Damn, this bitch is fine as a muthafucka!* Felix thought to himself. He gently and slowly stroked her hair, while he fucked her face. Rosa let him know how sorry she was for neglecting him by taking him all the way into her warm, wet, juicy mouth. *Mmm, it tastes sooo good,* she thought to herself as she feverishly worked her hands, neck and mouth. When she felt him about to explode, she caressed his balls to let him know that she wasn't done yet. She took her tongue and ran it up and down the shaft of his dick. When she felt it expanding, she went down so deep that he could no longer take it and he exploded. As his cum gushed deep down her throat, she swallowed every bit of his pimp juice until it was gone.

That was only the beginning of their night of passion as the action shifted into the bedroom. Once again, they started with a tongue-wrestling match. Felix sucked on her bottom lip and worked his way down to her big round breasts. He cupped each one of them with his hands and rolled his tongue around her nipples and gently bit and sucked them. She moaned her approval as he worked his way down to her awaiting coochie. He inserted two fingers to see just how wet he had her. Then he pulled them out, dripping with Rosa's juices, which turned him on tremendously. Her juices looked very tasty, so he decided that he needed to put his mouth were his fingers were. So Felix dove headfirst and gave her the best tongue work that she'd ever had in her life. He had her feeling so good that she cried tears of joy. After some thorough tongue love, he slid his dick in and smashed her brains out. The young couple took turns satisfying each other's needs until they fell asleep in each other's arms.

***

It was the middle of the night when Felix started to feel a little restless so he decided to get some air, while he was at it, he figured that he would check out a spot he'd seen on French St. the other day when him and Rosa was returning from visiting her family in Wagner projects in Harlem. When they were riding thru the hood, she noticed mad fiends lined up as if they were waiting for welfare cheese. Now it was time to go and see what the spot was all about.

 Felix lurked in the shadows across the street from the spot and watched the traffic flow in and out like grand central station, thus he decided to make his move today. The birds were chirping as the sun rose so he figured that the pitchers in the spot had to be as tired as he was and it would soon be a shift change. After a little more time and patients, sure enough his suspicions held true. The 10:30 rush was fizzling out when he spotted two young hustlers entering the house, which meant that they were replacing either the ones that were already there or they where there for the same reasons that he was. *This gonna be easier than I thought*, Felix said to himself as he made his move. When he eased up on them, he caught them totally off guard. The first shift workers were coming out of the house when he pushed them back in and entered behind them. "Rabbit ears muthafucka!" He shouted.

 The shocked Mexicans didn't give up any resistance when he forced them to the ground. Felix then retrieved the duct tape from his duffle bag and duct taped the four occupants of the house. Once he had them secured, he searched each of them and retrieved a zip lock bag full of bricks of heroin off each of the second shift workers and a zip lock bag full of cash off each of the first shift workers. He also recovered a street sweeper and a calico that they had stashed behind the radiator, along with two .9mm barrettes from the small of two of the Mexicans backs. *Pay Dirt!* He thought to himself.

He then searched the hallway closet there he found a carrying bag that was usually used for suites and used it to carry the guns, drugs and money instead. After the task was complete, he re-entered the room his victims were in, spit his razor into his hand

and stood over them.

"Hocus Pocus!" He said, before slitting their throats one by one before leaving the scene.

***

When Lady Pink, YoYo, Cameel and Iwaquim entered Duke's house, him and his henchmen were watching the Hopkins vs. Taylor brawl on his 60" plasma screen TV., sipping on some Moet and eating jumbo shrimp.

'I'm home boo!" Cameel was forced to announce.

"Grab me another bottle on your way in sweetheart!" Duke yelled.

'Yes daddy!" Cameel answered sweetly.

Duke and his henchmen were so engrossed in the fight that he didn't notice that it was Lady Pink who was handing him the bottle and not Camel, so he leaned over for a kiss. Iwaquim stood off to the side smiling, marveled at Lady Pink's smoothness. Damn that bitch is good! He thought. YoYo had the Glock .27 to Camel's head to make sure that she didn't try anything funny. Not receiving the kiss that he was all puckered up for accompanied by the horror that was in his man's eyes, prompted him to look up to see what was going on.

The bottle dropped to the floor.

Both Duke and his henchman went into shock because they really weren't street dudes. They just happened to take advantage of an opportunity that came their way. Never in their wildest dreams did they imagine anyone coming to his crib waving their guns.

'What the fuck you two fools setting there stuck on stupid for? Get yo' ass on the muthafuckin' floor!" Iwaquim demanded.

Both men damn near dove onto the floor, so as not to seem as if they wasn't going to comply. However, YoYo had to physically push Cameel to the floor next to them because she had a little more heart than the dudes.

Lady Pink was already searching thru the house and while Iwaquim held the marks down, YoYo went to find some rope. When she came back, she didn't have any rope, but what she did have was some handcuffs. A broad smile came across her face as she held them up.

"Ya'll some freaks huh?" She teased, causing the couple to blush and everyone else to laugh.

Being as though there were only two sets of cuffs, they only cuffed the dudes.

"Ya'll ready to show us the loot so that we can be out?" Iwaquim asked.

'Baby, show them where everything is," Duke spoke swiftly, hoping that they would take the stuff and go.

Duke didn't have a problem giving up everything that he had in the house. It wasn't even a fraction of what he and Camel had accumulated over the years. Reluctantly Cameel lead them over to the fireplace where she removed the grate and firewood. Then she reached up inside and pulled down one army bag full of money, then she reached back up there and pulled another bag down full of E-pills.

"Is that it?" Iwaquim asked.

"Yeah," Duke answered.

"I hope so, 'cause if my home girl comes down here with something else, it's going to be torture," Iwaquim warned.

"I promise that's it."

As if on cue, Lady Pink came walking back into the room.

"Nothin'," she said.

"We got it right over there." Iwaquim stated pointing at the bags.

Lady Pink reached for her ice pick, but Iwaquim stopped her and motioned for her and YoYo to take the bags and meet him outside.

Once they were out of the door, Iwaquim threw Cameel onto the floor next to the others. He then put two into the back of each of their heads, flashed a sinister grin and followed their footsteps.

***

Fifty minutes later they were all at Iwaquim's house splitting up 5000,000 ecstasy pills and the same in cash.

"It was good seeing you again Waq," YoYo told him.

"Don't be a stranger, there's plenty of more where that came from." Iwaquim said with a smile.

"You got me on the chirp nigga, holla at ya girl."

"No doubt! Make sure you shout my boys G Millions and Fame out and tell them that they some lucky muthafucka's!" Iwaquim gave them their props. "Ya'll some bad muthafucka all the way around the board."

"They ain't lucky; they just know how to pick 'em!" Lady Pink cut in, and they all laughed...

Chapter 19

"It's still on like Donkey Kong"

Pearl enjoyed her newly constructed, spectacular, oceanfront home in Long Beach, New Jersey. This was the house of her dreams; it was also G Millions dream to be able to buy it for her. Pearl prayed every day for her son's safety and thanked god for blessing her with such a beautiful home. It was in a perfect location for her to, not too far from Atlantic City, New York, Philadelphia or even New Brunswick. All of which she'd be spending time in at one moment or another.

Her home was exceptionally designed, with panoramic views of the ocean, a private catwalk to the beach, five bedrooms, 3 ½ baths, with an elevator and a roof top hot tub. It also featured exquisite details, 12 ft. ceilings in the living area, bamboo floors, granite counter tops, top of the line appliances and fixtures, round stair tower, fireplace, security system with electronic keyless entry and the list goes on.

She happily prepared a meal of flounder, fried chicken wings which was her grandsons favorite, baked macaroni and cheese, collard greens, pinto beans and rice, potato salad, corn bread and for desert, fresh cheese cake. Pearl looked forward to seeing her grandson. Her house was beautiful but lonely.

When they finally arrived, she was at the front door to greet them. Little G Millions ran into her outstretched arms.

"Grandma, I miss you!" He said, excited to see her.

"I miss you to baby!" Pearl hugged and kissed him, excited to see her grandson also.

Although it was his son, G Millions felt a ping of jealousy whenever his favorite girl showed anyone more attention then she gave him and she knew it to. So once her and little G Millions finished bonding, she gave her baby a hug and a kiss.

"Hey baby!" She smiled brightly.

"Hey mother!" He returned her smile.

"It's about time ya'll, I'm hungry," she informed rubbing her stomach.

"What we eatin'?" G Millions asked.

"I got the soul food in there, but you know I don't have any of that fancy stuff that you be wasting your money on. We're drinking some good old fashion kool-aid," Pearl informed and they laughed.

"Grandma, where's Polo?" Little G Millions asked, referring to her Presta Canava that G Millions brought her to guard the house.

He figured that the dog along with her Glock .27, would keep her safe.

"His big, greedy mean ass is in his kennel. That damn dog is as big as a horse and he eat like one too. Don't take your little badass out there by yourself either."

"Grandma…"

"What?"

"You said two bad words." Little G Millions held up two fingers to help make his point.

"Oh, I'm sorry baby; you know you're too smart. Gerrod, you're going to have to keep an eye on him.

"Ma, you ain't seen nothin', he chillin' around you."

"When I get the energy to keep up with him. I'm going to let him stay over for the weekend. Anyway, how is his mother?"

"She's damn near perfect. I couldn't be happier.

"Yes you could, when you stop doing what you're doing."

"What I'm doing brought you this house that Benz, sent you around the world and whatever else you want."

"Boy don't get smart with me! I don't care how grown you think you are, you're still my baby and I will still kick your ass!" Pearl scolded.

"Grandma!"

"Sorry baby, go to your room and play your XBox."

Dag, I always gotta go to my room when stuff getting' good, Little G Millions thought to himself while on his way to his room.

Once he was out of earshot Pearl continued. "Let me tell you something boy. Fuck this house, that car, those trips, fur coats, jewelry and everything else. I'd gladly trade all of that shit in just to see you happy and for me to be able to get a good night sleep. I already lost your grandfather, your father and Willie, all to that lifestyle. Granted they wasn't murdered, but the game caught up to them. They all had plenty of life left, but the devil sucked it out of them. God knows I hate to say, but you may not be so lucky the way the game is today. Back then, we got the bills paid and we had a little extra to do other things. But we didn't have to worry about nobody running up in our house robbing and killing us. We didn't have to worry about nobody snitching on us getting us life in prison. Lord knows I couldn't stand to burry you, or see you in prison for ever in a day," Pearl reasoned emotionally.

"Ma, I just can't up and retire, what am I goin' to do?" G Millions protested.

"Boy stop talking stupid! You already know I can't stand no stupid shit! You don't owe anybody but that boy in there anything," Pearl said, pointing at the room. "Cause if you don't teach him what he needs to know to be a man; you're going to be raising him in

Trenton State Prison. Plus you need to stop playing and marry his mother."

"We are married." G Millions joked.

Pearl shot him a stern look. "Boy you really tryin' to pluck my nerves ain't you! Now I know you didn't come to hear me preach. But I am your mother and I can't just sit here and not say anything knowing what's going on. Growing up, you saw and heard many things that you shouldn't have, but back then, I was a baby myself. I had you when I was 16 and I did the best that I could to raise you and grow up myself. But we made it thru all of that. Besides, you have enough money for your grand kids to be rich. You need to do something with it besides buying that nasty ass shit that you drink and most important you need to enjoy it.

"I can count on you to give it to me raw can't I?" G Millions said exasperated.

"That's the only way your hard headed ass understands it," Pearl said, hugging her son playfully.

They shared a tight embrace before G Millions changed the subject.

'You saw that Farrakhan special on TV the other day addressing the Louisiana flood situation?

"Yeah, I saw it. You know I love myself some Jesus, but that man sure know how to tell it like it is. They call him as racist as a smoke screen so that the people can concentrate on that instead of his message. The world is so blinded by money now a days that they find it hard to believe that there is anything wrong with this country. They replaced slavery with prisons to justify locking all of our young black men up by portraying ya'll to be criminals and all ya'll do is prove them right by robbing and killing each other for money."

"Ma, all I ever wanted was to be able to take care of you and my child as well as our family, without us ever being limited to having or doing certain things because of money," G Millions explained. "I still remember being in the children's hospital in Philly and you were there every day. I promised you that I was going to be strong again and that you would be proud of me. I promised myself that one day I was going to take care of you. I know that had to hurt your pockets, but you was there for me and that meant the world to me."

'Boy pleases, you're my kid, and I'd do it again if I had to. But much of what you said just proved my point. It ain't all about the money. Money ain't going to save your soul." She looked her son in the eyes. "Whatever happened to your dreams of opening up a community center? Wasn't it you who told me that if people wanted the gangster rappers to rap about something else then they needed to stop being hypocrites and help change the environment in order to give them something positive to rap about? The same thing goes for those urban books and them movies they be putting out." She pinched his cheeks for emphasis. "That was you wasn't it?"

"Yes mother that would be me." G Millions threw up his hand and smiled.

"Well I don't expect you to save the world. But a community center in our hood is a start. Lord knows you got enough, how ya'll say it, gwap!" she said and they laughed at Pearls attempt to sound hip.

"You made your point mother, handle your business."

"Good, I'll get the paperwork started Monday. Now go and get your kid so we can eat."

With that said, they hugged and kissed each other on the cheek. G Millions thanked his mother through body language that only she understood. Through the bond that they've built over the years, some things didn't need to be said, for the message to be received.

G Millions went and got his son and when they came back, they all sat down and ate. The three of them enjoyed light conversation over dinner. Little G Millions showed his ass and that's why you had to love him. Once dinner was over, Pearl wrapped up some plates for them and gave them each hugs and kisses on their way out of the door.

***

When G Millions reached his house, his little man was asleep looking like a little angel. Judging from how quite he looked, you would have never known he was such a terror. YoYo greeted them in their living room with loving hugs and kisses. After which her and G Millions went upstairs and tucked their son in. Once little G Millions was secure in his bed, they retired to the comfort of their bedroom.

After helping one another undress, YoYo gave her man a shoulder message. Satisfied that her man was nice and relaxed, she whispered in his ear.

"I got a surprise for you daddy," her voice was sexy and she twirled her tongue in his ear.

"Oh yeah, what's that?" He turned around to face her.

"Why don't you come with me and find out," she responded sounding sexy as fuck.

He stood up and she led him to the bathroom. G Millions patted her playfully on the rump all the way in.

"What you got for daddy?" He asked anxious to know what she was up to.

When they entered the bathroom, Lady Pink was setting on the Jacuzzi with two bottles of Dom on ice and the fattest, juiciest, reddest strawberries on the market. Also, on the counter lay the money and the ecstasy pills from the Delaware robbery. The sight of all of that money product and the prospect of jumping off with the two loves of his life, got his cock harder then scrap iron.

While it was true, that they knew about each other and they knew that he loved them both and they loved him. Never in his wildest imagination did he think that they would consent to a ménage.

"What are you whores up to?" He asked playfully.

"You know we gotta take care of you daddy!" YoYo peered while rubbing his chest.

"We gonna spoil you, like you've been spoiling us nigga! So stop asking so many questions and enjoy your treat!" Lady Pink followed up.

"Why wouldn't I?" G Millions responded with a smile as he went to inspect the money and the product, while YoYo joined Lady Pink in the Jacuzzi.

Once G Millions finished with his survey, he swaggered over to the Jacuzzi to enjoy his woman. When he hit the water, he immediately became the main attraction. The women completely focused all of their attention on him. He was fed strawberries and Dom P, while receiving sweet, tender kisses and shotguns. Jaheim's "Still Ghetto" was playing in the background for mood music. Slowly but surely their passion mounted.

After playing around in the Jacuzzi, the trio took their party to the bedroom where the girls laid them on his back and took turns licking and sucking his dick and balls, passing it back and forth, working it like a five speed. YoYo kissed her way from his feet and startled his meat. His two fine ass women double-teamed him all night long, draining him of his pimp juice, all the while fully enjoying multiple orgasms of their own.

***

Felix, Jux, and Al Capone lay watching the flow under the Highland Park Bridge, which separated Highland Park from New Brunswick in disbelief. Felix had gotten word from one of Rosas girlfriends that this was one of the Mexicans big money spots. He thought she was making it to be bigger than it was because just like his homeboys Jux and Al Capone, he regarded it as a spot for the homeless.

The Mexican hustlers made good use of the trees and bushes to provide a cover for their abundance of traffic that they had flowing thru. They even had the foresight to actually cut out an entrance and exit openings in the bushes in order to keep the traffic moving.

"Damn, these little big head muthafucka is smart," Jux spat.

"Yeah, they always talkin' that me no understand English bullshit. I'm telling' ya man, the next time one of them muthafucka tell me some shit like that, I don't give two fats rats asses if we on the fifty yard line, at half time of the super bowl. I'mma smack tequila taco bell outta they ass!" Al Capone promised.

The serious expression on his face made the statement that he'd made even hilarious and they all burst out laughing.

"Yo homes, stop makin' fun of my people," Felix added in between laughs.

"You ain't Mexican muthafucka, you nigga Rican!" Juxed snapped back and their laughter continued.

After deciding that they've seen enough. The youth made their way down the hill and separated in order to box the Mexican hustlers in. Once Jux got a closer look, he saw that they'd even built a clubhouse. Thoughts of fast money immediately kicked in as he crepted up on the side of the clubhouse. *These muthafucka's been getting' money down here all this time without problems, they don't even have lookouts*, he thought to himself. Once on the side of the clubhouse, he squatted like Caliph the mummy for Al Capone and Felix to make their move.

"Everybody on the muthafuckin' ground!" Al Capone shouted, making sure to run each of the customer's pockets as he lay them down. He installed the fear of god into them so that they wouldn't spend any more money in little Mexico.

Felix let loose a burst from his Mac11, gunning down four Mexican hustlers.

Just as Jux thought, five more spilled out of the clubhouse.

Their guns were blazing.

"Bang...bang...bang..." They were met by the hot led spit out of Jux's two favorite 45's.

What Jux didn't hit, Felix cleaned up. Al Capone ushered the customer's into the clubhouse and turned it into a slaughterhouse. Once there wasn't any more movement, they took the money off the Mexican hustler's, hit the stashes that they've already peeped during their surveillance and then left.

When they got to one of Jux's young girls house's in Bishop Towers, they were amazed by what sat in front of them.

"Damn, them cock suckas thought shit was sweet huh!" Felix said.

"Either that or them muthafucka was getting' more money than we thought," Al Capone responded.

"Yeah, 'cause a lot of them customers you ripped was holdin'. Which mean they were buying weight," Jux added.

"Yo B, we scored a half of bird of powder cocaine, another half of bird of cooked up coke, 78 bricks of heroin, 130 grams of raw heroin and 43 stacks in cash," Felix informed.

"Them pussies was getting' that scrilla out there right up under our noses," Al Capone responded.

"Yeah B, even though our scores are usually bigger, that was sweet for a street robbery. It's a lot of rice, beans, and broccoli eatin' goin' on in lil' Mexico!" Jux joked in his best Mexican imitation and they laughed.

***

When G Millions woke up, his son was at the foot of his bed playing with his XBox 360, which was one of the many gifts from the truck that Midget and Young Nitty jacked.

"Sup' lil' nigga?"

"Sup' dad."

"Where's your mother?"

"Her and Ms. Pink are downstairs cooking."

"You are a hard headed lil' boy, didn't I tell you about hookin' them games up to my TV." G Millions playfully mushed his son in the head.

"Yeah, but I wanted to chill wit' you dad."

"Oh, you got game huh." G Millions got up, rubbed his sons head ruffle, and wrestled him playfully.

'Ha, ha, ha you made me mess up dad. I got it from ya'll." Little G Millions giggled.

"What are you playin'?"

"Halo 2 and Call Of Duty, I like the games with the shooting on it. Cops, robbers, and stuff like that. I like to see the robber's get away."

"I told you he is just like yo ass!" YoYo said, walking into the room just as little G Millions finished his statement.

"Yeah I know," G Millions, answered nonchalantly. "Tell Lady Pink to call Fame and chop it up with him about what we discussed last night."

"You're really going to do it daddy?" YoYo asked, with a tear rolling down her face.

"Yeah baby, it's over." G Millions embraced her and his son lovingly.

After a family hug, they went to join Lady Pink for a breakfast consisting of pancakes, turkey bacon, cheese eggs, orange juice and fresh fruit that they had to make the little fellow eat.

Famous made his entrance just as they were finishing their breakfast. Little G Millions ran up to him and jumped into his arms as soon as he entered the room.

"Uncle Famous!" He shouted. "What's really gangsta?"

"Hey lil' man, you getting' too big, you damn near knocked me down," Famous said. "We gonna have to switch to high fives, and what are you doing talkin' like dat?"

"He get it from ya'll. He think he's a gangsta," YoYo informed. "I got a trick for his lil' ass though. He be talkin' like that in school too."

"Hey Fame," Lady Pink greeted trying to get her little man out of the hot seat.

"What's good ice pick," Famous joked.

"Fu…I mean forget you fool! You lucky lil' man here or I'd see you for that!" She laughed and everybody joined in on the humor.

"You always gotta start some shit. You want something to eat boy?" YoYo offered.

"You already know, I don't turn down nothin' but my collar and I don't wear them," Famous joked and everybody joined him for another good laugh.

"Boy you'z a fool." YoYo was still giggling while she fixed his plate.

After breakfast was over, G Millions and Famous sat in the living room, chopping it up and G Millions let his lifelong friend and partner know what was really good.

"It's over my nig, me, and you are already over 10 million strong and Lady Pink isn't far behind. That's not including the paper that continues to roll in. Product on the streets, businesses property etc. We've built a strong family, it's time to let the younginz' take over and get theirs. It's time to live B," G Millions stated, enthusiastically.

"It's been me and you from the sand box. More-less, you already know I ain't got nothin' but love for the family. Even though it has never been said 'cause it ain't your style. But you are the boss and if you say it's over, that's what it is. The fact that Candy Girl is pregnant shows that your timing is right as always," Famous said and they gave each other gangster love.

"Rally up the YG's and BG's and tell them to meet us at the studio. Congratulations on being a father my nig, we gonna toss it up tonight!"

"Where's Candy Girl at anyway?" YoYo asked as she entered the living room.

"She home chillin'. She wanted to come but I told her that she had enough excitement for nine months fuckin' wit' ya'll nutty ass whores last night. That paper was right on time tho," Famous said, with a wicked grin plastered across his face and they all laughed.

***

G Millions, Famous, and Lady Pink jumped in Famous's G Ride at quarter to eight in route to the studio. Famous called himself pulling out his BMW to keep a low profile for the day. They were all looking forward to announcing their retirement and letting their little homies get rich. The trio agreed that their run in the game was a success so there was no reason to push their luck. The decision to turn over the wheel to Jux and Al Capone was unanimous. The two proved their worth time after time. They also decided to split the rest of the cash amongst the three of them and give the rest of the product to the rest of the family. The way that all of the spots were pumping; they would be able to come up off it in no time. Not to mention the amount of product that the youth will be nheriting will assure them the opportunity to retire in no time also.

G Millions had been feeling a little uneasy all day long, but he chalked it up to the excitement. However, as they rounded the circle coming off route 18 to Commercial Ave, his feelings was conformed when Famous spotted a smoke gray X5 BMW that had been behind them for the past couple of minutes.

"Yo B, we got some Mexicans on our ass and they don't look like Jehovah Witnesses comin' to sell us the Hereafter."

G Millions and Lady Pink immediately pulled out, cocked their guns, and holstered them. Then Lady Pink slid G Millions the Russian AK with the short stock under the seat and gets hers locked and loaded.

"When you get to the top of the hill bust a quick left on George St. and go up by the college," G Millions calmly advised.

'I heard," Famous agreed.

No sooner then they crossed the light, the Mexicans put a monkey wrench in their game, when a black van full of gunmen suddenly exited the New Apartment parking lot and blindsided Famous, sending him spinning.

The Mexicans didn't waste any time pouncing on them.

By the time they came out of the spin, bullets where already flying in their direction. Although the Mexicans had the drop on them, they didn't panic.

Lady Pink took the X5 that was following them, while G Millions banged out with the occupants of the black van.

Under normal circumstances G Millions and Lady Pink's superior firepower would have been ended the gun battle, but the Mexicans ambush gave them the momentum that they needed to be able to bang out. Now there was a full fledge shoot out in broad daylight that was sure to end ugly.

After a few minutes of exchanging shots, the shoot out was beginning to turn one sided, leaning in the favor of the Mexicans. Their numbers and positioning gave them the advantage. Still, Lady Pink was un-phased by the gunfight, thus she proved to be the X factor with her quick thinking.

She swiftly hopped out of the back driver side door and opened up the driver's door for Famous who had been wounded. She then pulled him out, while G Millions continued to spray his chopper. He also had a slug lodged in the back of his vest. But his adrenalin along with the sight of blood leaking from his main man's head and neck wouldn't allow him to stop.

They used the car and the oncoming traffic as a shield. Lady Pink took over the reins while G Millions dragged Famous across the street towards Bishop Towers. Just as they made it across the street, G Millions was struck in the buttocks and high in the shoulder, sending him, Famous and their guns sliding across the concrete. As soon as Lady Pink spent to return fire, she was struck in the chest and knocked against a parked car.

Just as the Mexicans gunmen was about to close in and finish them off, Jux, Al Capone, and Felix arrived at the party letting their guns go.

The young gangsters had heard the shots from Jux girlfriend's apartment and when they looked out of the window to see what was going on, they saw their bosses in a heated gun battle. They nearly knocked the door off the hinges getting to their rescue. The young gangster's gunplay sent the surviving Mexicans scrambling to their X5 and getting the fuck out of dodge.

Sirens could be heard wailing in the background as they loaded Famous into the ML60. It was a tight squeeze, but it was their only chance to save their brother. Lady Pink had to peel off the vest that she wore faithfully ever since the Hotep incident in order to catch her breath. G Millions couldn't sit down and was breathless, but he was good because he knew that they were almost out of hot water. Famous wasn't looking good, so they were left with no choice but to rush him to Robert-hood Johnsons emergency room.

When they arrived, Butta and Grass was waiting on them. So G Millions, Lady Pink, Jux, Al Capone and Felix went to a private doctor that YoYo knew. Candy Girl arrived at the hospital in less than 20 minutes. A half an hour later the lobby was packed with the whole hood. It was the biggest turn out since the show. Some visitors couldn't even get in.

After about 3 ½ hours in ICU the doctor came out and informed the family that Famous was good. He'd caught a graze to the forehead that actually look worse then what it actually was, because it was in a tight skin area, which is subject to heavy bleeding. He also caught one in the neck that couldn't be removed because it was too close to the artery that pumps directly to the heart. His platinum and iced out chain acted as a vest for that one. The one to the back of the leg was removed and they counted several slugs to the front and back of his vest.

Homicide came thru and tested him for gunpowder residue, which was negative because he didn't get a chance to fire back. But they still threatened to charge him because they could do what they wanted too.

Saint I's, Jeffry Dommers, Young Nitty and Piff went berserk and was having Mexican target practice until Jux caught up to them and painted the bigger picture.

The crowd in the lobby went nuts when they found out that Famous would live, like the brokers on Wall Street after hearing an announcement of a rising stock. One thing was certain and two things were for sure, not only the Mexicans, but also the entire Tri-State area, was going to wish they had let them exit the game peacefully...

Chapter 20

"They should have let them retire..."

Two days after the ambush, Famous was fed up with lying in a hospital bed. So he took the IV out of his arm, the tube out of his penis and left Robert-hoods without signing out. As soon as the family got wind of the fact that he'd checked out they were at his front door.

Once they saw that it was all good, they made themselves right at home and ate, drank and smoked as much of his stuff up as possible. Of course, it didn't take long for the gambling to start, which put Famous back in his glory. Even in pain, he loved to gamble and be the center of attention.

"That's my word B, I'mma make them little big head muthafucka famous!" He shouted, pissed off about being hit up.

"That's my bad B, I under estimated that nigga Draggo," G Millions said, feeling responsible for dragging out the war instead of eliminating the problem immediately.

"Fuck dat shit B, you ain't no swami. Them niggaz done fucked up, they should have let sleeping giants lay," Famous ranted. "How they gonna pull some sucka shit like dat in my town."

"Fuck those heavy head muthafucka's! I bet they wasn't expecting no bang out like that either!" Lady Pink stated, attempting to make Famous feel better.

"Yeah, you that bitch!" Famous gave her, her props. "I fucks wit you all the time out of love, but you a prime time player for real!"

"Why wouldn't I be runnin' wit' a bunch of fools like ya'll!" Lady Pink attempting to shift the spotlight off herself.

Truth be told, the things she did came natural to her. So she wasn't looking for recognition, she was going to come thru for her team regardless.

"Shiit, if it wasn't for you and our young gangstas, our families would be in hard bottoms right now."

"Man, I got something for Draggo's ass!" G Millions snapped, banging his fist in the palm of his hand.

All the YG's were on the back patio shooting cee-lo, guzzling Moet and smoking sour diesel mixed with crank also known as wet, when G Millions stepped outside to join them. Piff and Young Nitty had the bank with a friendly ten thousand in it. Young Nitty was on fire, hitting head snaps back to back, trips and a stubborn bitch named Tracy that only Felix could manage to beat with a head snapper of his own.

Piff surveyed the money under every bodies feet, while each homey bet accordingly, stopping the bank thinking that their luck was about to run out. Young Nitty shook up the dice.

"Break yo self fools!" He shouted in his best Westside accent.

As the dice left his hand, he snapped his fingers once for each number 1, 1, 6.

"Lucky ass nigga!" Somebody mumbled.

"Head snappers!" He yelled, scraping up the dice, while Piff scraped up the money.

"Twenty in the bank," Piff challenged calmly.

"Ya'll some lucky ass niggaz!" Al Capone snapped, twisting up his face.

"Luck ain't got shit to do wit' this shit here," Young Nitty snapped back. "I'm a bad muthafucka!" While everybody placed their bets, Young Nitty continued to shake the dice and talk slick. "Yeah, I'm a bad muthafucka!" He reiterates as he let them go snapping his fingers 4, 5, 6.

"Cee-lo muthafucka's!" Piff yelled with excitement and the two of them laugh and argue over how much to put back in the bank after the split.

A light bulb went off in Grass's head while they were bullshitting around about the bank.

"Hold up, let me see them dice," he said beating Young Nitty to them.

When he picked them up and twirled them around in his fingers, he peeped the fact that one of the dice had all sixes.

"Man, these lil' niggaz cheatin'!" Grass exposed them in his slow lingo.

When he showed everybody the crook dice, they quickly turned on Piff and Young Nitty and playfully jumped them taking their money back.

"Why ya'll niggaz always shuckin' and jivin' me man?" Butta asked.

"We should take all ya'll bread," Felix chimed in.

"You ain't learn how to speak English yet fool?" Midget joked, causing everyone to break out into roaring laughter.

"You fools is the worst," G Millions interjected still chuckling. "Come on let's go and show Famous some love. Plus we about to have a meeting."

The family gave each other gangster hugs, playful punches and a few WWF wrestling moves while they filed into the house. When they entered the living room, Famous was in his leather recliner talking shit to Lady Pink as always. It was a beautiful thing to know that when the going got tough, the family got closer. Both Famous and Lady Pink addressed the family when they entered the room.

"What you fools up to?" Famous questioned.

"You know them fools up to something when they all get together."

Famous what you been teachin' these lil' niggaz?" G Millions asked.

"They must've slid that six in on ya'll," Famous said, knowingly.

"Yeah, the grimy ass niggaz tried us," Jux cut in.

"We would've had ya'll fools to, if it wasn't for Mr. Observant ass Grass peepin' gangsta," Young Nitty bragged.

"We would have cut you in big bra!" Piff joked and the room erupted in laughter.

Once the laughter calmed down and Candy Girl excused herself from the room, G Millions called the meeting to order.

"Yo, listen ya'll, before this issue came up, Famous, Lady Pink and myself were going to retire. We were confident that we were leaving the business in worthy hands," He scanned the room to see their reactions.

Sure enough, everybody was sitting there with long faces. Although they knew that they would have been seeing much more money, they enjoyed having their big brothers and sister around. G Millions and Lady Pink always made them feel just as important to the family as they were. Famous although more flashy and arrogant then G Millions always took the time out to show them different ways to get fast money and honeys.

"Ahh man-," The room groaned.

"Chill ya'll, hear my spiel. I'm not above admitting that I underestimated that nigga Draggo. So I take full responsibility for what went down and we gonna stick around to rectify the situation." Upon hearing the good news, the family cheered, clapped and gave each other gangster love. Once they calmed down G Millions continued. "We'll be finished with that issue in a couple of weeks after Fame get back right. I got big plans for us, we about to shock the world my niggaz! Everybody in here does their muthafuckin' thing. Just like a good athlete enters the state of body awareness in which the right stroke or the right movement happens by itself, effortlessly, without interference of the conscious will. This is a paradigm for non-action: the purest and most effective form of action. The gamer plays the game, the poet writes the poems, we can't tell the dancer from the dance etc… I got that from my man TAO TE Ching, but the point I'm making is that, that's how everybody setting here move, that's why we so successful. For the next couple of weeks we're going to stick close and be done with this minor issue at hand, and then we're going to take this robbery report to the next level!" G Millions continued the pep rally a little longer before the homeys went back to doin' what they do.

Over the next few weeks while Famous was healing, the hood was like Bagdad. There were shootouts and brawls all over the place. Although the incident with the family set it off, it was a long time coming, the tension between the blacks and Mexicans had been brewing.

After staying at Famous' house for two weeks, the homies must've watched every gangster flick and cowboy movie ever made. From Humphrey Bogart's Casablanca to Hoodlum and many more. Although they kept some shit going, they did build a closer bond. But the family was getting restless and craving to make somebody's robbery report.

On the 15th day, G Millions cell phone started doing the Harlem shake. He didn't recognize the number right away and started not to answer it, but against his better judgment, he answered it anyway.

"What's really gangsta?"

"Yo my nigga! I told you I was gonna bark at you!" Dump Truck spat thru the phone.

"Who this Dump Truck?" G Millions asked, getting excited.

"Why wouldn't it be? Like slide thru my dude. We can hoc spit, bullshit and make somebody have to write one of the reports, ya dig!"

"Say no more my nig, book a suite for me and my peeps, we on our way!"

"That's what it is; hit me on my hip as soon as you touch my dude."

"I heard."

When they ended the call, G Millions wasted no time telling Famous what it was.

"That was the boy Dump Truck we was boxed up wit', he want us to come thru."

"What we waitin' for then, this house is drivin' me nuts!" Famous said, giving his best pirate impersonation.

When G Millions rounded up the family and informed them that they were stepping out. They were happier than 100 niggaz and 1000 bitches. Everybody got fresh fast and prepared to do their thing in Camden NJ. While on their way out of the door, G Millions handed Famous a set of BMW keys. He was thinking that maybe they got his 745 fixed but when he laid eyes on the triple black 760i, fresh off the press, he damn near went ballistic. He immediately hit the keyless remote and diddy bopped over to his new toy.

G Millions, Lady Pink and the rest of the family surrounded the vehicle and watched Famous ease behind the wheel in comfort of the plush leather seats. He inhaled deeply and his nostrils were rewarded with the fresh sent of a new car. He slowly rubbed his hand across the wood grain, played with a few of his many gadgets and then a smile appeared on his face.

"It ain't the flyin' B, but it's a gift from the YG's and BG's. Lady Pink copped your Gianelle's and I threw in the body armor," Informed G Millions.

Famous knew that he had mad love, but this really touched him. He eased back out his new ride gave the family gangster love and he gave Lady Pink a hug and kiss, after which everybody hopped into their foreign cars and headed for Camden.

When they arrived in Camden, Dump Truck directed them to his hood in Parkside over the cell phone. When they pulled up on Hadden also known as the Ave., it looked like a car slash bike show, slash block party. All makes and model SUV's, cars and bikes lined the streets.

The onlookers watched as male and female riders did all types of tricks on bikes and four wheelers. *Lil' G would have loved this*, G Millions thought to himself. Although they're hot wheels blended in, they somewhat shut down the show until Dump Truck guided them to a spot to line their shit up.

Once everybody parked and hopped out, Dump Truck and a couple of his soldiers came over and greeted the family with hood love and a couple of bottles of Moet. Lady Pink couldn't help but laugh to herself because he wore his name well. Both families clicked immediately and it wasn't because of the Moet, it was because real recognized real.

"It's good to see my dudes in a better place, ya dig!" Dump Truck said to G Millions and Famous.

"You already know B, we told you what it was," stated G Millions.

"Ya timin' couldn't have been more perfect," Famous said. "What's on the antennary for the next couple of days?"

"I booked ya'll a suite at the Ramada Inn on Broad St. in Philly paid for, for three days. Tonight, we are going to ball at Chrystal and then slide thru the Doghouse after hours. You already know we gonna be the subject of somebody's Robbery Report, that's what we do. All them laps around the big yard wasn't for nothin', ya dig!?!" Dump Truck said giving them the run down.

"Me and Fame a little dented up my nigga, but our young gangsta's in animals," Informed G Millions.

"Yo like, holla at ya boy, like you already know we catch body's for trophies. Like just give me the nod and me and my soldiers will come thru like the tsunami, ya dig!" Dump Truck offered.

"That's how it is, but it's nothin' B, we gonna mash them pussies like cocka roaches," Famous said sounding like Tony Montana giving everybody a good laugh.

"That's gangsta my nigga. But dig this," Dump Truck changed the subject. "I'm already heavy like, so all I want is his hand and 25% of the jux," Dump Truck proposed. "Like as long as the boy outta my way, like the hood gotta bow down and ride in the Dump Truck, feel me!?"

'Fo' sure, its nothin' B, we got you," Famous assured him.

Everybody enjoyed the rest of the day popping bottles, smoking, setting up as for the night and gambling as always. The Camden hood-models were coming thru in doves and the saying that opposites attract was an understatement. Whoever had stocks in condoms as of that night shift was about to ski rocket over the next couple of days.

Lady Pink showed her ass when she got on Dump Truck's Ducati. She lifted it up from Park Blvd., past Sycamore, Wildwood, caught the green light on Cane in front of Donut Queen and didn't put it down until she got in front of Dunkies. Being as though she wasn't wearing a helmet, everybody knew she wasn't from the area. So all of those who missed the hot wheels rolling through strolled down the block to see what was going on. Dump Truck and his soldiers wasn't smelling nothing new getting started, so they ran them jokers back up top.

Later that night, Chrystal bar was all that Dump Truck said it would be. All of the top dogs was in the building with that shit on and the hood-models might as well have not been wearing anything as tiny as their outfits where. Make no mistake about it though, their outfits was from the top designers.

Between the two families, there were about twenty-five strong. They locked down the V.I.P and balled out despite the few minor scuffles that took place thru out the club. The fights didn't interrupt anything, the bouncers just bounced their ass right out of the door and the show went on.

"There go the boy I was telling you about right there," Dump Truck informed them pointing towards the exit.

When G Millions, Famous and Lady Pink looked, damn was the first thought that came to their minds. It looked as if Dante Culpepper was coming through with the whole offensive line. He was at least 6'5" 270lbs. and everybody that accompanied him besides the runway thin models was at least his height or taller and in the 300 club.

"What the fuck is them dudes, Eagle rejects!" Famous stated, causing everybody to laugh.

"The niggaz be tryin' to Debo shit too like. It was more of them then that, but we been letting the air out they ass slowly but surely," Dump Truck informed. "I been followin' the boy home like, you think he big, you gotta get a load of his crib. This fool even got the nerve to be calling himself David Koch the billionaire. I wanna see if he that cocky wit' that thing in his mouth." Dump Truck shook his head up and down while signaling for the bartenders. He then sends five yellow bottles over to their table.

Minutes later David Koch and his boys came to the table and slammed the bottles down along with a stack of big face hundreds and addressed Dump Truck falling right into his trap.

"Listen here nigga, take your bottles of piss that you spent your re-up on, take this ten stacks and get on board. Then maybe I'll let you come for me. We ain't no bitches and you can't afford ours. So don't send no more of that shit to our table." David Koch pointed at the bottles with an attitude.

"You my bitch and I'll turn these hoes you runnin' wit' into my stable nigga," Dump Truck responded calmly. "Like this is 2006, ain't no-body impressed by that brolic shit. I'll knock you the fuck out and spit in ya ass pussy!"

Before David Koch could respond, Young Nitty slung a yellow bottle and smashed one of his boys upside the head which started off the brawl of the century.

The young gangsters and Dump Truck's soldiers were on them like a pack of wild jackals. Champagne, Heineken and Corona bottles flew along with whatever else they got their hands on. As soon as they ran out of things to throw, out came the razors and hawks.

It didn't take them long to finally get tired of tussling with them big ass dudes and the bouncers, before the guns came out. When the guns started emptying out, so did Crystals. David Koch thinking his big nigga status was going to get him a win cost him a few good men. Never the less the doghouse never happened. But the jump off at the Ramada Inn did.

Once Crystals emptied out, the Donut Queen on the Ave. was packed. All of the young gangsters rekindled their courtships from earlier. They all headed over to the Ben Franklin Bridge to enjoy their own exclusive party. After the brawl, the young gangsters and the soldiers really clicked. It was as if they grew up together. To them they had proven themselves to each other. For them, it was like looking in the mirror.

While the dice games, smoking, drinking and fucking was taking place, Dump Truck, G Millions, Famous and Lady Pink were plotting.

"Yo B, I told you we was dented up!" G Millions said pointedly.

"I know my nig., but I had to put it on that boy to like insure that he'll be in the crib when the youngin's go up in there wavin' them things, you smell me?"

"It's all hood, we got it off and our family got to get off some of that aggression that been pint up these past couple of weeks," Famous added.

"Yeah, that shit was right up them young fools alley," Lady Pink cut in, "Ya lil' niggaz too."

"That's what it is, like everybody did what they had to do," Dump Truck smiled. "But like where did you learn how to use that ice pick?"

Famous sat there with a shit-eating grin on his face, while Lady Pink thought back to when she was thirteen.

Her older sister had sent her out to the store in order to purchase some GP20's so that her and her grimy ass girlfriends could bottle up the cocaine that they talked her sister into robbing her boyfriend for. When Lady Pink returned, two of her sister's girlfriends were holding her sister down, while the third one was penetrating her vagina with the barrel of a .38 special. Seeing and feeling her sister's discomfort and pain caused her to black out. The first weapon that she could get her hands on was the ice pick that she stuck thru the chick with the guns head, killing her instantly. Unfortunately, the gun went off and ripped thru her sister's insides killing her. Disloyalty cost her sister her life and Lady Pink her childhood. Until this day, she carried the same ice pick.

G Millions was the only person that she'd shared that nightmare with and he was the only one who was able to penetrate her cold heart. Famous, the YG's, YoYo and Candy Girl were working their way in slowly but surely, so she considered them family now. After the incident with her sister, she was consumed by guilt and loneliness causing her to eventually turn to dope in an attempt to ease the pain. It was fun at first, but after awhile she became miserable, needing it to wake up, eat, sleep, fuck and whatever else everyday life had to offer. That was up until G Millions literally ran into her life and saved her. Now her life was his.

"I learned from the best," Lady Pink forced a smile.

'Oh a'ight, that's gangsta," Dump Truck said, feeling as if he'd missed something.

For the rest of the night, everybody enjoyed doing what they do. The next day Dump Truck sent his soldier Robin Hood to show Midget, Jeffry Dommers, Young Nitty and Piff where David Koch laid to rest. The big time hustler lived in the exclusive section of Cherry Hill, New Jersey where many of Philadelphia's star athletes lived.

'See this is why I stay in the hood. These big scrilla gettin' ass niggaz don't wanna be around nobody and their nearest neighbors house is a mile away. They make this shit too easy for niggaz like us," Midget sported a broad smile.

'I trills you dog, our whole team is in the hood," Robin Hood replied. "You won't be able to tell from the outside, but like when you step in, you think you watchin' MTV cribs."

'I heard, let's go and collect this paper!" Piff urged, not beat for the small talk.

After Robin Hood and the YG's finished smoking their blunt laced with crank, they hopped out of his Chevy Tahoe in route to find an entrance. The youth moved swiftly thru the yard looking for an entrance. When they reached the patio and looked thru the glass doors, sure enough, David Koch was laid up, with gauze wrapped around his head like a mummy and he had his woman dressed in a one-piece nurse's uniform with the skirt part riding up her petite little butt, revealing her thong and ass cheeks. Her outfit was complete with stilettos and a nurse hat with the first aid sign on it and she waited on him hand and foot. *I'm glad I decided to ride in the Dump Truck, the boys a genius.* Robin Hood thought. While the YG's was thinking to themselves, *that has got to be the baddest chick in the world!*

Young Nitty had seen enough, so he picked up a patio chair and threw it through the glass door interrupting everybody's thoughts. But their thoughts didn't delay their movements. They rushed thru the broken glass doors as a couple of David Koch's goons appeared from out of nowhere surprising everyone.

Robin Hood and the YG's rose to the occasions with rapid burst from their machine guns, painting the walls and floors with blood, brains and skull fragments.

Koch's lady tried to aid him by grabbing his tech .9mm from under the chair and tossing it to him. But it was a little too late. *Too bad this fool ain't got no bitch on his team like ours.* Midget thought to himself. By the time he caught it, they were on him like piranhas'.

"Who else in the house muthafucka!" Piff hissed aggressively.

"Nobody," a fearful Koch answered.

Piff took David Koch's tech .9mm, put up his own twin .9mm Baretta and held David Koch and his woman friend down, while everybody else combed through the house looking for more goons and anything else in plain view. When they came back to the room, they had two small kids, a briefcase full of money, four kilo's of cocaine, a half of kilo of dope, another tech .9mm and two .50 caliber desert eagles.

After acknowledging Midgets signal Young Nitty took the kids back into the room to play video games.

"Please don't hurt my babies," Koch's wifey pleaded.

"You're the only one that could hurt your babies. By tryin' some super hero shit like you pulled earlier," Jeffry Dommers informed.

"My niggaz found this shit on ya'll bed, so I know this ain't shit. I'm only gonna ask you once," Piff got up in Koch's face. "Where the shit at?"

"Take them to the stash ma!" David Koch ordered.

His lady friend did as she was told and led Midget to the shed, which was bigger than the average niggaz house in the back yard. The way that David Koch glared at Robin Hood indicated that if looks could kill there would be a closed casket.

His lady friend led Midget thru the shed and into a basement that was located in a spot that nobody would have ever thought to look. She moved a few things around, and clapped her hands.

Her sudden hand movements caused Midget to pull the trigger and put one right in her temple.

Stuff started to shift and move, then pay dirt! Upon seeing the score Midget immediately called Jeffry Dommers.

"What's gangsta my nig?" Jeffry Dommers asked.

"I need help out here."

"Say no more!"

Minutes later Jeffry Dommers and Robin Hood reached the shed to find Midget waiting for them at the door. He led them to the back where the stash was and where the young lady laid in a pool of blood.

"What happened to her?" Robin Hood inquired.

"That bitch just started clappin' out of nowhere and I thought she was makin' a move, so I clapped her fine ass." Midget smiled.

"Ha...ha...ha...at least you got the stash first this time," Jeffry Dommers joked.

"Fuck you nigga, let's get this shit and get the fuck outta here before the one cop in this town get lucky or unlucky!" Midget stated holding up his .9mm and everybody laughed and loaded up the loot.

When they got everything loaded into the Tahoe, they went back in the house. David Koch could see in their body language that he'd lost his lady.

"Not the kids please?" He cried, pleading for his children's life.

"Oh hell naw, I know your tuff ass ain't bitchin' up," Piff antagonized him. "You was a bad muthafucka last night. What happened to that?"

"What the fuck we look like nigga?" Midget snapped. "We gangstas for real, you should've stuck to football!"

Jeffry Dommers pulled out his hatchet and addressed him. "You really should have taken them drinks, now you must be punished. Give me your hand."

Midget and Piff grabbed his hand and put it on the coffee table. In one swift motion, Jeffry Dommers brought down the hatchet and severed David Koch's hand from his wrests, which caused blood to squirt up in Midget and Piff's face.

"What the fuck B, if you gonna use that thing, learn what the fuck you doin'!" Midget and Piff complained while wiping off their face.

Robin Hood wasn't used to the butchering so he threw his guts up.

The angry Piff put two in David Koch's face.

Jeffry Dommers admired his handy work for a little longer before they all cleaned themselves up, barricaded the kids in the room, called DYF's and left.

When they arrived at one of Dump Trucks stash spots, everybody was patiently waiting. The YG's and soldiers passed around fifths of Hennessey, blunts of exotic weed mixed with crank and traded war stories.

By the time, everything was counted and Dump Truck got his 25%, it was close to the time for the Dog House. Jeffry Dommers walked up to Dump Truck who was admiring his new .50 caliber desert eagle, reached into his pocket and handed him David Koch's hand. Although the soldiers were shocked, they did their best to maintain their composure. Dump Truck had a surprised look on his face at the fact that they had really brought him the David Koch's hand.

The only thing that surprised the family was that the silly little nigga had been walking around with the hand in his pocket.

"Better late then never," Jeffry Dommers said, while shrugging his shoulders.

Dump Truck accepted the hand, walked over to Robin Hood and smacked the shit out of him with it. Then he jammed the desert eagle into his mouth.

Robin Hoods head damn near disintegrated.

Everybody in the room drew their weapons and trained on each other.

"At ease soldiers," Dump Truck ordered and they did the same.

"Easy cowboy," G Millions ordered and they did the same.

"If that nigga would cross his own uncle, like we ain't have a chance, smell me!" Dump Truck explained.

"Say no more B," G Millions gave him a pound.

Everybody resumed activity, then shot over to the bridge, stashed their shit and got fresh. When they arrived at the Dog House, they turned it into a closed door and all dudes had to go. XXX didn't have anything on what went down that night. The next day everybody showed their love gangster style, assured each other that, that was only the beginning then the family headed back to Jersey...

Chapter 21

"Time for another vacation"

Over the next few weeks, things went exactly how G Millions and Famous planned. The tension between the blacks and Mexicans died down for the most part. With the exception of a few isolated incidents, the beef between the two nationalities fizzled out. The whole family sat in their favorite suite at the Hyatt, separating stacks of money and product that they'd acquired from the Camden robbery. The ones who'd gotten tired of counting were spread throughout the suite, knocked out with a bottle in one hand and a hood-model's ass, coochie or titties in the other. You couldn't tell who was doing the most snoring, the hood-models or the YG's. I guess it was safe to say that they were all wore out.

The $475,000 was split twelve ways with the loose change distributed among Jeffry Dommers, Midget, and Piff. The same went for the 29 pounds of purple haze, the 62 kilos of cocaine and the 14-kilo's of heroin that would be shipped to the stash houses in order to be bagged, tagged, and put on the streets. Even though they didn't need any more, they also split the jewels.

G Millions, Famous, and Lady Pink were discussing their trip to Utah. Well actually, G Millions and Lady Pink dumped the plan making on Famous, when G Millions cell phone started humming. He really didn't feel like being bothered, but when he looked at the caller I.D. and saw the 804 area code, he knew that he had to answer it.

"What's really gangsta lil' sis?"

"Hey big brother, besides your nephew getting on my nerves, it's all hood," Toni answered.

"Tell him don't make me come down there, 'cause if I do, all hell gone break loose!"

"Yeah right!" Toni retorted. "You've been promising me that you were coming down forever."

"I know lil' sis, that's why I told you to come up here, because every time I get ready to come down something, happens."

"Well we only six hours away, four and a half the way you drive. So we need to see each other more."

When G Millions hung up the phone, he saw both Lady Pink and Famous in his mouth.

"What?" He snapped.

"Stop playin' all the time fool and tell us what's goin' on wit' lil' sis!" Famous urged.

"Them fools in Baltimore trippin'," G Millions responded.

"You know what it is daddy, just bring them on vacation with us," Lady Pink suggested.

"That's why you my bitch, you think just like me," G Millions wrapped her up in his arms excitedly and stuck his tongue down her throat.

"If that's how ya'll show how ya'll love each other, I'm about to hurl!" Famous joked, sticking his finger in his mouth as if he was about to throw up.

"Fuck you fool, you just mad 'cause Candy Girl all big now and you can't get none," Lady Pink retorted.

"Shiit, Lil' Fame gonna have a dent on top of his head how I be beatin' that thing up. Can't nothin' keep my dick out of that fine muthafucka," Famous said and they all laughed.

"Ma, after you make the drop off, I need you to slide by western union and send lil' sis' seven stacks," G Millions reached into his pocket to retrieve the money.

"I got it daddy," Lady Pink insisted while giving him a sexy kiss before grabbing the bags and heading for the door.

"Hold up sis, take a couple of youngins' wit' you," Famous strongly suggested.

"Damn, A'ight," She started to protest, but realized that he was right.

So she went and woke up Jeffry Dommers and Young Nitty. Ten minutes after they freshened up, they were out of the door.

Once they were gone, Famous chirped Thomas and had him gas up the private jet and book cabins in Lake Tahoe, Utah. After everything was taken care of, Thomas got back to Famous and informed him that the single cabins were too spaced out and the only way that they would hold the family is if they were packed in like the Mexicans that they were beefing wit.

Although for the most part they would be in the same cabin because that's how it always went down, they were going to need some space for the two weeks they were going to be gone. Unlike the Acapulco trip, they would be coupled up so they would need to stretch out and get some rest. Sleeping wherever your eyes closed was all right for a couple of days, but not two whole weeks.

Famous and Thomas agreed for him to book the five-cabin community. G Millions loved these vacations, not just to get away, but he also liked to see the excitement in the young gunners whenever they got the chance to get out of Jersey. Plus not only do they get to get out of Jersey, but also they're doing it in style, first class all the way. Being as though they didn't get out of the hood much, going out of state presented as much of a challenge to them as getting money, robbing and the bodies that they racked up.

***

When the day of the trip rolled around, everybody was like kids on Christmas Eve. Leeka Leek mobbed thru with his shorty and his right-hand man. The family rolled out the red carpet for them.

The atmosphere on the plane was much different on this trip, then the one to Acapulco. Whereas on the trip to Acapulco the YG's brought mistresses so, it was like free-style Friday. But on this one, everybody had their main girls. So even though the YG's was still being gangsters, they were much more refined. Instead of running around on the plane shooting cee-lo and wilding out, they sat their little asses down and watched Four Brothers on the G5's big screen. The fact that their shorties had them on lock down status didn't stop the smoke and drink from flowing.

G Millions, Lady Pink, Famous, YoYo and Candy Girl were getting a kick out of seeing the young couples hugged up. The women had started to whisper amongst each other.

'This is the quietest I ever seen them lil' niggaz," Candy Girl commented.

'Hell yeah, them lil' bastards are even loud when their sleep," YoYo agreed.

'I know that's right, but you know I gotta expose their little ass's though right!" Lady Pink added.

G Millions and Famous had overheard the conversation being as though the girls whisper was louder than normal due to the volume of the movie.

'Sis, please leave them fools alone while they're quiet!" Famous warned.

'Don't tell her nothin', then as soon as they get started, she gonna wanna ice pick a nigga," G Millions teased, flashing his million dollar smile giving everyone in around him a good laugh.

'Oh, you got jokes huh!" Lady Pink snapped.

'Ssshhh...Movie up!" Saint I's yelled, catching a flash back of the youth house day room.

"You ssshhh...That's why ya'll chicks got ya'll on snap!" YoYo set it off like Queen Latifah.

'Yeah, I ain't never seen ya'll this quite!" Candy Girl added a little coal to the flames.

'I see ya'll work home girls," Lady Pink cut in, putting a 12-volt energizer into the situation. "If ya'll got the pussy that snaps give me three claps."

Every girl on the plane clapped her hands three times and all hell broke loose. The rest of the trip was chaos. *Mission accomplished*, Lady Pink thought to herself. Those are the little brothers I know. I can't afford for them to get soft over no cunt on me now. We got work to do. G Millions noticed a slick smile on her face and just shook his head, knowing exactly what she was thinking.

When the plane taxied the runway in Utah, all of the commotion stopped. Everyone on the plane was hypnotized by the snow-filled mountains. When they walked through the small airport, they received stares, some wondering if they were celebrities and some just hating.

Once outside, they loaded up the awaiting chauffer driven SUV's and made their way up to the place where they would be staying at for the next couple of weeks. More and more of Utah's beauty unfolded before them as they headed for the cabins. Although it snowed in the hood, this was a far cry from the snow covered cars, trashcans etc. Instead of the drug free school zone signs, there were avalanche watch signs. The family caught the glorious sight on the camcorder for future references as they the trees and mountains whizzed by.

When their cabins came into view, it looked like something out of a Budweiser commercial. It was even more beautiful once they stepped outside into the brisk air. The cabins had the look and feel of the rugged outdoors, but it was loaded with all of the state of the art equipment. All of the cabins were identical with the exception of the dining cabin where the food was cooked and served. The staff stayed in that cabin as well. There was also another cabin, which held the snowmobiles and the rest of the snow equipment. Thomas already knew how the YG's did theirs, so he made sure there would be enough snowmobiles for the entire family.

Once everybody took their bags into their cabins, they all ended up in the cabin shared by G Millions, YoYo, Lady Pink, Famous, Candy Girl, Thomas, and his wife. Candy Girl blazed up the fireplace as the rest of the girls passed out the food and drinks.

The night before the trip, the girls got together at Saint I's spot and cooked fried chicken, fish, macaroni and cheese, potato salad, macaroni salad, fruit salad and the works. YoYo, Lady Pink and Candy Girl took care of the exotic food, while Felix and his shorty did the Spanish thing, minus the hog. Thomas and his wife put together the Italian and of course, the drink and smoke was plentiful.

Everybody took turns DJaying via CD's until everybody was full, tweaking and tipsy. They spent the rest of the night, just seating around coupled up in front of the fireplace trading war stories. G Millions was the only one lucky enough to be sitting between Lady Pinks legs, with YoYo between his.

The next morning the young gangsters wasted no time mastering the snowmobiles while waking everybody up in the process. Already in their fresh snow suites, they were hooping and hollering, flying back and forth thru the snow as if they'd been riding forever.

After finally giving up the possibility of sleep, everyone else got up, got fresh, and met in the dining cabin for breakfast. Once they filled up their bellies, everyone got smoked out, jumped on their snowmobiles and headed to the ski lodge for their morning ski lessons. Famous opted to stay in the ski lodge with Candy Girl while everyone else hopped on the ski lifts, which headed for the beginners slope. You couldn't get better comedy if you went to the Apollo. At first, neither of them could stand up on their skies, let alone ski. You had slides, rolls and crashes, but it was all in fun.

Halfway thru the morning the whole family had gotten a lot better. They all had also worked up an appetite along with being sore from working parts of the body that they never knew existed. So they headed back to the dinning cabin for lunch, after which they retreated to their cabins for some well-needed rest. This went on for a few days because the family had gotten addicted to skiing and their bodies hadn't adjusted to it yet. But as time went on their bodies seem to start to adjust and they spent even more time on the slopes. They also enjoyed the hiking trips that they went on. The mountain top views and the animals of the wild were something to be seen. It was a beautiful thing for them to be able to see something besides wild cats, rats, and dogs.

After the first week, their bodies started to recover, so they were able to enjoy fuller days. They also got tired of the bland food in the dinning cabin, so the girls got rid of the cooks. Lady Pink and YoYo made out a grocery and alcohol list and snatched up Leeka Leek's shorty and her home girl to accompany them on their mission. Everybody had pretty much learned the area since they'd slowly but surely gotten around during their time in the mountains. The girls hopped in the H2 rental and went on their way.

***

Meanwhile G Millions, Famous, the YG's, Leeka Leek and his partner had just come in from ice fishing and they were arguing about who was the nicest on the snowmobile. Leeka Leek was smelling himself from getting all of the dope money he had been getting and was blind to the obvious.

'The only thing you can beat is my cock!" Leeka Leek said arrogantly, causing everyone to laugh, not with him but at him.

G Millions and Famous locked eyes and read each other's thoughts. They were thankful that the YG's shorties were in the other cabin. Judging from the look on Jeffry Dommers and Midget's faces, it would have gotten uglier then it was supposed to.

'I got ten stacks nigga, let's get there!" Jeffry Dommers challenged.

"Fuck it B, ten G's a man!" Midget added.

'Let's do this then, winner gets the pot!" Leeka Leek accepted.

With an issue to settle, they all filed out of the cabin and hopped back onto their snowmobiles. The race was set to go three miles and back. The course that they were taking would lead them thru the tree's, over hills etc. And the first one back would win all of the money. G Millions, Famous, Jux and Piff fell back. Everybody else lined up and waited for Famous to drop the black flag. Once he dropped it, it was on and popping, the youth went hard. Leeka Leek counted the money in his head, already plotting on what he was going to buy.

By the time they made it to the landmark and were making their way back, Leeka Leek led the pack with his partner running a close second. Just as they made their way thru the trees, Leeka Leek was struck in the back by Jeffry Dommers hatchet causing him to veer off cutting his partner off. He went slamming into a tree head first killing him instantly. The excruciating pain in his back caused Leeka Leek to lose control and flip his snowmobile. He was sprawled out on the ground and desperate to relieve the pain in his back. He was trying desperately to reach the hatchet when Jeffry Dommers and Midget rolled up on him. Midget stood directly over him, placed a timberland boot on the back of his head and pushed his face in the snow.

"Let me get that for you my man!" Midget's words reeked of sarcasm.

"What the fuck is wrong wit' you nigga?" Leeka Leek screamed.

Midget already done with the issue kicked him in the mouth, ridding him of several teeth.

"You know what your problem is?" Midget hissed. "You talked to fuckin' much!" He answered his own question before Leeka Leek got the chance to and kicked him in the groan. "The next time you invite somebody to your little cock; make sure it's a bitch!" Midget spat before walking away to retrieve some rope.

No sooner than Midget walked off, Jeffry Dommers chopped him in the throat so hard that he damn near beheaded him. When the rest of the YG's pulled up, they hooked the bodies as well as the totaled snowmobiles up and headed back to the cabin where they covered them up with tarp until nightfall.

While the girls were on their way back to the cabin, the inside light of the H2 came on indicating the tires needed air.

"Fuck!" YoYo complained. "This can't be happening.

"What's wrong?" Lady Pink asked.

"One of the tires is going flat," YoYo, informed her. "I don't believe this shit; it's too cold to be out this bitch fuckin' around wit' a fuckin' dirty ass tire!"

"Hell yeah and these tires are big as fuck!" Lady Pink agreed.

"I can't change no tires, I'm pregnant," Candy Girl protested.

As they pulled over the girls continued to haggle back and forth over who was going to change the tire. Lady Pink Finally got fed up. She got out in order to inspect the damage while the other ladies sat restlessly hoping that they would be able to ease out of this situation without getting dirt under their manicured nails.

After conducting her inspection, Lady Pink opened the driver side door and interrupted everyone's thoughts.

"Listen, this is what it is; either we can try to fix it ourselves or call them fools. But you already know we ain't gonna hear the end of it."

"Yeah, fuck that!" YoYo said. "I'm not beat for that shit them fools gonna be hollerin'."

All of the women agreed to go ahead and fix the tire. Lady Pink took out the car jack and placed it under the body of the trucks driver side while the other girls waited on the SUV's passenger side.

Lady Pink signaled for Leeka Leeks girlfriend to come and help her. Once Leeka Leek's girl made her way around the truck, she bent over next to Lady Pink in order to assist her. Her girlfriend, whom also decided to help in order to get back to the cabin faster, arrived just in time to witness Lady Pink sticking her ice pick thru the back of her girlfriends head. The shock of the sudden violence caused her to freeze temporarily. Once she began to regain her wits, she started to back away. But just as she was about to turn and run, she bumped into YoYo who was on her with the tire iron. Luckily, for her she saw it coming in time to dip it. *I ain't goin' out like my girlfriend!* She thought to herself before taking off thru the woods, closely pursued by YoYo and Lady Pink. *Damn, I stay in some shit fuckin' wit these wild ass whores!* Candy Girl thought to herself while exiting the truck to clean up the mess that her home girls left behind. She quickly dragged the girls' body into a shallow off road ditch and covered her up with snow. Then she got back into the truck, turned on the heat and hoped for the best.

The pursuit was short, YoYo closed in on the fleeing young woman, close enough to whack her upside her head with the tire iron sending her crashing to the snow. As soon as the girl hit the ground YoYo pounced on her and started cracking her skull. YoYo lapsed into a zone and Lady Pink had to pull her off the girl and take away the tire iron. Thinking fast, Lady Pink ripped the girl's shirt off and wrapped it around her head in order to delay the blood and brain leakage. Then the two of them dragged the girl's body back over to the truck. It was a struggle for them, but they finally got the body into the back.

"What happened to the other bitch?" Lady Pink asked.

"I buried her over there!" Candy Girl informed her, pointing to the spot that she'd buried the body. "You bitches seem to keep forgetting that I'm pregnant."

"You should've stayed your crying ass back at the cabin!" YoYo snapped.

"Yeah right, then who would ya'll have to clean up behind ya'll," Candy Girl responded pointedly.

"Whateva!" Lady Pink cut in, sucking her teeth, giving her the hand to talk to.

YoYo and Lady Pink quickly retrieved the body, put it into the truck on top of the other one, and headed back to the cabin. When they arrived, the YG's helped them with all of the groceries and then they stored the bodies in the equipment cabin along with the other ones.

After the bodies were safely tucked away, they got smoked out, and engaged in a snowball fight, with men against women. Everybody acted like fools for a little over an hour before going back to G Millions and Famous' cabin for more party and bullshit. It didn't take long for them to stroll off couple by couple to their own cabins to smash. At around 3:00 a.m. the YG's met back up so that they could dispose of the bodies. It was just their luck that it was snowing heavy outside, it made it easier for them to take the bodies to where they went ice fishing earlier that day. They put weights on the ankles of the bodies and pushed them into ice fishing holes. At least they would be together.

Everyone was snowed in for the next couple of days, so they took it as an opportunity to catch up on their rest. Although they enjoyed the trip, they were getting home sick and were ready to go back to the hood.

The trip back was uneventful. When the jet landed back in Jersey everybody hopped in their vehicles and went home to get ready to go back to work the next day…

Chapter 22

"Back to work"

Ever since they arrived back in town, G Millions and Famous had been flexing in Famous' brand new 2006 Bentley Continental Flying Spur also known as the Flying B. They had been running errands and putting together the pieces to make the Robbery Report of the century. This robbery was guaranteed to not only make the whole family millionaires, but also put them in the position to be famous.

To pull this one off would make both of their dreams come true. Although the two of them were already millionaires ten times over, this robbery would put them in the elite class of robbers and sure make them Famous in the underworld. After this, one there was only one place for them to go and that was international. The scavengers could have what was left in the hood.

"Yo B, we gotta be two of the best that ever did it and got away wit' it," Famous bragged. "And we did it all without a connect."

"Yeah B, but dig this. We only got what our hands called for, you smell me!"

G Millions agreed with his partner. "We led this hood full of treasure hungry gangsters by example. Our loyalty for each other filtered down to them and it's paying off. Loyalty will take you further then griminess and hate any day."

"Fo' sure my nig., that grimy shit ain't about nothin' and I never could understand how a man could hate on another man. Not when you got the physical capabilities to get off ya ass and get your own. I'm sure Gangsta can attest to that," Famous joked and they laughed.

After their laughter subsided, Famous whipped out his Nextel and chirped Thomas.

"Hey Famous, how's my guy?" Thomas's voice came thru the cell phone.

"What's really gangsta my dude?"

"So far so good my man, I'm working on a few angles. Some shit is going to be hard but money talks, so we'll get it done. It's gonna cost you though," Thomas informed.

"I know it will. You always come thru, so don't worry about the paper, you just make sure everything is flawless and it's all good, ya dig!"

"I can dig it. Hey, we'll have dinner in a week or so."

"Say no more." Famous disconnect the call and put his phone back on the clip.

"I see you handlin' ya business," G Millions said.

"Know doubt, you already know what it's hittin' for. That's my favorite white boy!" Famous joked and they laughed.

"Mob thru the hood and see what them fools are up to," G Millions instructed while chirping Jux.

"Bleep…bleep…bleep…Jux."

"Bleep…What's really gangsta?"

"Bleep…Where you fools at?"

"Bleep…The pit."

"Bleep…A'ight, stay right there."

"Bleep…Shiit, I ain't goin' nowhere, this money too sweet!" Jux laughed while closing his jack.

***

Ten minutes later, Famous pulled up in the back yard of the house that the YG's invested their money in for jump offs upstairs and dog fights in the basement, which they called the pit.

Dog men came thru from all over the country, they weren't just limited to Jersey. The funny thing about dog men was that they all thought that they had the best looking and the toughest pit in the world. So whatever amount of money that they had on them wasn't anything to let ride. Many of the hustlers came with their dogs and left without them. Most of the times they were killed by other dogs, but in many instances, they died at the hands of their masters. Although the loyal dogs fought hard for their masters, not wanting to disappoint them, when they came up short, nine times out of ten their reward was one to the head. Ten out of ten times if they cured. Meaning, after they were broken up and taken to their corners during the fight, if they refused to come back out, it was complete humiliation to their masters, punishable by a mandatory slug to the head.

As soon as they arrived down stairs, G Millions spotted his cousins Wild Style and Dan. Wild Style was originally from New Brunswick and Dan was from Queens, New York. The two of them put their money and heads together and moved to the Southside of Richmond, Virginia in the late 80's. G Millions, who hadn't seen his cousins in a while, burned down on them immediately.

"Wild Style, Dan what's really gansta wit' you fools?" He greeted and they gave each other gangster love.

"You already know I'm doin' what I do, 'cause I'm wild and I got style!" His response gave them all a good laugh.

"I'm chillin'," The more laid back Dan answered.

"I see you ain't change B," Famous cut in, giving them love also.

"Hells no…Why would I? Shiit."

"How's the family?" G Millions asked.

"They're good, but mommy mad at you though."

"I know I gotta get at her."

"Which one of your ugly ass dogs you got with you today?" Famous bailed his partner out.

Dan being his usual laid-back self amused by the conversation, just stood to the side, and enjoyed the exchange.

"Hit man!" Wild Style responded proudly. "That muthafucka so mean that when I feed him, I gotta back out of the kennel. He is an ugly muthafucka though."

"How's business?" G Millions asked after he recovered from the last laugh that Wild Style gave them.

"You know me still flattin' them birds," Wild Style, answered referring to him not selling any weight.

"I got some business to take care of right now, but holla at me later and I'mma give you somethin' to take wit' you," G Millions informed him. "Just make sure you holla at my aunt and take care of Toni and the kids."

'Fo sure."

After everyone showed each other love, G Millions and Famous worked their way through the room on a mission to find Jux. When they rolled up on him, he was standing next to Al Capone, Felix and a few of the up and coming gangsters from the hood, with his Brendel pit-bull in his kennel waiting for his turn to fight.

'What's really gangsta big homeys?" Jux greeted.

After everybody exchange gangster love, G Millions and Famous eased off to the side. The pit was a bloody mess and the hustlers were enjoying every minute of it.

'What's really wit' that issue?" G Millions asked

'Midget, Jeffry Dommers and Young Nitty said that they took care of it," Jux responded.

'So were the nigga at?" G Millions probed.

'They said that they got him stashed."

'First of all, you send three of the loosest fools in the family," G Millions scolded. "Then on top of that, you ain't find out exactly what was goin' on?"

"Nah, but usually they on point 110%," Jux justified.

'Yeah, but usually it doesn't matter if a nigga dead or alive," G Millions pressed. "We need this nigga alive."

"I feel you big homie, my bad I'll take care of it," Jux assured.

'Don't worry about it, I got it," G Millions said, putting his hands up signaling for Jux to continue doing what he was doing.

G Millions then signaled for Famous and they both stepped off leaving Jux standing there heated. When they caught up to Jeffry Dommers, him, and Young Nitty were smoking crank and watching Midget fight Terror, his championship bread red nose. When they saw their big homies walk up, they immediately tightened up.

"It's all hood my niggaz," G Millions said noticing their shift in moods.

"What's really gangsta?" Jeffry Dommers asked.

"Ya'll handle that issue B?" G Millions G Millions got straight of the point.

"More-less that issue was taken care of yesterday," Young Nitty proudly informed.

"Where they at," G Millions asked, trying to be patient.

He knew that this type of shit came with having a bunch of cannons in the family, but it still worked his nerves.

"In my trunk," Jeffry Dommers answered with a wicked grin on his face.

"What the fuck is he doin' in the trunk?" G Millions was losing his patients slowly but surely. "Jux didn't tell you to leave the muthafucka alive?"

"He is alive, I checked on him this morning," Jeffry Dommers justified, not understanding what the problem was.

"We got his wife, son and bodyguard too," Young Nitty cut in, figuring he might as well get it all out now because G Millions seemed to be on the verge of erupting.

"So were they at?" G Millions paused. "Never mind, just take me to them. As a matter of fact, all you little muthafucka meet me at your G Rides!" G Millions scolded. "Ya'll got until Midget fight is over to get everybody together and meet outside!"

After he ran his spiel, he and Famous headed for the door. The two partners walked back to Famous's "Flying B" in silence, both still processing what they'd just heard. When they got in the G Ride Famous turned on the system. The sounds of Nore could be heard at a low volume while G Millions and Famous talked.

"You a'ight B?" Famous questioned. "I haven't seen you like this in a while."

"Yeah B, I'm good," G Millions answered, although he was still agitated. "Those little dudes are psycho," He shook his head.

"Stop frontin', you know you like their stlye!" Famous teased in attempt to to lighten up the mood.

"Fo' sure, that's why I fucks wit' 'em like that, dig me. But I can't afford to let 'em know right now," G Millions explained. "This Draggo shit ain't 'bout nothin'. I need them fools to be on point for real. They gotta bring their A game to the big score, you smell's me!"

"I heard...You already know I'm wit' you B."

Fifteen minutes later, the YG's came out of the house. Once they secured the dogs, they strolled over to the "Flying B".

"One of ya'll wanna tell me exactly how this shit went down?" G Millions asked.

"We followed them on their little family day out and made our move in the Red Lobster parkin' lot. We was gone take them to the safe house but our jacks been jumpin' and we been busy scoopin' up our paper and makin' drop offs. That E money crazy right now," Midget explained. "Between that and our other product and the rest of the shit that's been goin' on out here, we never get them to the house."

At this point, all G Millions and Famous could both do is shake their heads.

"So let me get this straight. It's nine of ya'll and ya'll couldn't split the duties?" Famous spoke up. "Stop shuckin' and jivin' me man, just say ya'll fools got ya little jollies off of ridin' around town with ya trunks full."

"Yea B, we figured that, that would be a good start on shakin' them up. So it would make it a little easier to get Draggo to cooperate." Jeffry Dommers reasoned.

"You fools got the right idea, but we can't afford for one of them super cops to get lucky," G Millions said.

"We thought about that, but fuckin' wit' us their luck would have ran out!" Young Nitty stated confidently, flashing his two 45 automatics.

'A'ight cowboys, pop the trunk and let's see what it's hittin' for," Famous laughed.

They all walked over to Jeffry Dommers and Young Nitty's Ford Taurus hoopties and popped open the trunk so that G Millions and Famous could inspect their handy work. Draggo, his family and bodyguards hands, eyes, mouths, and legs were duct taped. Seeing that they were secured they closed the trunks.

"Take them to the safe house and feed them. Then get rid of body guard right in front of Draggo and his wife and keep the kid in a separate room," G Millions sternly instructed. "I'll holla at ya'll tomorrow, by then Draggo should be nice and loose."

With that out of the way, G Millions felt much better. So he and Famous peeled out confident that business would be taken care of properly. Not only well made, but he also knew that his YG's wouldn't take him getting like that too good and Draggo would definitely pay for it.

The YG's were determined to get results after the scolding that they took from their big homies. Up until today, they'd never saw G Millions get like that. So they weren't smelling that shit at all. However, they had sense enough to know that not only was he right, but he also had their best interest in heart.

Once they had the tarp down, they ushered Draggo and his wife to the chairs that they had ready for them and began to work on the bodyguard. When Young Nitty removed the duct tape from the couples eyes they wanted to laugh bad as hell because the duct tape took all of their facial hair with it, including their eyebrows. But they knew that this wasn't the time or the place for jokes, so they kept their game faces on.

Midget pulled out Draggo's cell phone and handed it to Jux.

"Listen Draggo, this is what it is homes. We know everything about you and your entire operation, including the fact that you copped ready yesterday and your spots will be dryin' up two days from now. That's when you'll have your people go to your stash spot to make sure your stock gets refilled," Jux explained. "We also know that you run a tight ship, so they ain't gonna move wit' you m.i.a. So you gonna call your people and tell them that your family in the BX ran into some problems and you had to go to their rescue, so they gone have to pull everything out early. Your also gone give us the combo to that vault you had built in your crib to hold all of that paper you were getting in the hood before you sends it to Mexico. Cooperate and save your family and your bodyguard. You don't and all of your rice and bean eatin' ass is gonna die slow and we'll find everything ourselves."

Draggo looked at his already battered bodyguard, and then his wife who seemed to be relieved knowing that he was going to save them.

"Fuck you muthafucka! You must don't know who I am. I'm Draggo known in little Mexico as Jesus! My people worship me like Christ! If somethin' happens to me, ya'll some dead muthafucka!"

His wife and bodyguard looked at each other in disappointment and horror. They weren't delusional enough to think for a moment that the hoods standing before them were playing games. Unlike Draggo who'd just cost them their lives by letting his emotions over ride his intellect.

First Midget walked over to the bodyguard and hit him with the taser. Then Young Nitty and Piff taped him to the chair, after which Midget walked over to him and hit him with some more voltage. The rest of the YG's stood around smoking haze, drinking Remy Martin and enjoying the show.

Once the bodyguard was secure, Jeffry Dommers whipped out his hatchet and brought it down swiftly on his shoulder blade. The sickening sound of bone crushing accompanied by the blood squirting thru the air caused Draggo's wife to pass out. Draggo just sat their foaming at the mouth with murder in his eyes. Jux had a smile on his face when he addressed him.

"Don't worry, as I already told you; we know everything about you, including how you off it. But I got somethin' fo' that ass!" Jux let out a demonic laugh.

Before Draggo got a chance to reply, Midget hit him with the taser again rendering him unconscious again. The YG's simply went over to the corner of the room and entertained themselves via cee-lo until G Millions and Famous arrived.

When G Millions entered the basement of the safe house, the stench from urine and feces caused their faces to twist up involuntarily.

"Yo B, how can you fools stand that smell?" Famous asked.

"We was just about to clean them stinkin' muthafucka's up, but you already know strippin' the dudes caused an argument. So we decided to let the old girl strip dude and we strip her," Midget smiled.

"I bet ya'll did," G Millions laughed. "Jeffry Dommers, when are you going to get ya hatchet out of dudes shoulder?"

"When his bitch ass wake up," Jeffry Dommers answered nonchalantly.

G Millions walked over to Draggo and company. Then he returned back over to the YG's and give Saint I's and Grass the nod to cut the lady loose so that she could strip the men. The YG's formed a circle around them to make sure everything went smooth. Once she got Draggo's clothes off, Midget hit him with some more voltage and Saint I's sprayed him down with the hose. His wife hearled at the sight of the bodyguard's gory shoulder wound.

"You better get right bitch, 'cause the way your husband acting, ya'll in for much worse," Grass warned, which was all of the encouragement she needed to handle her business.

The bodyguard was losing blood rapidly, even more so after Jeffry Dommers removed his hatchet. Instead of the YG's stripping Draggo's wife, they allowed her to do it herself, revealing a body that would put video vixens to shame. They all watched Saint I's spray her down, while thinking about how they were going to bust some body's ass when this was over.

As soon as Grass re-taped her, Jeffry Dommers put the hatchet thru the bodyguards other shoulder, causing him to shriek in pain and her to pass out again. G Millions caught a hint of emotion as he watched his body guard scream in agony and his wife pass out from horror, so he gave Jeffry Dommers the nod and he proceeded to chop up the body guard like he was fire wood. The scene was so sadistic that even Draggo had to close his eyes.

After Jeffry Dommers was complete. Butta and Piff rapped the bodyguard up in one of the tarps, dragged his mangled body to the corner of the basement, and replaced the tarp for Jeffry Dommers next victim.

"You're really beginning to aggravate me homes," Famous whispered to Draggo.

Draggo just stared at him bleakly, which infuriated Famous even more, so he motioned for G Millions to bring over the acid that they'd retrieved from one of their drug spots. The acid was normally used for disposing of product, but it also came in handy for times like this.

G Millions motioned for the YG's to back up as he walked over to Draggo's wife, grabbed her by her beautiful hair and caressed her face.

"You have a beautiful wife. I strongly suggest that you make that call if you want to keep it that way," G Millions warned.

Draggo gave G Millions the same blank stare that he gave Famous, which pissed him off also. Without hesitation G Millions picked up the bucket of acid and threw it in Draggo's wife face causing her to pass out immediately from the excruciating pain. Draggo nearly tipped his own chair over as he witnessed his wife skin bubble up and began to peel. Her hair was also smoking as if someone lit a firecracker dud. Sensing that Draggo was primed and ready for the kill, Famous motioned for Jeffry Dommers to go and get his son.

"You think this a game muthafucka?" Famous yelled."

Finally seeing that Draggo was ready to fold, they put on the full court press. When Jeffry Dommers re-entered the basement with Draggo's son in one hand and the hatchet with blood still dripping from it in the other, he was ready to throw in the towel. But seeing the look on his sons face when he saw the disfigured woman sealed the deal.

"Okay, okay, you win, don't hurt the boy!" Draggo begged for his son's life.

G Millions, Famous, and the YG's were all relieved. Not even Jeffry Dommers wanted to kill the kid. Famous gave Jeffry Dommers the nod to return the boy to the room that he'd brought him from and G Millions gave Felix the nod to bring Draggo his cell phone.

"Don't even think about tryin' to get over wit' that meda, meda bullshit either. My man Felix here knows that shit too," G Millions warned and Draggo nodded his head as if to admit defeat and made the call.

For the next hour or so, Draggo gave them all of the information that they needed, including the location and number to the vault. He also gave them the pass to the security system. After putting Draggo's wife out of her misery, Famous took Al Capone, Butta, Grass, and Young Nitty to Draggo's estate in Edison N.J. in order to retrieve the money, which went like clockwork. Jux, Felix, Jeffry Dommers, and Piff took care of the bodies.

G Millions having thoroughly done his homework found out that the Mexicans were responsible for 85% of the drugs entering the United Sates at the time and although Draggo wasn't even close to putting a dent into that percentage, he was definitely getting his little piece of the rock. Draggo was purchasing so much drugs that he had a direct pipeline to the border. His arms also stretched further then New Brunswick's little Mexico.

***

Equipped with night vision goggles, walkie talkies, police scanners, AK47's, MP5's and back up hand guns, G Millions, Famous and the YG's broke up into two teams and patiently awaited Draggo's divers to bring in the stash from the bottom of the Raritan River. The thick fog gave the atmosphere the feel of a horror movie.

G Millions, Jux, Felix, Saint I's and Piff made up the ground crew. They camouflaged themselves amongst the trees and brush on both sides of Donaldson Parks launch ramp where Draggo's team would be bring in the stash, and the YG's would be there to intercept it. The divers were completely oblivious to the fact that the truck drivers were already sleeping with the fish at the bottom of the river, which made them easy prey.

Famous, Al Capone, Midget, Young Nitty, and Butta sat on their jet skis, blending in with the trees watching the divers make one trip after another, retrieving the stash.

Lady Pink, Grass, and Jeffry Dommers kept Draggo on ice until the mission was complete. Jeffry Dommers performance had Draggo's tuff ass so shook that it was doubtfully that he would even sneeze the wrong way, never the less try something.

After what seemed like an eternity, Draggo's men cranked up their boat and headed for the launch ramp. As soon as they started moving, G Millions gave Famous the signal for him and his team to follow at a safe distance. Both the fog and the night vision goggles gave them the advantage that they needed.

G Millions had Jux back up the pickup truck that was waiting for the boat to be hooked up to the launch pad. When the boat pulled in and the passengers got off, G Millions and his team quickly converged on them taking them completely by surprise. A few of them wanted to reach, but upon seeing that they didn't have any wins, abandoned the idea. Famous and his team saw that their comrades had the situation under control, but played it safe and went thru the boat anyway to make sure there wouldn't be any surprises. Once they were satisfied, they hooked the boat up along with the jet skies and made Draggo's men take their last swim while they made their getaway.

***

Lady Pink, Jeffry Dommers and Grass delivered little Mexico Draggo, their Christ, whom Jeffry Dommer's nailed to the crucifix. They made sure to send a strong message by putting him on display for everybody to see. The French St. Clock which sat smack dab in the middle of little Mexico couldn't have been a more perfect spot.

The kid wasn't a threat in no shape form or fashion, so they removed his blindfold and let him go a couple of blocks away from his pops. This power move they pulled on Draggo and little Mexico deserved to go in the hood history books...

Chapter 23

"In Between Time"

The next day, news of Draggo's death on the crucifix was not only buzzin' thru the hood, but it was also big news in the papers and televised media stations. They both showed pictures of Draggo next to Jesus, both of them on the cross. They also made mention of his missing wife and body guard. The pictures of his traumatized son was saddening and even worse were his claims that his mother and father deaths were the result of some type of new monsters wearing gas masks and all black.

There were many different conspiracy theories, but as always, none of them was correct. The Mexicans had a candle lit visual and placed, flowers, candles etc. by the clock where Draggo was found. Felix quickly took advantage of little Mexico's vulnerability by putting his people in place. In light of the impending robbery, this would only be a temporary arrangement. But for the time being, Felix would add insult to injury by pumping Draggo's product through his own hood. The fiends' only loyalty was to their drug of choice, so to them it didn't matter whom or how the void would be filled as long as it was filled. Their only concern was that it was filled.

The whole family took a full week to count the take from the Draggo score, get their minds right and relax. Everyone was well aware of the fact that their next one could be their last. But they already knew that once in a lifetime scores like the next one that G Millions had set up was what the Robbery Report was all about, get it until you get it, was their motto.

'Damn daddy, that fool was holdin',' Lady Pink stared at the box of cash and mountains of product.

'Hells yeah, I knew that pussy was stackin', but not like that," G Millions agreed.

'Yeah, son was going hard," Famous, agreed.

"You ain't never lied, twelve mill cash, two hundred keys of yay, a hundred and ten keys of smack and an arsenal for a day's work ain't bad at all," G Millions said, flashing his million dollar smile.

"I don't know who he thought he was fuckin' wit'," Jux chimed in.

'Yeah B, like we was gone let him get all that gwap in our town and not go and get that!" Al Capone added.

'That fool musta been stupid and retarded!" Midget joked and everybody laughed.

'Niggas ain't heard by now that we travel the seas like pirates and if you got treasure we can smell it," Piff stated seriously.

"Shut ya high ass up fool, you ain't no philosopher!" Young Nitty cracked.

"Fuck you nigga, I know you ain't talkin', as many blunts as you done steamed up over the years," Piff snapped back, giving everyone another good laugh before jumping on Young Nitty wrestling him to the ground playfully.

At the end of the day, everybody got two million apiece. Famous made dinner arrangements with Thomas at Justin's in Harlem to discuss some important issues concerning the big robbery that they had lined up. He also arranged to get Thomas his six million up front for his connects to get the whole layout and everything else that they needed done. Famous would make a way to get his other four million to him once they recouped from the street sales. This was also another good time for them to get at everybody that they met when they were locked up who was getting money in and out of Jersey, they all of the dots, now it was time to connect them.

G Millions, Lady Pink, Candy Girl, and YoYo all got G'd up to have dinner with Thomas and his wife. While the YG's secured their cut off, the loot and got the product to all of the stash spots.

When the Family arrived at Justin's, they spotted Thomas's Bentley GT double-parked and pulled the Masserati and Flying B behind him. Just as Thomas was assuring them that they were good where they parked, there vehicles were roped off.

Upon entering Justin's they immediately took to the atmosphere. The lights were dim and the music mellow. On the way to their reserved seats, they passed by a few celebrities and ballers on and off the court. Of course, they blended right in with their expensive furs, jewelry, and reptiles of their own.

When they made it to their tables, Thomas ordered a couple of bottles of Dom P to go-to-go with their salad and soft butter biscuits. After about forty-five minutes of small talk and two more bottles, their steak and lobster tails came. Candy Girl feeding two and vexed because she couldn't drink, took it out on her food, which everybody at the table got a kick out of.

The YG's were feeling them, so they got dressed up and hit Club Platinum. Club Platinum was a local club that everyone went to, to shine. Instead of going in the limo's or the labels Excursion like usual, they all pulled out their hot wheels. When it was ShowTime, they came thru in S600, 760i, Range Rover, Cayman S, and the Suburban 2500, everything was fully equipped with all of the gadgets and fresh kicks also known as rims.

The YG's shut it down as always. They rarely played the local scene these days, so now whenever they did the love was crazy. Plus they got the celebrity treatment at Platinum.

The family was 90% responsible for bringing all of the hot rappers through making the owner a lot of cash and the bar was without a doubt brought out. Unlike their boys and home-girls, they weren't donning the furs and reptiles. The sported the trademark Boston Red Sox skull cap, black snorkels, designer jeans fresh construction timberlands and of course the jewelry was sick. The YG's that didn't carry their machine guns had at least two handguns on them, their vests and a knife or a razor. Jeffry Dommers had his hatchet. Getting in with their tools was never a problem and when they made it to V.I.P. their bottles of Champaign was already waiting on them. But they still had the waitress bring them fifths of Remy Martin, Hennessey and Absolute.

The music was banging and the YG's showed their asses. When the new street banger "Gangster Degree" came screaming thru the speakers. The YG's rapped along with their homeboy Throw Backs verse. *"And if you see me at the Platinum, I ain't dancin'; I'm plottin' and puttin' together schemes to have us filthy and rotten!"* It just so happened that Pay Dirt was in the building also.

All of those who had love for them came thru and paid homage. All of those who hated did so from affair. The hood-models were out in force pushing up aggressively. Although they let them all back in the V.I.P. with them and enjoy themselves in their presence, only the top of the line, which didn't always have to be the prettiest or the thickest etc., it just had to be something about her to make her official and get chosen. Being as though mostly everybody knew who was in the Platinum, the courtship just consisted of conformation of a jump off for the night.

After having their private party in V.I.P. the YG's snatched up shorties of their choice and headed for the exit. As soon as their entourage spilled out onto the pavement, they ran smack dab in the middle of some ruckus between some cats from another hood and the police. The cops had been up to their usual which was harassing one of their dudes. It just so happened that they'd decided to harass a live nigga that didn't give a fuck, so one thing led to another and an all out brawl issued.

Once dude and his home-boys popped off, other onlookers who was tired of the bullshit and police brutality that was constantly being dished out joined in. The brawl quickly turned into a gunfight and that's when the YG's grabbed their lady's and was out.

As much as they would have loved to participate, they couldn't see celebrating their newly acquired millionaire status in the county jail. Nor did they want to explain getting locked up to their big homeys with so much on the line. All they needed was for their names to pop up in some bullshit and that would have put the whole family in jeopardy.

When they reached Crenshaw, they showed each other love, relieved that they all made it there safely. They stood on line in McDonalds doing a little mingling while waiting for their food to get ready and as soon as it came, they went. Once they reached their suit, they discussed how they were all too big for that small town and there wouldn't be any local clubbing. Their shit could have been fucked up just that fast. The hood-models aggressiveness caused the conversation to end just as quickly as it started and Club Platinum ain't have anything on their jump off.

***

The dinner at Justin's was going well and they were tightening up the plan when Thomas had to break the news that he'd been avoiding all evening.

"Everything is set, but I have some good news and some bad news. Which one you want to hear first?"

"The bad news," Famous answered.

"I found a weak link in the chain," Thomas informed.

"What's so bad about that?" G Millions asked.

"He wants ten million."

"No problem, we set up the payment, push him, and take our bread back," Lady Pink suggested.

"I thought about that one myself and obviously dude did to, that's one of the reason why he wants to do a wire transfer."

"This cock sucka!" Famous shouted drawing mad stares. "What's the other reason?"

"I wanna be long gone when shit hit the fan."

"Fuck it B, ten million is like a thousand with the type of paper we talkin' about," G Millions stated calmly.

At that moment, Thomas popped open his brief case and handed each of them a folder.

"Here's all of the information you need on dude so that you will know that what I'm saying is official," Thomas smiled. "Wouldn't want ya'll to think I'm on some other shit."

"Knock it the fuck off Tommy boy, we been doin' this too long!" Famous assured.

"Speak for yourself nigga!" Lady Pink snapped.

"Yo, why you always got some slick shit to say?" Famous shot back.

"Cause I can fight and I'll stick a nigga!" Lady Pink hissed thru a sinister grin, causing everyone to enjoy a good laugh.

After they savored the flavor of some good cheesecake for desert, they headed for their cars. As the two couples watched, Thomas and his wife pull off, G Millions addressed Famous.

"Rally up the young gangstas, we got an extra ten million to get and I'll be damn if i comes out of any of our pockets, ya dig."

"I heard!" Famous replied and they sealed their understanding with a high five.

With that said, they hopped in their cars and headed back to New Brunswick. On their way, back Famous chirped Al Capone and had him inform the YG's of the meeting. The YG's weren't too enthused, about having to leave their orgy, but business was more important and they could always get back to the ladies. Besides for the type of money that they were about to touch, they would be able to jump it off with exotic woman all around the world.

The YG's were bullshitting and talking slick when G Millions, Famous, and Lady Pink walked in.

"Yo B, you see how greedy that bitch Deseral was guzzlin' down that Cryst Young Nitty pissed in'?" Midget asked.

"I guess it's safe to say, she was pissy drunk!" Piff answered, causing the room to erupt in laughter.

"Ya'll niggaz wild!" G Millions said, still laughing.

"Why wouldn't we be?" Young Nitty agreed.

They bull shitted around for a little while longer before Famous brought the meeting to order. This time Famous did all of the talking and G Millions just listen along with everyone else.

"More-less, ya'll already know what it is, so we need all of you fools off of the streets. We gonna have buyers from all 52 states coming thru. So we need ya'll for that, 'cause they gone be coming to buy weight. Ya'll can keep the spots poppin', but everybody in charge of a hood, bump niggaz up so that ya'll can be free," Famous explained. "Saint I's will collect everything from the streets and turn it in to Al Capone or Jux. Every now and them for the right price and the right people somebody may have to take a trip. But for the most part, they will be comin' thru to see us. We getting close to "Pay Dirt" so we need everybody to stay focused and not take any unnecessary chances don't stop being gangstas, but keep ya mind right!" Famous coached his team like Larry Brown.

After the meeting was over, everybody did his or her regular in the studio well into the wee hours of the morning. The sun was bullying its way out of the darkness when they finally decided to go to their homes and enjoy the little things in life. Which was their houses that they worked so hard for, those who had main girls enjoyed them and their babies. The jump off girls got a free suit for the night.

Once the word filtered thru the underworld that the family was giving their product away like Crazy Eddie, they couldn't hold on to it. Clientele was coming thru from all over the map to see them and whenever they had to travel the prices went up.

After going hard in the streets for a month straight, they were worn out. But they had enough money to pay Thomas and a little something for their pockets. With everything falling in line, at the YG's request they went on a carnival cruise to the Caribbean Islands. With the up and coming robbery, both G Millions and Famous agreed that, that would be a good idea. That way they could clear their thoughts and have a little fun at the same time. They also decided not to take any women with them. But of course, Lady Pink got a pass because she was part of the team. The other women knew or at least hoped that there would be plenty of time to travel. They were rich and they already knew that they were main chicks. Candy Girl on the other hand wasn't taking it too good.

"Why can't I come daddy? She whined.

"Didn't I make you come last night?" Famous joked, trying to duck the question.

"Stop playin' all the time boy. You know what I'm talkin' about," Candy Girl persisted.

"I told you ain't none of the women comin'. Now stop aggravatin' me about this shit," Famous said, trying to remain patient.

"I bet Lady Pink goin'!" Candy Girl continued, hitting him with a low blow.

"Like I said ain't none of the women goin'!" Famous spat back sarcastically.

"Ooh, I'm tellin' her what you said nigga," Candy Girl teased, holding her hand over her mouth. "Plus I'm tired of you leaving me here by myself, shit I'm about to have little Fame."

"First of all, I didn't say nothin' about Lady Pink that I wouldn't say to her face. Second, you always workin' wit' the bullshit! Third, why the fuck am I even arguing wit' you? Hop on a jet and go visit your parents or Angie."

Famous' last statement hurt her feelings causing her to cry. When he moved in to comfort her, she made her move pressing her lips against his. He pushed his tongue into her mouth and her hand traveled down to his hardness. She took it out, stroked it, then bent down and deep throated him. As every inch of him disappeared down her throat, she was loving it and refused to choke. Ain't no bitch gonna do the shit I do for my daddy.

"You ready to taste your pussy daddy?" She asked between slurps.

Famous responded by maneuvering them into the 69 position. After they were both satisfied, he made his move to get on top of her to slide it in. But Candy Girl pushed him back on the bed and continued to suck him hungrily. She worked her way down to his balls, and then slid her tongue across his ass hole. After causing him to squirm and beg for mercy, she got up just before he lost control. She then got on her hands and knees face down ass up and rubbed KY jelly on her anus for lubrication. Famous didn't waste any time guiding himself inside her ass. While she was backing it up on him, he reached around, messaged her clit and long stroked her anal canal to ecstasy. The couple made love repeatedly for the next few hours.

***

When Famous reached "Pay Dirt" studios, the family was in full force. Although the YG's was getting use to vacations, the atmosphere was still like that of the first. They were wide open in front of the building with plenty of smoke and drinks circulating, the dice game was in full swing. Everyone was sure to check the dice this time.

When Famous hopped out of his Bentley, it amused him to see Lady Pink shaking the dice and G Millions leading the bets. When Famous walked up to the game, everybody gave him a nod acknowledging his presence and continued to do what they do.

Two hours later, they were on a red eye flight to Florida, where they would catch the ship headed for the Caribbean. When they got to the ship, the YG's were amazed at its size. They were in awe even more when they boarded it. After they took their bags to their rooms, they all met back up in the hallway. As they took their tour of the boat, they were like tourist going thru New York, Los Angeles, or Chicago for the first time.

The huge boat consisted of many big label stores that you would shop at in the mall. There were also plenty of clubs, casinos, restaurants, bars etc. you name it the boat had it. The family was so excited about the packs of shorties in flavors like Baskin Robbins, who seemed to be outnumbering the men 20 to 1. All of them being gambling men, placed bets on who would get the most women in the week that they would be on the boat and island. They even bet on the island pussy, none of which could be paid for beyond smoking and drinking. Cash, clothes or trinkets of any kind was strictly prohibited and an automatic loss.

They also bet on how many shorties they could get on camcorder. The cameras were rolling and snapping at all times. Not only would they get to enjoy this later, but their comrades serving time would appreciate this action, just like all of the other events and vacations.

After the tour of the boat, they returned to their cabins, which were the size of a small hotel room to rest up for the night's festivities. Being as though they didn't come there to sleep, their rest was short.

Later on that night, everybody got dressed up and put their jewelry on. Then they headed for the clubs to mingle with as many women as possible. At the end of the night, the score was even because the YG's found a gang of freaky ass snow bunnies who were up for an all night orgy.

Over the next couple of days they ran a tight race with Butta leading the pack and Midget running a close second, which didn't come as a surprise being as though they were both the pretty boys of the family. G Millions and Famous opted not to participate and allowed the young gangsters to have their fun. Plus G Millions, Famous, and Lady Pink decided to chill and get their minds right.

When they hit St. Thomas the first thing that they noticed was the beautiful clear water. Jux saw it in San Juan and Felix grew up around it, but the closest the other YG's came to it was Belmar, Atlantic City and a few other beaches in New Jersey. The second thing that they noticed was the four wheelers that seemed to be calling their names.

Once they paid their rental and security fee, they proceeded to race up and down the beach like maniacs. Just before it was time to get back on the shit, they bet $5,000 on a race down to the water and swim to the reef and back. Saint I's collected that.

The conversation in Jux cabin during the smoke session was about how unbelievable it was that they could actually see their feet and exotic fish in the water. G Millions and Famous was in the corner carrying on their own conversation.

"Damn B, it feels good to be chilling, no cell phones or nothin'," G Millions said.

"You already know B. From here on out, we don't have to worry about the streets. Once Jux collect our gwap from the cats renting the block, it's a wrap," Famous agreed expressing his relief.

"Yeah B, that shit ain't about nothin'. We always gonna get millions and be Famous. Now we put ourselves in the position to score bigger then a big league contract, ya dig!"

"I heard my nig'. We been getting' that fast money forever and we some good dudes. If don't nobody else deserve it, we do."

"Thomas will have everything straight when we get back. It's time to move on to the next level B. The greatest show ever, ya dig!"

The two partners enjoyed a good laugh then went to join the family who was engaged in a dance contest trying to see who could do the A Town stomp and the shoulder lean the best.

Famous spent the rest of his time in the casinos, while the YG's got their freak on. They were having orgies like crazy on the boat. No sooner then they hit the island they continued their female scavenger hunt.

The cruise ended too fast for them. The more they traveled and got to see how the other half lived, the more they wanted to get out and see the world. G Millions and Famous made a pack to travel more once they had completed their upcoming robbery…

Chapter 24

"The Big Day"

A new bank was scheduled to open up in New Burg, New York. An armored car was to drop off the banks money supply in the city first and then proceed to the other upstate New York banks. G Millions had gotten the word on the armored truck operations over the years. Although it cost him a pretty penny, he looked at it as an investment. He, Famous and Thomas had been master minding a way to pull off the job. Now the big day had come and it was time to make all of their hard work pay off in a major way.

The U.S. agency was located in Washington D.C. and it was responsible for printing, cutting, counting and distributing currency to every major bank branch across the country. Its armored car service was scheduled to arrive in New Burg that day carrying more than two- hundred million dollars. For the family, this would not only be the score of a lifetime, but they would be living every hustler's dream.

The sun shined brightly as they chilled in the cut. Thomas rigged up their souped up Ford Excursions specifically for the heist. Thomas had his people put full body armor and role flat tires, with a sliding door. The back seat was removed and the middle seats where turned sideways against the driver side doors, which were welded, shut. The 50. Caliber, which was the gun, used in the movie The Terminator that kept spinning even after it was empty, was mounted to the floor. The killing machine was compliments of Vinny the chin.

The whole family was armed with an assortment of assault rifles, machine guns and their favorite handguns. They were all ready to go to war with a small army. All parties involved had secret service earpieces in place, including YoYo and Candy Girl who was holding up at the local hotel listening to their nationwide police scanner.

Thomas had his people posted up at designated points on the route, in order to report the time and progress of the trucks movements. The plan was going perfectly and according to schedule. The weather had enhanced the whole family's mood and had them absorbed in their own thoughts, excited about how good their future was looking once they pulled the heist off.

Famous was growing tired of his silence, so he decided to loosen up the troops with a little bit of humor.

"Hey Tommy baby, I hope ole' boy know what he doin'. I don't want any of that dead president shit," Famous teased, drawing uneasy chuckles thru the earpieces.

"I see you got jokes huh Fame. But I'll tell you what, ole' boy better not fuck this up or it's gonna be more then them dead fuckin' presidents!" Thomas's Italian accent boomed thru the earpieces giving everybody a good laugh.

Each one of Thomas's people was situated along the armored truck route. Once they made their report, they peeled out. Thomas was the last and closest to the action, when the trucks road past Thomas's spot they would be that much closer to the ambush.

***

The women were getting restless sitting in the hotel, wishing that they could be a part of the action with their men. All Candy Girl could do was rub her stomach and hope for Famous to make it back safely in order to be there for the birth of their child. As if reading her mind, YoYo offered her words of comfort and reassurance.

"Don't worry Candy, we dealing with some real live niggaz, they gonna come up out of this just like they do everything else."

"I already know, I just want little Fame to have both parents like I did plus you gotta admit the stakes are much higher on this one."

"Oh knock it the fuck off girl," YoYo insisted. "We fuckin' wit' winners and they're gonna win today just like always."

Candy Girl knew YoYo had a point, so she simply threw up her hands in defeat. However, she still couldn't help but worry. The two women gave each other a hug and went back to work.

***

The entire crew was now charged. They'd been banging the Lot Boy rider music all the way, up until they got into position. They'd been looking forward to this day ever since they first got wind of it. They lived to be the unknown entity of the law enforcements robbery reports and it didn't get any better then this. They considered their leader to be a ghetto genius and felt he never let them down. This was the big leagues now they knew and considered themselves major league players. This is what they lived for.

Although the occupants of the armored trucks were trained to be alert at all times, they'd made these trips of million times without incident so they had no reason to believe this trip would be any different. Besides, they believed there wasn't anyone stupid enough to try to take Uncle Sam's money. But that statement was far from being the truth.

While everyone was sitting carefree one of the guards caught sight of a silhouette out of the corner of his eye. Reflexively he rapidly reached for his Glock while reaching for the walkie-talkie with his other hand. He never got the chance to get a shot off or word out.

Thomas pressed the button on the remote causing a blast to erupt from under the seat of the vehicle sending the driver and passenger to their makers. The guards in the gun ports were startled and injured in the back of the truck, but they weren't dead. The explosives on the back doors did their jobs and popped them open without destroying the currency. The team of assailants broke off into two groups. Each group took a truck and splattered the guards' brains everywhere before they knew what hit them.

With his job being done, Thomas retreated to the hotel room with the girls. Lady Pink monitored the stopwatch and the drivers stayed behind the wheel. G Millions, Famous and the rest of the family loaded up bags and neatly stacked them in the trucks as planned and practiced in record-breaking speed. The task of loading up the trucks had the whole family drenched in perspiration. All of the drugs, alcohol, and sex were taking its toll on the entire squad. But the idea of retiring on their own private island somewhere gave them their second wind and energy needed to continue and get it done.

"It's time to get the fuck outta here," Lady Pink shouted, just as the first helicopter came into view.

However, the young crew was in their zone and didn't hear her signal or didn't pay it any attention. The sounds of automatic gunfire woke them all up and snapped everyone back to reality.

"Time, lets ride!" Lady Pink screamed again.

As the first helicopter approached Jeffrey Dommers fired on it, causing the pilot to have to rise it's altitude in order to avoid the bullets. The gunfire interrupted the news chopper's footage. Getting the result he was looking for, Jeffrey Dommers hopped into the truck with G Millions, Famous and Lady Pink with Jux behind the wheel as they made their exit from the scene.

The rest of the family believed in their .50 caliber saws, assault riffles, and fully armored trucks. Their greed caused them to push it to the maximum limit and tried to get every dollar. Their decision to gamble with their freedom and lives was a bad choice. By the time they were done, it looked as though every law enforcement agency in existence rounded the same curve that the armored trucks rounded just minted prior and was rapidly approaching.

Felix and Midget, who were behind the wheel of the other trucks pulled, parallel to each other so the 50. Calibers were facing the direction the authorities were coming from.

"Lets go, it's over!" Midget shouted. But it was too little too late.

All agencies closed in from both angles along with both news and police choppers, which hovered over them like a bunch of hungry buzzards. The remaining YG's wearing gas masks and full body armor under their black fatigues didn't waste any time positioning themselves. They knew this was where court was going to be held and ended and they were ready to be trialed.

***

When the news of the shootout came across the hotels TV screen, Candy Girl broke down. They had already lost their connection to the earpieces around the time the first news chopper showed up, making it impossible to communicate.

YoYo had her work cut out for her trying to keep Candy Girl calm, listening to the scanner and watching the news. When she finally got Candy Girl quiet, she gathered as much information as possible from the news reporter who was covering the crime scene. "We are reporting live from over the scene of a wild shoot out between law enforcement agencies and several unknown assailants who are out numbered but not out gunned. Law enforcement agencies are having extreme difficulties trying to apprehend the suspects who attempted the brazen robbery of several armored trucks headed for the grand opening of the New Burg First National as well as other first national banks located up state New York. Our sources say the armored trucks were believed to be carrying an estimated amount of two hundred and thirty million dollars. As you can see, we are also having problems covering the story because we can't get close enough to the stand off. The daring suspects are firing at both the news and law enforcement choppers. Also, law enforcement is contending with hand grenades and an unlimited arsenal of military weapons. That's all of the information I'm able to gather at this time, but I'll keep you posted as the scene unfolds and we gather more."

YoYo surfed thru the channels. The stand off was on every channel from NJN to CNN.

"It was hard to see because of the view, but it looked like only two trucks out there. Hopefully my eyes are not deceiving me and our men made it out already in the third truck," YoYo said to Candy Girl who seemed to be in her own world.

No sooner then the words escaped her lips, Famous, G Millions, Lady Pink, Jux and Jeffrey Dommers came strolling thru the door. Candy Girl damned near tackled Famous, while YoYo, Lady Pink, and G Millions calmly hugged each other.

"Hey we don't get no love?" Jeffrey Dommers asked, and everyone laughed nervously and hugged each other.

After their short union, they all parked in front of the TV and watched the rest of the family hold it down to the best of their ability in the streets. Everybody hoped that by some miracle their comrades made it out of there alive. But the feeling that they had deep in the pit of their guts told them something different.

***

The scene of the shootout was ugly, bodies and body parts were sprawled and scattered about the highway. Both patrol and unmarked cruisers were on fire and flipped on their sides. The units that weren't victimized by grenades where peeled like tuna cans by the saw and assault riffles. The well-trained officers of the law were running around like chickens with their heads cut off. When they were first called to the scene in no way were they prepared for this type of action.

The YG's were not only calm and getting a kick out of the gun battle. They were also confident that they were going to make it out of there and to another one of their vacations. Miraculously the scales were tilted in the YG's favor and at that moment, they were just waiting for an opening to make their great escape like their idol Kenyatta.

"Yo B, I know ya'll havin' fun, but we gotta get the fuck outta here before the National Guard come!" Butta shouted over all of the mayhem.

"We could have been up outta here, but them wild ass niggaz fucked the roads up wit' the hand grenades," Saint I's said. "Now what ain't blocked by burning cars, the police got blocked off."

"Grass gonna have to hold us down on the backside wit' the saw, while we clear out a path in the same direction that Jux and them made it out of," Young Nitty stated, before going to tell Grass their plan.

They were confident they were coming up out of there. As Young Nitty made his way back into position, he was struck right above the left eye by a police bullet. The unexpected shot ended his life on impact.

At that moment, the fun was over and the gun battle intensified. Piff threw a hand grenade recklessly in the direction of the bullet, which caused the back blast to temporarily altered Grass' flow and injured him after being hit by shrapnel, but he continued his mission.

***

Everybody in the hotel room was cheering their family on as if they were watching the Super Bowl. The first two smoke bombs took the officers by surprise. They all ducked for cover or scrambled to get out of the way, thinking that it was another hand grenade. They recovered just as the smoke started to rise and fire wildly flowed in the direction of the YG's. When Saint I's finally made it back to the truck, he noticed Grass slumped over the 50. Caliber. He shook his head in grief. As soon as he bent over to slide the door closed, he himself was struck in the back of the head. The shot split his head in half. Piff and Felix dropped two more smoke bombs as the rest of the YG's jumped into the truck for their getaway. Within a minute, the entire area looked as if a major fog came over it. Midget got behind the wheel and pulled down his night vision goggles while the rest of the YG's followed.

The hotel room fell silent when the screen went blank from the smog. G Millions, Lady Pink, and Famous couldn't help but be concerned about their little homies.

***

Meanwhile the news and the police choppers were lost. The YG's finally got the opening that they were looking for before they lit up the area with smoke and was almost at the drop off spot by the time the National Guard arrived on the scene.

Satisfied that the coast was clear, the officers moved in. They ran around frantically as the fog lifted, finding one surprise after another. Tow trucks had to be called in to clear the wreckage so the ambulance and coroner could get in to do their jobs.

***

The television cleared and the news reporter was finally able to give an update.

"The smoke has finally lifted and we are able to see again. It looks as if there is only one of the suspect's trucks on the scene. Thus, the robbery suspects are at large. From where we sit it appears to be many shell casings scattered about."

Everybody in the room was relieved to see that there was only one truck and hoped that their peoples made it out in the other. *Damn, them some hardheaded muthafuckas,* G Millions thought to himself.

"Why couldn't they have rolled when we rolled?" He stated to nobody in particular.

"Them fools was in a zone," Famous spoke up.

The ladies were comforting their men when the reporter came back.

"*This is Ranee Gilmore giving you a live report from the CNN ground crew at the scene of the most daring and destructive armored car heists in United States history. Bodies of law enforcement agents are still being tallied up. The total death count as well as the identities have yet to be confirmed. As for as the robbers, the suspects seem to be teenagers.*"

***

A genuine feeling of sadness swept over the room. Tears escaped everyones eyes, including Jeffrey Dommers. Not all of the preparation in the world could prepare them for losing the young members of their squad.

When the rest of the YG's walked into the room, everybody temporarily snapped out of their funk in order to greet them. Butta and Al Capone came thru the door first, followed by Midget, Piff, and Felix. The love was felt when they walked thru the door.

"Ya'll little niggas don't know just how good it is to see ya'll!" Lady Pink exclaimed thru tearful eyes. "Ya'll gotta tell us what happened."

"We'll fill ya'll in, but we need something to calm our nerves first, I need something to smoke. Shit man," Piff chimed, feeling grief for the loss of his brother and friends.

"Yeah, my nerves are fried," Butta, agreed. "That shit was fun at first, but it got hectic at the end.

"Why ya'll didn't come when homegirl gave the signal?" Famous asked.

"I feel you Fame, but we wanted what we came for, ya dig!" Piff explained.

"I wish we would have listened," Midget confessed. "Being fuckin' greedy caused us some good dudes, including my big bro," he expressed regretfully. "The gunplay wasn't about nothin', but damn what I'mma tell my mom?" Midget shook his head.

"I know it ain't the time, but it is what it is. That's why I tell ya'll to stick to the script. Whenever I put something together for us my main concern is that we all make it out alive," G Millions explained. "Shit, we already touchin' paper, so I'd rather have my little brothers any day. For certain scores you gotta put that wild bull shit on pause."

"I hope ya'll learned from this," Lady Pink cut in.

Everybody in the room nodded in agreement, while the smoke and drink made its way around the room. The room was silent, everyone drifted off into there own thoughts.

***

While the rest of the family was smoking and drinking, Thomas was taking the money from the robbery back to New Jersey. *Fame gotta be crazy to trust me with all of this money and I gotta be crazier not to get him,* Thomas thought to himself while letting out a slight chuckle. Fame lucky he my main man or I'd be in Sicily somewhere. Damn, my mind playin' tricks on me let me get my boys their money. Thomas took the money to the stash house and soon after was home in the safety of his mansion with his family. Grateful to be home, he put on some Victor La' Mone to relax and took it down.

***

Back at the room, the loss of three family members was the only thing that stopped the atmosphere from being a full-fledged celebration. When the subject of the shoot-out came back up Midget took the floor.

"Yo B, cats be killin' each other out in the streets for sport, but no sooner then the police come, they bow down. But you know how we do, we was givin' it to all them pussies!"

"Yeah, them muthafuka is pussy, just like the next man," Piff agreed.

"I don't give a fuck about none of them pigs, Feds, D.E.A., A.T.F., anybody can get it!"

Felix cut in and everybody laughed, while popping champagne.

"That shit was fun too, up until our homeboys got popped," Midget stated sadly.

"It's a good thing we built Ford tough or we might not have made it out of there," Piff added.

"Yeah, the average team would have folded," Midget, agreed.

"We came up outta that muthafucka on some James Bond type shit!" Felix spat.

"What you know about James Bond?" Jux teased. "Ya'll don't watch that shit in San Juan."

Fuck you muthafucka," Felix snapped causing everyone to burst out laughing.

"Yo, how long we gonna hold up in this dump?" Al Capone complained. "We running out of bud."

"Ya'll some young junkies," Famous stated. "It's about a quarter pound in that bowl."

"That's what I'm talkin' 'bout, we getting low B," Al Capone responded. "Don't hate on us 'cause you don't get down."

"He don't know what he missing either," Butta said in between puffs.

"Fuck what ya heard, I gotta be at my best when I grace the big screen, ya dig," Famous retorted.

"Oh boy, ain't nobody in their right mind gonna let you play in their movie," Lady Pink teased.

"I don't know what the fuck you talkin' 'bout ice pick," Famous shot back. "It would be a privilege just to have a nigga like me on the set."

The whole family laughed at Famous' last statement.

"On some real live shit though, what they need to do is make a movie about all of the shit we done did in the last few years. The world needs to see that," G Millions bragged. "Bitch's will pay millions just to see me walk, ya dig!"

"Our shit too raw for television, picture them showin' that shit Jeffrey Dommers be doin' on the big screen," Famous said. "Plus, you, the rest of the YG's or myself ain't too far behind."

Once again, Famous drew laughter from the family. They stayed up for the rest of the night and most of the next day. They left the hotel about 4:00 a.m. that morning and headed back to New Brunswick...

Chapter 25

"Shit just gettin' started"

After getting the hard part out of the way, this was to explain the deaths to the families, G Millions called a meeting at the studio concerning the funeral arrangements. At the meeting, he suggested that no one attend the funerals, however the YG's didn't agree. Midget and Piff had to attend Saint I's and Grass's funeral anyway because they were their blood brothers. Their responsibility to their families was a priority that G Millions had to respect. Butta and Al Capone refused to let them go alone, so they agreed to attend all three funerals. Candy Girl and YoYo agreed to attend in the place of their men who weren't going within a hundred miles of the places.

The YG's understood. However, personally, they wouldn't have been able to live with themselves had they not attended. Although their money was as long as church choir song now and were ahead of the game, they wouldn't feel like winners until the fourth quarter buzzer sounded.

G Millions, Famous, and Lady Pink knew better so they didn't feel good at all about the situation. Jux, Jeffrey Dommers, and Felix agreed with them. The only reason Candy Girl and YoYo decided to attend was that they figured they could go virtually unnoticed.

The funerals were held one day after the other and just as promised their fallen comrades were sent out in style. All of the services were standing room only, the outside was packed, and so was the whole town. Gangsters came in from all over in order to pay their respects.

The family arranged for a horse and carriage to carry the caskets, riding thru each one of the YG's hoods, followed by limos and all different types of luxury vehicles. The first two funerals went as good as a funeral could go. But Saint I's funeral, which was held last, had F.B.I. agents posing as family members. There they arrested Butta, Al Capone and Piff, who had made the unfortunate mistake of leaving there guns in the car.

Nobody ever even bothered to question the presence of the agents because they had no way of knowing all of the family and friends. The sight of three young dead men at the funeral was too much for the massive crowd to except and all hell broke loose. Both Midget and Felix decided to attend that one. Sensing the imminent danger of being captured they were forced to make a rapid exit. The two were able to slide out at the sight of the agents approaching. Moments later they were on the New Jersey Turnpike South bound riding dirty enough to put them under the jail. They chirped Jux to give him the heads up on how things had un-folded at the funerals.

With Grass, Saint I's and Young Nitty dead, Butta, Al Capone and Piff in federal holding and Midget and Felix on the run, things seemed to be falling apart. G Millions along with Famous and the rest of the crew that were still alive and free knew time was running out. They knew they had to tie up any loose ends or lips if they wanted to strengthen their chances of survival.

Thanks to YoYo's computer skills, Thomas was able to trace the wire transfers to where the insider fled to and made sure he would never get to enjoy his cut of the money or run his mouth.

***

When Famous swaggered into Thomas' office he had just finished boxing up the ex-insiders twenty million and his ten million. When he saw Famous walk thru the door he looked up at him sporting a he smile.

"Fame my main man, I knew you was the shit when we first met," Thomas confessed. "Fuckin' wit' you is always profitable."

"You know a winner when you see one," Famous responded.

"Things couldn't be better right now. I took care of everything you asked, but I gotta admit Fame, I'm a little nervous about the guy's who got pinched, I mean they are a little young," Thomas wore a look of concern on his face. "Do you think they will be able to hold up under the light?"

At that moment, Famous felt as if Thomas had spit in his face, but his poker expression concealed how he felt in front of Thomas.

"Tommy baby, all the time you've spent around my little homies, do you really think they give a fuck about the feds?" Famous questioned.

"You can never be too careful in this line of work Fame," Thomas replied smugly. "We dealin' wit' millions here and not just money, years too," Thomas added as a matter of factly.

Famous smiled to himself. He and G Millions had anticipated a problem out of Thomas and discussed how they had a feeling that he would get flaky. They already knew the only reason he hung around was that he knew how dangerous they were. The thirty million was plenty to keep Thomas around without having to worry about health problems for himself or his family.

Famous kept his poker face on.

"Don't worry Tommy baby, not only are our lawyers on the case. But we are in full control of their cut," Famous informed him convincingly. "You already know how me and G Millions do so relax."

Thomas let out a sigh of relief and took a few of remaining stacks off the desk leaned over to place them in the box, while at the same time retrieving his. Being no stranger to the threat of danger instantly the hair on Thomas's back stood up warning him of the danger that he was facing behind him. He quickly reached for his Ruger and spun around, but not quick enough. Famous was two steps ahead of him.

His .45 whispered three times, dumping lead into Thomas's face and neck.

After splattering Thomas's brain matter all over the office, Famous re-holstered his gun and loaded up Thomas's van with the money. He tripped over Thomas's half-naked wife's body while on the way out of the door with the last box. Thomas had been acting funny ever since the dinner and G Millions and Famous felt uneasy about keeping him around. Although he'd been very useful in the past, they had a feeling he was no longer to be trusted so they decided he had to go. Too bad his wife was home thought Famous, knowing she had only been a casualty of war. Famous chuckled at his own quick-witted humor, and kept it moving…

Chapter 26

Everybody greeted Famous with love as soon as he walked thru the door and then went back to what they were doing. G Millions had been feasting on some crab legs and drinking Moet, while Jeffrey Dommers and Jux gambled on NBA-Y2K.

Famous walked over to G Millions and Lady Pink and took a crab leg. Knowing he'd need something to wash it down with Lady Pink got up and got him some lemonade. When she returned Famous was telling G Millions what went down with Thomas. "Yo B, you must be a psychic, that fool was on some bullshit just like you said he would be," Famous gave G Millions his props for being on point.

"Yeah B, Thomas was good for certain things, but when the stakes change, people change, ya dig," G Millions explained.

"You already know," Famous agreed. "I can't believe that nigga had the nerve to question our little homies loyalty with all of them dago's out in the deserts of Arizona in witness protection."

"Yeah, but you let them tell it they the real gangstas and everybody else can't be trusted," Lady Pink added, twisting up her face. "But they the quickest to role over."

"I gotta admit the pussy had balls though. I thought I was rockin' him to sleep and all the while, he was reachin' for his Ruger. But he ain't know my a.k.a. is Quick Draw Magraw," Famous laughed and everybody else joined in.

"Bleep...bleep...bleep...Get ya ass to the hospital!" YoYo yelled thru Famous' chirp interrupting their laughter.

"Bleep...What happened now?"

"Bleep...Just get down here to St. Peters, your wife is about to have your baby," YoYo informed him.

"Grab the camcorder, I'm about to be a dad," Famous screamed.

Everybody piled up in Jeffrey Dommers Suburban and headed for St. Peters. Everybody else was just as excited as Famous. They had lost family members they couldn't get back, but new life had a way of soothing the pain.

Famous showed his natural black behind at the successful birth of little Famous. He came into the world feet first at 8lbs. 7 ounces. It was the proudest Famous had ever felt in his entire life. Everyone expressed their congratulations and left the family to their quality time together. Three days later Famous carried his son out of the New Brunswick hospital while escorting Candy Girl to the car. As soon as they walked thru the door everyone yelled surprise, waking the baby up causing him to exercise his lungs. The whole family took turns comforting him. Rose, Pearl and Joe hogged him for the rest of the day, occasionally allowing little G Millions to play big brother. The rest of the kids just ate up everything and ran around like maniacs.

G Millions, Famous, and the YG's were on their best behavior because they knew Rose and Pearl didn't play. Joe was flirting with a few young girls while the other girls played hostess. With all of the gifts, pampers and formula everyone brought, little Famous would be straight for at least a year.

Towards the end of the night G Millions, Famous and Lady Pink sat in the master bedroom discussing a few issues they were faced with, mainly their little homies.

"Shit looking pretty good for our home boys considering," Famous informed.

"Score one for the home team. The lawyer said that they tried to charge them with capital murder for each body. But the judge ruled against it because of their age and the fact that they're only going to live once," G Millions said. "Plus they really don't have anything on them except the fact that they are associates of our fallen comrades."

"Thanks to our friend Thomas's donation to their legal fees, it looks like they might just wiggle their way outta that shit all together," Lady Pink added.

"I'm confident that they'll be a'ight once all the media coverage and shit die down." G Millions reasoned. "They should be able to slide out on the low."

"I told Felix and Midget to bring they little asses back up here, but you know they on that we gone ride till the wheels fall off and when they fall off we gone walk bullshit," Lady Pink stated.

"Them wild ass bastards done found a spot to set up already," Famous added. "The don't give a fuck about bein' on the tri-state top ten."

"We gonna have to chop it up wit' them fools. They don't need to do that shit, they got retirement money waiting on them and that ain't including what they already had before the jux," G Millions reasoned.

"They addicted to the lifestyle baby," Lady Pink justified.

"Well they better take their ass to rehab," Famous joked.

Rose and Pearl burst into the room interrupting their conversation.

"The party is out there!" Rose announced, pointing towards the door.

"Ya'll always sneakin' off somewhere," Pearl added.

"And ya'll always bustin' in somewhere," Famous retorted.

"Remember when we were young and ya'll bust in on us jumpin' off with Ms. Dee Dee?" G Millions reminisced.

"Hell yeah, and we whupped that bitch's ass!" Rose shouted.

"Ya'll was some little grown fucks," Pearl reminded them, causing everybody to laugh.

***

Meanwhile in the federal building on located at One Police Plaza, in lower Manhattan, New York. Butta, Al Capone and Piff were heroes. Although they were all on different blocks, the results were the same. Everybody had seen the shootout on the news and was expecting to see some hardened criminal types like themselves. Not the frail baby faced pretty gangster niggas that were in the building. Al Capone was the oldest at 18 but he could still pass for a juvenile. Butta and Piff who were both sixteen would be tried in an adult courtroom because of the nature of their crimes.

Although they looked young, the other prisoners seen it in their swagger that they were ahead of their time. Their eyes told the same story, so their fellow inmates wanted to be around them to see if their observation was accurate. The YG's weren't beat, especially after being interrogated for days on end. However, being as though they learned from the best, they took advantage of the situation and got the things they needed. The first thing they did was find a mule so that they could smuggle some weed into the building, which would make it easier for them to pass their days. In addition, too the pictures, magazines, the phone and trading war stories with fellow prisoners would help the time.

It made them feel good to be living good in jail and even better that their boys and home girls on the outside were taking care of them. Between their street family and their real family, they didn't want for anything...

Chapter 27

For the next couple of months, everybody was laying low, doing the family thing. G Millions was very hurt and disappointed because even with a top selling single out and alot of tours, Pay Dirt and the Green Team couldn't stay off of the streets. Nor would they hire professional-armed security causing them to catch gun cases in several states. Although they were out on bail with great lawyers, it was highly unlikely that sooner or later they would be seeing prison.

G Millions and Famous both thinking ahead as always started grooming a new group called "Lot Boys" but quickly found out that they might have been just as wild or wilder then both other groups put together. So now, they were looking to recruit R&B Chris Brown and Ne-Yo types. They were also looking to catch fellow cake-alcoholics to invest in Robbery Report the movie that G Millions had been working on.

In the meantime, the family stayed close and kept work hour schedules in their business office or wherever. They also went out to dinners on weekends and had little family get together. You rarely saw anyone unless you caught them going to work, the store or the mall or something like that, other then that they stayed under the radar.

Little Famous was getting big fast and you couldn't tell little G Millions that, that wasn't his little brother. Jux had gotten use to just chilling out. But, Jeffry Dommers was getting bored, so he drove down the highway to be with Midget and Felix, who didn't care whether they wound up on Americas Most Wanted. They refused to come back until caught or the smoke cleared, fuck being caged up like animals. They were getting fast money out of town, the shorties down there were betting on their dicks and they were feeling it. They didn't even need their cut of the loot for the moment so they let it stay in the stash.

G Millions, Famous, and Lady Pink didn't want any parts of their little brothers business down the highway. To keep them extra comfortable, Jux gave them the money coming in from renting out the blocks whenever he went down to join them once a month for a little excitement. He also made sure that they had whatever else they needed.

"I see ya'll poppin' off down here already!" Jux recognized.

"Why wouldn't we be?" Midget answered.

"You betta act like you know!" Felix added.

"I know one thing; ya'll fools betta act like ya'll know these good ol' boys ain't playin that wild cowboy shit down here," Jux teased.

"Shiit! They betta act like they know, they can get the hachett to!" Jeffry Dommers retorted rubbing his hachett, giving everybody a good laugh while passing around the smoke and drink.

***

Famous had just gotten finish-having sex with Candy Girl for the fourth time that evening. Feeling a little restless, he slid on his polo flip-flops and his matching smoker's jacket, lit up a Cuban cigar, stepped out onto his balcony to gather his while taken the fresh air. Life had been good to him and his family barring the lost and imprisoned homeboys. Him, G Millions and Lady Pink had been plotting on a little island right outside of Florida exclusively for the family. Unfortunately, they have been having some trouble shuffling around the paperwork. It was times like this when they missed having Thomas around, but he had no regrets. He had learned not to trust people who couldn't trust his judgment when it came to handling his affairs in his own house.

Famous' thoughts were interrupted by what he thought was movement off in the distance. Hennessy and Gin were both in their kennels and whatever it was that was moving, was too big to be there, his first thought was the F.B.I., but when he caught the movement again, he saw tall dark shadows with what looked to be towels wrapped around their waste.

"Hotep!" He shouted.

A barrage of spears hit the balcony as soon as he turned to run back into his bedroom.

"Go get the baby and barricade yourselves in his room, hide in the closet, call G Millions and tell him that his dream is comin' true!" Famous yelled. "Hotep is in the buildin'!"

Candy Girl grabbed the MP5 from under the bed and followed his instructions. Famous flipped over the mattress and grabbed his Russian AK47 with four extra banana clips. *These muthafuka can't be serious, bringin' speers to a machine gun fight*, he thought to himself. The technique usually worked for the Africans because they moved swift, silent, and unexpected. It just so happened that Famous was up at the right time.

"Blllat… blllat… blllat…" Famous mowed down the Africans as they closed in on him.

His mini mansion quickly turned into a slaughterhouse. Candy Girl couldn't stand to stay in the room and let her man fight alone, so she came on the scene to join him in battle. However, she never got the chance to pop her MP5, nor was she able to reach G Millions, YoYo or Lady Pink.

After the smoke cleared, Famous made his way around the inside and outside of his property as swiftly as possible to make sure that there wasn't any more Africans lurking before going back to retrieve Candy Girl and little Fame.

Candy Girl dug little Famous out of his room, gave him a tight hug, and then informed Famous that she was unable to reach G Millions.

"Go to my mother's house with the baby, I gotta go bail out my homey," Famous yelled on his way to his BMW.

Candy Girl grabbed the baby and ran behind Famous to the garage. They both jumped into their cars and went their separate ways. Famous lived forty-five minutes away from his partner and pushed his 760i to the limit to try to cut it to twenty.

***

G Millions woke to a foul smell and tied up along with YoYo and Lady Pink.

"Yo, ya'll smell that?" He asked, sniffing the air.

"What the fuck is that smell?" Lady Pink added, answering a question with a question.

"Eww that shit stinks!" YoYo continued.

What they smelled was Sable and Lynx on a spec roasting like pigs by Hotep's men. All three of them thought that their minds were playing tricks on them. The sound of the jungle drum being tapped lightly in the corner of the room, while they struggled to adjust their eyes from the black magic induced sleep.

"What the fuck?" YoYo shouted after noticing that they were tied up.

At that moment, G Millions and Lady Pink noticed they were tied up. When Hotep's men saw that they were coming around from the dust they had sprinkled them with the sounds of drums got louder. The Africans stood around the bed with lit candles.

"What the fuck! Is this a dream or dejavu?" G Millions said loudly to no one in particular.

"These are the same muthafuka that was in my dream on the way to the garden."

"No wonder you was sweating," Lady Pink joked, excepting her fate.

"This shit ain't funny, these ten feet tall muthafuck's 'bout to eat us!" YoYo spat.

Hotep's men were just about to make their move when the door burst open.

The room was illuminated with the flash of automatic weapon's gunfire.

G Millions, YoYo and Lady Pink layed there in disbelief. Not only did they all feel lucky to have escaped death, but the person that stood in the doorway and responsible for saving them was the last person they expected to see. Still somewhat dazed, from the African's dust, the three of them could not figure out the method behind their new ally's madness. A millions thoughts ran through their minds as their savior entered the room...

-To Be Continued-

A New Quality Presents...

☐ My Manz And 'Em	☐ Down In The Dirty
☐ Ride Or Die Chick	☐ Ride Or Die Chick 2
☐ Heaven & Earth	☐ On The Run With Love
☐ Have You Ever...?	☐ Back Stabbers
☐ Massacre	☐ From Incarceration To Incorporation
☐ Robbery Report (Ava. Dec 2010)	☐ Ski Mask Way 2
☐ The Dutty Way (Ava. March 2011)	☐ Around The World

Name _____

Address _____

City _____ State _____ Zip _____

Each Book: $15.00 – Shipping $2 – Each Additional book: $1
Please include a Money Order or Cashier's Check with all orders
Send Payment to: New Quality Publishing * PO Box 589 * Plainfield, NJ 07061

FREE S/H TO CORRECTIONAL FACILITIES ONLY!
For wholesale purchases: Book store chains contact Ingram distributors or Mid-Point distributors, Maryland area contact Afrikan World, Philadelphia Pa area contact Black N Noble or Brodart Inc, Chicago area contact Lushena books, New York area contact Maxwell of JNC distributors, Harlem Book Center or Sea Breeze distributors, New Jersey area contact Baker & Taylor or any other areas contact A New Quality Publishing.

A New Quality Publishing Welcomes...
Erica K. Barnes
Author Of Upcoming Novel
"Allure"

Allure: to exert a very powerful and often dangerous attraction on somebody
Antonym: Dissuade

Kamryn Mackey is a beautiful and vibrant 19 year old girl with a heart centered in the city of Los Angeles. She and her best friend, who is gay male, only source of income is through boosting from high end department stores. But Kamryn soon has a change of heart about her illegal profession and decides to call it quits, so she thought. During a relapse and a lot of persuasion from her crime partner, Kamryn runs into a mysterious and overwhelmingly handsome brother who catches her eye.

When New York native Ricky Wade first visited Los Angeles at 17 years old, he only had ambition and a few hundred dollars. After a connecting with a heavy hitter in the LA drug world, Rick moves from The Big Apple to The City Of Angels and never looks back. Now at age 32, he has it all. With a focused hustle and a tiny circle of trustworthy partners, Rick has managed to evade law enforcement, while building a drug empire which stretched across the Southwest region. These days, Ricky Wade is looking to expand his business. But first, he finds a love interest in Kamryn and decides to focus on pleasure.

Soon after meeting Rick, life Kamryn once knew changed right before her very eyes. She immediately recognizes the cons of his type of work, and proceeds with caution. From shopping sprees to exclusive vacations, Rick stops at nothing to win her over. Kamryn secretly adores his prolific lifestyle, one she could only dream of having. Within time, their whirlwind relationship takes off and Rick finds his place in Kamryn's heart. After being introduced to his finer way of living, Kamryn unexpectedly drops her guard and falls head over heels for Rick. After introducing her to his world, Kamryn soon becomes Rick's rider and ultimately the couple's relationship soar to new heights.

For Kamryn, things couldn't be better thanks to Rick. She begins to believe that together there is nowhere else to go but up... Until she finds herself in the terrifying center of a man's intrigue.

With Rick's fate handed down to him, it'll be Kamryn fighting for her own freedom... And a price will have to be paid for it. The question is... Who will pay it? And how much?

At age 18, Author Erica K. Barnes made her debut into the literary game with the novels I Ain't Sayin She's A Gold Digger and Immortal. But her upcoming novel Allure under A New Quality Publishing show how much the California native has grown in the past two years, as a writer and as a person. Erica is proud of her accomplishments, but feels she is just getting started. Erica still resides in Southern California where she is already working on the second I installment of her trilogy and can be reached at Facebook/AuthorEricaK

Coming Soon January 2011
Memoirs Of An Accidental Hustler
By J.M. Benjamin

Prologue

I can't believe this shit! I'm back in this hell hole again. Caged like a fuckin' animal; helpless. All alone in this cold and desolate place they call a jail holding cell. I never thought it would turn out like this, that I would turn out like this. I never thought I'd have to feel the tight grip of these metal bracelets around my wrist again, digging into my flesh to the point of nearly cutting through my skin like a razor blade. I never thought I'd be sitting on this silver metal bench, staring at these gray paint chipped walls, absorbing the toxic smell of stale urine from the urinal or feeling the chill from the coldness of this cell and air condition combined ever again. I never thought these butterflies fluttering in my stomach would ever have to return or that life as I once knew it would be flashing before my very own eyes again. I never thought I'd be wrapping my hands around these bars and clenching them tightly until my palms begin to sweat profusely, fingers begin to cramp and knuckles turn white or that I'd be banging my head in between the six inches that separated them, cursing myself until my head began to pulsate from the pain again. I never thought I'd have to see the look on my girl's face when they came for me. I never thought my mom would have to get that phone call telling her she had lost another child. Damn! I promised them. What the fuck was I thinking? I just never really thought it could happen, never really thought about it period. But then again, that's a lie, because I actually did. And I was reminded all the time that it could, but I just kept right on doing me and disregarded the signs. I knew there was a strong possibility! I knew. And I knew better. The signs were right there in front of my damn face, everywhere I looked, but I pretended not to see them and just ignored them. I knew this shit was lurking around the corner, just waiting for my ass to turn and run right into it. I knew the clock was ticking and it was just a matter of time before it stopped. I knew time waited on no one and it wasn't on my side. I knew better, because I sat and watched those before me and closest to me time run out and saw what happened to them. I knew better because it was up under and all around me despite me being shielded from it in the beginning. They tried to warn me but I didn't listen and they tried to show me but I didn't want to learn. And now because of that, I've lost everything...My family...My freedom and yes...Even my life. And this is how it happened... This is my story...

The Beginning...

August 3rd 1982, it's Saturday morning and I am extremely happy, because today I get to see my father. It's his birthday. Any normal eight-year-old kid would be overwhelmed by the fact that it's their dad's birthday, but I'm more than that because I don't get to see my dad every day since he doesn't live with us anymore. "The Bad People" have him. That's what my mom says. "The Bad People" came to our home in Brooklyn New York and took him away from us when I was six. Since then, he's been with them in New Jersey. I only get to see him on the weekends for a couple of hours, which is not a very long time, especially when I have to split it with my brother, two sisters, and my moms. Even though I don't like the place my dad lives, I look forward to taking the trip each weekend to see him. I like to look out the window at the stores while we're riding down Canal Street and see all the different color of people shopping and walking. I also like going through the Holland Tunnel because my mom told us it was built under water so I imagine us in a special type of sub marine-car floating to New Jersey. The place where my dad lives is huge. It's kind of shaped and looks liked The White House where the President lives but it's light green and brick and there's a pond in front of it with ducks and geese. A few times I saw some rabbits hopping around and around Thanksgiving I saw wild turkey's walking around. I know my mother feels the same way I do about where my dad lives because the words, "I hate this place," is mumbled under her breath every time we pull up. I can tell my mother misses my dad because she's always crying, kissing, and hugging him the whole time she spends with him, and then when we get home she cries some more. I miss him too, but I cry when I'm in my bed, while it's dark so no one can see me. I know my brother can hear me though, because I can hear him too. We share a room together. I think my dad would be disappointed if he knew that my brother and I were crying, because he always tells us how we have to be strong, and that we're the men of the house now that he's gone. My brother Kamal is a year older than me, but you'd think we were twins. Not just because we look alike, only he's darker, but because we act, and think alike too, plus like the same things, which is why we do everything together. I also have two sisters. My oldest sister name is Monique and she's ten. Jasmine, who is only five, is my little sister, and me, my name is Kamil, the next to the youngest.

"Everybody better be getting dressed," my mother shouts from her bedroom.
"You know today's your father's birthday and I want to get there on time, cause you know how he is when it comes to being late."
"I'm all ready ma," I yelled back.
"I'm all ready ma!" my brother mocks me sarcastically.
I started to rush him because he know I don't like to be teased but I knew it would end up in wrestling match and didn't want to get in trouble for messing up my clothes.
"Monique, do you have your sister dressed yet?" My mother continued with her yelling.
"Yes mom, I'm finishing up with her hair now, and I just have to put my shoes on."
"Okay, I expect everyone to be in the car within the next ten minutes, and make sure you get your daddy's food package from out the kitchen."

"Kamil, you bet not try to get in the front seat either boy!" Monique pops her head in my room and threatens, knowing me like a book.

She knows how much I like to ride in the front seat of my dad's 1980 Cadillac. I know if he wasn't away he'd have a 1982 model like my uncle Jerry does, because he used to trade his in for a new one every year. His "80" still looks just as good as the "82's" though. It's cream with a white leather top and the seats to match, and it has shinny spokes with the best tires that money can buy. At least that's what I used to hear my dad say. All the other kids in the neighborhood admired my dad and uncle's cars. When he was home, he and my uncle Jerry were inseparable. I guess that's where Kamal and I get our closeness from.

Although I'm a boy and boy's are suppose to be tougher than girls, I wasn't taking any chances going up against my sister, because I had seen her in action plenty of times before to know better. One time she was in a fight with this bully at the private school we go to, who was much older and bigger than me, and I remember what she did to him. That alone was enough for me to know not to mess with her, so I let her have the front seat.

Every since my dad had been gone though, Kamal and I had become over protective of our sister's, especially Jasmine, because she was the youngest and was at the age where she would get into any and everything, within reaching distance anyway. Her and Monique were so pretty, that my brother and I knew we were going to have to beat a bunch of boys up for trying to talk to them when they got a little older. Even though we were younger than Monique still we had already chased a few guys away, and they began getting the hint that our sister was off limits. She would be mad at us for doing it but that's what brother's are for my dad told us.

"Monique, give me your sister's hand and get your daddy's package out the back seat. Kamal and Kamil, go get in line while I take your father's bag over to the desk so we don't have to wait too long to get in," my mom tells us, as we do what she says.

As usual, after she sent Kamal and I to the grocery store to get everything she had written down, my moms slaved over the stove nearly all night to make sure my dad had all of his favorite dishes when we came to visit him. He didn't eat meat, red or white so everything really consisted of vegetables. He was something called a Vegan. We were not Vegan's but my mother and father only allowed us to eat certain meats and forbid us to eat pork.

"I hope dad got some junk food or something set up for us in there like he usually does, cause I'm getting tired of eating all that healthy stuff ma be feeding us. She be buggin' with all of that," Kamal complains.

"For real, she be trippin', but you know dad is gonna hook us up. Knowing him, he probably even got a cake with candles up in here for his birthday," I said.

"Yeah, you right, knowing dad, he probably does. I know he gonna be surprised that we came early today."

"I was thinking the same thing," I agreed with my brother. Normally my mother would bring us to the afternoon visit, but today she wanted us to spend the entire morning and some of the afternoon with my father on his birthday.

"Numbers sixty through ninety-five," the dark skinned Bad Guy called out.

He was almost as big as my dad, I thought to myself, as I stared at him, wondering what it was my father had done so bad that it would make this man not like him so much, that he'd want to keep him away from us. I wished that he knew my dad the way that we did, then maybe he would let him come home with us. I wasn't used to seeing the "Bad Guy" because this was the first time we had came to see my dad so early, but he looked no different then the ones I was used to seeing in the gray and blue "Bad Guy" uniforms. As our number was called, we all trailed behind my mother as she casually made her way towards the front part of the area where you have to get searched and scanned by the "Black Thing" that beeps and looked like something from Star Wars. Countless of different fragrances people wore tickled my nostrils as we were crammed together with other visitors the way sardines are bunched together in a can.

"Key up!" that's what the "Bad Guy" always yells right before the huge rusted metal doors open just enough for us to walk through to get to where they were holding my dad. My mother always took her time, keeping us close to her and all the while careful not to bump anyone or step on anyone's toes. I'm sure she moved this way due to the many fights that break out between women for those very same reasons. One time I saw a woman actually get trampled over after falling down from being forcefully pushed through the cracked door. As I walked through my heart started racing with excitement like it was when I first woke up this morning. I knew in just a few moments my dad would be wrapping me up in one of his famous bear hugs and then tossing me up in the air like I was lighter than a feather then doing the same to my brother and sisters. When we stepped in the visiting area, as usual the place was crowded. People were everywhere, men, women, and children. I was looking all around trying to spot my dad, but I was so short that I couldn't locate him in the crowd. I couldn't see a thing. Apparently, my mom's must've spotted him, because she began pushing her way through the crowded room of visitors as we followed. Then all of a sudden, she just stopped. I immediately began looking around for my dad. I was sure that any minute now he would be busting through the crowd. To my surprise, as the crowd parted, I looked up, and there was my dad sitting right there in front of us. He was smiling and looked to be having a good time. His muscles were bulging through his shirt, and his afro was all neat the way it always is. Everything looked to be normal, except for the fact that he was being fed cake by some pretty looking light-skinned girl, not prettier than my moms, but a lot younger though. He was enjoying his self so much that he didn't even see us standing there. It wasn't until my mom's called his named that he noticed us. In record breaking speed, my dad had made it from where he was sitting to directly in front of my mom and us. I could see the tears beginning to roll down my mother's face, as she tried to find the words to say to my father. And then they just spilled out.

"I-I hope that tramp was worth your family, because you just lost it!" Her words started out weak but ended strong.

None of us knew what was really going on, but I knew that something was wrong, and seeing the unfamiliar look on my mom's face confirmed it all, as she turned to us and said, "Kids, let's go!"

Just as we were about to exit the room, my father came up behind my mom and grabbed her by the arm. He began to try to explain whatever it was that needed explaining.

"Wait a minute, hold up!" he yelled.

"That broad back there don't mean nothing to me. You're the only woman that I love and I'm not tryin' to lose you over some nonsense. How you think I've been makin' all that money I've been sending home for you and the kids?" he asked, answering his own question. "Because that broad been bringing me stuff up here that I would never ask you to bring, cause I love you, and care about you and the kids too much to disrespect you like that," he said, looking around, as he lowered his voice. I could tell whatever he was talking about he didn't want the "Bad People" to hear him. But not only did the Bad People not hear him, neither did my moms. It was if as though his words had fallen on deaf ears. Wiping her face, my mother calmly spoke. "I won't play this game with you anymore. I love my children and myself too much to throw my life, time, and love away on someone who only cares about himself. Who thinks they can buy everything and that fast money is the best money. Money isn't everything, you can't buy love and happiness and the fast way isn't always the best way Jay. How can you say you love me and you'd never disrespect me? What do you call having another woman up here, when you have a wife and kids?" my mother stated.

My father started to answer, but my mom's cut him off.

"Save it Jay, I don't even want to hear what you have to say, I'm tired of all of your lies, I can't take it anymore, it's over!" She cried out. Since I was the closest to her, my mother took hold of my hand and began walking away leaving my dad standing there, with my brother and sister's trailing along. Hearing my mother's words and not knowing when the next time I'd see him, I couldn't help but take one last look back at my dad, as I walked along side my mom. I'll never forget the expression on his face as long as I live, as he watched us leave. He had the look of someone who had just lost something very valuable and didn't know where to find it as he stood there shaking his head. I didn't fully understand at the time but that day marked the first day of a new life for all of us and that was the last time I had ever saw my dad again while he was away...

CHAPTER ONE

20 months later….
"Grandma, I finished my homework, can I go outside now?"
"Okay, but if you go on the other side don't cross those train tracks walk your tail around and stay away from that handball court. Don't let me catch or hear your butt was over there Kamil, you hear me?" My grandmother warns. The handball court was where all the older people hung out doing illegal things. I knew better than to defy her. She didn't play when it came to following the rules, or rather her rules. Besides, I knew it was because she was concerned about my safety.
"Yes," I answer without hesitation.
"Can I go too grams? I'm done," Mal, asks straightening up his books.
"Yeah you can go too, but what I tell you about calling me grams, like I'm some old woman or something, I told you before about picking up that street talk and bringing it up in this house with you boy."
"Excuse me grandma," Mal corrected.
With the exception of her long silver hair, nothing about my grandmother indicated that she was an old woman. She had smooth almond colored skin and a perfectly round face. Even though she had given birth to my moms and six uncles, she wasn't a big lady and stood only five feet. I had seen pictures of her when she was a teenager and she still looked the same. She was small in size but huge in heart and was full of life and full of energy. She always said, "You're only as old as you feel, and I'll be twenty one years young on my next birthday."

After the last time we saw my dad, things began to change. Actually, everything began to change. We moved out of our neighborhood in Brooklyn and moved in with my grandmother in the projects she lived in out in New Jersey, where my parents were originally from. We started seeing less of my mom's because she was now working two jobs. When my dad was there, he did all the working. Even when the "Bad People" took him away from us, he use to send money to my moms, but then he just stopped. I never really knew what type of job he had, but I knew that it had to be a good one because we never wanted for anything, and never had to struggle, up until now anyway. All I knew about my dad's job was that he use to travel a lot and would sometimes be gone for days, even weeks at a time. I guess he was some type of traveling salesman, so when asked about what my father did for a living I just use to say he was a businessman. In spite of my mom's working, there would still be a lot of strangers coming to the house demanding money when we still lived in Brooklyn. At first, I use to think that they were Jehovah Witnesses, but then I knew that it couldn't have been them because she wouldn't have opened the door. I didn't figure out all the strangers were bill collectors until the gas and electric got turned off, and we had to move from our brownstone because my mom couldn't maintain the rent while raising four kids on her income. Don't get me wrong, Jersey was okay, but still it's wasn't New York, so like anything else that's new or different, you have to get use to it. I knew a lot of the kids out here in the projects though, because every summer my mom's use to send Mal and I to my grandmother's to spend time with her, not knowing that my brother and I had to fight the whole time we were out there just to prove that we were tough New Yorkers. Jersey kids thought New York kids couldn't fight. They thought that we only knew how to rob and steal or in our case, thought we were too uppity to know how to defend ourselves, but my dad and uncle use to box, and they taught us. After all the fights that we had, we were finally accepted in the Jersey ghetto as one of the boys and looked forward to our summer trips to Plainfield.

"Yo Ant, what up?" my brother spots one of our homeboys from building 532.
"Chillin, chillin, what up with you?"
They gave each other a pound and embraced one another.
"We tryin' to see what's goin' on out here in the hood," said Mal, jokingly.
Ant was 12 years old. 2 years older than me, and 1 year older than Kamal, but treated us as if we were all the same age. We learned a lot from Ant because he grew up in the streets, so he was more hip to how things were running out there. His father was where we used to go visit my dad but he told us that his dad was away for selling drugs. It was Ant who broke me out of saying "The Bad People" had my dad and started saying he was "Away". The more he began to educate us about where we now lived, the more Mal and I began to question what it was our father was really away for. Ant also had a brother that sold drugs. He was only 17, but already had a 1980 Caddy, similar to the one my dad used to drive. Ant told us how his brother always brought him the freshest clothes. They were fly too, and Mal and I were envious, especially since we were still wearing some of the same gear we had since we moved from New York and now had to share our clothes and wear hand- me- downs from the Salvation Army.
"Let's go over Trev's crib and see what's up, see if we can put together a free for all or something," Ant said.
"Bet," Mal and I agreed.
Trevor lived in building 120 on the Elmwood side of the projects, and he was Ant's best friend. Their families were actually two of the first to move into the Elmwood Gardens housing projects back in the 60's and were close, so it was only right that when they were born and grew up they became close themselves. I found out my grandmother was one of the first to move around here after my grandfather had died from a heart attack and she couldn't afford to pay the mortgage on the house they had lived in for four years until his death.
"Who is it?" you could hear Trevor asking through the other side of the door.
"It's the police, open up before I kick it in!" yells Ant, trying to disguise his voice.
"Kick it in and you're gonna pay for it nigga," Trevor yells back, as he opens the door and embrace his best friend, recognizing Ant's voice.
"Trev, what it is?" says Ant.
"You know, maxin' and relaxin' that's all. Mal, Mil, what up? We got muthafuckin' New York in the house!" He shouts, and laughter begins to fill the little apartment.
"Forget you," says Mal laughing along with them.
It was something we were used to, not being from Jersey. It was our own little joke. Once Trevor closed the door behind us, the rest of the crew began pulling their beers, cigarettes, and weed back out. Everyone had hid whatever they were doing when Ant pretended to be the police. All of our boys hung out over

Trevor's crib doing the things they knew they couldn't get caught doing at home, except for Ant, unless they wanted to die at a young age, but Trevor's crib was cool because his moms worked mostly all day, so he practically had the house to himself Monday through Friday.

"Nigga why you gotta play so muthafuckin much?" Shareef asked Ant.

"Man cool out, Trev knew it was me."

Outside of Trevor, and Shareef, the rest of the gang consisted of Troy, Shawn, Mark, and Black. Everybody was pretty much around the same age, between the ages of eleven and fourteen. In fact, I was really the youngest out of the bunch, and the littlest too, but was accepted just the same, because I had heart and wasn't afraid to fight.

"Yo Mil, come hit this spliff nigga, this that shit right here," said Black, coughing from the smoke. Black was the oldest and had the most experience around the projects. His real name was Benard but he earned the name Black from the darkness of his complexion.

"Nah man, you know I don't smoke kid, I don't even know how to," I answered shaking my head. I knew he was trying to be funny because he knew my brother and I didn't smoke or drink already.

"Oh that's right, I forgot you a young whipper snapper," Black joked. "But you still my nigga, even if you don't get any bigga," he added in a laughing manner, while taking another pull of the joint.

"This is for you baby boy!" He held out the weed wrapped in white paper in my direction before passing it to Troy who gladly accepted it.

"Yo Trev, we was comin' over here to see if we could get a football game goin' on the other side, but you niggas up in here getting' all high and shit, so that cancels that," Ant said disappointedly.

"Maaaan, ain't nobody all high and drunk up in here nigga," Trevor said defensively. You always comin' at us sideways every time we tryna have a good time, actin' like we some of them junky and whino muthafuckas out there on the block. We just havin' a little fun, know what I'm sayin'?" Trev stated. "Besides, the alcohol and weed make me play better and harder anyway, so let's rock you ain't sayin nothing!" He concluded with a smile before Ant had a chance to rebut. We were all used to them going at it like brothers. It was comical to us and knew it was all love. At some point, we all had gotten into it with one another, but the next day we would be right back to kicking it again like the boys we were.

Everyone jumped up hearing Trevor's words and one by one we began spilling out of his apartment headed over to the field on the other side of the tracks.

"We ain't got all day mama's boys," Black was the first to yell as we approached the field.

"Word up," Shareef followed up.

While everybody else crossed the train tracks to get to the other side of the projects, Mal and I walked around remembering what our grandmother had told us, so they all had to wait on us. Kamal stuck up his middle finger at Black's comment while I stuck mine up at Shareef. Before it could escalate to anything else, Trevor started picking teams.

"Me, Troy, Shawn, and Mark, against you, Mil, Mal, and Black," he said to Ant.

"Reef, you ref the game."

"Why the fuck I gotta ref the game?" Shareef questioned.

"Nigga you know why you gotta ref the game, cause ya ass is whack and you don't know how to play," Trev said, as we all burst into laughter. Everybody around the projects, with the exception of Shareef was good in everything we played from football, to basketball down to baseball. Although we weren't originally from the projects Mal and I loved playing sports just as much as we did watching them, but when it came to God handing down skills and talents in the athletic departments Shareef was standing in the wrong line. He couldn't catch a football even if it landed in his hands, he couldn't swing a bat if his life depended on it and he couldn't dribble a basketball unless he used two hands, no matter how many times we tried to teach him.

"But I can fight," Reef spit back. That was his response every time.

"I bet you won't win if we jump ya punk ass, nigga," was Ant's comeback each time, as we laughed even harder.

Up ahead from the field was the handball court. All of the older teenagers and old heads hung out up there, either hustling, getting high and drinking, shooting dice, shinning up their rides, kicking it to girls, playing ball, or just coolin' out.

I was always good with remembering faces and names, so I knew all the hustlers. And the cars they drove too, and they knew who Mal and I was, through my dad and Uncle Jerry. It wasn't until Ant's brother told him that my dad was a street legend out there, that I began to realize my father wasn't any type of traveling salesman. The more we hung around Ant and the rest of our friends the more Mal and I learned. I didn't want to at first but as time went on I had no choice but to believe what they were saying about my father. In passing, my brother and I would hear some of the hustlers saying things like, "Their dad was clockin' major doe," or "Their dad was paid." Because of who he was in the streets, we received a lot of respect from the people who hung out by the handball court.

While we were out there playing football, we noticed that guys were beginning to scatter, running all over the place, and then we saw the police jump out of their unmarked and patrol cars from everywhere, both in plain clothes and uniforms. Some guys sprinted into the housing projects complex while others made a mad dash for the bridge and the train tracks. Just as I was about to move out of the way, one of the fleeing runners seemed as if he was about to hit me with a football tackle. I tried to maneuver out of his way but it was too late, he was already up on me. I braced myself for the hit.

"Lil Mil, hold this," he said as he continued to fly right pass me headed in the direction of the train tracks.

I knew who the guy was. Everybody knew. His name was Mustafa. He was a 19 years old hustler from the projects that was known for being thorough, a ladies' man, and one of the best dressers in the hood. Ant told us how he was well respected by all in the streets, young and old, and didn't take any junk from nobody. Without giving it a second thought, I took what Mustafa had handed me and shoved it into my left sweatpants pocket. A few seconds later one of the out of breath police men who was giving chase came to a complete stop in front of all of us.

"Hey you kids, did you see anybody drop anything by you?" The plainclothes officer asked us.

"No sir," we all answered in unison, knowing that even if we had we still wouldn't have answered him truthfully.

"Alright, well we need you to clear this area so we can search it," he said. We were used to one of our playing sessions being broken up because of something that had happened up by the handball court. It was always something going on in The West End Gardens housing projects known as the Bricks. Because the ones we lived in were newer, they called the Bricks The Old Projects and ours The New Projects. Hustlers from both sides would go back and forth over the train tracks hanging out and hustling unless they were beefing with each other. When that happened, we weren't allowed to play on the other side. But for the most part everyone got along. As we were leaving, Ant saw his brother hemmed up against the police car with handcuffs on, along with a few of the other local hustlers from our side of the projects.

"Man my mom is gonna kill Terrance when she finds out they caught him again," Ant cried.

"This is the second time this month he's been in the youth house."

That's what they called the juvenile detention center for anybody under the age of 18 years old. It's a type of jail for young people that hold you until you're released to the custody of your parents by the judge. All the guys that Kamal and I hung with, except for Ant, had already been there before at least once, and they bragged about it as if was a fun place to be or it made you cool. Speaking of the youth house, if the plainclothes officer knew what I had in my pocket, I would've been right alongside of Terrance and the rest of them, handcuffed and on my way to the detention center. My mother would've killed me if that had happened. She wouldn't have understood the position I was in at the time. I know my dad would have though. It was either take what Mustafa handed me and do exactly what I did with it, drop it and let the cops find it or hand it to them. If I didn't take it then I would've been looked at as a sucka by my friends, if I would've dropped it and somebody saw me I would've been looked at as a coward and if I would've gave it to the police then I would've been looked at as a snitch. Even though I knew, I had no business accepting what Mustafa had given me to hold, I knew I didn't want to be labeled as a sucka, coward or snitch. We all went our separate ways, slapping one another fives. I couldn't wait to tell Kamal what Mustafa had given me back there. No one had seen him give it to me. I really didn't know what it was myself, but I was curious to find out. I took a glance back to make sure our boys were out of range before I spoke. They were already up the rocks and on the tracks crossing back over.

"Mal, guess what?" I said looking around to see if anyone else could hear me.

"What up Mil."

"Yo, when Mu ran pass us in the field he tossed me something and told me to hold it," I said waiting for his reaction.

"What? What is you talkin' about?"

"You heard me. Mu tossed me something to hold when we were back there in the field playin football."

"And you took it?"

"What was I supposed to do?" He was runnin', I couldn't catch up to him and say no, I can't hold this, take it back. And I couldn't turn it over to the cops cause that would've been snitchin', and I don't want no rep like that cause nobody respects a snitch or rat."

"Where you learn that at?" Mal asked

"I heard dad say it one time when him and Uncle Jerry was in the living room talking, and Trev and them said it a few times too when they be talking about the youth house."

"Yeah you right, I remember, and plus mom and dad taught us to always mind our business. We don't see nothin', we don't hear nothin', and we don't know nothin'. Yo, whatever you got don't pull it out here though, wait until we get in the house and make sure you act normal when we get in there cause grandma ain't slow. She's from the old school and she'll know somethin's up." My brother had said a mouthful. My grandmother was a sharp as they come. For someone who never really left the house she always knew everything about everything. Whenever she would be talking to my mom, one of her friends that came over or on the phone she would always start out saying, "It's not any of my business but you know so and so did this," or "Such and such happened to so and so." There wasn't anything that you could do or say without my grandmother not catching wind of it.

"I'm not, and I know, grandma be on point," I agreed with my brother.

"You boys are back early, is everything alright," my grandmother greeted us with as soon as we walked through the door and pass the kitchen. We could smell what she was cooking the moment we entered the building. No one's fried chicken smelled better than my grandmother's.

"Some boys got chased and the police broke up the game," Kamal answered for us.

My grandmother just shook her head. We prepared for the, "I told you about," speech but surprisingly it didn't come. I made my way to our room as Mal followed.

"Did you lock the door behind you?" I asked Mal, as I pulled the plastic sandwich bag out of my pocket.

"Yeah its locked boy, stop being so paranoid like you used some of that stuff already," Kamal whispered back.

I shot him a look that made him know that I thought he was talking out the side of his neck, saying something like that.

When I opened the plastic bag, inside of it contained a bunch if tiny little balloons, some red and some blue, 35 red's and 15 blues to be exact.

"What the heck is this?" I said aloud, surprised to be seeing balloons instead of drugs.

"Don't be stupid," said Kamal. "It's drug's. The drugs are in the balloons goofy."

"How do you know?" I asked curiously.

"Because I used to hear the guys out there hustling yellin' I got that "Boy" and "Girl", and then I'd see the fiends lined up to spend their money in exchange for the balloons. I asked Ant and he told me and said the boy goes for five dollars and the girl goes for ten."

"So you mean to tell me that these little balloons are worth four hundred and twenty five dollars?" I asked my brother, as I calculated the value in my head, which was easy to do because math was my strongest subject in school as well as my favorite.

"Yep," Mal replied.

"Dag! Mu must be rich if he got it like that."

"Man that ain't nothing. They be out there with more than that on 'em. Put all that stuff back in the bag and tie it back the way it was before you opened it," Mal told me.

"Tomorrow as soon as you see Mustafa, we gonna give him that stuff back, and I don't want to hear about it again," Kamal demanded.

"I'm with you on that bro, I don't want no parts of this either," I agreed.

The next morning, before Kamal and I went off to school, we looked for Mustafa, but he was nowhere to be found. Out of fear of moms or grandmother finding the package in the house, I took it to school with me. Here I was, about to turn 11 years old next month, in school with over four hundred dollars worth or drugs in my pocket, not able to do any school work, waiting for class to let out so I can get back around the projects and give Mustafa his stuff. At 2:45 school had let out, I waited for Mal out front.

"Yo you a'ight bro? You look like you about to pass out," Mal says to me.

"Man, this stuff been drivin' me crazy all day being in my pocket. I don't know how they do it, standin' out there like that around the way, cause I feel like five-o gonna run down on me any minute now.

"I wish dad was here, then we could've gone to him for help, cause if moms found out she'd flip-out and probably try to keep us in the house until we turned 21."

"You got that right," said Mal.

As we turned the corner, approaching the projects, I heard my name.

"A yo lil Mil!"

When I turned around to look, I saw Mustafa rolling down the black tinted window of a pearl black 318 BMW, with gold rims, and a gold front grill to match. You could tell it was brand new, because it still had the dealer temp tags in the back window.

"Yo get in," he leaned over toward the passenger side and shouted. I wanna talk to you for a minute, lil Mal, you too," he gestured.

Mal and I both knew what he wanted to talk about, but we still were a little nervous about getting in the car with him. We knew if our moms, grandmother, or someone who knew them saw us getting in this car we'd be in serious trouble. I looked both ways to make sure the coast was clear then walked over to the passenger's front door and hesitantly opened it to get in the front seat, as Kamal opened the back door and hopped in. When we closed the doors, Mustafa drove off to the sounds of the latest Run DMC cut "Here We Go", rolling the tinted window back up. This was the first time I'd actually ever been in a drug dealer's car, but being in the car with Mustafa felt like being with any other ordinary person's ride, with the exception of his appearance. When we got in, the inside of the Beamer smelled like he had just came from the barbershop. His sharp chin strap line and goat tee confirmed. As he drove, I tried not to stare but I couldn't help it. He was sharp from head to toe. On his left hand, he had a two finger gold ring, with a dollar sign on it that covered his pinky and ring finger. He had two separate rings on his middle and pointing finger, one had a "M" and the other had a "U". On his right hand, he had a four finger ring on, with lion heads on both sides, with red rubies in their eyes. I could see the name "Mustafa" in between them, on the plate of the ring. Around his neck, he had three different size gold rope chains, with medallions on them. He wore a pair of silk pants with a silk shirt to match; only the shirt was yellow, and the pants were black.

To top it off, he rocked a yellow and black beanie with a tassel dangling from it and had on the black and yellow British Walkers. Everything he had on matched and coincided with his ride. I was in awe. The sound of his voice snapped me out of my daze.

"Yo, remember yesterday when I ran pass you?" He stated rather asking me as he lowered the volume of his music. I tried to answer but instead I was only able to nod. I wasn't afraid, I was just nervous. I had never been so nervous in my life. Maybe because I knew what I had done was wrong and knew the consequences behind my actions. I just wanted it all to be over.

"What did you do with that?" Mustafa asked in a cool tone.

"I got it right here, just the way you gave it to me Mu, and I didn't tell anybody, well except for my brother, but he didn't tell anybody though," I rambled.

"Relax, Mil, I believe you and I'm not gonna hurt you either so chill," he said with a grin on his face.

"Okay." It wasn't so much of what he said but how he looked when he said it that put me at ease.

"Yo, Big Jay ya pops right?" he asked

"Yeah," I answered, never hearing anyone refer to my dad as "Big Jay" before, but I knew that they called him Jay, which was short for Jayson.

"Your pops is a good man so I knew the apple didn't fall far from the tree," Mu said. I was too young to understand what he meant by the statement.

He must've sensed that he was talking to a couple of kids, because he broke it down so Mal and I could understand.

"What I mean is, I figured you were just like your pops," he rephrased his comment. "That's why I trusted you like that with my stash."

All I could say was thanks, not really knowing whether what he had just said required a response, but out of politeness, I was only responding to what I believed to be a compliment.

"Lil Mil, stay the way you are and you'll go far in this world," he told me.

"Cause a man is measured by three things in life," his tone changed. It became smoother but serious.

"And that's his loyalty, respect, and most importantly his money," he quoted as if he read the lines straight out some philosophical book. Then he pulled out a knot of money filled with nothing but hundreds, bigger than both of my hands put together. My eyes grew wide from his knot. I noticed that he didn't have any twenty's, ten's, fives, or singles in his bankroll, as he peeled of two hundred dollar bills and gave one to me and one to Kamal saying, "This is for you, for holding it down, and this one is for you Kamal, for havin' your brother's back. Always hold each other down, no matter what," he told us as he took the sandwich bag from me. "And stay away from this," he said in a much sterner tone holding the bag in the air. "Cause this shit will kill you! You understand?"

Mal and I both nodded yes.

Mustafa pulled over, up the street from the projects and let us out by the vegetable garden on the corner of West Second and Liberty Street. Just as he was about to pull off, he rolled down his window.

"If either one of you ever need anything, just let me know."

Then the words of Whodini's latest cut "Friends" flowed out of his sunroof and filled the air as he pulled off.

From that day on, I had a different outlook on drug dealers…